# PRAISE FOR COOKING FOR CANNIBALS

One terrific and fascinating idea for a novel, delivered with quick wit and sparkling humor, this new Rich Leder tale is one of the most entertaining books of the time! Highly recommended.

GRADY HARP, HALL OF FAME AMAZON
REVIEWER

I just can't recommend *Cooking for Cannibals* highly enough. The language is bad, the bad guys are despicable, the old folks are randy, the love story is everything you could sort of wish for in a book where rats kill by peeling the flesh off their victims, and the laughs are nonstop. Rich Leder pulls off the last minute, wonderful, hopeful twist that we all need to read. 5 Stars!

BARB TAUB

Devastatingly funny, dark, and unputdownable. *Cooking for Cannibals* is one of the year's best thrillers!

BEST THRILLERS

# PRAISE FOR COOKING FOR CANNIBALS

Darkly mischievous, vigorously manic, and surprisingly touching and tender, *Cooking for Cannibals* is for readers with strong stomachs, a dark sense of humor, and a need for some off-the-rails, comically violent catharsis in these crazy days. If that's you, then Rich Leder's delightfully bizarre book may be just the ticket!

INDIEREADER

*Cooking for Cannibals* is a fast-paced, Raymond Chandler-esque creep-thriller with a *very* funny and sardonic edge.

YET ANOTHER CRIME BOOK BLOG

Fascinating and original are two words that come to mind when I think about Rich Leder's *Cooking for Cannibals*. Surprising and funny are two more. This book is brilliant and entertaining from the start until the end. 5 Stars all the way!

RABIA T FOR READERS' FAVORITE

# PRAISE FOR COOKING FOR CANNIBALS

Leder mixes his dark humor with a compelling storyline full of twists and turns that is immensely readable and hard to put down. *Cooking For Cannibals* is ideal for lovers of fast-paced high-concept thrillers. As the insanity continues to build exponentially throughout the book, it becomes more and more difficult not to read "just one more chapter" as you find yourself craving to find out just how crazy things are going to get. The perfect book for a binge read!

BESTSELLERS WORLD

At times hysterically funny, at others times thrilling, and sometimes both at once, *Cooking for Cannibals* will appeal to readers of medical thrillers, satire, speculative fiction, and horror, to start. Part zombie fiction, part something you've never read before, Leder pulls off a novel that is at once a black comedy and fast-paced thriller, setting it apart in the crowded thriller genre, and existing in a genre of its own

SELF-PUBLISHING REVIEW

# PRAISE FOR COOKING FOR CANNIBALS

*Cooking for Cannibals* is one of the best horror comedies to come along in years. Rich Leder has created an irresistible dark comic thriller that keeps you involved with plot and character until the end. Books and movies are saturated with cannibals and science gone amok, so obviously it's time to have a little fun with the genre, and that's exactly what this author does. He writes a solid story about cannibals that pulls you in with the expected tropes but puts a comedic twist on it that's refreshing and fun. He also gets into the characters more deeply than you might think, and there's a sweet side to the story as well. Today's troubling times could use a little—or a lot—of humor. This one is tailor-made for the big (or small) screen. If you're looking for escapism in the vein of *Pride, Prejudice, and Zombies* or *Shaun of the Dead*, then treat yourself to *Cooking for Cannibals* by Rich Leder!

TAMMY R FOR READERS' FAVORITE

Oh my goodness! Like nothing I have ever read before. Hilarious, shocking, funny, dark, and gross—what a ride!

VERONICA J FOR COOKIEBISCUITS BLOG

# PRAISE FOR COOKING FOR CANNIBALS

What a hilarious and thrilling shitshow of a story! The characters are quirky, evil, unnerving, and freaking awesome. The plot is brilliant and fast-paced, with this reader eager to find out how they all get out of the mess they're in. If you like a rollercoaster thriller filled with partying geriatrics, lab rats, psychopathic hitmen, dodgy parole officers, diehard reporters, dogged cops, an unlikely couple, and a drug to change the world, give this book a try. I guarantee you won't be able to put it down!

THE ECLECTIC REVIEW

Without a doubt, *Cooking for Cannibals*, delivers a bizarre, far-fetched, darkly humorous motorcycle ride into Los Angeles madness. It's a tongue-in-cheek reading pleasure for any lover of dark comedy, so grab a copy, climb onto Johnny Fairfax's Harley, and read off into the sunset! 5-Stars.

CPMA BOOK REVIEW

A thrilling helter-skelter of a book!

33 SOUTH TEXTWORKS REVIEWS

# COOKING FOR CANNIBALS

RICH LEDER

# APOLLO AND HERMES

GOD OF MEDICINE AND GOD OF THIEVES (AMONG OTHER THINGS)

# CHAPTER 1
# A MODERN MARVEL OF MEDICINAL MANUFACTURING

IT WAS an unprecedented feat of pharmaceutical engineering with a kiss from Mother Nature and a whisper from God. Carrie could tell without technical measure, with her naked eye, with the touch of her hand, that the rats were younger this week than last, younger today than yesterday. There was indisputable clinical corroboration to authenticate and validate her professional observations. The most rigorous laboratory methodologies had been employed. The results had been questioned and challenged time and again. Every test, trial, study, and calculation confirmed the conclusion. The aging process in all nine rats had been definitively and profoundly reversed.

The drug worked.

Carrie stood hidden in a dark corner of Lab No. 3 holding a rolling pin. Her knuckles were white from choking the handle. Her heart was beating like the bass drum she'd played for a short time in the New Brunswick High marching band back in New Jersey when she was fourteen (an unpleasant memory even now), all those years and three thousand miles ago. If she didn't keep her mouth closed, she thought, her heart would pound its way up her throat and shoot across the lab floor.

In all her thirty-five years, she'd never hit anyone on the head with a rolling pin. Never broken the law. Not a speeding ticket. Not a gum wrapper on the ground. Panic was a reasonable reaction given the circumstances. Shortness of breath, rapid pulse, and excessive perspiration were expected outcomes. Amplified adrenaline wreaking emotional chaos and intellectual havoc was a predictable and projected response. But Jesus Christ, she hadn't planned on being such a nervy mess.

To steady herself, she focused on her alibi. Technically, she wasn't here. Her car was parked in a lot on the other side of the San Fernando Valley. Witnesses had seen her with a beer in the Foxfire Room in Valley Village. There was a bartender who would confirm it. She'd used a colleague's card to scan her way back into the lab. If anyone was here with Old Tom, the security guard who worked Wednesday nights after hours, it was Stuart Langston, Alsiko's biostatistician, the smarmy math creep no one liked.

To calm herself, she focused on the courage it took to do what she was doing, how far she'd come in her own personal development to be brave enough to commit this kind of compassionate crime when her career and life were laid out before her as clear as California. She was a behavioral gerontologist, not a thief, for Pete's sake, with a good job and a steady income, a purpose and a conscience. Maybe a criminal could sneak into the lab, bonk Old Tom on the head, steal the drug, and be done with it—no remorse, no regrets—but Carrie?

She'd rue the day, but she would do it. She would make this one illegal detour in her otherwise straitlaced life, get back on the freeway, and avoid the rearview mirror as best she could.

Unfortunately, she looked straight into the rearview mirror and saw her parents, Joanna and Lawrence Kromer, fifty-one and sixty-one years old the day she'd been born back in New Jersey. Her mother had been a college librarian at Rutgers University for four decades. Her father had been a sullen research biologist —and a mean drunk. They'd never meant to marry—for God's sake, it was one inebriated night at a university cocktail party.

Her mother wasn't even supposed to have been there. But Joanna had gotten pregnant by mistake, and the respectable solution was to give the kid a family. The fact that neither parent had wanted to get married or desired a child was immaterial.

Lawrence had died of a nasty disposition (and cirrhosis of the liver) on Carrie's twenty-first birthday, about the best present she could have asked for. Joanna promptly retired with her and her late husband's university pensions and moved to Los Angeles to live her golden years in the Golden State.

Carrie went with her. She'd just graduated from Rutgers (tuition-free because she was the offspring of a university professor and a university librarian) with a degree in psychology and had gone on to earn two master's degrees and a PhD from UCLA by the time she was twenty-eight. Each degree was in the field of gerontology, the scientific study of old age, the process of aging, and the particular complications of growing old. But it wasn't the chemical equations or the biology of aging DNA that fascinated her; it was the application of the principles of applied behavior analysis in the elderly. Why old folks ticked the way they did as they got older. How to analyze elderly behavior and the lives of senior citizens.

Carrie's curiosity about the elderly had been sparked to life at an early age—when she'd realized Joanna and Lawrence were old enough to be the parents of her classmates' parents. And her intellectual captivation had only grown stronger as her mother and father packed on the years.

From her father, Carrie had inherited the research gene—the desire to set a scientific system in place and follow the process to its technical result. There was no good or bad about it, only the attention to process and analysis of the data. Lawrence would often take her to the lab because he had no time or patience for ballet and soccer and so on. As a university biologist, Professor Kromer often worked with lab rats, and Carrie found a connection with them. She liked working with them, enjoyed watching them live their little rat lives, as short and unglamorous as they were. There was a lot to learn about human comportment, she discovered, by observing lab rats in carefully controlled conditions.

From the beginning and for reasons she never understood, she found quiet pleasure in naming them. Not surprisingly, in elementary school, a certain segment of the student population had called her Rat Girl. She'd been smarter than those kids, of course—smarter than most kids. So she'd accepted the name as a matter of observable fact (she liked rats, and she was a girl) and stopped the tease in its tracks.

It wasn't that she'd been disliked. She just hadn't had a lot of friends. She was the wallflower geek introvert who preferred science club to glee club, who spent more time with rats than with kids, and whose parents had come over on the *Mayflower*. But no one had considered her an anti-social loner, a mentally unstable loser, or an emotionally dangerous outsider. There'd been no reason for anyone to think of her like that. She'd never hit anyone on the head with a rolling pin, for instance.

*Although*, Carrie thought as the Lab No. 3 door opened with a whoosh and Old Tom came in on his rounds, *that's about to change*.

From Joanna, Carrie had inherited strength of purpose, commitment to task, and devotion to order. When she hadn't been in the biology lab with Lawrence, she could often be found in the library with her mother, who'd enjoyed the company of books far more than the company of men, especially her husband. Which meant Carrie hadn't had a parental role model for romance. And that was fine as far as she was concerned. Like her mother, she didn't need a man to feel fulfilled. Her mother had found self-realization in her reference librarian research, in the row upon row of books that filled the university library; Carrie had found gratification in the lab, studying the behavioral effects of old age. Her mother had been forced into a loveless relationship after one careless night of debauchery; Carrie would not make the same mistake. If the right man came along one day

—her standards were exceptionally high—fine. If not—and, really, how could any man measure up?—also fine. But so far, she'd never met a man who'd understood her or even wanted to.

*And that includes Old Tom,* Carrie thought as the security guard crossed the lab to where she hid in the dark shadows.

She listened to his footsteps as he walked past the wall of rat cages and thought about the Greek Gods—well, the nine rats in the proof-positive group Carrie had named after them.

*Rattus norvegicus.* She'd chosen brown rats over black rats, *Rattus rattus,* for Alsiko Labs because of their longer life span— two to three and a half years for the domesticated class—and started with an assembly of several hundred of various ages. She had analyzed their behavior as they'd aged and died for the full six years she'd been working for Dr. Leo Sikorski.

The first two hundred had expired of old age—or from one of the many dozens of Sikorski's failed drug trials—so Carrie had brought in another two hundred for continued testing and analysis. Many of that second assembly had died as well, more and more of them from the drugs. And while Sikorski's endless iterations of experimental white powder had increasingly produced anti-aging properties, they'd also delivered some terrible, sometimes bizarre, side effects—death, of course, being the worst.

Until now.

Now, the drug worked wonders. After six years, Sikorski's magic white powder had unequivocally made the old brown rats —her Greek Gods—not just younger but much younger. And with no apparent side effects. It was a modern marvel of medicinal manufacturing. Sikorski's drug would change the course of human history if and when it was approved by the cogs in the arcane machinery of the U.S. Food & Drug Administration. But that was too big an *if* for Carrie Kromer—and too long a *when.*

She readied the rolling pin, positioned herself to strike and, as Old Tom went by, stepped out of the shadows and cracked him on the back of the head.

He hit the lab floor face-first. Carrie looked at him splayed out like a rag doll and hoped she hadn't hurt him too badly. She didn't dislike Old Tom. Truthfully, she hardly knew him.

*Sorry, Old Tom.* The words were ready to fall out of her mouth, but he groaned. She had to hurry.

She crossed the hallway to Lab No. 2 and went straight to Sikorski's pharmacy. She pulled a mini pry bar from her purse, broke open the locked drawer, and saw the only vial of magic medicine on the planet.

## CHAPTER 2
# DIDN'T KNOW I HAD A NEW PAROLE OFFICER

JOHNNY FAIRFAX WAS A ROCK-STAR BUTCHER—
POSSIBLY one of the best butchers in LA, certainly one of the most badass. How badass a butcher was he? If Johnny Fairfax took a How To Be A Butcher certification class, the other wannabes would want to be Johnny Fairfax, that's how badass. Of course, he'd never taken a butcher certification class—Johnny had hated school in any conformation, and school had hated him back.

He was thirty-eight years old. His arms were covered with tattoos, two colorful sleeves of chaos. Both legs too. And his chest. And his stomach. And his back. Johnny had what most people would consider to be a shit-ton of tattoos. His hair was long. His beard was scruffy. He was tall and lean, wiry and wild. He rode a beat-to-hell Harley and never wore a helmet. Like all rock-star butchers, he had every knife, carver, and cleaver in the book. Knives to die for was what Johnny had.

But Johnny Fairfax didn't want to be a rock-star butcher. Cutting wholesale slabs of beef, pork, lamb, and veal into steaks, chops, ribs, and roasts did not fulfill him. And though he did it with the power of Keith Moon, the energy of John Bonham, and the madness of Ginger Baker, being a butcher did not make Johnny's mojo jo.

Johnny Fairfax wanted to be a rock-star *chef*.

Before and after both of his stints in prison, he'd worked in steakhouses around LA. But a bad attitude and imperceptible patience meant he'd never stuck it out long enough to move onto the line—from butcher to cook. No matter how many times he told his chef he could cook like a freak of flambé, like a rogue of rotisserie, like a sultan of sauté, they'd tell him to pay his dues and wait his turn. But Johnny had paid his dues—done his time, as it were—and he was ready for it to be his damn turn right now. He could cook, he'd tell his chefs before he bounced, like a hellcat in a kitchen.

"What are you doing, Johnny?"

Ian Ferguson was the head chef at Melvin's, a steakhouse on Ventura Boulevard in Studio City, not far from Laurel Canyon, where Johnny had been working as a butcher for four weeks.

Johnny was standing at the stove, cutting cubes of beef and vegetables, adding them to a pan and sautéing them over a low flame—wine, beef stock, cream ready all around him. It was early Thursday morning.

"Making a fricassee," Johnny said.

"Who gave you permission?" Ian said.

Johnny kept cooking, cutting more meat and vegetables, adding more spices, careful not to brown the dish, adding the wine and then the shallots, sea salt, and fresh ground black pepper, braising the beef with textbook technique. He'd had similar conversations at a dozen steakhouses and knew that when kitchen tête-à-têtes started with questions about permission, bad news was in his immediate future.

"It's a French stew, Ian. No big deal. Most people make it with chicken, like you do. But it's better with beef. You should taste it."

"Don't tell me what I should and shouldn't do in my kitchen. Why are you here so goddamn early?"

"Was out too late to go home, so I came in to cut steaks, had time to spare, thought I'd make a little fricassee." Johnny added enough cream to the pan to turn the sauce white. "Beef. It's what's for breakfast."

"Put the knife down. I have to talk to you."

"No caramelization. That's the trick."

"Put the goddamn knife down."

Johnny turned the flame to a low simmer and locked eyes with the chef. In his younger years, his teens and twenties, Johnny would have beaten the living shit out of anyone who'd talked to him like that, even someone bigger than him—someone like Ian Ferguson, for instance, who had forearms like Popeye and red hair like the devil and was the size of a small building. A barrel-chested, hot-headed Scotsman.

Just like Johnny's father.

Johnny had been two years old—too young to remember—when his birthmother, an eighteen-year-old girl whose first name had long been lost to time and circumstance but whose last name was Russo or Romano or Rotolo or something Italian, had walked him down the block to the house of Patrick and Meredith Fairfax, rung the bell, and left the boy at the door with forty-three dollars and a note saying his name was Johnny and that he needed a family. The birthfather wasn't in the picture, the note said, which meant even the boy's birthmother didn't know who he was.

Merry had miscarried half a dozen times, and the doctor had said that was it, no more pregnancies for her and Patrick. Young Mrs. Fairfax had been devastated and told her husband God Himself had come to her in a deep dream and said she'd be a mother one day, so they must adopt. But Proud Pat had refused to raise someone else's child—not to mention adoptions cost more money than the fledgling butcher had in his bank account —so he and Merry had remained childless.

And then God had delivered their son to the front door. At least, that's what Merry had told Pat, and this time she wasn't taking no for an answer. Johnny Russo or Romano or Rotolo or whatever had become Johnny Fairfax, and Pat and Merry raised him as their own.

"Say please," Johnny said to Ian.

The badass tattooed butcher was not to be fucked with—especially when he was holding a knife. The chef flinched first.

"Fine. Please put the goddamn knife down," Ian said.

Johnny didn't put the knife down. He kept cooking. A metaphor for his life.

"Melvin spoke to your new parole officer," Ian said.

*Bad news*, Johnny thought.

"The fucked up part of that," Ian said, "is that we didn't know you had *any* parole officer, never mind a new one. You didn't put that in your application—the part about you being a two-time ex-con."

"Maybe I forgot," Johnny said, tasting the fricassee, adding a touch more wine.

"Grand theft, assault and battery, breaking and entering. Ring any bells?"

"What's your point?"

"My point is Melvin doesn't want ex-cons in the kitchen, especially when they lie on the application. My point is Melvin's investors aren't happy about it either. His lawyer, his insurance agent—nobody's happy. My point is you're fired, Johnny."

Johnny tasted the fricassee one last time, nodded that it was good to go, and reached for one of the warm plates stacked above the stove. "I'm a hellcat in a kitchen, Ian."

"I'll never know."

Johnny plated the fricassee, wiped the edges of the plate clean, garnished the dish with rosemary and thyme. It looked like Paris and smelled like heaven. He figured he had a day, maybe two, before his new parole officer caught up with him. If he had a job when that happened, he could talk his way out of the trouble he was in right now. He took off his apron. He'd set a place for himself at the counter—cloth napkin, small flower vase, wineglass, all the trimmings. He put the plate down, pulled up a stool, and started to eat.

"I just fucking fired you," Ian said. "What the hell are you doing?"

Johnny ignored the question. If Ian was too stupid to know what Johnny was doing, then fuck him. Anyway, he was lost in the flavor of the broth, the tenderness of the beef, the subtle snap of the vegetables, the headiness of the creamy aroma. "Didn't know I had a *new* parole officer."

"Well, you do. And he told Melvin he was going to call your landlord."

Johnny stopped eating, pushed back from the counter. "Bad to worse to fucked."

By the time Johnny pulled the Harley up to his hellhole, one-room apartment on Inez Street between Whittier and East 6th, the lowest low-rent region of the downward spiral known as Boyle Heights, it was too late. His landlord, Rodrigo Ramirez, an old gangbanger turned slumlord, had put Johnny's meager possessions in the front yard. Rodrigo, called Rodney the Wrecker by everyone in the hood, sat in a ten-dollar folding lawn chair surrounded by his posse.

"What the fuck, Rodney?" Johnny said, crossing the crab-grass to the ring of Walmart lawn chairs. Rodney and his boys were drinking cans of PBR at nine forty-five in the morning. There was a healthy stack of crushed empties in front of them.

"What the fuck?" Rodney the Wrecker said. "I tell you what the fuck. Your new parole officer call me to find out how you doing. You got a job? You walking a straight line? You living a clean life?"

"*Had* a job," Johnny said. "They just fucking fired me."

"'Cause you never tell them you a ex-con," Rodney said. "'Cause you never tell me. *That* what the fuck, amigo."

"I need a place to live, Rodney. It's part of my parole," Johnny said.

"I hear you, compadre. But can't be no convict in my castle," Rodney said. "Can't raise no eyebrows at this address."

Johnny nodded. Rodney ran a drug lab in a back room of the house where Johnny had lived for the past few months—until this morning.

"You're a fucking ex-con too, Rodney," Johnny said.

"Don't tell no one," Rodney said, putting his index finger on his lips. "Is a secret." The old gangbangers, ex-cons one and all, laughed out loud.

"Now I need a job *and* a place to live," Johnny said.

"Yeah, you do," Rodney said. "Parole man send you back up, is what he thinking."

Johnny shook his head in defeat. One of the old gangbangers handed him a PBR. Johnny popped the top and drank half the can.

"You a cook?" Rodney said.

"I'm a cook," Johnny said.

"Got some guy know some guy quit his job this morning on account of he can't get to work no more on account of some guy break his legs on account of he take something don't belong to him," Rodney said. "I ain't saying what he take or who he take it from or who break his legs. Just saying the guy was a cook at a place on Palm Avenue called Copacabana. West Hollywood. Job come with a place to live. What they call that, Santiago?"

Old gangbanger Santiago, teardrop tattoos on his face, drained a PBR while crushing the can. "Room and board."

"Room and board," Rodney said.

Johnny ran to his Harley. Called back over his shoulder. "You got time to watch my stuff?"

"Yeah, I got time," Rodney said to his posse as Johnny fired up the bike and accelerated into LA's morning madness. "Time for a yard sale."

# CHAPTER 3
# THAT'S WHAT EDUARDO WOLF WILL WANT TO KNOW

CARRIE ARRIVED for work Thursday morning. There were no police cars in the Alsiko parking lot, though there should have been a handful of cruisers and a couple of unmarked sedans.

For one thing, either Old Tom had died—*Sorry, Old Tom*—in which case someone would have found his corpse first thing this morning, or he'd regained consciousness and reported the crime to Sikorski, who should have alerted the police, in which case a crime scene team would still be dusting for prints, searching for evidence, and combing for clues.

For another thing, an experimental revolutionary drug, the honest-to-God Fountain of Youth, the only capsules in existence, had been stolen as soon as its efficacy had been confirmed.

From either angle, every pharmaceutical lab across the country should have been crawling with cops because contacting law enforcement when investigational new drugs went missing was what sensible, accountable, and lawful labs had to do and always did.

Yet Carrie wasn't surprised by the lack of LAPD presence. She hadn't expected anyone to notify the authorities. Alsiko Labs wasn't simply under the research radar; it was entirely off the investigational grid. And for good reason—Dr. Sikorski's drug would be worth billions and billions, not to mention change the path and plight of humanity. Absolute silence and secrecy were essential.

The lab was located on Sherman Way, between Reseda Boulevard and Wilbur Avenue, in the town of Reseda, the hub of the West Valley, meaning the San Fernando Valley. The main entrance faced Sherman Way, but the lab staff used a door from the parking lot on the left side of the building—an unattractive, two-story, concrete office block they shared with a lowbrow tax preparer, who rented the first floor. A muffler shop, a Carl's Jr., a tire place, and a McDonald's were nearby neighbors. This string of bargain-basement blocks had been built in the 1970s and was showing its worn-out, cut-rate retail age—like so many other strings of blocks across the Valley.

The directory in the lobby gave no mention of Alsiko. The lab's front door was blank as well. There was no lab phone. The mailing address was a post-office box in Van Nuys assigned to a shell company called Reseda Sciences. If you wanted to find Alsiko Labs, you'd have to work at it. If you wanted to know what drug Sikorski had been researching, developing, and testing for the past six years in this building—and had finally, miraculously manufactured—you'd have to work harder.

Dr. Sikorski had half a dozen lab techs who'd come and gone like a Redondo riptide. Carrie rarely bothered to learn their names, knowing in a matter of months they'd be dragged out to sea and replaced by six more. While the techs followed Sikorski's R&D directions to the letter, none of them were privy to what anyone else in the lab was doing or how any one piece of research might affect the final pharmaceutical outcome—a drug whose purpose remained a mystery throughout their brief tenure.

Only Carrie and Stuart had been with Sikorski from the beginning. Sikorski needed his data organized and analyzed with meticulous precision. That way he knew where he'd been, how he'd arrived at his current chemical combinations, and what subtle changes should chart his next trial. Stuart, for all his douchebaggery, was a wizard with lab stats, and Carrie was irreplaceable because she could read the rats like no one else. Only they knew the nature of the drug Sikorski was creating. Only they knew he'd succeeded beyond anyone's wildest pharmacological dream.

"Is he alive?" Carrie said to Sikorski.

He'd met her at the Alsiko side entrance and told her the terrible news: late last night, someone had whacked Old Tom's skull with a heavy blunt object, maybe a baseball bat, the attending physician had surmised. Old Tom had suffered a concussion—confusion, nausea, vomiting, blurred vision, headaches, memory loss—and was in a state of shock.

Sikorski was well under six feet tall and weighed one hundred thirty pounds soaking wet. He had a skeletal skull with a receding hairline that accentuated the size of his forehead, which was as wide as Wyoming, like some extraterrestrial come to Earth to eliminate the tragedy of aging. His hair was gray and long, wild and wiry, Einstein hair shooting out at crazy angles. His teeth were crooked, as was his smile, which appeared only for fleeting moments of sardonic irony and nothing else. He was void of humor.

"Memory loss?" Carrie said.

Instead of traversing the hallways, they took the shortcut through Lab No. 3—Carrie's rat lab, where she'd clocked Old Tom—and headed toward the back of the building.

"Does he remember what happened?"

"He doesn't remember what city he lives in," Sikorski said.

Alsiko occupied a five-thousand-square-foot space bisected by two long hallways, side to side and front to back, creating four large rooms, all with multiple entrances. Three of the rooms were labs. The fourth room, in the rear south corner, was divided into several smaller spaces, including a storage closet, the restrooms, the breakroom, and Sikorski's private office.

All three labs were stocked with state-of-the-art scientific equipment. There was no way to anticipate that this butt-ugly building in the middle of this low-rent Reseda block had an über-modern, heavy-hi-tech, investigational drug research and development laboratory on the second floor. Alsiko was as mechanized, computerized, and space-age as the drug incubators at Merck, GlaxoSmithKline, Eli Lilly, Pfizer, and Johnson and Johnson.

An off-the-reservation scientist like Sikorski had no business owning and running a lab like this. Virtually every big-ticket item had been purchased regardless of price. From amino-acid analysis instruments to automated biomolecular interaction analyzers to blood-bank automation systems to bacteria-colony counters to gas chromatograph mass spectrometers to animal pulse oximeters to cell culture incubators to automated solid phase extraction systems to liquid handling robotics to multi-mode microplate readers to DNA shearing sonicators to vortex evaporators to ultrasonic homogenizers to every cutting-edge piece of pharmaceutical gear betwixt and between, no expense had been spared.

It had cost a fantastical fortune. Whoever the investors were, they'd bet two hundred million or more on Sikorski's search for the Fountain of Youth—and now their drug had come in.

They arrived at Sikorski's private office, a large room made claustrophobic with math and science. Sikorski's desk dominated the far wall. Reports, charts, and graphs were stacked high into the air—both on his desk and in piles across the floor. The bookshelves behind his desk overflowed with periodicals and papers and books by the thousands. A whiteboard covering the wall opposite his desk was filled with chemical equations written with multi-colored markers—a complex parade of computations that could only be the work of a madman or a genius. Which was what Dr. Alexander Leonard "Leo" Sikorski was—impossibly intelligent in some particular respect but to the exclusion of all other personal, professional, private, and social behaviors. Sikorski's special genius was biochemistry. In all other regards, he was an awkward, little, sixty-eight-year-old man.

A conference table, also drowning in scientific manuscripts, stood between the desk and the white board. Stuart Langston was already seated. He was forty years old, long and lanky.

Carrie and Stuart looked at each other as Sikorski shut the door. It was unusual for them to be together in the boss's office. To be together anywhere. Stuart had hit on her their very first day at Alsiko. His come-on line was that he'd been married and divorced three times because women, it turned out—wives in particular—weren't at all like statistics that could be forced into orderly columns and made to behave as he desired. He was as arrogant and emotionally stunted as he was mathematically brilliant.

Carrie had advised him that the minute they'd met, she'd developed an incurable, contagious sexual disease. He'd gotten the point, and for the past six years, they had silently agreed to be lab colleagues who disliked each other.

And while they were at it, neither one of them liked Sikorski, who didn't like either one of them in return. All in all, an emotionally dysfunctional laboratory family who'd somehow managed to make a miracle.

"Old Tom's attack is terrible but not the worst of it," Sikorski said, moving to the end of the conference table, where Carrie now sat with Stuart. "The assailant broke into the pharmacy drawer and stole the capsules."

Carrie acted stunned. Stuart didn't have to act.

"Did you call the police?" he said.

"No," Sikorski said. "I can't call the police."

*Didn't* and *wouldn't* made sense. But *couldn't*? "Why not?" Carrie said.

"Because my investor agreement forbids all contact with American agencies unless such contact is approved by the investor," Sikorski said. "The Los Angeles Police Department would be defined as an American agency. Contact was denied."

"Because?" Stuart said.

"Because my investor is prohibited from doing business with United States companies by the Federal Office of Foreign Assets Control, which handles licensing and oversight of the government's international economic sanctions," Sikorski said.

"Your investor is sanctioned by the federal government?" Stuart said.

"It's complicated," Sikorski said.

"You probably shouldn't have told us that, Leo," Carrie said.

"You would have found out soon enough," Sikorski said.

"What does that mean?" Stuart said.

"It means one of you stole the capsules," Sikorski said. "It means my investor has an individual on retainer who handles these matters for them. His name is Eduardo Wolf. He's their fixer, and he has been alerted."

Carrie was taken aback, though not surprised, by Sikorski's accusation. She knew she had to tread carefully. A melodramatic defense would be a dead giveaway seeing as how she'd never once been remotely melodramatic. She would have to *act* her way through this, a skill she hadn't used since her short stint in the New Brunswick High School drama club, where she'd played a handful of minor roles until realizing that the drama backstage was even less tolerable than the drama onstage.

"I know *I* didn't steal them," Stuart said, looking at Carrie. His indignation was genuine, part of his persona. "The odds of getting away with this are microscopic. There are too few suspects on the board. Too few avenues of escape. Too few doors to hide behind. It's not worth the mathematical risk. Eduardo Wolf will play the angles clean and nail you to the wall before Friday."

"He won't nail *me* to the wall because I didn't steal them either. I don't steal things. My mother taught me honesty is the best policy. And I would never hurt Old Tom," she said with feeling but without shedding a tear. That she was lying through her teeth with some success made her think she should have stuck with the drama club after all.

"You are the only ones with means and motive," Sikorski said as if analyzing the results of an Alsiko experiment. "Only you knew the drug had been successfully tested, the location of the capsules, and Old Tom's security schedule."

"Or you could have stolen them," Stuart said. "You had the same information we had. Dr. Leo Sikorski, the aggrieved scientist. I'm sure your investor is thinking that as we speak."

"Why would I steal my own drug?" Sikorski said.

"That's what Eduardo Wolf will want to know," Carrie said.

Sikorski's face fell flat. He took a seat at the conference table. "Do you know the expression 'Leave no stone unturned'?"

Carrie and Stuart both nodded.

"We are all stones," Sikorski said.

# CHAPTER 4
# THE NATIVES ARE RESTLESS

IN THE ROARING TWENTIES, West Hollywood was an unincorporated area in the middle of Los Angeles County, where gambling was illegal. To escape the long arm of the LAPD, which stretched everywhere but the unincorporated area, casinos, nightclubs, and other unsavory joints grew like Locoweed along Sunset Boulevard. Even after the Sunset Strip lost popularity with local Los Angelinos, it continued to be a hot ticket for tourists.

Russian Jews migrated to these autonomous neighborhoods by the thousands in the late 1970s and then again in the late 1980s; and the gay community, who'd called the freewheeling district home base for thirty years before that, grew bigger and bolder, more confident, more flamboyant.

Most of the Russians and the LGBTQ crowd were renters. In the early-to-mid 1980s, when Los Angeles County decided to do away with rent control, the unlikely allies banded together and, with help from the Coalition for Economic Survival, voted to incorporate as the City of West Hollywood. In their next breath, they passed one of the toughest rent-control laws in America.

That was good news at the Copacabana, one of several dozen Palm Avenue, low-rise courtyard apartment buildings not far from the Strip, around the corner and down the boulevard from The Roxy Theatre, The Viper Room, and Whisky a Go Go—three world-famous nightclubs showcasing rock bands playing for movie stars, hangers-on, and other assorted LA deadbeats, all of them doing drugs and drinking high-end booze until sunrise on Sunset.

It was good news at the Copa because an elderly Russian immigrant with money to burn had bought the building and turned it into a rental for less fortunate Russian retirees, who could now and forever find an affordable apartment. Over the decades, as the original tenants met their maker at the Frozen Gates of Siberia in the Sky and the original owner sold out, the Copa continued as a low-rent rest home for old folks even as much of Palm Avenue went condo, younger people poured in, and WeHo, as it came to be called, became a hotspot.

How hot? Sal Mineo had a house on Holloway Drive—before he was murdered in his carport. Sinatra, Flynn, the Gabor girls, John Wayne, and Howard Hughes all lived (at one time or another) in Sunset Tower. Filmmakers found West Hollywood and studios were built, movies were made, and big things happened, including the largest Halloween street party in America, where more than three hundred fifty thousand costumed lunatics living the high life gallivanted through town like the most crazy-colorful cavalcade on Earth. It was called the West Hollywood Halloween Carnival, or as the locals liked to say: Tuesday.

With exactly none of West Hollywood's history in his head, Johnny Fairfax parked his Harley between two cars right in front of the Copa, rear tire kissing the curb, bike perpendicular to the sidewalk—creating his own spot out of thin air, as it were—and went up the tiled steps and through the gap in the gate.

Like many of its neighbors, the Copacabana was a two-story, rectangular structure. The entrance faced Palm Avenue. A free-form, kidney-shaped pool dominated the courtyard. Classic ceramic pavers gave the courtyard a California feel. Potted plants, flower boxes, and couple of trees brightened and shaded the outdoor space. Disparate loungers and chairs were scattered around the pool. To Johnny's left, the north side of the Copa, were three outdoor dining tables with large shade umbrellas, colors faded by the year-round sun, weighted by concrete bases below the tables. Each table had six mismatched chairs that looked to have wandered in off the street and found a home. Johnny hoped he could do the same.

Seven ancient human beings sat at the tables—three men, four women, all wrinkled with age, shriveled with arthritis, eyes clouded with cataracts, hard of hearing, hair thin, bones brittle, minds drifting through memories of lives once lived. Wisps of the people they'd once been. Fragile folks. Their canes, walkers, and wheelchairs were parked nearby. The youngest was eighty-eight if she was a day.

Johnny had no experience with old people. His grandparents had died by the time he was ten. His mother, Merry, had lost her life to cancer when Johnny turned sixteen, and Patrick, his father, had been hit by a bus crossing Fairfax Avenue the day Johnny turned twenty-one.

There'd been no old people in Johnny's professional life either. Commercial kitchen work was for young men and women who were strong and sturdy and had stamina to spare. The hours brutal. The labor backbreaking. The stress unrelenting. In all the restaurants Johnny had worked, he'd never come across anyone older than sixty. No eighty-eight-year-olds at the after-hours bars where Johnny drank tequila and smoked weed until dawn.

He knew nothing about old people. Didn't know how to talk to them or how to listen to them or what they were thinking about him or what he was thinking about them. He'd always imagined it would be horrible to be very old. His first minute at the Copa had not convinced him otherwise. Because in addition to advanced age, these people had something else in common: they were not happy.

Where the hell did you start with unhappy old people? He didn't want to come off as having never been a chef anywhere, but he didn't want to ruin his chances either. *Fuck it*, he thought. *Even old people have to eat.*

"I'm here about the cook job," he said.

They stared at him. Had they heard what he said? Did they not understand?

"I heard your cook quit this morning," he said. "I want to apply for his job."

The old folks looked at each other, looked at Johnny, looked at each other, looked at Johnny, and still said nothing.

*Shit*, Johnny thought. *I'll probably have to spoon-feed them.*

He spoke louder and slower. "I want to be your cook."

"What's your name, Tattoo Boy?" one of the women said. An oxygen tank was attached to her wheelchair. A cigarette hung in her mouth. She was African American. Her name was Lillian.

Johnny stepped back. *They heard me all along. They're checking me out.* "Johnny Fairfax."

"We're not getting any younger, Fairfax," said a man who Johnny thought might be asleep and drooling but, in fact, was just drooling. His name was Arnold. "What the hell took you so long?"

"What?" Johnny said.

"Going to be time for lunch before we eat breakfast," another woman said. Her skin was weathered and burnt like the dark leather of a Wild West saddlebag. Johnny wondered whether she'd gone out to lie in the sun sometime last decade and never come back inside. Her name was Betty.

"I just—" Johnny said.

"Kitchen's that way, Fairfax," another man said, pointing to a first-floor door behind the tables. The man was in his nineties and wore black glasses big enough for a person with a head three times his size. His name was Norman.

"Ask for Joanna," a third woman said. She was even older

than the guy with the black glasses but had bleach-blonde hair. Her name was Dolores.

*Must have been a looker sixty years ago*, Johnny thought.

"She's captain of the kitchen committee," said yet another man in his mid-nineties. He was Black and wore a suit and tie. His name was Bernard.

"Make it snappy," said the fourth woman, the oldest of the group. "The natives are restless." She was so small, so thin, so aged it was like she was invisible. Her name was Helen.

Nearsighted Norman lifted a bony finger and pointed again at the first-floor kitchen door. Johnny walked to it, then paused a moment to take in the Copa. He would have checked it out when he'd first walked in, but his attention had been drawn to the arthritic assholes waiting for food.

Four sets of steps—one in each corner of the courtyard—led up to the balconied second floor. Three apartments lined the north side. Two were on the backside, three more on the south side. All could be accessed from the covered walkway that wrapped around the courtyard.

On the first floor, the courtyard level, on the north side (the side that Nearsighted Norman had pointed to), what would have been three apartments matching the layout on the second floor had been built to be the cook's apartment (closest to the building's front entrance), the interior dining room (in the event of bad weather), and the kitchen (closest to the back of the building).

Staying on the courtyard, there were two more two-bedroom apartments along the back side of the building, and coming back down the south side (like the north side across the courtyard), what would have been three apartments matching the layout on the second floor had been built to be, from back to front, a laundry room, a card room in the middle with several tables and a television, and a two-bedroom apartment that had been turned into a kind of guest room/fitness room combination, with yoga mats, free weights, and a massage table.

Johnny was torn. Part of him wanted to walk into the kitchen and apply for the job. Another part wanted to run for the Hollywood Hills. So he turned back to the old people thinking maybe one of them could tip the scale one way or the other.

"My goddamn breakfast's not going to make itself, Fairfax," Drooling Arnold said.

"Don't waste your breath, Arnie," Oxygen Tank Lillian said. "Tattoo Boy couldn't cook his way out of a paper bag if he tried."

# CHAPTER 5
# UNPRINCIPLED BEHAVIOR IS TO BE EXPECTED

JOANNA'S BONES were disintegrating inside her eighty-six-year-old body. Though she was thin, her legs could no longer support her weight, so she used a wheelchair. She could get from her wheelchair to the bed or the toilet or the car, but she couldn't stand for more than a minute without collapsing. Her bones hurt; her muscles hurt; the blood moving though her veins hurt; it all hurt all the time.

Hard as it was to handle the relentless decay of her physicality, harder still was the reconciliation that her mind had not lost half a step as the decades disappeared—she was aware of every degeneration. Would it be worse to lose your mind while your body stayed strong? Joanna conceded that either way was a curse. God did not reward the elderly for living long lives. He punished them one way or the other. She knew God had to be a man because a woman would not have so severely, so cruelly defined aging. Only a man would have made it so desperately painful.

*When I see God,* she occasionally thought, *I'm going to kick Him in the nuts, see how He likes it.*

She'd moved to Los Angeles fourteen years earlier after a lifetime in New Jersey, where she'd been a Rutgers librarian for almost half a century. She'd traveled three thousand miles to recover from—celebrate—her husband's death. She'd been seventy-two at the time. Carrie, her twenty-one-year-old daughter, had come with her.

Joanna's health deteriorated soon after they'd arrived in Southern California. When she'd needed more attention than Carrie could provide, she'd moved into the budget-friendly Copacabana, where her meals and laundry and housekeeping were taken care of.

The Copa had been home for six years. For half that time, she'd been the Copa Kitchen Captain, supervising the cook and the kitchen—menu planning, food preparation, inventory organization, equipment upkeep and cleanliness, financials, wait service, and so on.

Joanna took her kitchen responsibilities seriously and ran a tight ship, just as she'd buttoned up the Rutgers library—a place for everything, and everything in its place. She'd expected the Copa's Mexican cook to follow suit. And before he'd resigned without notice this very morning, Carlos Castillo had done just that, steering the stove through three meals a day, six days a week, fifty weeks a year.

Castillo had been far from exceptional. His recipe and menu development had been unremarkable, meal prep and presentation passable, sanitation suitable, and resident communication below average. But he'd always provided a vegetarian option for Joanna, and he'd been reliable, never missed a shift throughout her tenure, a big check in his plus column. Which was why she had been so surprised when he'd called early this morning to say he'd accidentally fallen down the stairs, broken both legs, and would not be coming back.

Knowing Castillo's childhood gang history and hearing the fear in his voice, Joanna doubted the accidental part of the accident. It seemed even less likely that her Copa kitchen committee could cook breakfast for the rest of the residents without destroying the kitchen and each other.

Three residents, average age eighty-nine, made up the committee. Bob was six feet five inches in his socks and still as handsome as Clark Gable. But while his body remained ramrod straight and disease-free, his mind was melting to mush. He'd sold women's shoes for a living, moving from store to store up and down the California coast until he couldn't remember what shoes he was looking for in the stockroom (or what store the stockroom was in). At that point, he'd hung up his shoehorn and moved into the Copa.

Joining Tall Bob were Walter and Brenda. He'd worked for the United States Postal Service in Albany, New York, for fifty years and received a reasonably nice watch on the occasion of his retirement. A Black man with white hair and a voice so deep and resonant that the Reading Room Committee often asked him to recite poems to the Poetry Club. He was continually cantankerous and did not always say yes.

His main squeeze, Brenda, had been a bubbly residential real-estate receptionist in Pasadena. She was zaftig—plump, pleasing, and pleasant.

They were an unlikely pair, living proof opposites attract. They'd met at the Copa and shacked up soon after. Neither had any intention of marrying the other. *We're living in sin before it's too late*, Buxom Brenda said when anyone asked. *Ain't nobody's damn business*, Cranky Walter would say.

He'd never cooked anything in his life except maybe a can of soup, but Buxom Brenda had made him join the kitchen committee because, she said, she was trying to socialize him. So far, it hadn't worked.

*There will be knife wounds and burn victims*, Joanna thought as the committee attempted to make pancakes and bacon on the griddle. The three of them were covered with flour and milk and raw eggs. There was bacon grease in their hair, on their faces and clothes, and all over the kitchen. Fresh-squeezed orange juice seemed too tall a task, even for Bob, who was very tall indeed. It had been so many years since any of them had prepared a meal for themselves, not to mention a large group, that they might as well have set out to steal the Hollywood sign. Joanna shook her head and began writing the want ad for a new cook.

"I'm looking for Joanna," a voice behind her said.

She spun her wheelchair. A tattooed man stood by the kitchen door. She narrowed her eyes. *Transient. The Groundskeeping Committee failed to fix the front gate, and a panhandler has wandered in looking for a free meal. Although he asked for me by name, so there might be more to this than vagrancy.*

"I'm Joanna."

"I'm Johnny Fairfax. I want to apply for the cook job." He looked around the room in slack-jawed amazement. "The room-and-board job."

*Aha. More than vagrancy.* "Is that so? What makes you think we need a new cook at the Copa, Mr. Fairfax?" Joanna said.

The committee noticed the tattooed man but continued flinging food around, losing their battle with breakfast, looking like some kind of Asian television game show contestants where the winner is whoever creates the most astounding mess.

"Because your old cook quit this morning."

"And how do you know that?"

"Heard it from a friend of his."

"Did you hear why he quit?"

"Someone broke his legs, the guy told me."

"Was it you?" She didn't trust transients. If you couldn't put down roots, unprincipled behavior was to be expected.

"I never met him," Johnny said. "Why would I break his legs if I never met him?"

"Because you're a tattooed man, and tattooed men cannot be trusted," Joanna said with her librarian's discipline voice. "Tattooed men are hiding something under their ink, hiding in their own skin. What are you hiding, Mr. Fairfax?"

She stared into his eyes and looked absolutely through him like only a lifelong librarian can. He was hiding something important, lying to her, to himself, about something grand. Not about breaking the cook's legs but about something larger, something monumental. And if he was lying about something that big, he'd certainly lie about something small. And if he'd lie about big things and small things, then he'd lie about all the things in between. If she'd learned one thing after more than forty years in the Rutgers library and twenty-one years in an empty marriage, she had learned that.

Johnny said nothing. For Joanna, it was more evidence he was indeed hiding something.

"That's what I thought," she said. "Thank you, Mr. Fairfax. You can apply with everyone else when the job appears in the local paper."

She turned her wheelchair back to the committee but sensed Johnny had not left the kitchen, despite being dismissed. She spun around. "Is there something else?"

In that brief moment she'd turned away, his countenance had changed. He was less intimidating, more despairing.

"I'm an ex-con," Johnny said. "I lost my job and my room for not coming clean about that. If I don't have work and a place to live by tomorrow, I'll be in violation of my parole, and my new parole officer will send me back to prison. I can't go back. I'm not going back."

"Are you saying you served time in prison?" Joanna said. She wasn't surprised, given his appearance and demeanor.

"Twice," he said.

"For what crimes?"

"Grand theft, assault and battery, couple other things, nothing good."

"I don't care for criminals. They offend my sense of decency, my fondness for law and order. Especially order."

"I don't like them either, if that helps."

"It most certainly does not."

"I need this job."

"You sound desperate, Mr. Fairfax."

He nodded. She drilled him with her eyes. He was an ex-con,

and now he needed a job and a place to live more than he needed anything else in the world.

"Can you cook?" Joanna said.

"Like a hellcat in a kitchen," Johnny said.

"Let's find out if that's true," Joanna said. "There are eleven of us, and breakfast is late. Clean this mess, make us something wonderful, include a vegetarian option, and we shall see what we shall see. Are we in agreement?"

"Damn straight," he said.

"Splendid," Joanna said. "There are three tables beside the pool—I'm certain you saw them on your way in. That is our outdoor dining room. We are served family style. Pots and pans are above the stove. Knives and utensils are in the drawers. Platters are on the rack. Plates, glasses, coffee cups, and silverware are in the cabinet. Everything is labeled. The big rolling cart is against the wall. The refrigerator is full, we have every spice under the sun, and the entirety of the Copa commercial kitchen is at your disposal. Shall we say breakfast in thirty minutes?"

Then she shooed Buxom Brenda, Cranky Walter, and Tall Bob out of the room, and the four of them joined the others. Joanna explained to the community what had happened this morning to Carlos and what was happening right this moment with Mr. Fairfax.

For the next half hour, they carped about the old cook and complained about the tattooed criminal in the kitchen who might be the new cook. Joanna assured them that would never happen but hardly participated in the discussion, instead regretting she'd used the ex-convict's desperation against him.

Not so much that she'd done it—mislead him to cook their breakfast *while* making him believe this one-time stint was a prelude to the position *while* knowing full well she would never hire a convicted felon—but that she'd lowered herself to his level of indecency and disorder.

Yes, of course, even a convicted felon deserved better than to be lied to if they were trying to straighten their life, but who knew if Mr. Fairfax *was* trying to straighten his life? She hadn't gotten a good read on that. In any event, the tattooed criminal—*criminal* mind you!—had said he could cook, and she'd led him down the garden path. There was no taking it back.

But she could be excused this one trespass, couldn't she? For the greater good of the Copa? No matter. It was likely that Mr. Fairfax had lied about his cooking prowess in the same way she'd lied about breakfast being his audition, so in that regard she'd simply defended her territory.

The outcome seemed evident: the Copa crowd would eat Mr. Fairfax's mediocre breakfast because they were famished, they would voice their disapproval of his character, his tattoos, and his food, and she would dismiss him and place the want ad in the paper.

But just as Bleach Blonde Dolores was dialing the Yeastie Boys Bagel Truck in the event Mr. Fairfax had flown the coop, the kitchen door opened, and Johnny pushed the big rolling cart into the courtyard.

All eyes were on him as he put the plates and glasses and silverware on the tables. The old folks set themselves up while Johnny went back to the cart for the platters. Eggs scrambled with gruyere cheese, sautéed sweet onions, and red peppers; bacon and sausage and grits; toast and butter and jam; melon and berries and whipped cream; fresh-squeezed orange juice and hot coffee. Three platters of hot food, three baskets of toast, three bowls of fruit, three pitchers of juice, three pots of coffee.

Johnny served each table one of everything, wished them bon appetite, moved back to the cart, and wiped it clean.

The old folks looked at each other and at the food and at each other and at Johnny and at each other and at the food. After thirty minutes of concurring that breakfast would not be served and if it was served, would be unappetizing and inedible, the tattooed criminal had presented them with a sumptuous morning meal that smelled as good as it looked.

The Copa crowd ate like mad men and women, consuming

everything in reach. Joanna ate too. She knew the food was good —better than good—and this worried her because she couldn't hire a convicted criminal, a tattooed man on parole. She couldn't, and she wouldn't. She would put her foot down if she had to.

"Done deal for me," Nearsighted Norman said.

"Sign him up, Joanna," Saddlebag Betty said.

"Chain Tattoo Boy to the stove," Oxygen Tank Lillian said, only half-kidding. "Don't let him get away."

"I agree," Tall Bob said. "What are we talking about again?"

"We're talking about Mr. Fairfax, Bobby," Suit and Tie Bernard said. "How he's going to be the new cook as soon as Joanna offers him the job."

"Offer him the job, Joey," Drooling Arnie said.

"He *is* a criminal," Joanna said. "Are we sure he's the right cook at the right time? Perhaps we should—"

"Vote on it?" Cranky Walter said. "Good idea."

"Yes, let's vote," Buxom Brenda said.

"All those in favor?" Invisible Helen said.

Every hand went up except Joanna's. She couldn't believe it. There would be no putting her foot down after all. The residents had hired an ex-con out on parole to be the new cook. Johnny Fairfax would be her responsibility.

"I got the job?" Johnny said to Joanna.

"Three meals a day," Joanna said, rolling herself to the kitchen to see if he'd cleaned up after himself. "Six days a week, fifty weeks a year in exchange for room and board and a paycheck. Lunch is served at noon. I suggest you get started."

# CHAPTER 6
# DO YOU THROW DARTS, DR. SIKORSKI?

HE WAS a man of many nations, a citizen of the world. He had a briefcase filled with dozens of identifications he used according to the client, the country, and the conundrum he'd been contracted to correct. For the United States alone, he had seven separate passports.

His client roster was international in nature, anonymous corporate entities with global reach, monetary muscle, and political pull. To these multi-national conglomerates, there was no such thing as a small problem. A ghost in the morning machine, a blip on the afternoon radar, or an anonymous overnight hiccup might translate into billions blown in tomorrow's trading. An unanticipated slip of the tongue could be the difference between a lost opportunity and twenty years of market domination. From their executive suites above the ebb and flow of the public square, the faceless folks who called the shots at these dividend-driven enterprises did not leave such things to chance.

They left them to Eduardo Wolf.

This was not his name. It was the persona he employed while working in Southern California. He imagined it made him sound like a Hollywood mogul. Certainly, he looked the part—ten-thousand-dollar Kiton suits, seven-thousand-dollar Cartier watches, two-thousand-dollar Ferragamo shoes.

From his Brazilian mother, he'd inherited his Latin looks—dark hair, stylishly unruly; smooth-as-silk olive complexion; smoldering eyes. From his German father, he'd inherited his physicality. Six feet tall and one hundred seventy pounds, lean and muscular, fast, agile, and uncommonly strong.

His parents had divorced when he was five, and he'd lived with his hot-tempered, fashion-model mother in Brazil, spending two weeks each year in Germany with his construction-foreman father, until he'd turned eighteen. Then he'd moved to Germany and joined the military, the KSK, Germany's Special Forces Command.

He'd become impatient with the KSK's adherence to rules and regulations, frustrated at having his hands tied to the organization's moral mast, and maneuvered himself into the *Bundesnachrichtendienst*, or BND, the German Federal Intelligence Service, looking for an opportunity to stretch his muscles, so to speak. He was a dream special agent, highly educated and impeccably trained. He spoke six languages fluently, all with pitch-perfect accents. He was drop-dead handsome and didn't look the slightest bit German.

BND had given him the international espionage experience he'd been hoping for, but he'd outgrown government intrigue and become anxious to see what his skill set was worth in the world market.

It was worth a fortune. He was exceptionally well-compensated for his efforts. Global corporate clients set up layers of subcontracting shell companies in far-flung countries and paid whatever price he quoted. His methods were non-traditional, frequently unfriendly, often injurious, and occasionally deadly. His employers cared nothing about the unorthodoxy of his techniques because his ends justified his means.

He did not have a home address. He lived in high-end hotels around the world, changing locations and identifications in patterns that even seasoned secret agents couldn't track. He had no listed cell phone number. No registered email address. No credit cards. No social media accounts that could be traced back to anywhere or anyone. Clients contacted him through an ultra-exclusive, exceedingly secure Swiss communications agency. Repair requests were managed as if they'd never been made. Payments were personally deposited in international bank accounts, electronically transferred to other countries in different currencies, laundered judiciously, and finally delivered as dollars to safety-deposit boxes around world.

In other words, there was no Eduardo Wolf unless an anonymous board of directors discovered a procedural snag in, say, Southern California that required immediate repair. Then, Eduardo Wolf existed in ways you did not want to experience firsthand.

Eduardo leaned against Sikorski's desk. It was five thirty, Thursday afternoon. Just this morning, he had been in Quebec, enjoying the company of a professional escort who made more money than a member of Congress. While he and the escort had bathed in the afterglow, sharing a room-service breakfast of champagne, poached eggs, and croissants, he'd received word from the Swiss agency that a certain pharmaceutical client had requested his services.

As soon as the required deposit had registered in an Argentinian brokerage account, he'd flown first class to Los Angeles International Airport. There, he'd hired a driver to take him directly to Alsiko in Reseda.

He was experiencing some jet lag, it was true, but not so much he couldn't immediately administer a little restorative justice to get the ball rolling.

He'd instructed Sikorski to empty the office at five sharp so he and the biochemist could share some quality time alone in the lab. He had arrived at five fifteen. After the usual pleasantries had revealed nothing regarding the missing capsules, Eduardo had applied the right amount of pressure for precisely the right amount of time in exactly the right location on Sikorski's throat, causing the scientist to lose consciousness. He'd then placed Sikorski's desk chair in front of the whiteboard wall, stripped the biochemical genius down to his boxers, zip-tied him to the chair, and waited.

"I did not expect you to look like this," Sikorski said, regaining consciousness.

"What did you expect?" Eduardo said, reading through private papers on Sikorski's desk.

"Rough around the edges, I suppose," Sikorski said. He looked down and discovered he was practically naked and zip-tied to his chair.

"Thank you," Eduardo said, "but I'm certain you'll find me to be quite rough around the edges as we spend these next few moments together."

He put the papers on the desk and walked across the room to the whiteboard. Sikorski swallowed hard.

No one ever expected Eduardo Wolf to look as he did. Handsome as hell. Benicio del Toro handsome. The same droopy eyes. The same devastating smile. The same intimidating glare. He'd chosen thin, tight-fitting, black leather gloves, a gorgeous suit with no tie, and handcrafted dress shoes. Long goatee, black with flecks of gray, not overly manicured, as fashionably unmanaged as his thick head of hair. He was fifty years old.

"I have one question to begin," Eduardo said, standing in front of Sikorski, "and I am going to ask it until I'm convinced your answer is honest and true. Only then will we move on to my second question and to my third and so on. Do you understand?"

"Please," Sikorski said, his voice disappearing into a wormhole of terror.

"Where are the capsules?" Eduardo said.

"I don't know. That's why I called the company. If I knew where they were, if I knew who took them, why would I call?"

"I've come a long way to see you, Doctor, and I left the

company of a lovely young woman to do so. Don't add insult to injury. You would call to cover your tracks, to buy time, to point me in the wrong direction. Your call does not raise you above suspicion. It makes you suspect number one. Where are the capsules?"

"Why would I take them?"

Eduardo nodded. He'd heard this same question in one form or another a hundred times. He moved back to the desk, opened his briefcase, and removed a beautiful, hand-carved wooden box.

"Perhaps you became displeased with your profit participation. Perhaps you received a better offer from a pharmaceutical competitor. Perhaps you realized the power of your creation and decided to play God all by yourself. I can think of a dozen reasons you might take the capsules."

He moved back to Sikorski and opened the box. The inside of the box was lined with soft red felt and contained eight, professional-quality, handmade darts, each in its own pocket, steel tips as sharp as knives.

"Do you throw darts, Dr. Sikorski?" Eduardo said.

Sikorski made a high-pitched sound that resembled the word no.

"I play when I'm in Great Britain, which is more often than you might imagine, so I can say without hesitation the Brits do love their darts." He lifted a dart out of the box and held it in front of Sikorski's face. "These are custom-made, Wolfram steel-tip tournament darts. Wolfram is Tungsten in its purest form."

"I'm a chemist," Sikorski said weakly.

Eduardo laughed. "That's funny, Doctor. But if we can get past the irony, you must also know that using a high-pressure, ultra-fine injection molding process that produces a uniform atomic structure for exceptional strength and beautifully balanced weight distribution will result in a flawless dart." He turned and took three strides from Sikorski. "The official distance from board to toe line is seven feet, nine and a quarter inches, but under the circumstances, eight feet will suffice."

"What are you going to do?" Sikorski said, whimpering as if he knew the answer.

"I can't compete with professionals," Eduardo said, imagining the toe line and setting his feet, "but I'm better than average."

"How much better?" Sikorski said, practically crying the words.

"I will try not to hit a main artery or an internal organ, but I cannot make any promises," Eduardo said, lifting the dart, measuring the distance, and focusing on the target. "Now then, where are the capsules?"

"Oh God, I don't—"

*Ssswwwttt*. Eduardo threw the dart as if he were playing for pints in a London pub. It hit Sikorski in the left bicep, went into the muscle, and drew blood.

Sikorski screamed in pain, looked down at the dart sticking out of his arm. "Oh my God!"

Eduardo readied the next dart. "Where are the capsules?"

"Stop ... please ... I don't—"

*Ssswwwttt*. Right thigh. The scientist screamed bloody murder—mostly because there was blood flowing from his wounds.

"Oh my God, please ... no more ... stop throwing darts at me ... please ... stop ... please ..."

Eduardo smiled. He so enjoyed this part of the process. Some people chose chocolate but a touch of torture satisfied like no other indulgence.

"Where are the capsules?" Eduardo said, another dart raised and ready.

"The drawer was locked. The security guard was in the lab. It had to be an inside job, but it wasn't me. I can't tell you where—"

*Ssswwwttt*. Left shoulder. More blood. More pain. More

screaming. Spittle flew from Sikorski's mouth. Snot ran from his nose. His eyes bulged out of his skeleton skull.

"Where are the capsules?"

"No, no, please ..."

*Ssswwwttt*. Left thigh. Sikorski wailed like a banshee. There were four darts sticking out of his stripped-down body. Blood dripped all over him. He was in shock, overwhelmed with fear and horror and disbelief. He was hyperventilating.

"Where are the capsules?"

"I don't know, I don't know, I don't know, I don't know ..."

Eduardo lifted the fifth dart. "If pharmaceutical research and development doesn't work out for you, Doctor, I'm certain you'll find work as a professional dart board."

*Ssswwwttt*.

# CHAPTER 7
# SIDE EFFECTS OR NO SIDE EFFECTS

"YOU'RE HOME EARLY," Joanna said.

Carrie walked around the pool to the umbrella-shaded dining tables. The Copa crew were drifting down the stairs and across the courtyard for dinner. It was ten minutes to six. Upon becoming the Copa Kitchen Captain, her mother had instituted a schedule that called for the evening meal to be served at precisely six o'clock. Not five to. Not five after. Six o'clock.

"Leo sent everyone home at five," Carrie said.

From Alsiko, she'd taken the 101 to Laurel Canyon to Holloway to Palm—a fifty-minute drive one way with normal traffic. She did it twice a day. She occasionally listened to jazz during the trip, an appreciation she'd learned from her father, but more often than not let the silence wash over her, hoping it would remove the epidermal layer of stress she'd developed during the day.

"I'll tell you about it at dinner. What's Carlos making?"

"Carlos isn't making anything," Joanna said. "Carlos quit this morning because someone broke his legs."

"What? That's terrible. Really? Someone broke his legs? Who would do that? And who's in the kitchen if Carlos quit?"

Carrie had liked Carlos. He'd never said two words in all the years he'd been cooking at the Copa, which meant he'd never said anything nice but also meant he'd never complained about anything either.

"I'll tell you about it at dinner," Joanna said.

They shared a look that carried an entire tit-for-tat conversation, and Carrie started toward her apartment on the courtyard level at the far end of the building.

A sixty-six-year-old woman (a youngster) did the Copa's laundry and cleaning. Her name was Maureen Breen. She was from Ireland and had an accent so thick you couldn't cut it with a hacksaw. None of the residents had any idea what she was saying, but their linens smelled like an ocean breeze and their rooms were tidy, so Maureen's unintelligibility became part of the landscape.

Maureen worked five days a week. Not enough for the Copa crowd, who needed cleaning and laundry services more or less every day of the year, so when Carrie's Sherman Oaks lease had come up two and a half years ago, and Buxom Brenda had moved in with Cranky Walter, she'd taken the weekend Copacabana job in exchange for Brenda's old apartment and a break in what was already the lowest rent in LA. Not to mention, it was a chance for her to be near her mother as Joanna's health went south.

It was the ideal second job. During the day, she monitored her rats, and on weekends, she watched her Copa crew. It was like going from one gerontology lab to another. She never felt she was giving up anything by working weekends. She'd chosen long ago not to spend her free time on frivolous social comings and goings. Never understood the nightclub hubbub. Experimenting with drugs and drinking and staying out late had never interested her. Maybe if she'd met someone special, she would have tried that lifestyle on for size, but that had never happened, and she'd been too busy for that kind of carousing anyway. She had her work to attend to, she had her mother to take care of, she had the Copa crowd to consider, and she had the Fountain of Youth capsules hidden in her purse.

Dinner was divine. A crisp green salad with homemade lemon vinaigrette followed by chicken piccata over orzo with grilled zucchini followed by homemade butterscotch pudding with fresh whipped cream. Heaven on a plate. Carlos, on his best day, before someone had broken his legs, had never cooked anything this good, although his Friday night special enchilada casserole (Mexican lasagna) had always been a crowd pleaser.

"So, your turn," Carrie said. "Who is he? What did he make for lunch?"

"His name is Johnny Fairfax. Grilled gruyere on sourdough with tomato soup and fresh-baked chocolate-chip cookies with lemonade," Joanna said.

"Sounds good."

"Unfortunately, yes. "

"So where is he?"

"Cleaning, of course."

Carrie had changed her clothes and come to the tables a few minutes past six, dinner already served, so she'd missed meeting Johnny because he'd returned to the kitchen as Joanna had instructed.

Her mother explained that Mr. Fairfax had stayed for the meal during his breakfast audition, but after he'd won the job, she'd informed him that after serving, he was expected to continue working in the kitchen until the residents had finished eating. Not because he wasn't welcome, though he wasn't, but because there was much to do and not enough hours in the day to do it. Afterwards, he would clear the tables, finish doing the dishes, prep for tomorrow—as far in advance as was realistic— make his shopping list, meet with Joanna, and then go about his business. His nights were his own so long as the work was completed to Joanna's satisfaction.

"He has to satisfy *you*?" Carrie said.

"Indeed he does," Joanna said.

"So today's his first and last day?"

"One would hope."

Carrie listened while her mother told her about Johnny being a convict out on parole. About his being in prison twice for grand theft, assault and battery, breaking and entering, and who knew what else.

Her kneejerk reaction was revulsion. *How could anyone assault someone and take something that didn't belong to them?* But while eating orzo drizzled with lemon, capers, butter, and white wine, she realized she might have to temper that feeling now that she'd rolling-pinned Old Tom and stolen the capsules. *Still, how could you all hire an ex-con?*

Except she didn't just think it. She said it loud enough for all three tables to hear. "How could you all hire an ex-con?"

"We were backed into a corner," Saddlebag Betty said.

"Like hungry animals," Oxygen Tank Lillian said.

"And hungry animals will do anything to survive," Suit and Tie Bernard said, wearing a suit and tie. "Marlin Perkins taught me that."

"I had a thing for his assistant," Bleach Blonde Dolores said.

"Jim Fowler was a dish," Invisible Helen said. "My husband had a conniption every time I turned the TV to *Wild Kingdom*. Let me tell you, I would've gotten wild with Jim Fowler."

The Copa crew laughed until Tall Bob forgot what they were laughing about.

"Anyways, we took a vote," Cranky Walter said.

"And we voted to hire him," Buxom Brenda said.

"But he's a violent criminal," Carrie said. "You can't put a violent criminal in the Copa kitchen."

"Carrie, this is Mr. Fairfax," Joanna said. "Mr. Fairfax, this is my daughter, Carrie."

Carrie choked down her last bite of chicken. He was standing right beside her.

Johnny lifted Carrie's empty plate. "Relax," he said so only she could hear him. "I'm not going to beat anybody's ass on my first day."

He'd meant it as a kind of joke, but the humor was lost in translation. Not surprising given his hardcore history and lack of comedic practice in prison. And Carrie didn't have the most finely tuned sense of humor either, seeing as she'd spent much of her time talking to rats. It was a swing-and-a-miss moment for both of them.

"I don't think that's funny," she said.

"You call me a violent criminal, and I used to be one, so I get it, so I make a joke about it to break the ice, let you know I'm good now...that's funny as shit."

She'd heard that smartass tone before. It pegged her as a stick in the mud.

They locked eyes. Carrie took him in. He had the tall, gaunt, scruffy look of a hard-drinking, drug-taking troublemaker, just like the greasers she'd known back in New Brunswick. She'd despised those New Jersey jerks, with their small brains and big egos, their muscle cars and macho bluster. And now she was well on her way to detesting the new Copa cook with the tattoo-covered arms. She knew what they were called: sleeves. He was exactly the kind of person she'd loathed all her life.

"Not even mildly amusing," she said.

He took her plate, cleared the rest of the table, and moved away. Their exchange had taken ten seconds. The Copa crew had missed it. Joanna had not.

"Your turn," Joanna said.

"My turn to what?" Carrie said, watching Johnny roll the cart filled with dirty dishes and platters and glasses and silverware back to the kitchen.

"To tell me why Leo sent everyone home at five."

Carrie nodded, refocused on what was important. She took the capsules from her purse and put them on the table.

"You took them," Joanna said

"Yes," Carrie said.

"I wasn't sure you could ... or would," Joanna said.

"Neither was I."

"Are you in danger?"

"Leo's investor sent a fixer person to find them, but I was careful. My alibi is foolproof. Whoever he is, he can't track the drug to me."

They were quiet for a moment. Mother and daughter staring at the drugs on the table.

"It really works?" Joanna said.

"The rats are younger, stronger, faster, smarter. More alert. More awake. More playful. They have more stamina. More energy. Increased appetite. The aging process has been absolutely reversed. Yes, it works."

"There are no side effects?"

"None that have presented. Which is not the same thing as saying there are no side effects. There are no side effects in evidence, that's all we can say."

"That's all you need to say."

"I'm having second thoughts. I need to say that too."

It was true the drug worked. Indisputably true. But the next step in the FDA approval process was not to steal the capsules and give them to your mother. The next step was to formally apply for human testing. Except FDA approval procedures were long and tedious, and once approved, the testing process was longer and more tedious. Carrie had no problem with assessing longer-term results on people she didn't know—that was how drug development worked—but she did have trepidation about her mother being human test subject number one. On the other hand, Joanna could not wait years and years for FDA approval.

Carrie and Joanna had become close as adults in Los Angeles —closer than they'd ever been in New Brunswick, where they'd bickered and battled throughout elementary, middle, and high school. Carrie thought their California friendship might be a result of their cross-country adventure as well as an emotional reaction to the march of time, the failing of Joanna's health, and the nearing of the inevitable end. Joanna had told Carrie she hadn't wanted to be a parent in the first place and had struggled with motherhood, which was why those years and their relationship were dreadful.

But as hard as they were, Carrie saw the Jersey days in a different light. She remembered her mother stepping between her and her father whenever he'd lost himself to the gin and blamed Carrie for his underachievement. Throughout her childhood, Joanna had been all that stood between Carrie and her father's emotional abuse. When Carrie was older and stronger and better able to defend herself, she'd returned the favor when her father directed his drunken rage at Joanna. They weren't so much mother and daughter as they were a wrestling tag-team.

The basics between them hadn't changed; their relationship was still contentious, always measure for measure. But the truth was they had always needed each other. Which was why Carrie had stolen the drug, to try and stretch their time together.

And why she had second thoughts. *We would have seen a serious side effect by now, wouldn't we? Of course, we would. Right? Wouldn't we?*

"I'm not having any second thoughts," Joanna said. "My bones are turning to dust inside my body. I can feel them disintegrating, bone by bone. I'm wracked with arthritis. It hurts to breathe. My body is frail and failing. I'm in pain when I wake up, and I'm in pain when I go to bed. The doctor says I have a year to live. Growing old is not for the faint of heart. There are days—many days—when I think, Shoot me now. Let's get the afterlife show on the road already—"

"Mother—"

"But then I think, No, hold that curtain. I don't want to go yet. My mind is not ready to abandon ship. I'm willing to take the risk. Side effects or no side effects, if the drug works ..."

"It works."

"Then I'm taking it."

Joanna lifted the vial and opened the lid as Johnny arrived

and served homemade butterscotch pudding with fresh whipped cream.

He put a bowl in front of Carrie and met her eyes. "It was definitely funny."

She caught the undercurrent in his voice. The New Brunswick greaser disdain. The immaturity. *What a fucking fuddy-duddy killjoy,* the undercurrent said.

"It definitely wasn't funny."

While Carrie and the cook decided not to like each other, Joanna put a capsule in her mouth and swallowed it a with swig of black coffee.

# HEBE AND DIONYSUS

GODDESS OF ETERNAL YOUTH AND GOD OF RITUAL
MADNESS (AMONG OTHER THINGS)

# CHAPTER 8
# THE MIDDLE OF THE MIDDLE

"AM I GETTING PAID?" Stuart said to Carrie. "If I'm here, I should be getting paid. Are we open? Are we closed? What are we doing?"

"I don't know," Carrie said. "I'm sure we'll find out."

Friday morning. Lab No. 3. *None of the other employees are here,* Carrie thought. *And no one else is coming.*

Sikorski had texted her and Stuart late Thursday night instructing them to be in the rat lab first thing Friday morning, and that was all he'd said. She'd texted him back asking if he'd learned anything, if he'd located the drug, if he'd heard from the fixer, but Sikorski had not replied.

Stuart bitched on and on about his paycheck, about how underappreciated he was, and about how this was his last Alsiko straw, but he had less than five percent of her attention. Carrie was focused on the Greek Gods.

The rats moved through the tabletop maze and reached their food with ease. They seemed to be toying with the maze, seeing how fast they could go, creating new shortcuts. Obstacles that had baffled them mentally, taunted them physically, and tortured them emotionally as they'd aged were now a simplistic game. They had become so strong they were climbing up and over the impediments just so they could get to the food in a straight line. Carrie had never seen rats behave like this in any experiment ever.

She lifted Hermes up to her face. The rat knew her. She was friend, not foe. A source of food and affection. Carrie knew the rat better than the rat knew her. She'd basically raised Hermes from birth. She held him firmly but gently, feeling the tautness of his back and his belly, the ropey musculature of a much younger, healthier, and stronger rat—Hermes in his prime, except better than his prime. Not long ago, before he was given the drug, Hermes was old and soft and flabby. Now his thin and patchy fur was thick and healthy. Cloudy and confused eyes had become clear and focused. Teeth worn to the bone by age were now sharp and strong. It seemed impossible to Carrie, but the evidence was in her hands.

"If you don't give them back the drug, we're all out of work," Stuart said. "You know that, right? So long, Alsiko. So maybe you should give them what they want so your bank account and my bank account and everybody's bank account doesn't get blown to fucking bits."

As was her habit since she was a little girl in Lawrence's lab at Rutgers, she held Hermes up to her face, nose to nose so the rat could get the closest sense of her. She smiled, put him back in the maze, and turned to Stuart. "Maybe *you* should give them back the drug."

"Certainly, one of you should."

A man had silently entered the lab with Sikorski at his side. Leo looked like a living corpse. Paler than usual. Even more skeletal. Limping on both legs. He held a blood-stained bandage to his cheek.

"What happened to your face?" Carrie said to Leo while looking at the man.

All her life, she'd been attracted to sultry Latin men: Julio

Iglesias, Antonio Banderas, Andy Garcia, Javier Bardem, Benjamin Bratt. There was something inexplicably charming, something unscientifically enticing about their smoky, seductive Hispanic looks that drew her in and pushed her buttons.

But with the exception of one Bolivian biology boy at UCLA, Latin men had not been interested in her. She was not homely or unattractive—on good days, she thought she might even be pretty. Clear skin that had nearly never seen the sun, hazel eyes, wavy brown hair that fell below her shoulders, and a pleasing face. She was curvy, just not in a Victoria's Secret sort of way. She was, as her mother often said, the dreaded pear-shape—that no hairstyle or tan lines could fix. Small breasts, big hips, heavy thighs, and a broad butt. She had a tummy but wasn't overweight. She was simply wider and thicker than was considered commercially attractive. Julio Iglesias, she told herself, would never be in the market for a pear-shaped woman, and neither would Enrique, his fine-looking son.

"I'm afraid that one got away from me," the man said, answering for Leo. "I'm better than average but not professional, and it turns out Dr. Sikorski is a bleeder."

Carrie had no idea what that meant but knew it wasn't good. Sikorski looked terrified and relieved at the same time. *Leo found out what that meant in person,* she thought.

"Who are you?" Stuart said. "And what the hell does that mean?"

"I am Eduardo Wolf," Eduardo said. "I'm here to recover the stolen capsules—"

*The fixer.* A shiver ran down her spine—one part fear, one part physical attraction. She did everything she could to disregard the attraction part.

"And what that means is Dr. Sikorski has been tentatively eliminated as a target."

The acerbic irony was not lost on Leo, who smiled briefly because the pain in his cheek where Eduardo's dart bit him still hurt a great deal. And was still bleeding.

"So now you need to eliminate one of us," Carrie said.

"One of you has taken a drug that does not belong to you," Eduardo said.

"Who does it belong to?" Stuart said.

"Yelchin," Eduardo said, referencing the colossal, state-owned Chinese pharmaceutical company. "Although the research and development of Dr. Sikorski's drug was funded by a Chinese venture-capital company that does hundreds of millions of dollars' worth of business with both Yelchin and North Korea, intermingling their monies and pharmaceutical investments through a complicated web of ancillary business interests that I don't pretend to understand."

"So you work for Yelchin?" Carrie said.

This was bad news if it was true. Yelchin was a brutally competitive drug conglomerate that took no prisoners when it came to its R&D. Rumors of mob-like violence were as much a part of their worldwide corporate reputation as law breaking, price gouging, document shredding, lab burning, formula stealing, regulation dodging, environment polluting, and profit worshipping.

"Neither directly nor indirectly," Eduardo said.

"North Korea?" Stuart said.

"An embargoed nation?" Eduardo said. "That would be bad business on my part, don't you agree? In this particular circumstance, I am on retainer with an international law firm that consults with a subsidiary of a shell company that is in and of itself a subsidiary of a shell company that has tenuous ties with a consulting firm that has an informal relationship with a spin-off company of a spin-off company ... I imagine you can complete that picture without my help."

"You're not here," Carrie said, her pulse racing.

"I'm not anywhere," Eduardo said.

"It's a few dozen capsules," Stuart said. "Can't Leo just make more?"

Eduardo shook his head. "If the drug appears in the world,

as it now seems likely to do, Yelchin cannot be connected to its research and development, seeing as how its principal partner is an embargoed nation. Such an association would compromise Yelchin's other American pharmaceutical interests, which are significant."

"Then close the lab," Stuart said.

"That's certainly possible, but the profound nature of this individual drug and its astronomical monetary upside is not something Yelchin wishes to walk away from without first seeing a comprehensive effort on my part to locate the capsules and salvage their investment," Eduardo said.

"So who's next?" Carrie said.

He nodded. "Thank you for understanding. I'll start with Stuart."

"The hell you will," Stuart said. "Get the fuck out of my way. I quit."

Carrie knew Stuart worked out regularly at Gold's Gym on Cole Avenue. Besides manipulating complex biostatistics, the only other thing he excelled at was fitness. He was wiry, he was strong, he was arrogant, belligerent, and cocky by nature, and right now he was pissed off to no end. Certainly, he was a jerky douchebag, but when Stuart got big and wide, all six-foot-three of him, she could see how someone could find him imposing.

Stuart got big and wide and went for the door where the fixer stood. But before he could push his way out of the room, Eduardo hit him hard in the throat, below the Adam's apple, with the knuckles of his right hand, which he'd locked together like a single piece of steel. It didn't look like a punch from a boxing match to Carrie. It looked like a martial-arts blow delivered with bad blood and intended to incapacitate on contact.

Stuart's eyes shot open in pain and shock. He would have screamed, but he couldn't breathe. He bent at the waist because he also would have vomited, but he couldn't do that either because, again, he couldn't breathe.

Eduardo took Stuart's right hand, found the pressure point in the fleshy connective tissue between the thumb and index finger, and applied enough force to bring Stuart to his knees. If Stuart was hurting before, now he was in agony, paralyzed with pain—and he still couldn't breathe.

"If you go to the police," Eduardo said, "they will not find me. But I will find you. I hope that's become clear. Carrie? Leo? Stuart?"

Carrie and Sikorski nodded.

Stuart did the best he could. Narrow bands of breath were now making it into his lungs, so since breathing was possible, the biostatistician could fully concentrate on the excruciating pain he was experiencing.

"Excellent. Stuart and I are going to the breakroom to continue the elimination process. I saw an InSinkErator with powerful pain potential. I will see you both in the lab after lunch, say around two?"

And then, using the pressure point on Stuart's hand, Eduardo lifted the biostatistician off his knees and led him, like a dog on leash, out of Lab No. 3. Carrie and Sikorski locked eyes.

"If he doesn't get the capsules back," Sikorski said, "he'll destroy all evidence of the lab, any indication that the drug's R&D happened here. Remember how yesterday we were stones?"

"Yes," Carrie said.

"Today, we're evidence." He turned and limped out of the lab.

Carrie couldn't move her legs, but her mind was running. She wasn't thinking about the beating Sikorski had taken or the beating Stuart was about to take or what the Latino fixer would do to her when he was done with the biostatistician. Instead, she was thinking about her mother, who had taken the drug last night, which made her evidence in in Eduardo's world. *I have to get to the Copa and keep the capsules quiet.*

She glanced at the Greek Gods, who were now leaping through the maze more like antelopes than lab rats, then exited for Sikorski's office. She would tell him she was going home, would be back after lunch, and would he please convey that to Eduardo Wolf so the smoldering fixer didn't think she'd skipped town? No point pissing him off. Look what he'd done to Leo and Stuart when he was in a good mood.

Carrie went past the breakroom/kitchen. The door was shut, but she could hear hushed voices. No painful protests. No blood-curdling screams. Just inaudible whispers. Maybe some begging for mercy. It was hard to tell.

Farther down the short hallway, Sikorski's office door was ajar. He was on the speakerphone, standing at his desk, facing away from the door, his back to Carrie, bandage still held to his bleeding cheek. She could hear both sides of his conversation.

"How long has drug been missing?" a man with a Russian accent said.

"I discovered its disappearance Thursday morning," Sikorski said.

"Is Friday. Is there reason you don't call yesterday?"

"I thought I could find it and avoid bothering you."

"You don't call anyone else?"

"Who would I call? Pfeiffer is my only investor."

Carrie's mouth fell open with such force she imagined Sikorski must have heard her jawbone unhinging, but he was other-wise involved...*with Pfeiffer*, the Russian drug conglomerate with its nefarious, state-owned fingers in pharmaceutical develop-ment around the world.

Leo had lied to them about their being his only investor. And if he'd lied to Pfeiffer—to *Pfeiffer*, for God's sake—it stood to reason he'd lied to Yelchin as well. *Jesus*, Carrie thought. *He's playing both ends against the middle, and the ends are Russia and China.*

The bad news was Yelchin had a worldwide reputation for employing the use of violence as a means of protecting their pharmacologic territory, real or imagined. The worse news was

Pfeiffer was known for condoning the use of force as a means of claiming medicinal property that didn't belong to them.

*If the middle is the miracle drug*, Carrie thought as she quietly closed Sikorski's door, *then I'm the middle of the middle.* As she went back down the hallway past the breakroom, Stuart roared like his spine was being pulled out through his throat. The InSinkErator growled beneath his screams.

# CHAPTER 9
# THE POINT OF PAROLE

JOHNNY FAIRFAX DID NOT GIVE EVEN a little shit about his new parole officer, but he did give a great big shit about not going back to prison, so being late for his first meeting wasn't an option because he had to wipe his slate clean with the guy, whoever he was. The new parole officer had called Melvin's and learned Johnny was no longer gainfully employed. Then he'd called Rodney the Wrecker and discovered Johnny no longer had a permanent residence. That Johnny had found the Copa job with room and board that same day would be to his credit, but there was bad behavior against him he would need to address if he was going to stay on the outside.

Johnny served breakfast to the Copa crew (oatmeal with fresh berries, cinnamon toast, poached eggs), cleaned the kitchen, prepped for lunch, showered and changed his clothes, and decided not to take the 10 to the parole office—the Santa Monica Freeway could be a mid-morning parking lot if someone sneezed the wrong way. Instead, he took Palm to San Vicente to West Olympic to Arlington to West Washington to East Washington to Alameda. He arrived at ten twenty-five. His meeting was at ten thirty. Plenty of time to erase the board and get back to the Copa before lunch.

The parole office was in a nondescript, two-story gray building in a beat-to-hell industrial neighborhood near Johnny's old Boyle Heights stomping grounds—old meaning two days ago, when Rodney had thrown him out and sold his possessions at an impromptu, gangbanger yard sale.

The inside was drearier than the outside. Johnny waited in the first-floor reception area with five other paroled ex-cons and the usual handful of visiting cops who could always be counted on to ruin the party. There were a dozen uncomfortable chairs and several decades-old coffee tables piled with publications that had expired years ago. Johnny flipped through a ten-year-old fishing magazine and stopped at a full-page picture of a bass or a trout or some river fish with a hook in its mouth being dragged out of the water.

*I'm that fucking fish*, he thought.

"Mr. Fairfax," the receptionist said, "Mr. Boston will see you now. Room 211. Top of the stairs, turn right, end of the hall on your left."

The gray upstairs carpeting hadn't been changed since the seventies, when the building was constructed. There were equally old gray file cabinets on both sides of the hallway. It was snowing parole papers every which way. Johnny knocked on 211.

"It ain't locked, Fairfax," a Barry White voice said from inside.

Johnny pushed the door open and stepped into the room. It was small and cluttered, drab and bland. Army-issue file cabinets, possibly from the Korean War, lined three of the four walls. Stacks of files and reams of parole papers covered every inch of horizontal space. An ancient credenza was centered against the wall opposite the door. A mismatched desk stood in front of the credenza. Two metal chairs from different decades faced the desk. And seated behind the desk was an extra-large Black man.

"Just so we straight from the top," the man said, "I'm Ben

Boston, your new parole officer, and you're Johnny Fairfax in violation of your parole. Shut the door."

Boston stood and pulled a file from a cabinet along a side wall. He wasn't just extra-large; he was a Mack truck of a man. Maybe forty-five years old. Maybe older. Maybe younger. It was hard to tell because he was so damn big. Six-eight, three hundred ninety pounds. Fat *and* barrel-chested. He could have been a nose guard for the LA Rams or a bodyguard for a Death Row Records rapper.

He was impeccably dressed. Fashionably styled in an NFL gangsta sort of way. Tailored royal-blue, three-piece pinstripe suit, vest buttoned up. Baby-blue dress shirt with a cranberry paisley tie knotted with a slick Half Windsor. A cranberry handkerchief decorated the breast pocket of his suit coat. Big black beard. Tortoise-shell glasses. Expensive brown dress shoes. Chic brown fedora.

*Hard-ass prick. Fuck you and your fedora.* "I'm sorry," Johnny said, "I know I was supposed to call you as soon as—"

"You fucked up your parole? You got that right, you skinny tattooed fuck." The big man took a menacing step toward Johnny and held up the file labeled Fairfax in a massive hand. "This says you a two-strike convict, motherfucker. Three strikes, you fucking out."

Johnny knew what he wanted to do. He wanted to hit Ben Boston in the nuts so hard the asshole parole officer would bend down so Johnny could bash his brains out with one of the metal chairs. He also knew he couldn't lift a finger because he wasn't going back to jail, no matter what. He took a breath and forced himself to be respectful.

"I got a new job and a new place to live the same day I lost the old job and the old place to live," Johnny said. "I know I'm supposed to tell you when shit like that goes down, but I also know you're busy, so I took care of it so you wouldn't have to waste your time. I thought I might get points for being a good citizen, but I can see now it was a mistake."

"Your whole life's been a goddamn mistake," Boston said. "Ain't that right, Fairfax?"

"Pretty much," Johnny said. "But that's the point of parole. Chance to turn shit around. That's what the parole board told me."

Boston glared down at Johnny, took another half step toward him. Johnny knew not to take a step back. He had to hold his ground or Ben Boston would own him for the rest of his parole. He'd learned that life lesson from his hotheaded father in his father's butcher shop, Fairfax on Fairfax, from jackass chefs in a dozen LA steakhouses, and from dirtbag convicts in prison—both times.

"Sit down," Boston said, heading back around the desk. "Big Ben about to educate your ex-con ass pertaining to the point of parole."

Johnny sat in one of the metal chairs. It was hard and cold and uncomfortable. Boston sat in his desk chair.

"Parole is a privilege," he said, lifting Johnny's parole agreement and pointing at Johnny's signature. "Comes with a contract you signed before your release, conditions you agreed to live by. These conditions require you to meet with your parole officer on a regular basis, so said parole officer can assess your ex-convict behavior and adjustment to life in the lawful world. Your parole officer monitors your conduct on a weekly, sometimes daily basis to determine whether you in compliance with your parole certificate, whether you playing with drugs or alcohol or weapons or whatnot. Whether you gainfully employed. Whether you permanently residing in a copasetic setting. Or whether you full of shit about your shit. Should your parole officer find that you *not* in compliance with your parole certificate, if you have *not* lived up to the conditions of your parole as determined solely by your parole officer, then a warrant is issued for your arrest, and your ex-convict ass goes back to prison until a parole violation hearing can be arranged. For a two-strike motherfucker like you, Fairfax, a parole violation is the difference between you living the rest of your maggot life on the outside or you living the rest of your maggot life on the inside. You follow me so far?"

Johnny had a bad feeling about where this was going. "So far."

"The California Department of Corrections and Rehabilitation divides the state into four Parole Divisions. Los Angeles is the smallest division in terms of area, but it is the most densely populated and is home to more than sixteen thousand parolees assigned to a dozen different units. Parole officers are overwhelmed with work. Your everyday average parole officer carries a caseload of between fifty and sixty parolees. As you might imagine, that is a shit-ton of parolees to organize and supervise. As you might also imagine, your everyday average parole office is overworked and underpaid. As you might finally imagine, I am not your everyday average parole officer."

"I'm getting that," Johnny said, his feeling going from bad to worse.

"Your previous parole officer retired to sell insurance or shoes or some shit, and I was told to take his caseload because our unit is understaffed and underfinanced, meaning additional compensation did not come with the additional work. But that don't bother me, Fairfax, because I am an entrepreneurial parole officer, meaning I see the parole business as a business. Which brings me back to the point of parole, which is how much money are you making a month at your cook job at the Copa, which you acquired without the consultation of your parole officer, which from the get-go is a violation of the principles of your parole?"

"Two grand, plus room and board," Johnny said.

"Then your cost of compliance is two hundred dollars a month."

"I pay you?"

"If you want to be violation-free for the remainder of your term of parole, two years and ten months, then, yes, you do."

Even though he'd been right about the bad-to-worse feeling, Johnny wasn't surprised to find out corruption was part of his parole. He'd discovered dishonesty and exploitation everywhere he'd ever been. Some kind of extortion was a part of every game he'd ever played. Every fiber of his soul said he should shut his mouth and pay the man the money. He even said it inside his head—*Shut your mouth and pay the man the money*. What was two hundred dollars a month compared to a lifetime of freedom? He was a two-strike violent offender. Strike three was the end of the line. Two hundred bucks was nothing—a small price to pay. He opened his mouth to say, *Done deal*, but instead said, "Fuck you, you fat motherfucker. I'm not paying you shit."

Big Ben Boston leaned over his desk. "The parole system is meant to rehabilitate a high percentage of released convicts, but not all of them. If one hundred percent of released convicts were rehabilitated, that would mean the system be broke because how in the fuck can every damn one of sixteen thousand convicts be rehabilitated? At least one of them would have to be a skinny-ass, tattooed cocksucker like yourself who violated his damn parole on the first day with his new officer. The first fucking day. And that's the good news, Fairfax. Because for the California Department of Corrections and Rehabilitation to prove the viability of its parole procedures to the public, it must fail at least a few dozen ex-cons every goddamn year. It's the only way to know parole works when it works and don't when it don't. You understand? The parole community *needs* you to go back to prison. It *requires* you to violate your certificate. To fuck it up and fuck it up fast. Your return to prison is how we know we're successful. Which is to say that not one motherfucker on my side of the law will question my decision to issue a warrant for your arrest. They will slap me on the back and say, 'Goddamn, Big Ben, you done it again. Thank you for proving the system works. Now go back about your business with this official letter of commendation.' Except letters of commendation don't pay my bills. Which is to say the cost of your compliance is now two hundred fifty dollars a month." Boston sat back. His chair groaned in agony.

If Johnny had hidden a gun in his pants, he'd have shot Big Ben between the eyes. But having a weapon was a violation of his agreement, so he didn't.

"I'm not going back," he said. "But I'm not paying you either."

"Your confusion is duly noted," Boston said, making notes in Johnny's file. "Likewise, it is also duly noted that you are in violation of your parole, and since the first step in the process of calling in a warrant for your arrest is a site inspection, I am scheduling one for Tuesday. Give you a few days to reconsider your serious situation."

Boston came around his desk, took Johnny by the arm, and lifted him out of the metal chair like a rag doll. The parole officer towered over him, blocking out the sun and moon and every thought between them except one: Johnny would have to come up with the money or go back to prison unless Big Ben Boston met with some form of fatal misfortune between now and then. Since that didn't seem likely, Johnny was screwed.

Boston opened the door and dumped him in the hallway. "Keep in mind that you will fail this inspection with flying colors unless you put three hundred dollars in my pocket on Tuesday." With that, he shut the door in Johnny's face.

"Fuck Tuesday," Johnny said.

# CHAPTER 10
# A BEAUTIFUL DAY FOR A DIP

AS SHE DROVE BACK to the Copa, Carrie should have been thinking about how much trouble she was in, about Eduardo Wolf waiting for her at Alsiko, about giving him the capsules and hoping for a no harm / no foul verdict when she returned to the lab after lunch. In a way, she *was* thinking about all of that, except as the traffic crawled from Reseda to West Hollywood, her thoughts took the following form: *I am not a virgin.*

She had done it twice. Once with a boy named Daryl Sasso in his parents' basement after a high-school science club meeting, and once with the Bolivian biology boy at UCLA.

Daryl had liked swimming, which was why he'd been on the swim team, and physics, which was why he'd joined the science club, but he'd been obsessed with militaria and had worn vintage Army jackets no matter the season. He'd known the names and identification numbers of every plane, ship, tank, and rifle across all branches of the service. He'd also been tall and gangly with plenty of teenage acne.

It had not been an act of pity on her part. She had not felt that way about Daryl. She'd understood his captivation with all things military in the same way he'd comprehended her fascination with all things rat. They hadn't been physically attracted to each other and weren't particularly friends. They'd simply shared a lab station in science club and found a level of coexistence that didn't include discomfort, contempt, or condescension —not too shabby for high-school wallflower science geeks.

It had been an act of kindness. Premeditated but not entirely selfish. Carrie had considered the consequences of a sexual encounter and concluded that she and Daryl would both benefit from their conjoining. Carrie could check off losing her virginity and feel as if the femininity facet of her high-school development was more or less on track, and Daryl could tell the swim-team bullies he'd been laid, and maybe they'd leave him alone for a few weeks. Daryl had agreed with her assessment.

She barely remembered anything about the sex except for the World War II model jet fighters suspended in mid-battle from Daryl's basement ceiling and the fact that neither of them had enjoyed the clumsy encounter.

On the other hand, she remembered plenty about seducing the Bolivian biology boy, a freshman undergrad who spoke enough English to ask for help with his bio homework. She'd been a grad school teaching assistant. It was the start of the semester. He'd only just arrived in America and didn't know anyone. They'd had coffee and gone back to her room to study, but soon they were in each other's pants, and she was whispering his name—*Alonzo, Alonzo, Alonzo, Alonzo*—and running her hands through his hair. Heart pounding, room spinning, body shaking. She couldn't risk losing her TA position, so it had been a one-time-only affair.

Anyway, the reason she was thinking about Daryl and Alonzo and not being a virgin was because it had crossed her mind that Eduardo Wolf would assume she *was*. It would not be a conscious consideration. More a brief flash in the back of his mind: *Is this pear-shaped, rat-loving behavioral gerontologist still a virgin? Yes, I imagine she is.*

That nugget of underestimation would permeate his world view of her. Eduardo Wolf would never believe she was capable of smacking Old Tom in the head, stealing the capsules, creating an airtight alibi, and pulling the wool over his smoldering, sexy eyes. Throughout her life, men had underestimated her, and the fiery fixer would too. He would finish interrogating her, the spotlight would return to Leo and Stuart, the lab would close, the whereabouts of the capsules would remain a mystery, and Carrie would extend the length and quality of her mother's life for however many years Sikorski's drug would provide—*if* it worked with humans like it worked with rats.

"Robert still hasn't fixed the front gate," Carrie said to the ladies beside the pool.

"He will, dear," Invisible Helen said, "as soon as he remembers it's broken."

She was lying on a lounge chair, wearing a massive straw sunhat that covered the entirety of her body. It was as if there were only the hat on the chair and the hat itself had replied.

"Forget the gate, girl," Oxygen Tank Lillian said. "Tattoo Boy brought home a hog."

She was in her wheelchair, cigarette in her mouth, oxygen tubes in her nose. She wore a one-piece swimsuit, though she was decades past swimming and had never once been in the pool. She'd slathered herself in impenetrable sunscreen from head to toe. The sun would look at that layer of creamy goo and move straight on to the next person.

"A hog?" Carrie said.

"Poor boy came back from meeting his new parole officer and was hauling half a hog," Saddlebag Betty said.

She was on the lounge chair next to Lillian, wearing a two-piece and holding a suntan face reflector to make sure she didn't miss a spot, though she hadn't missed a spot in twenty years. She and Lillian were roommates and smoking buddies. As the years clicked by, Lillian had needed more and more help and Betty hadn't wanted to be alone, so she moved into Lillian's apartment, and Betty's apartment had become the gym.

"He wasn't a happy camper," Lillian said.

"He was upset about the meeting," Helen said. "It didn't go well."

"What happened?" Carrie said.

"He's in there chopping it to pieces right now," Lillian said.

"I mean at the meeting," Carrie said.

"We didn't push him for details," Betty said,

She looked like a crispy piece of bacon in a frying pan. Carrie heard sizzling but could have been imagining it.

"That would be like his grandparents asking if he had a boo-boo on the inside," Helen said. "Not a good approach for man like Johnny Fairfax."

"Tattoo Boy would turn us off like a radio," Lillian said.

"But he'll talk to you," Betty said.

"You're his age," Helen said. "You can relate to each other."

"We have nothing in common," Carrie said. "We speak different languages."

"Well, somebody has to find out what the hell happened with his parole officer or

Tattoo Boy will fly the Copa coop," Lillian said. "And we don't want to lose him. We're eating like kings and queens."

"Where's my mother?" Carrie said. "She's the kitchen captain."

"We haven't seen her, dear," Helen said.

"She didn't come to breakfast," Betty said.

"We knocked on her door, and she said she was fine," Lillian said.

"She sounded fine," Helen said.

"She said she was having sweet dreams and was going to keep on sleeping and dreaming," Betty said.

Joanna slept in fits and spurts—forty minutes here, thirty minutes there. The pain would wake her, she'd recover for a few minutes, fight her way back to sleep, and the pain would wake her again. And so on. For six years.

*If that's all the capsules do, let my mother sleep and have pleasant dreams,* Carrie thought, *then they were worth stealing.*

"Fine. I'll talk to him," she said, heading for the kitchen, "but I don't know what I'm supposed to say."

"Tell him we don't want to lose him," Helen said.

"Tell him we like his food," Betty said.

"Tell him we're eating like kings and queens," Lillian said.

Carrie entered the kitchen and stopped on a dime. Johnny was behind the counter. Shirt off. The hog lay on the counter in front of him. It wasn't wholly whole anymore. Johnny had been busy butchering, and the swine had been cut into four large but more manageable pieces known as the primals—shoulder, loin, belly, and ham, plus the tenderloin, leaf lard, kidney, and head.

Carrie didn't know what to react to first: the butchered hog or Johnny's tattoos. He had a riot of ink on his chest, on his stomach, running up and down his rib cage, and on his sides. A lion and a buffalo in a warrior standoff on his stomach. Above them, the word *California* in an arc beneath his rib cage, a dome above the animals. The word *Beast* across his chest beside the word *Chef*. Carving knives and cleavers, bald eagles and race cars, and what looked like prison bars. A ten-thousand-dollar bill above the words *In Johnny We Trust.* Matching tombstones—one that said *Merry* and one that said *Patrick*—and the Guns N' Roses album cover *Appetite for Destruction*. The flag of Scotland tattooed on his left side. The flag of Italy tattooed on his right side. And others too small for Carrie to see clearly. Numbers and names. A woman's face Carrie couldn't make out. Unlike his sleeves, you could see skin between his torso tattoos. She couldn't see his back, but she had no doubt it was covered as well. Either way, as far as Carrie was concerned, it was a hell of a lot of ink.

But she couldn't concentrate on the tattoos because Johnny's butchering ability demanded her attention. He was phenomenal. An artist with the knives. She knew nothing about butchering, but she'd always had a feel for talent, and Johnny had it.

His lean body glistened with sweat as he butchered the hog into cuts of meat she recognized: ribs, chops, roasts, tenderloins, ham, and bacon. He seemed to be in some kind of passion-fueled trance, a lonely zone of fury and resentment, as if his world had faded into unfocused color except for the hog and the knives and whatever it was that was eating him from the inside. She sensed the anger in his butcher body language, saw the bitterness in his eyes, felt the tension in his jawline. But beneath his wrath and rage, she recognized an underlying vulnerability, a deeper emotionality composed of pain and hurt. She had seen it in herself enough times to pinpoint it in Johnny.

She stood watching him until, finally, he stopped cutting and their eyes met.

"This is wildly unsanitary," Carrie said, her voice softer than she'd expected. "My mother would fire you on the spot if she caught you working without your shirt. Can you please put it on? The ladies by the pool don't want to lose you."

He put the knife down, moved to the side, grabbed his shirt, and went back to the hog. He continued to butcher it down to size, still brilliant with the cleaver and the carver, but the manic energy, the feverish focus, had turned to mist. The spell had been broken.

"Where did you learn to do that?" Carrie said. "I've never seen anyone butcher a hog like that."

"You ever seen anyone butcher a hog at all?" he said.

"No, but I bet they don't do it like you."

"Not too many. My father was a butcher. He owned a shop on Fairfax. He showed me the ropes. I took it from there."

"Your father's not a butcher anymore?"

"He died on my twenty-first birthday."

She was stunned. "*My* father died on *my* twenty-first birthday."

"Bullshit."

"He did. It's true."

Their eyes met again. She crossed the kitchen to the counter. He went back to butchering. The hog was between them.

"The ladies by the pool wanted me to ask about your new

parole officer, about what happened at your meeting," Carrie said. "They saw you were upset and, like I said, they don't want to lose you. I'm sure you don't want to talk about it, but they want you to know they really like your food. They're eating like kings and queens. That's what they said. Kings and queens."

A small smile crossed Johnny's lips, and he told her the basics —how and why he'd violated his parole, Big Ben Boston's blackmail, the site inspection on Tuesday.

"You have five days counting today," Carrie said. "What are you going to do?"

"All I know is I'm not paying him," Johnny said, "and I'm not going back to prison."

"Aren't those your only options?"

"Right now. Some options don't happen until later."

Just then, Helen appeared, sun hat barely able to fit through the doorway. "Come to the pool, Carrie," she said breathlessly. "It's your mother. You've got to come right now. Hurry."

Carrie looked at Johnny and sprinted across the kitchen, her mind racing faster than she could run. In the three seconds it took to reach Helen at the kitchen door, she imagined a slip on the wet tiles, a stroke, and a coronary, any of the three leaving her mother physically or mentally incapacitated or dead on the ground.

She zoomed past Helen, peripherally aware that Johnny was behind her, and went through the kitchen door into the courtyard. When she was ten feet from the pool, she stopped so hard and so fast that Johnny nearly knocked her over.

Joanna stood by the lounge chairs, wearing a bright blue swimsuit, a colorful beach towel over her shoulder. Betty and Lillian were quite literally frozen with amazement and shock. Betty had dropped her suntan reflector, the first time she'd let it go in decades. Lillian's cigarette dangled from her mouth.

It was such an incongruous vision—her mother in a swimsuit with a beach towel slung over her shoulder—that Carrie could hardly reconcile the first part, that her mother was *standing*. No walker, no wheelchair, no cane, no nothing. Standing easily, comfortably, solidly on her own two legs.

*Oh my God*, Carrie thought.

She opened her mouth to call out to her mother but no sound escaped.

Joanna waved. "I'm fine, Carrie. Never better. No need to worry. The capsules came through. The drug works. Thought I'd go for a little swim. It's been years. Why don't you put your suit on and join me? It's a wonderful day for a dip."

Carrie's first feeling was *horror* at the idea of wearing a swimsuit in public. Actually, that feeling was tied for first with the feeling of *dread* that Helen and Lillian and Betty had heard her mother say there was a drug that had worked, that there were capsules that had made her mother not just *feel* but *be* younger and healthier, more vibrant and alive. That was the very opposite of keeping the capsules quiet.

It wasn't just the ladies at the pool who had heard the news. The Men's Copa Card Club—Norman, Arnie, Bernie, and Bob— had come from the card room to the courtyard to see what the fuss was about. And Maureen Breen was watching from the second-floor walkway with Dolores. And Brenda and Walter were crossing the courtyard to get a closer look at Joanna on the diving board.

*Jesus Christ, she's on the diving board*, Carrie thought. *What the hell is she doing there?*

Joanna smiled at her dumbfounded friends surrounding the pool, waved up at Maureen and Dolores, set her jaw, took three bounding steps to the end of the board, bounced high into the air, and did a perfect jackknife into the water.

# CHAPTER 11

# NO TACOS FOR TINO TODAY

HIS NAME WAS NOT Constantine Antonov. That was the name he used because he liked to be called Tino. He lived in a handsome home hidden in the hills above Coldwater Canyon Drive, the twisting two-lane that traversed the Santa Monica Mountains and connected Beverly Hills to the San Fernando Valley, a busy thoroughfare winding through an affluent LA neighborhood of studio and network executives, actors, agents, writers, directors, producers, and other professionals. The house was surrounded by an eight-foot privacy wall with heavy wooden entrance gates. Tino did not rent the house. He also did not own the house.

He was a custodial consultant on permanent retainer for a board of directors comprised of mysterious Russian oil, shipping, and pharmaceutical oligarchs who had created an offshore holding company whose name was a series of random numbers and whose only stated business was "diverse international custodial services." He was the only consultant on retainer. There were no employees. His job was to clean up whatever corporate mess had been made in whatever country the mess had been made in using whatever mess-cleaning methods he needed to use.

The offshore Russian holding company had paid cash for the house, purchasing it through a real estate brokerage shell company that was owned by a subsidiary of the holding company's spin-off investment capital company. Meaning nobody actually owned the house. Tino drove a two-hundred-thousand-dollar Mercedes. Nobody owned that either.

He parked the Mercedes in the lot beside the Alsiko Labs building. The passenger side front door opened, and Sikorski leaned in.

"Mr. Antonov?"

"Tino."

"I am Dr. Sikorski."

"I know who you are, Leo baby," Tino said with a thick Russian accent. "Get in car. We do lunch like Hollywood hotshots."

He'd been born in Belgorod, a mid-size Russian city near the Ukraine border, about nine hours south of Moscow. As a young boy, he'd been good-looking, athletic, and intelligent, a high achiever by most measures. But he was not what Russians or Americans or anyone would consider normal. From an early age, two things had set him apart from his family, friends, neighbors, and classmates: he liked fire, and he liked to hurt people. He hadn't started out liking fire and causing people pain. At first, he'd liked fire and torturing animals. He'd grown into hurting humans.

This magical combination of character traits—amiable intelligence and good looks blended with a talent for cruelty and a psychotic disregard for any ethical behavioral boundaries—had eventually drawn the interest of the Russian Federal Security Service, who'd enlisted him, nurtured him, trained him, employed him for a decade, and handed him to the corporate oligarchs, who in turn had covertly contacted the Kremlin requesting cleaning services for their international business binds, singular custodial assistance to protect the cash flow that poured into Putin's pockets.

He traveled quite a bit but was home in LA a lot too. In the shadow of Tinseltown, he'd become enamored with the Hollywood lifestyle—the paper-thin, movie-star ethos of the place that made it so easy to become someone other than who you actually were—and had professionally framed posters of his favorite motion pictures on the walls of his Coldwater Canyon house. He had a special fondness for tough-guy Hollywood icons—Jack Nicholson, Clint Eastwood, Gene Hackman, Robert De Niro, and Sylvester Stallone—and believed he was spiritually connected to the characters they played.

"Where are we going?" Sikorski said

"Hyperion Public," Tino said. "By the people. For the people."

"I've never been there."

"South of Boulevard, Leo baby. Studio City. Best grilled sea-bass tacos in Valley. Only twelve dollars? What? Are you kidding me with that price?"

Though twelve bucks was indeed a good price for grilled sea-bass tacos, Tino had a distorted view of how the world worked. Who could blame him? He'd been rewarded for inflicting pain and suffering for nearly two decades. He had more money than he could spend, and he'd never cashed a paycheck. Instead, on the first day of every month, a briefcase full of American dollars was delivered to the Coldwater Canyon house, more than enough money to live life large. If he needed even *more* money, say for an assignment in San Salvador, then he would place the empty briefcase by the front door with a note asking for additional funds. A second briefcase, this one jam-packed with whatever currency was required, would be delivered without delay. He had all the clothes, caviar, vodka, and women he could buy. Whatever he wanted whenever he wanted it. All he had to do in return was clean up the mess.

To give them plenty of time to talk, Tino had taken Ventura Boulevard instead of the 101. He was a Sunday driver every day of the week, cruising casually at the speed limit no matter how fast the traffic around him moved. Partly because he didn't like to rush and partly because he drove with his knees. That's how he guided the Mercedes. With his knees pushed up against the steering wheel. One hand holding a cigar, the other hand holding a drink—often a coffee, more often a vodka. He adored Barbra Streisand and played her greatest hits on the surround sound Bluetooth audio system at an ear-splitting volume while smoking cigars and drinking vodka and driving with his knees.

Though he wanted to crank it, Tino kept the Streisand volume low so he could hear Sikorski's story. Old Tom cold-cocked, Sikorski calling the Pfeiffer emergency number, Carrie Kromer, Stuart Langston, the rats, and the missing capsules. There was no mention of Yelchin or Eduardo Wolf.

He nodded now and then, asking questions to clarify time-line omissions or thinly developed character arcs, but found Sikorski's performance unconvincing and did not believe a word the biochemist said. *Two thumbs down, Leo baby*, he thought and drove past the entrance for Hyperion Public to the red light at Coldwater Canyon.

Sikorski turned in his seat and watched the restaurant disappear behind them, becoming even more distressed, which was saying something because he'd been both anxious and disconcerted since Tino had lit his cigar, poured a vodka, and taken the wheel with his knees. Not to mention he had Pfeiffer and Yelchin on two ends of the same leash.

"You drove past the restaurant," Sikorski said.

"No tacos for Tino today," Tino said.

"But they're the best in the Valley," Sikorski said, his voice cracking.

Tino put his drink in the cup holder, opened the center console, and removed a blindfold. "Put blindfold on, Leo baby."

"What? No. Wait. Why?" Sikorski said, his anxiety level shooting through the roof of the Mercedes.

"Because you not see where we going," Tino said.

"Where *are* we going?"

"Is mystery. Put on blindfold."

"No."

"No?"

"I'm not putting the blindfold on."

"Okay, Leo baby. You win. Come close. I tell you where we going." The custodial consultant turned to Sikorski, leaned toward him.

Sikorski slowly, reluctantly began to lean into Tino, to meet him over the center console, but in a blinding second, Tino reached out, grabbed the back of his head, and pulled it forward. At the same time, he thrust his own head toward Sikorski. Their skulls met in the middle like two trains on the same track. The collision was epic, a Hollywood headbutt for the ages. Sikorski was knocked unconscious. Tino leaned him back into his seat.

The light turned green. He picked up his vodka and made the left onto Coldwater Canyon with his knees.

# CHAPTER 12
# THE FABULOUS EFFECT OF THE FLAMES HE LURED TO LIFE

USING JUST ENOUGH flammable adhesive to give additional spark to the fire, Tino attached the fuse to the soft skin between the big toe and the second toe of Sikorski's left foot. It was a white fuse with a slightly golden hue, twelve inches long and as stiff and straight as an especially thin breadstick. Thinner, even, than Sikorski, who was strapped to a metal chair bolted to the floor. The biochemist's legs, stretched straight out, were strapped down tight on a matching and similarly bolted metal ottoman. He was, of course, barefoot. Pants rolled up above his ankles. He was conscious. Eyes wide with horror. The duct tape across his mouth muffled his fear.

"I make fuse myself." Tino sat in front of Sikorski, drinking chilled vodka from a *Dirty Harry* coffee mug with a picture of Clint Eastwood holding his .44 Magnum on one side and the words *Make my coffee* on the other. "Potassium nitrate, sugar, water. Steady burn, three seconds per inch, pretty little flame. I think Rambo make same fuse to burn mountain town to ground, to burn sheriff who start fight in first place." And then he sang the chorus of the Bob Marley classic, adjusting the lyrics as he always did. "I shoot the sheriff, and I also shoot the deputy."

In total, eight fuses were glued to the skin between Sikorski's toes, each sticking out twelve inches from the soles of his feet. When the flames reached the end of the fuses, they would burn long enough and hot enough for Sikorski to remember the pain —the blackened and blistered baby skin between his toes burning like hell—for the rest of his life, all the way to the moment of his death. Even if Tino had to kill him at the end of the week.

Tino patted Sikorski's cheek and crossed the room to a stainless-steel cabinet he used as an office bar. A high-end wine refrigerator had been built into the bottom of the cabinet. On the countertop, a bottle of vodka stood in a bucket of ice. Next to it, a plate of black caviar and blinis. Tino poured another shot of vodka into the Dirty Harry mug, turned to Sikorski, and held up the bottle.

"Beluga vodka, Leo baby. From Russia with love. Hundred bucks a bottle. Made with water from Siberian bedrock. I want you to taste, but you don't tell me truth, so no Beluga for you."

He placed the bottle in the bucket, the spooned caviar onto a blini and popped it into his mouth. He carried the mug back over to Sikorski and sat down facing the eight fuses.

"No worries, Leo baby. I tell you truth. In next fifteen minutes, you going to have second-degree burns between your toes. Lot of swelling, lot of pain. Big pain. You going to blister, Leo baby. You going to blister bad. Don't burst blisters. Use antibiotic ointment. Change dressing two time per day to remove dead skin. Fire not fun for you. But fire fun for Tino, so *za zdarovje*. To health."

He lifted the mug and downed the vodka. Sikorski's eyes were popping out of his head. His expression was one part incredulity, one part abject terror.

Tino leaned in and grabbed an outer edge of the duct tape. "I take tape off like Mommy used to. Count to three. One—" He ripped the tape off Sikorski's face.

Sikorski screamed.

"What? That not how Mommy do it?" Tino said. "That how my Mommy do it." He held up a box of large kitchen matches and rattled the box in front of Sikorski's face. "Maybe you tell Tino who take drug before flame reach foot. Have thirty-six seconds." He struck a match.

"No, no, please, don't, *no*—"

Tino lit the fuse between Sikorski's second and third toes on his right foot. The fuse sparked to life and the flame marched in a steady straight line, three seconds per inch, just like Tino had said it would.

"Who take drug, Leo baby?"

"Stop, stop, I don't know, I don't—"

The flame reached the end of the fuse, hit the flammable adhesive, and sparked into a momentary mini inferno.

Sikorski screamed again. Longer and louder this time.

Tino savored the flame and thought fondly, as he sometimes did, of Martin Vanger, the psychotically sick millionaire murderer from *The Girl with the Dragon Tattoo*.

Tino admired Vanger. They were not the same sort of psychopath, of course. He was a real-life Russian custodial consultant working in the actual world; Vanger was a fictional character in the best-selling novel and mega-million-dollar movie. Tino was usually good about telling the difference between Hollywood and reality, although he did lose himself in the middle from time to time, as psychopaths sometimes do. That fact notwithstanding, Tino appreciated the further fact that both he and Stieg Larsson's sadistic CEO killer were top-tier professionals when it came to perpetrating pain and suffering and that misery and torment were happy byproducts of their true passions.

Vanger's hunger was for kidnapping. Torture, murder, and mayhem were delightful derivatives of his abductions. Tino's singular brutality—and perhaps his one true love—was fire.

Agony, anguish, and cruelty were the fabulous effect of the flames he lured to life.

"Who take drug, Leo baby? Tell Tino."

Sikorski hyperventilated. Tears rolled down his sunken, skeletal cheeks. His voice was a shaken whisper. "I don't know. I don't—"

Tino struck another match ...

"I swear to God. I don't know. Please, no—"

... and lit the fuse between the little and fourth toes on Sikorski's left foot. The flame moved down the fuse with purpose.

The biochemist puffed up his cheeks and desperately tried to blow the fire out before it reached the end of the fuse at his foot. It was futile. Tino laughed as if he'd never seen anyone do that before.

"Five seconds, Leo baby. Three, two, one ..."

Sikorski shrieked as the fire between his toes raged for three seconds and then went out.

"Such a pretty flame," Tino said. "So sad to see it go. Oh, look, six more fuse."

He lit a match and looked at the flame. "So beautiful. I always like fire.

Yes, he had. Since early childhood. He'd liked its hypnotic dance, swirling and playful when happy, wild with violence when enraged. He'd liked that it was insatiable. He'd liked that it burned without prejudice, without regard for race or creed or color or ethnicity or religion or politics. He'd liked that it would burn boats and buildings; businesses and homes; cars and trains and planes. He'd liked that he was the servant and it was the master; that his coaxing it to life was a privilege; that he had no choice but to obey its mystic power, old as mankind; that if he was reckless or inattentive, it would burn him as it burned all that crossed its path.

The match flame licked Tino's fingers. He blew it out.

Sikorski groaned with exhaustion, pain, and defeat.

"Time to tell Tino who take drug?"

"Yes."

"Good. Everybody actor in Hollywood, Leo baby. Next-door neighbor on CSI. Make me believe. Light, camera, action. Who take drug belong to Pfeiffer?"

"I want to tell you, but I don't know," Sikorski said feebly, faintly.

"Cut, cut," Tino said and lit another match.

# CHAPTER 13
# PEAR-SHAPED GIRLS DON'T DIVE

CARRIE COULDN'T CONCENTRATE to save her life, though she sensed saving her life was the next thing on her agenda. Traffic on the drive back to Reseda was heavy, and she should have been focused on the constant cruising in and out and back and forth at speeds calling for a crackup, not to mention her impending interview with Eduardo Wolf. But all she could think about was her mother diving during lunch.

Johnny had served a superb midday meal—pan-fried salmon sandwiches on toasted sourdough with lettuce, tomato, and cayenne mayo; homemade potato chips; endive salad with a champagne vinaigrette; and a sparkling lemon sorbet for the finish—and Carrie had not taken a bite because her mother had spent all of lunch doing front flips, back flips, cannonballs, and can openers into the pool.

So instead of staying put in the precarious here and now of LA automotive madness, Carrie traveled back to when she was nine years old in New Brunswick, New Jersey. Joanna, already sixty, had taken her to the Rutgers natatorium, a massive indoor athletic complex that featured an Olympic-size competition pool, two auxiliary pools—one with multiple diving platforms and boards —and bleacher seating for a thousand swim-team supporters. Her mother insisted Carrie learn to dive and join the local youth aquatic team, socialize with other diving children instead of with Lawrence's lab rats. At least, that's what Joanna had said. The truth, Carrie had learned later, was something other than that.

Joanna had been athletic as a girl, tall and slender, graceful and swift—she'd run track and field in her student days, played tennis too, and had been on the school diving team. The experience had served her well. She'd discovered discipline, order, and commitment, both physical and mental, charismatic traits that had propelled her through school and life and marriage and motherhood. She'd been determined that her daughter be athletic as well and cultivate those qualities in herself.

Behavioral skills and character development. That is what Joanna had *said* was the point. And, yes, even at nine years old, Carrie had known there was truth in her mother's words—just not the whole truth. Carrie knew—because she had already become an accomplished little scientist and was exceptionally aware for her age—that what Joanna *meant* was that if Carrie ran around like the other children, she might not turn out to be like Lawrence.

But the die had been cast. Carrie had inherited her father's physique and all of his athletic prowess, which was to say none at all. The tennis experiment had been a disaster surpassed only in futility by the track and field experiment.

So it had come down to diving. They were at the Rutgers pool, and Joanna was twisting and spinning like Aileen Riggin, who'd won gold in Antwerp in 1920 at fourteen and kept right on diving and swimming into her old age. Meanwhile, Carrie was nine and frozen on the three-meter platform, embarrassed to be in a bathing suit, terrified to jump, never mind dive.

When it had been clear that all the coaxing and coaching in the world wouldn't produce a single dive from her daughter that day or any day, Joanna had said, "Not to worry, Carrie. It's not your fault. Pear-shaped girls don't dive."

After that, Joanna had let Lawrence, a bitter and boozy seventy-year-old, finish making her daughter into a scientist.

And then it was two o'clock, and Carrie was parked in the side lot next to Alsiko. She tried to gather her wits before going inside to see Eduardo Wolf, but the only thought she could think was, *Jesus Christ, my mother dove better today than that day at Rutgers twenty-seven years ago. Better at eighty-six than at sixty.* Scarier still was the fact that Joanna had gotten better—younger and stronger—as the lunch hour ticked by, better by the end of lunch than at the beginning.

The Copa crew had been equally astonished by Joanna's sudden strength and stamina, dumbfounded by her newborn vim and vigor, thunderstruck by her improbable, impossible girlish energy. Not that it had stopped a single one of them from eating everything in sight. As they devoured lunch, they had stared with wonder and awe and confusion at Joanna and glared with demanding curiosity at Carrie.

*They'll want answers at dinner,* Carrie had thought as she left the Copa.

She opened the door with her security keycard. The empty silence instantly reminded her that all work at Alsiko had been suspended since the drug had been stolen. She walked to Lab No. 3, where Eduardo Wolf was watching the Greek Gods make a mockery of their maze—they were sprinting through it backward.

"These nine rats are living proof the drug is a miracle," Eduardo said. "Is that correct?"

"Yes," Carrie said. "The Greek Gods. Proof positive."

"Perfectly named, then."

Carrie nodded, not because she agreed the rats were perfectly named, but because she'd asked herself if Eduardo Wolf was not the hottest, sexiest man she'd ever met.

He was dressed in black: jeans, shoes, T-shirt, sport jacket. He wore skintight, black leather gloves. He smiled and stepped toward her. There was something menacing about him, but also something intensely sexual. Her pulse pounded.

"What happened to Stuart?" she said, her voice a whisper. *Why am I whispering?* she thought. *It's not a library.*

"Stuart was evidence," he said. "Compromised beyond capture. He had to be eliminated."

"He's dead?" *Stop whispering. It's not a funeral.*

"In the breakroom. Yes, he's dead."

*Jesus, it is a funeral.* He was still coming toward her, smiling that devastating smile. Was it getting hotter in here, or was it her? *It's me. I'm burning up.*

"Are you going to kill me too?" she said.

"No, Carrie." He stopped three feet in front of her, voice husky and soft and sensual. "I'm going to seduce you."

"Oh my God." Her heart was thunder in her chest. *He can hear it. It's leading him on. Stop it, heart. Stop that pounding.*

"You want me, yes?" He took another step toward her. Two feet away now.

"Is it obvious?" It didn't sound like her normal voice. It had come from some forbidden place in her libido. She didn't recognize its tone or tenor. It was her but not her. "I mean no. I mean yes. I mean no. I mean yes..."

"You can have me, Carrie." He took another step. One foot in front of her. Which was very much the same as zero feet in front of her. "I will make love to you until you beg for mercy."

"Oh my God," she said. *Who the hell's voice is that anyway?*

He smelled like Irish Spring soap, or at least how she imagined Irish Spring soap would smell if a man who'd showered with it stood this close to her and talked about making her beg for lovemaking mercy. His breath was hot like a Santa Ana wind sloping down through the mountain passes, like strong whiskey in a smoky Brazilian bar.

"Tell me what you did with the drug, and I am yours." He touched her cheek with his gloved right hand and leaned in as if to kiss her.

She'd never felt leather that soft and melted into his hand. Her eyes closed. Her lips readied to receive his kiss. She swooned for the first time in her life. Words formed in her mind. *Yes, I took the capsules and gave them to my mother. I thwacked Old Tom on the head and stole the drug. Yes, yes, I did it. I'm the one. Yes, oh God, yes. Now make love to me, Eduardo. Take me in your arms and make me beg for —*

But the words were stopped by an unexpected vision. Johnny Fairfax, of all people. Shirtless, butchering the half hog in the Copa kitchen. Tattooed body glistening with sweat, filled with focused rage fueled by pain and loneliness. His vulnerability had touched her heart without her knowing it. It was preposterous, the idea of this ex-con cock making her feel something real, something mysterious and unspoken, and yet...and yet...

She slid away from Eduardo Wolf. "I didn't take the capsules."

He smiled and followed her across the floor, past the wall of rats, past the maze and the Greek Gods. "I know you did, Carrie. Leo didn't take them, and neither did Stuart. It was you."

He wasn't threatening her. He was, as he'd said, seducing her. It was harder than hard for her to resist his Latin looks, his Hispanic heat. Still, she backpedaled across the lab. He kept coming.

"I couldn't have taken them," she said.

"Because?"

"I can't be in two places at the same time."

"You have an alibi?"

"Yes."

Her back bumped up against the wall. He stopped in front of her, close enough to embrace her without moving. He brushed a few loose strands of hair from her face. His voice was soft, erotic, insistent.

"Can you tell me what it is?" he said.

"Yes." Her voice was barely there.

His eyes were hypnotic. She was lost in them. His breath was fire on her neck. *Don't pass out*, she told herself.

"Tell me, Carrie. I'm listening," he said, his voice already making love to her.

Her knees were weak, her blood boiling, her head spinning. "I left the lab at six thirty on Tuesday. I went to the Foxfire Room in Valley Village for a beer. I knew the drug worked, and I wanted to celebrate Alsiko's success. I don't usually have more than one beer, but I made an exception because of the drug, because the Greek Gods were younger."

"You stayed at the bar until what time?" he said.

*Jesus*, she thought, *don't breathe on my neck. Stop breathing on my neck. Don't. Stop. Don't. Stop. Don't stop, don't stop, don't stop ...*

"I was there from about seven fifteen to maybe eleven fifteen," she said. "Played darts. Sang karaoke. 'Don't Stop Believin'' by Journey. I don't even like Journey, but we never stopped believing in the research, in the drug, and I had a few beers."

"And then?"

"I got my car out of the lot down the block and drove home."

"Well done." He leaned in and kissed her cheek.

Her knees buckled. She wondered whether she should visit the emergency room for the third-degree burns his lips had left on her face.

He handed her a black business card printed with only a white phone number. "In the event you come across the capsules before we meet again."

"We're going to meet again?" she said, and she felt herself swooning anew. "I mean, so you believe me?"

He moved away from her, looked down at the Greek Gods, and smiled. "As much as I believed Stuart."

## CHAPTER 14
# NO WONDER JOHNNY NEEDED TO GET STONED

IT WAS Johnny's second day on the job, and he was already catching the Copa rhythm, the pace of the place as far as being the cook was concerned. As for the tempo of the rest of his life, he couldn't have found the beat if Buddy Rich were playing drums.

Lunch had been looney tunes. No other way to describe it. His mind had been blown. His boss, Joanna, an eighty-six-year-old woman who walked with a cane when she wasn't in a wheelchair, whose bones were so weak she couldn't stand for more than a minute, had spent the hour diving like she was fifty-six. Until the end, when she was diving like she was forty-six.

He'd seen it with his own eyes—a woman younger today than yesterday—and he hadn't smoked any dope. None. He'd been completely straight.

Calling to Carrie across the courtyard from the diving board, Joanna had said something about capsules coming through, about a drug working. *What the fuck drug does that?* Johnny said to himself as he'd cleaned up lunch and prepped for dinner. *What the fuck drug makes you younger?*

He'd never heard of a drug that could turn back time, never seen a drug that could turn back time, never used a drug that could turn back time—and he'd used a world of drugs in his thirty-eight years. In his teens and twenties, aggressive and reckless and wired for trouble, he'd done drugs aplenty that could mess with the perception of time. And he'd done drugs galore in prison, where it was nothing to get any drug you wanted to help you do your time. But he'd never done a drug that could actually reverse time. No fucking way. Not a single drug from his early days or his prison days had made him eighteen instead of twenty-eight. Since he'd gotten out this last time, he'd preferred weed over anything else he could swallow, smoke, snort, or shoot. Used daily, he'd discovered, marijuana mellowed him out —hothead to pothead—and made him feel like there wasn't anything a Fatburger with chili cheese fries couldn't fix. What pot definitely *didn't* do was make him any fucking younger.

But he couldn't fully focus on the freak show that was Joanna because he was also thinking about his new parole officer. There wasn't a Fatburger big enough to fix Ben Boston.

That extra-extra-large asshole was about to make an insurmountable mess of Johnny's life. The site inspection was Tuesday. Today was Friday. Johnny had refused and still refused to pay Ben Boston's extortion fee because it wouldn't stop with the money. Once that parole piece of shit had control of Johnny's life, he could demand anything. More money maybe. Or something worse. Something illegal that Ben Boston wouldn't do himself. If Johnny didn't play the angles just right, he could easily end up as Big Ben's bag man. Or hit man. Or sex slave. Who the fuck knew what bad news was on the horizon with a bitch like Boston? Still, it was that or back to prison. That's what made it so hard to figure out.

He hadn't come up with an answer yet, but when he finished prepping for dinner, he'd smoke a joint and think it through. He didn't like his prospects, but he'd never liked his prospects. His life had been a shitstorm since his mother had left him at the Fairfax front door when he was two years old. He had no memory of that moment, but how could it not have been the beginning of every wrong turn he'd made since then? Merry had sat him down and finally told him the truth of his abandonment when he was ten. *Better to be honest than dishonest,* she'd said.

*Better for you,* Johnny had thought.

He was no shrink, but even a high-school dropout turned two-time ex-con knew that if you couldn't make a connection with your own fucking mother, you were never making a connection with any woman ever.

And that's what had happened. It had been sex and drugs and one-night stands since he was fourteen. He'd only been attracted to wild women, women like him, women who lived lives like the one he was living, women he'd picked up in bars who weren't looking for a commitment he couldn't give. Gang girls. And only wild women had been attracted to him. Law-abiding women had never shown any interest in Johnny. None. Zero. Ever. So what? No promises, no guarantees, no vows. Just a good time this time. That's who he was and who he'd always be.

He never thought about relationships and commitments and shit because he didn't need it or want it. Hadn't thought about it in decades. Which was why today, his third day as the Copa cook, the same day Ben Boston had blackmailed him and Joanna Kromer had gotten younger, he couldn't concentrate on either the parole officer or the Copa Kitchen Captain. Because when he'd been butchering the half hog and Carrie had come in and watched him work, something had happened. A connection had been made that wasn't sexual, drug related, or dangerous. It had been—he knew the fucking word for it—*real.* Genuine and human. An ex-con cook and a geek girl who hardly knew each other and didn't like what little they knew finding an unlikely emotional connection at an unexpected time.

She wasn't his type. No fucking way. She'd made that clear. He wasn't her type either. She'd made that equally clear. And yet it had happened. Their fathers had died on the day both Johnny and Carrie had turned twenty-one. What were the chances? It was a moment of connection. They'd both felt it. He'd seen it in her eyes. She'd seen it in his. It wouldn't lead to anything. It couldn't. It would be stupid to think that. But it had happened and there were residual after-feelings to be felt. And if you put that fact on top of the Ben Boston fact and those facts on top of the Copa-Kitchen-Captain-getting-younger fact, then no wonder Johnny needed to get stoned.

But instead of getting high and riding his Harley to the beach, he went back to his room, took off his shirt, smoked a fat Marley, laid down to think about Ben Boston, and fell asleep.

He had a terrible dream about Big Ben pimping him out in Pacoima, of all places. He was in a seedy motel room, and he was pounding on the door to get the hell out. And then he woke up, and someone was knocking on the Copa cook's apartment door.

"Yeah." He crossed to the door and opened it.

It was Carrie. They looked at each other for a long time.

"Do you ever wear a shirt?" she said.

"What do you want?"

"I work weekends for Maureen—laundry and cleaning—and I sometimes help the cook. And it's five o'clock, and dinner's in an hour, and I stopped by the kitchen to see if you needed help, and you weren't there, so I knocked on your door to see if you quit or were asleep or sick or dead."

"That's fucking morbid."

"People die all the time. Illness, accidents, old age."

"Nobody dies of old age around here."

They both knew what he was talking about and didn't say much after that.

He put on a shirt, and they went to the kitchen, and he made dinner—grilled pork cutlets with a rosemary cream sauce, basmati rice, and thin-sliced eggplant baked with fresh-grated Romano followed by an icebox chocolate-peanut butter pie that Merry used to make.

While he cooked, Carrie gathered the plates and glasses and

silverware and set the poolside tables. She was in and out, but when she was in, Johnny caught her watching him out of the corner of her eye out of the corner of his eye.

"I don't mean to be morbid," she said, busting his balls, "but how did he die?"

He knew she would ask him that, and figured she knew he knew, which was why she'd asked it like they were in the middle of that conversation, except it was a conversation they were having with their minds, which was a stupid fucking thought to begin with, so he let it go.

"His butcher shop was called Fairfax on Fairfax," he said.

"I already don't like where this is going."

"I'd been working there since I was sixteen. I hated that place. Or maybe I hated him. Same thing, I guess. On my twenty-first birthday, he surprised me with a new sign for the front door. Fairfax and Son."

"Not a good surprise."

"I told him I wasn't going to be a butcher on Fairfax Avenue like him all my fucking life, and we had a shouting match about it, and he was in my face, and I shoved him, and he picked up a cleaver, and I knew he was going to kill me, and I ran out of the shop and across the street, and he ran after me, waving the cleaver like a fucking madman, and he got hit by a bus."

"I'm sorry." It was clear she meant it.

"It was always coming to that."

They didn't say anything for a long time.

Later, when he was putting the pork on the platters and she was taking the platters from the counter and placing them on the rolling cart, he said, "What about you?"

"He was a hard drinker," she said. "Old and bitter and resentful. He blamed me for the mediocrity of his teaching and research career. He was abusive. Emotionally, I mean. He was very smart and very troubled. Hard to believe words could hurt that much. But he tore me apart."

"How old is old?"

"Eighty-two when he died. Liver failure."

"Sorry."

"It was always coming to that."

He put the rice in three large bowls. She put the bowls on the cart. Their eyes met.

"You going to tell me or not?" he said.

She took a breath and told him about Alsiko and Sikorski and Stuart. About the Greek Gods and the drug and Old Tom, who couldn't remember what city he lived in after she'd hit him on the head with a rolling pin and stolen the capsules.

He nodded at the Old-Tom-and-the-rolling-pin part like she'd grown somehow in his estimation of her. "Been there, done that."

And she told him about giving the drug to her mother. About Eduardo Wolf, even the bit about him seducing her instead of killing her, and about her failsafe alibi.

"He can't kill you yet," Johnny said. "He has to bust your alibi first, prove you took it. If he does that, he'll come for the drug, and then he'll kill you."

"And if he can't bust it?"

"Then he'll just kill you."

Johnny plated the eggplant, and they rolled the cart out of the kitchen to the poolside tables, where the Copa crowd, including Joanna—looking every bit a fit and fabulous forty-five—were waiting with ravenous appetites.

"You didn't have to tell me," he said.

"I had to tell someone," she said. "I have no one to talk to."

He nodded, knowing just what that felt like.

"I can't tell my mother," she said. "She's too old."

"Not anymore," he said.

# CHAPTER 15
# ONE GODDAMN DAY LIKE JOEY HAD

THE PORK WAS SO TENDER, Carrie could have cut it with a spoon. The tension at the tables, however, was tough enough to need a chainsaw.

The Copa crowd ate like there was no tomorrow, but never took their eyes off Joanna, who looked gorgeous in a red, sleeveless sundress cut above the knee. Her legs were smooth and shapely, her arms firm and fabulous. She looked remarkably healthy—eyes bright, hair shining, skin radiant. Her aura, if you believed in that sort of thing, was damn near glowing. Her age appeared to have stabilized at forty-five, but since her Olympic performance at lunch, she had continued to become stronger and healthier, more confident, more beautiful, more alive, better by far than the best forty-five any of them had ever seen. Amazingly vibrant. Incredibly youthful.

When they weren't watching Joanna, the Copa crowd glared at Carrie. She knew, what they were demanding. On the one hand, she wanted to comply. Her life's work had been the behavioral study of aging. Who knew better than she the challenges, the pain, and the suffering of growing old? Either the body failed, or the mind failed, or they both failed. And with that physical and mental degradation came a hopelessness that often led to life-sucking lethargy, a graceless disintegration of the will to live, a demoralizing giving-up and giving-in, a psychologically vanquished march to death.

She saw it in the Copa crowd every day. She'd seen it in her mother until six hours ago. She didn't want that inelegant ending for any of them. This was her extended family. Sure, she was a scientist trained to keep her emotional distance, but she was involved in their lives, knew their fears, their regrets, their frustrations and frailties. She did their laundry and made their beds on the weekends, for Pete's sake. She was desperate to relieve their pain, refill them with life, renew their spirits, rebirth their souls.

Then again, Carrie had no damn business whatsoever giving these people the drug. How could she? Besides breaking every pharmaceutical law in the known universe, she'd be exposing them to Eduardo Wolf. They would be younger, yes, but they'd also be evidence. And as the Yelchin fixer had made clear, all Alsiko evidence was doomed for destruction—RIP Stuart Langston. Giving them the drug meant returning their youth and signing their death warrants.

She was terribly torn between the choices she knew were coming her way, but the fixer was the difference. She wasn't handing them over to him. No way.

"Carrie, dear, I think the break between dinner and dessert is the perfect time to address the miracle in the room," Joanna said, standing. "Do we all agree?"

The Copa crowd voiced their consent as Johnny arrived from the kitchen and began bussing the tables.

"Very good. Starting with the obvious—there's a drug that makes an old person young." Joanna walked around and between the tables as she spoke, giving physical presence to her words. "And that would be enough, even if it were as simple as being young again. But that's not the case. The drug does more than make you younger. The drug makes you *better* than you were when you were younger. Better by far than you've ever been. This is the fact of the drug. I am the living, breathing, diving proof."

"Tens from every judge, Joey," Norman said, wiping his extra-thick lenses. "Even I could see that."

"Thank you, Norman," Joanna said, putting her hand on his shoulder.

Everyone laughed, but there was an anxious quality to their amusement, a sense of urgency, a surge of edgy electricity.

"Continuing with the obvious, the drug works quickly. I took a capsule twenty-four hours ago, and I've never felt better," Joanna said.

"You look like a million bucks too, Joey," Tall Bob said.

"So do you, Bob," Joanna said.

"Thanks. What are we talking about again?" Bob said.

"About Carrie's drug," Invisible Helen said.

"It's not my drug," Carrie said.

"It is since you stole it," Lillian said, smoking a cigarette while sucking in oxygen from the fresh tank attached to her wheelchair.

"Moving onto the not so obvious," Joanna said, "we have questions to which we hope you have answers. The floor is open, everyone."

"Does the drug make you younger and younger the more you take it?" Saddlebag Betty said. "Am I going to be twenty-eight and then eighteen and then eight?"

"I don't think so," Carrie said. "The rats stabilized at more or less midlife, though strength and stamina, speed and agility, mental acuity, sensory responsiveness...all of that continued, still continues, to improve—not getting younger, just better. And their behavior grows more correspondingly energetic as well."

"You got lab rats diving like Olympians," Bernard said, straightening his tie.

"Kind of," Carrie said.

"How many capsules did they have to take, dear?" Helen

said from somewhere, though she was so invisible tonight, Carrie couldn't see where.

"Is there enough for everyone, is the question," Walter said, crankier than usual. "It's all for one and one for all. That's how we roll."

"No one gets left behind," Brenda said, taking Walter's hand.

"We gave them the equivalent of three human doses," Carrie said. "The first dose reversed the aging process. The second two seem to have locked that age in and improved athletic performance, physical appearance, sensory perception, mental range and rapidity...everything. And, yes, there's enough for everyone, but you can't take it."

"Why not?" Dolores said.

"Are there side effects?" Betty said.

"Just one I'm aware of," Carrie said.

"But it's not serious," Joanna said. "You said you would have seen any serious side effects by now."

"I've seen one, and he's a doozy," Carrie said.

She told them about Eduardo Wolf. You could hear a pin drop in the pool, that's how silent the Copa crowd became as they listened to Carrie tell the tale of the fixer and Sikorski, and the fixer and Stuart, and the fixer and the destined destruction of all Alsiko evidence—them included if they took the drug.

Even Johnny, who'd returned with a cart of coffee and dessert, stopped moving around to hear the story...and he'd already heard it.

None of them had ever imagined a man like Eduardo Wolf. He was the side effect they weren't expecting, and they remained silent when Carrie finished speaking.

Finally, Arnie stood up. By all appearances, he'd been dozing and drooling, but appearances could be deceiving. He hadn't been dozing; he'd been contemplating. And he wasn't drooling, he was crying.

"If it's five days, three days, two days...if it's one day, I want it. If I croak the next day or if the fixer flattens me, it doesn't matter. Side effects or no side effects, Wolf or no Wolf, I want one goddamn day like Joey had. I'm in."

Walter stood. Brenda with him. "Fucking A for Arnie," he said. "We're in."

Helen stood, though it was hard to tell. "Me too."

Then Betty and Bernie and Norman. Then Lillian and Bob (who wondered why he was standing) and Dolores. They all stood. They were all in.

Carrie froze. Deciding their fate—miraculously recapturing their youth and becoming Alsiko evidence that Eduardo would destroy versus the agonizing downward decline to death—was the most profound pronouncement she would ever make, and she couldn't make it alone. She needed support.

She turned to Johnny.

Johnny locked in on her eyes and saw that she needed help, needed *him*. "When we're that old, we're going to want one goddamn day like that too."

She exhaled for the first time in what seemed like a lifetime. She'd felt the same way but been too guarded to acknowledge it. She opened her purse, took out the vial, and gave everyone a capsule. They washed it down between bites of pie.

# LYSSA

GODDESS OF MAD RAGE AND FRENZY (AMONG OTHER THINGS)

# CHAPTER 16
# AN EMOTIONAL RESPONSE CARRIE COULDN'T ANTICIPATE

MONDAY MORNING, Carrie drove to Alsiko to check on the rats. There were still two hundred forty or so that needed food and water and attention—plus the Greek Gods, who needed Lord knew what. Some day in the very near future, she imagined, Eduardo Wolf would come for the rats and make them disappear, but that day was probably not today because the Alsiko rat population, excluding the Greek Gods, could not easily be identified as evidence.

Under normal circumstances, being with the rats, caring for them in the cool comfort of the lab, calmed Carrie's nerves and forced her to focus on the science of her observations. But not today. Not after the emotional fun-ride of a weekend she'd just had. Today, she couldn't take her mind off the Copa crowd.

They'd been younger on Saturday. Much younger. Like Joanna, the Copacabana residents had miraculously become the best mid-to-late-forties versions of themselves in all regards. Better than they had ever been. Joanna, who'd taken the drug Thursday night at dinner, twenty-four hours before the rest of them, was even stronger-sharper-fitter on Saturday than she'd been on Friday—and she'd been spectacularly vigorous on Friday.

All day Saturday, Carrie had done their laundry and cleaned their apartments while they'd gathered around the pool and reveled in the radiance of their recovered youth. She'd taken plenty of breaks throughout the day, watching them as both behavioral gerontologist and surrogate daughter. She'd seen them embrace and bond—physically, spiritually, intellectually, emotionally—in ways she'd never seen them do before. They'd become friends by virtue of their happenstance: all of them in their late eighties to mid-nineties, all of them decaying and degenerating, all of them marking time at the Copa as their collective clock wound down to certain, unceremonious death. But with their recaptured vitality, they had closed ranks on a deeper level and become a family of miracles.

Carrie had watched them share tears of joy, shock, and disbelief. The thrill of this impossible second chance was, of course, unmistakable to her scientific sense of them. But there was also an equally evident odd sort of sorrow they all seemed to be feeling. It was some kind of philosophical sadness brought on by the profoundly refreshed memory of the years they'd all squandered when they were younger and now had a chance to relive. It was the full-frontal internalization of the fact that none of them had lived their lives to their own self-determined potential. They had all, every one of them, at some point settled for jobs, behaviors, relationships, and lives that were less than what they'd expected of themselves, what they'd hoped for. They hadn't reached for the stars when it counted, not any of them, and their regret had been brought into impossibly sharp focus by the chance to do it again.

It was an emotional response Carrie couldn't anticipate. As a credentialed behavioral gerontologist, she recognized and understood the full spectrum of changes that accompanied growing *older*. But while watching the Copa crowd on Saturday, she realized she couldn't comprehend the same spectrum of changes going the other way, growing *younger*.

She'd wanted to talk to Johnny about it, since he was the only other person who knew the Copa crowd had taken the drug, but he'd been busy in the kitchen all day with Joanna, and then he'd gone out on his Harley at night after dinner.

That was Saturday.

The Copa crowd had been even brighter-bolder-better on Sunday. Carrie had been back at it as well, cleaning the dining room, card room, laundry room, and fitness room, and had once again taken lots of little breaks to watch the residents' reactions.

Their residual regret and sadness had washed away like the years of their lives. Sunday had been about celebrating their strength, speed, and stamina, rejoicing in their collective fantabulous health. The men had done calisthenics at a furious pace, pounding out push-ups and sit-ups, and had played a casual game of touch football. (*Where did they find a football?* Carrie had wondered.) On the sidelines, the women had done cheerleading routines dating back to their high school days, cartwheeling across the courtyard like professional gymnasts.

For lunch, Joanna and the Copa Kitchen Committee had rolled the gas grill out by the pool and, since Sunday was Johnny's day off, cooked themselves burgers and steaks. They'd feasted all afternoon and well into the evening. Their appetites had been insane. They'd finished two cases of wine—a Napa Valley cabernet and a chardonnay from Sonoma.

Carrie joined them during dinner and signaled for silence. She reminded them that Eduardo Wolf was coming and that they were living evidence of the wonder drug. So if the fixer (or anyone) came to the Copa, they had to keep the capsules quiet and act their age—an odd thing to demand of ninety-year-old folks who'd turned back time.

"You mean forty-five?" Walter had said in his crankiest voice. "Goddamn right, I will."

He was as strong as a meat packer and must have been imposing as hell when he was that age, which was the age he was again right now. But then he'd laughed out loud, and everyone had laughed with him. Even the Yelchin fixer couldn't kill the Copa mood.

When Carrie wasn't thinking about Copacabana poolside football (*just where the hell did they find a freaking football, anyway?*) and cheerleaders leaping along the sidelines, she was thinking about Stuart Langston. She couldn't stop wondering if he was dead in the breakroom, blood everywhere, what was left of his arm still jammed in the InSinkErator, armpit over the edge of the counter, body blue with death. She couldn't stand Stuart, but nobody deserved to die like that. Was he still in there? Had the fixer literally left him hanging over the breakroom sink? What would be the rush to clean up the mess? *No one's coming to the lab ever again, except me and Leo—and we could be dead soon too*, she thought.

She had to know one way or the other, so she left Lab No. 3 and walked to the breakroom. She held her breath, put her ear to the door, and listened for...what exactly? The final sounds of death? The buzzing of flies? The InSinkErator's ever-grinding gears chewing Stuart's arm to bone dust? She heard nothing.

*The long, sad silence of death*, she thought. *He's in there.*

Still holding her breath, she opened the door, steadied her nerves, and stepped into the breakroom.

It was empty. No Stuart. No bloody stump of an arm stuck in the InSinkErator. No blood splatter on the walls and cabinet doors. No overturned chairs. No smashed plates and glasses. No signs of struggle. Nothing amiss. Just the strong smell of lemon-fresh bleach. The breakroom was spotless. Void of germs. Absent of evidence. The cleanest it had been in six years.

Maybe Stuart wasn't dead after all. Maybe Eduardo Wolf's specialty was scaring the bejesus out of his suspects until they told him what he wanted to know. Maybe the fixer's game was *psychological*. Maybe that's what Eduardo Wolf had been up to with his threats and seductions and sensual Latin looks.

She found Stuart's number in her cell phone contacts and

called him—she had Stuart and Leo saved as favorites, though neither one had ever been a favorite for her. It rang three times.

"Hello, Carrie. You can't call Stuart anymore. Stuart is dead."

Eduardo Wolf. His voice made her head spin. She hung up without saying a word, left the breakroom, and returned to her rats.

On the way back to Lab No. 3, she thought about Johnny.

He'd flown the Copa coop Saturday night after dinner and hadn't returned on Sunday, not by the time she'd gone to bed anyway. And he hadn't been in the kitchen this morning before she'd left for the lab around nine thirty. She worried he'd hopped his Harley to Houston and was never coming back. She wouldn't blame him for choosing a life on the lam over cooking at the Copa. Better to jump parole and vanish somewhere deep in the Lone Star State than deal with Ben Boston or feed forty-five-year-old ninety-year-olds three times a day for the rest of time, whatever the hell time meant now.

At first, she'd thought she was worried because she knew how aggravating it would be to find, train, and adapt to a new Copa cook, especially given the circumstances. But then she thought she might be worried because she already missed him— *after only four days*—and that was worrisome indeed. Because if she could have feelings for someone like Johnny Fairfax, an uneducated, hard-drinking, drug-taking, tattooed ex-con butcher with whom she had absolutely nothing in common, then who the hell had she become? He wasn't her physical type. He wasn't her emotional type. He wasn't her intellectual type. So what the hell was it about Johnny Fairfax that she couldn't stop thinking about him? If she could miss Johnny Fairfax, want to see him, talk to him, be around him, then she was as foreign to herself as the rejuvenated Copa crowd had become. And yet there was this feeling in her heart and in her head that she could neither deny nor understand. She felt it for sure but couldn't define it, couldn't put her finger on it...and then she could. It was sadness. Yes, that was it. Sadness. At the thought he might be gone, out of her suddenly insane life just when she'd found someone—*him*—to share the insanity with. Just when she'd needed him.

*Jesus Christ*, she thought as she opened the Lab No. 3 door, *if I can have feelings for Johnny Fairfax, then what the hell else can happen?*

She stepped into the lab and stopped on a dime. A man stood by the wall of rats. She'd been so focused on whether Stuart was dead in the breakroom, she hadn't heard him come in. And how the hell had he gotten in anyway?

The man wore cowboy boots, blue jeans, a *Terminator* T-shirt with a striking image of Schwarzenegger—evil red mechanical eye glowing like the devil—a blue windbreaker, and a blue LA Dodgers baseball cap. Like some slick Hollywood producer looking to pick up the rights to a story he'd heard about but couldn't believe. But Carrie knew he wasn't a producer because his skintight leather gloves gave him away. He turned to her and smiled.

"Come in, Carrie baby," the man said with a Russian accent. "Tell Tino why you take drug."

# CHAPTER 17

# SHE HAD AN EXCEPTIONALLY BAD FEELING ABOUT THE LIGHTER

"STUART STOLE IT," Carrie said. She'd heard his voice before. He was the Pfeiffer man on the phone with Leo. "Or Leo did."

"How you know was one of them?" Tino said.

He walked along the wall of rats, smiling at her. Lab No. 3, like Lab No. 2 and Lab No. 1, was a thousand square feet, give or take. The other walls were lined with counters and cabinets cluttered with cutting-edge laboratory accoutrement that measured any and all quantifiable results from whatever test, trial, or technical investigation was working.

"Because it wasn't me," Carrie said.

"Process of elimination?"

"Yes."

"Way ahead of you, Carrie baby. Leo already eliminated."

*Not good,* Carrie thought. *Not good for me, and definitely not good for the already eliminated Leo.* "Who are you?"

"I am Tino Antonov. Pfeiffer custodian," Tino said. "I find drug, close lab, make mess disappear. I am cleaner."

*The cleaner, of course,* Carrie thought. "Is Leo dead?"

"He's home, Carrie baby," Tino said. "Burned both feet bad. Worse than expected. Very hot flame. He won't walk for few days, maybe week. But not dead yet. Not like Stuart, who is very dead."

He slowly opened cabinets and drawers, perused papers and printouts, flipped through files and folders. He was a rough-looking man. Bad skin covered by a scraggly, Hollywood-movie-star-style beard. Short, fashionably messy hair. Big nose. Pitiless eyes. That's what scared her, his eyes. There was cruelty in them, plus some insanity.

She knew Stuart was dead. Eduardo Wolf had told her so. But how had Tino known? And if he knew Stuart was dead, did he also know about Eduardo Wolf? About Yelchin being in bed with Pfeiffer unbeknownst to either of them? Leo might have told Tino about Yelchin when his feet were burning (whatever *that* meant), but she couldn't be sure. Either way, she wasn't letting that two-headed cat out of the bag.

"What do you mean, not like Stuart? Stuart's dead? Is that what you're saying?" she said in her most shocked voice. "How did he die?"

"Car crash on Friday," Tino said. "Police say Stuart drive into brick wall. Car blow up in blaze of glory. By time finish fighting fire, nothing left but bones. No skin. No hair. No blood. Just bones."

"That's terrible," Carrie said. She meant it too. She couldn't stand Stuart, but she didn't want him to die like that—even though she knew he *hadn't* died like that. He'd died in the break-room. The crashing car was Eduardo Wolf's fix to eliminate the evidence. She felt sure about that.

"Police say Stuart's right arm look like chewed in blender up to elbow," Tino said. "That not from car fire. That from torture. Who torture Stuart before car crash? Wasn't Tino, I tell you that. Anyway, Leo not take drug, and Stuart not take drug. Process of elimination, Carrie baby. Just the way you like it."

He stopped at the large table in the middle of the room, Carrie's custom-constructed maze, the home of the Greek Gods. It was eight feet wide by twelve feet long and was the height of a regular dining table. An eighteen-inch perimeter "wall" kept the rats in the maze, on the table. Inside the wall were dozens of different shaped pieces of wood that could be placed in countless positions on the pegboard tabletop to create an endless variety of mazes for an infinite number of tests, depending upon what behavior Carrie was monitoring at that moment. One zone served as a kind of corral, a home base for the rats. Carrie called the corral Olympus.

"When Leo's feet are burning, he tell me about you, Carrie baby. He say you like rats." Tino looked down at the Greek Gods in Olympus. "He say you like rats more than people. Is true?"

There was an underlying tone to his voice that scared Carrie. "I like them more than some people."

"That what Leo say," Tino said. "Especially Greek God rats. Leo say you talk to Greek God rats. Hold them. Kiss them. Love them. You know each rat individually. Give names, Leo say. You give names, Carrie baby?"

She wanted to say, *Yes, I named them. I know them. Each one of them. They're my friends. Please don't hurt them. They're special. They're important to me*, but she didn't answer because he took a long-wand butane grill lighter from his pocket and clicked the switch, turning the flame on and off, on and off, on and off. After hearing Tino talk about Leo and his burned feet, she had an exceptionally bad feeling about the lighter.

"Leo say you like Greek God rats best of all rats," Tino said. "You know what? I look at your face, I think is true. Is true, Carrie baby?"

She wanted to move to the maze, protect the Greek Gods from his voice alone, but her feet were frozen with fear. "Yes." The word was barely a whisper.

"Is funny. You know why? Because I hate rats. Let me tell you story. When I was boy in Russia, town have too many rats. How do you say...infestation. Shitload of rats. No one like rats in Russia. People in town say who can get rid of rats, but no one can do it. So I burn them. I burn hundred rats, and nobody say one word because rats carry disease, make mess, and have no value to people in town. So I keep burning rats until all rats are dead. Moral of story is I hate rats, but I like burning them."

With his left hand, Tino clicked the switch, lit the flame, and let it burn.

"Now you tell me story, Carrie baby. Tell me what you did with drug or I burn Greek Gods."

Her feet came unstuck, and she moved toward the table to stop him somehow. But before she could do or even say anything, he pulled a Sig Sauer pistol with a 9mm silencer and pointed it at her.

"What you do with drug?" Tino said, eyes back and forth between Carrie and the rats.

"I didn't do anything with it. I didn't take it."

No one had ever pointed a gun at her in her entire life. She couldn't remember ever being in the same room with someone who'd had a gun. And a silencer? *What the hell? Nobody has a silencer in real life. Only movie stars have silencers, and only in the movies. Jesus Christ. A silencer?* If it wasn't for the fact that the cleaner was about to burn her rats, she might have fainted.

"Two thumbs down, Carrie baby."

"What?"

"Siskel and Ebert. Two thumbs down."

He shook his head, as if not understanding how Carrie could have missed the reference, lowered the lighter into Olympus, and used the flame to separate one rat from the others. Dionysus.

"It couldn't have been me." She watched the flame dance dangerously close to Dionysus. "I have an alibi."

"What alibi?" He flicked the flame, trapping Dionysus in a corner of the corral.

Her heart was a jackhammer. "When Old Tom was knocked unconscious and someone stole the drug, I was at the Foxfire Room in Valley Village."

"What time leave bar?"

"After eleven, maybe eleven fifteen, I don't remember exactly.

I'd had a few beers to celebrate the success of the drug, then I got my car out of the parking lot down the street and drove home. There are people who saw me. Ask the big bartender, Justin. Leo's lying. Leo took the drug."

If anyone was going to get thrown under a bus, it was going to be Sikorski or Stuart but not her—although Stuart had already been figuratively thrown under a bus, so it was going to be Sikorski.

"I check alibi," Tino said. "But first I burn rat for old time sake."

Carrie took another step toward the table, up against it now. Eight feet away. The maze between them. Helpless to stop him. She wanted to cry out, but her voice got stuck in her throat. The Russian aimed the gun at her chest.

"Don't move, Carrie baby."

With his other hand, he lowered the lighter deeper into the corral. Dionysus was backed against a wall. The lighter moved closer and closer and closer. Tino's eyes filled with a sick sort of pleasure—a fond memory of the pain and suffering and death he'd delivered. Still with the gun pointed at Carrie, he glanced at her and winked. He wasn't kidding. He did like to burn rats.

She thought she might vomit or pass out or both.

And then one split second before the flame touched its fur, Dionysus leaped up and out of the way of the flame. Though not like a rat at all, not like any rat Carrie had ever seen. More like a wild gazelle—graceful and strong. The rat jumped away from the fire, yes, but not back, forward and to the side, just enough to dodge the flame head on, the tip of the lighter and then the long wand parallel to its body. The rat jumped, Carrie thought, like an Olympian, straight at Tino's hand, and bit him hard.

"Shit!" He dropped the lighter and pulled his hand out of the corral. "Fucking rat bite me. Goddamn fucking rat bite me. I'm going to need fucking stitch..."

It was true. He was bleeding all over himself. Dionysus had

taken a nasty, ragged chunk of skin from the back of the cleaner's hand.

"Fuck you, you fucking rat," Tino said, and he whipped his hand into the corral, grabbed the rat, and threw it like a baseball, like a Clayton Kershaw heater, at the wall of cages. Dionysus smashed into the wall and fell to the ground, nearly dead. Tino moved to the Greek God, looked down at it with something between pleasure and hatred, and stomped on it. Once, twice, three times. Mashing it to a bloody pulp.

Involuntary tears came to Carrie's eyes. The brutal violence of the moment made her heart stop. How could there be a human being who behaved like this? One of her miracle Greek Gods was dead on the ground, the cleaner was walking toward her, and she was in shock.

The Russian stopped in front of her, blood all over his hands and arms and clothes. "Not as good as burning, Carrie baby, but will do in pinch."

# CHAPTER 18
# A MOMENT OF, WELL, EUREKA

SATURDAY NIGHT, after he'd cleaned the Copa kitchen, Johnny had gone out. He'd smoked weed and done shots of tequila and worked his way up and down the mountain of strange shit on his mind. And what he'd come to, the bottom line of all the weird shit and bad shit and impossible shit that had happened since he'd been fired from the steakhouse and hired at the Copacabana was this: *Fuck all that shit.*

He'd returned to the Copa at seven o'clock Sunday morning, still stoned from the weed and wired from the tequila, packed his clothes, fired up the Harley, and gone north. He was headed for Alaska, planning to disappear in the frozen wilderness, never to be found. *Because who's going to look for me in fucking Alaska? Who's going to look for me anywhere?*

Rodney the Wrecker? Rodney had sold Johnny's stuff at an impromptu, gang-banger yard sale and likely erased Johnny from his brain cells immediately thereafter. Rodney wasn't leaving his drug-lab homies behind to track Johnny into the frozen wilderness.

Big Ben Boston? That fat asshole wouldn't travel three thousand miles to extort two hundred bucks from Johnny's meager Alaskan paycheck—if Johnny even had a meager Alaskan paycheck. Johnny skipping out on his parole would be proof positive that the system worked as intended—a lot of wins, a couple losses—and Big Ben Boston would go about his dirty business without anyone being the wiser. Big Ben was not following Johnny to Alaska.

The Copacabana crew? That mutant freak show was like nothing Johnny had ever seen in his life—and he'd been to prison twice. The Copa crowd were so wrapped up in their bizzaro world Fountain of Youth they wouldn't even notice Johnny was gone. How could they? One day they were ninety years old, and the next day they were forty-five. Who would notice anything other than *that* if it happened to them? Not to mention it was against the laws of nature, against the laws of the universe, against the laws of the FDA, the FBI, the CIA, and the LAPD. Getting the hell out of town before all kinds of law enforcement arrived was the smart play. No one from the Copacabana would be wasting their newfound youth chasing him to Alaska.

Patrick and Merry? His parents were dead, so they couldn't physically follow him, though that wouldn't stop their ghosts from guiding Johnny to his Alaskan grave. Even still, they couldn't mess with Johnny's life in Alaska any more than they'd already messed with it in LA, so they didn't count in this particular equation. The parental damage had been done.

No matter how he'd added it up, Alaska was his last, best chance to leave behind the hurricane of crap he called his life and start again.

But at six o'clock Sunday evening, after eleven hours on the road, when he'd rolled into Eureka, not far from the Oregon border, he'd had a moment of, well, eureka: *Carrie might look for me.*

His eureka moment was immediately followed by a what-the-fuck moment because what he'd really meant was: *he* might look for *her* if *she* ran off to Alaska.

*That can't be fucking true,* he'd thought as he sat on his bike and looked north. *I barely know her.*

But he couldn't deny he'd thought that thought and *had* been thinking it since Carrie first told him about Eduardo Wolf. He'd heard something in her voice when she'd said Wolf's name, a lilt of some kind, a subtle change of tone. And he'd notice a look in her eyes that gave away her attraction to the fixer. *And by the way, how in the fuck could I understand the look in her eyes when I've only just met her?* But he'd seen the look and heard the lilt, and now he felt a feeling that was something close to, well, jealousy.

*Jealousy?* Really? Johnny jealous? Of some fucking fixer named Eduardo? No way could he be jealous of that asshole. *Fuck Eduardo Wolf,* Johnny thought, sitting on the Harley in Eureka facing north. *Eduardo Wolf should be jealous of me.*

*Wait. What?* Why in the world should Wolf be jealous of Johnny when it came to Carrie Kromer? Johnny had never been attracted to, interested in, or dated a woman like her. For shit's sake, he'd never *dated* any woman. What he'd done was have short-term flings and affairs that were purely physical with women who were rail thin and covered in tattoos, like he was. Chain smokers, drug users, heavy drinkers, party girls—women looking for as much of a commitment as Johnny was looking for, which was no commitment at all. He'd never been with anyone who'd ever been to college, forget graduated college, double-forget anyone with *multiple* graduate school degrees. Maybe a handful of the women he'd slept with had been to cosmetology school, but it was more likely they'd been to prison.

He wasn't attracted to Carrie. *Except she has a pretty face, good hair, and a nice smile.* They had nothing in common. *Except our fathers both died on our twenty-first birthdays.* He liked his women wild, and she had no wild streak. *Except she knocked out the security guard and stole the drug from the lab.* He was turned on by the threat of danger, and there was nothing dangerous about her. *Except the fixer is part of her picture.* He was a two-time ex-con, so she could never really know him because she had never been to prison. *Except that could change if I'm not there to watch her back.*

Those thoughts were immediately followed by this thought: *What the fuck am I thinking? I'm going to goddamn Alaska.*

But he'd fired up the Harley, pointed it south, and roared back to LA. He'd drained Red Bulls on the hour and stopped only to get gas or take a leak. Throughout the eleven-hour haul, he'd had one thought, *I'm out of my fucking mind.*

He'd rolled into Los Angeles at half past six Monday morning, gone straight to the Copacabana, taken a shower, chugged his last Red Bull, and was in the kitchen by seven.

The Copa crowd ate Johnny's breakfast burritos—goat cheese, grilled onions, fried eggs, and chorizo sausage—like they were the last food on the face of the Earth, then told him they were headed to the beach to spend the day bodysurfing and sun-worshipping, something none of them had done in decades—except for Betty, who'd been on a first-name basis with the sun for as long as anyone could remember.

Though they were all astoundingly middle-aged, bodies tight and toned, skin gorgeous and glowing, eyes sharp and shining—Nearsighted Norman had no need for glasses—Johnny was most taken by Tall Bob.

Despite the disintegration of Bob's memory, he had remained six feet five inches tall and handsome as hell well into his eighties. But as a phenomenal forty-five, he was a sight to see—straight and strong as steel. Pro-athlete gorgeous. Johnny learned Bob had played football at San Diego State, where he'd been a hellacious tight end until a serious concussion knocked him out of the game for good. He'd dropped out of school after that and drifted into women's shoes because it was an excellent place to meet women—and Bob had been something of a hound dog. He'd managed a store in downtown San Diego until his mind started to melt away, then he moved up and down the California coast, from shoe store to shoe store. Women had loved buying from Bob and then showing off their shoes for him after hours.

But what made Johnny's jaw drop wasn't Bob's physicality or striking looks. It was Bob's memory, which had returned with sparkling clarity and living color. Bob now remembered every damn thing about every damn thing. Including how to hit on women.

While the Copa crew inhaled breakfast burritos, Bob flirted with Bleach Blonde Dolores, who instead of ninety-six was forty-two and looked like freaking Marilyn Monroe. Dolores flirted right back at Bob. And everyone was in on it. All the talk at the tables was deep double entendre. Everything was sexual innuendo. The Copa crew was carnal and erotic at eight in the morning.

*What will they be after a day at the beach?* Johnny thought as they loaded into the Copacabana passenger van.

Oxygen Tank Lillian was the last one in the van. She didn't look a day over forty. Her wheelchair and oxygen tank were now part of her distant past. (*Saturday!*) She had a cigarette in her mouth because bad habits die hard.

"We'll be back after dark, Tattoo Boy," she said. "We're thinking beef brisket sliders and pork ribs. Get us a keg of Sam Adams."

They were gone by eight fifteen.

Johnny cleaned the kitchen, felt himself crashing, went back to his room, slept from nine fifteen to three forty-five, took another shower, and was back in the kitchen at four.

Eduardo Wolf was waiting for him.

# CHAPTER 19
# CRAZY CARTOON NETWORK SHIT

"HELLO, JOHNNY," the fixer said.

He was leaning against the stainless-steel prep counter, arms folded across his chest. He wore charcoal gray slacks and a black dress shirt that had been tailored to fit him like the black leather gloves on his hands.

*Eduardo Wolf,* Johnny thought. *Jesus Christ, he looks just like Carrie described him.* He remembered Carrie had said everyone needed to keep the capsules quiet because the fixer was no joke. He was a badass here to, number one, collect the stolen drug if he could find it and, number two, eliminate the Alsiko evidence —whether or not he was successful with number one.

*Fuck this scumbag,* Johnny thought as he moved into the kitchen where Wolf was waiting. "You a sales rep?"

Eduardo almost laughed. "No. I am Eduardo Wolf. I'm here to retrieve the capsules Carrie stole from the lab and repair the damage done as a result of her crime. You know who I am. You recognized me immediately. I saw it in your eyes. You must be a miserable poker player."

Johnny hated poker. He'd lost cigarettes, candy bars, and cash money in biker bars and prison yards all his life. He moved to the sink and washed the dishes he'd left for later. He didn't like the sound of "repair the damage done as a result of her crime," especially since he and everyone else at the Copa was now part of that deal—although they'd been renewed as opposed to damaged.

*I hate this motherfucking fixer*, Johnny thought. "Poker's for pussies. If you're not a sales rep, get the hell out of my kitchen."

This time Eduardo did laugh. "If we're going to have a productive conversation, and we *are* going to have one, then first we need to get past your macho posturing. As a show of good faith, I will start."

He moved to the dishwashing sink and leaned against it, right next to where Johnny was working, facing him, uncomfortably close to him. "Carrie mentioned the new Copacabana cook during our candid conversation at the lab. I did my homework to prepare for this meeting, so I know precisely what kind of loser you are. You're a bitter, angry punk. A two-time ex-con out on parole—or more accurately, in violation of your parole—who can't control his temper. You are unable to hold a job. You have no friends. You have no family. You are a non-contributing member of society. You are alone, you are stupid, and you are weak. Knowing Carrie as intimately as I do, though not as intimately as I will, I felt sure she would tell you and everyone else in residence about my arrival in Los Angeles, particularly given how she's made you accessories that require termination, thereby confirming she did indeed take the capsules. Knowing I was coming, why would she tell you if she had not involved you? As expected, you have verified that with your transparent obstinance, so thank you very much. Now it is your turn, Johnny. Where is everyone?"

Johnny sprayed down the dishes, slid the rack into the commercial washer, hit the start button, and glared at the fixer. Then he moved around the kitchen, gathering everything he needed to make beef brisket sliders and barbecued pork ribs.

Eduardo remained by the sink, but Johnny could feel the fixer's eyes on him. Still, he played it cool, which wasn't easy because self-control was not a character trait that ran in his family. His Italian birth father hadn't had enough of it to stay with the woman he'd impregnated, and his Irish adoptive father had a temper that could stop a train—but not a bus, seeing as how one had flattened him on Fairfax Avenue while he was chasing Johnny with a meat cleaver. Piss-poor self-control was the reason Johnny had been to prison twice, the reason he couldn't hold a job, the reason he was alone, the hallmark of his life.

The smart move, Johnny knew, was to bide his time, to make the case that he'd only started the job the previous Thursday and didn't know any fucking thing about any fucking drug. He *knew* that was the smart move.

But he could feel the heat of hell burning his spine. He'd felt it many times throughout his life, the heat of hell. It had always led to a loss of control, to trouble, to violence. Eduardo's words about being intimate with Carrie had hit a raw nerve.

*He pissed me off on purpose,* Johnny thought. *He's trying to make me lose my shit so I'll fuck up and give Carrie away, admit I know she stole the drug and gave it to the old-timers, which is going to be bad shit for everyone involved. So the new smart move is to fuck the old smart move. The new smart move is to kill this motherfucker right here, right now, and make this whole fucking fixer clusterfuck a memory.*

"Everyone who?" Johnny said.

He'd considered it on the long ride back from Eureka—killing the fixer—but it had been a passing fancy, background noise overpowered by the screaming wind.

It wasn't like he'd never killed anyone. He'd done it twice, in fact. The first time he'd been nineteen and caught a crazed junkie, wild with meth, stealing his motorcycle in the shadows behind Cook's Corner, a biker bar in Trabuco Canyon. The junkie had come at him with a knife. Johnny had killed him, kept the knife, jumped on his bike, and taken off into the night. No murder weapon. No witnesses. No Johnny. Just a random dead junkie no one gave a shit about. The second time had been on

Johnny's birthday, which he'd celebrated in prison while serving his second sentence. Some scumbag skinhead had accused him of stealing cigarettes, which Johnny hadn't done. What kind of idiot stole cigarettes from a skinhead in prison? The skinhead had come at him with a shiv in the prison laundry, where they'd both worked, and Johnny had choked him to death behind the huge commercial machines, then stuck him in a dryer and kept on keeping on washing prison clothes. By the time they'd found the skinhead, there was no way to pin it on Johnny or anyone. All they'd had was a dead skinhead on tumble dry. Even the guards hadn't cared. "At least he's not wet," one had said.

"The old people," Eduardo said. "Where are they?"

Johnny glanced at the knives hanging on the magnetic rack—cleavers, carvers, and chef knives. *The ten-inch carver in your fucking back*, he thought. *That's where the fuck they are.* "They took the van after breakfast. I think they went to a medical center somewhere. Group checkup or something. I'm the cook, not the activities director."

"Do you know where Maureen Breen might be?" Eduardo said.

Johnny had not seen her come in that morning. "No idea. Maybe her dog died. Fuck do I know where she is?"

Eduardo took a letter from his pocket, moved to the counter, across from Johnny, and held it up. Johnny glanced at the letter while he assembled the ingredients for his barbecue sauce.

"Ms. Breen placed this letter in the mailbox as I was arriving," Eduardo said. "I spoke with her before she hurried home. She was, as the saying goes, spooked. She refused to step foot on the grounds. Odd behavior for someone who's worked here as long as she has, and as recently as Friday, don't you think?"

"I think it's against the law to take somebody's mail in America," Johnny said. He blended minced onion and water into a puree and poured it into a heated saucepan coated with olive oil. "Maybe I'll make a citizen's arrest." He laughed in a way intended to imply he wasn't kidding and tested the temperature of the puree in the pan, adding crushed garlic, apple cider vinegar, tomato paste, Worcestershire, dry mustard, cayenne, and pepper. He turned the flame to low and let the sauce simmer.

"Skipping her formalities," Eduardo said, "Ms. Breen writes: 'What happened to Miss Joanna on Friday was the devil's work. Old people are old and young people are young. That's the way God made us, and that's the way He wants it to be. Miss Joanna's been touched by the hand of the devil. I quit, and I'm never coming back.' So, her dog did not die, and something extraordinary happened to Miss Joanna. Something to do with old people being old and young people being young and the hand of the devil. As an aside, that's what they should name the drug, Hand of the Devil, though marketing is not my forte. Fixing problems is my forte, so even you should be able to understand why I want to talk about Maureen Breen and the stolen capsules."

"I got nothing to say about Maureen," Johnny said. He stirred his barbecue sauce. Tasted it. There was no recipe. There never had been. Johnny cooked by memory and feel, by taste and vibe. "I met her maybe three times. I don't know what the fuck she's talking about."

"She's talking about the capsules Carrie stole from the lab and gave to her mother," Eduardo said. "The drug that reverses the aging process."

"Crazy Cartoon Network shit," Johnny said. "Nobody gets younger. You get born, you get old, you die. Or you die before you get old. Either way, you don't get younger."

Johnny opened the oven, removed a cast-iron pot and placed it on the counter. He took the lid off and let the steam evaporate. Using two forks, he lifted the brisket onto a cutting board. It was perfectly cooked, charred all around, fall-apart tender all the way through. He grabbed the ten-inch carver and trimmed the outermost layer of fat from the meat.

"Either way, it doesn't matter to me." Eduardo walked

around the prep counter to where Johnny was working, leaned against it, facing him, encroaching on his personal space.

"Then what are you doing here?"

"I am here because you are my wild card," Eduardo said. "I understand the logic and motivation of Dr. Sikorski. I appreciate the instinct and reasoning of Carrie Kromer. I eliminated the problematic participation of Stuart Langston. I recognize what a mystical Fountain of Youth would mean to the residents of the Copacabana. All of these pieces fit neatly into this improbable puzzle. All but you. You are my wild card. I can't comprehend your involvement. Are you romantically connected to Carrie? That would be a shame because love leads to impulsive, sometimes volatile behavior, and that is unacceptable given the circumstances. Combining your emotional attachment with your low IQ and ex-con temper, you may well be ready to risk your life to protect hers."

Something across the kitchen caught Eduardo's attention. He turned his back to Johnny and took two steps in that direction, putting a few feet between them. But he kept talking, comparing Carrie and Johnny to Romeo and Juliet, doomed to die dreadful deaths in the name of romance, musing how he might kill Carrie in the middle of making love to her while Johnny watched, just to rub it in Johnny's face.

Johnny listened, but what little control he had left had checked out. His spine was an inferno, the back of his neck was in flames, and his brain was burning like a house on fire. He knew what he had to do to save Carrie and the old folks, to save his job and maybe his life. He lifted the ten-inch carving knife. *No one has to know. Same as the junkie and the skinhead. I got no choice. It's live or die. I got to do it. I want to do it. I want to kill this son of a bitch. I hate this fucking fixer.*

Johnny raised the knife above his head and pounced at Eduardo like a big cat—with speed and strength and deadly purpose. In a split second, Eduardo Wolf would be dead on the Copa kitchen floor, and all this fixer shit would be over.

Except in a mind-boggling blink of an eye, like he'd been waiting for it, like he'd lured Johnny into it, Eduardo spun, stepped to the side, grabbed Johnny's wrist, and slammed him face-first into the floor between the counter and ovens—like some fucking mixed-martial-arts master.

Johnny was stunned, nearly knocked out. He saw stars. Tasted blood from his nose. His head pounded with pain as it bounced off the floor. The fixer slapped the knife from his hand, flipped him onto his back, pinned his arms beneath him. He put a knee on his chest, a powerful forearm on his neck, and started to choke him.

Johnny struggled, but the fixer was too strong and too fast, much stronger and faster than Johnny had thought possible. He was immobilized on the kitchen floor. His lungs screamed for air. Every muscle burned. His head throbbed. He thought his chest might cave in from the pressure.

"She took them, Johnny," Eduardo said. "You know she did."

"She has an alibi, asshole," Johnny said, barely spitting the words out.

"We will see." Eduardo applied more pressure to Johnny's throat, making it harder and harder to breathe. "Actually, I will see. You will be dead because a wild card with a violent temper is unacceptable."

Johnny couldn't move, couldn't breathe. He was blacking out. In thirty seconds, he would, indeed, be dead.

"And while it would give me great pleasure to cut the tattoos from your skin while you watch," Eduardo said, "suffocating you in close quarters will do nicely."

"Hey, anybody here? Freedom Beverage. I got a delivery. Keg of Sam Adams."

Eduardo released the pressure. Johnny gasped air into his lungs.

"Yes, the cook is on the floor." Eduardo stood, came around the counter, smiled at the Freedom guy, walked past the keg and out of the kitchen. "He slipped and fell and had the wind knocked out of him. He's fine. Just needs a minute."

The Freedom guy looked around, didn't see anyone else in the room but heard someone stirring behind the counter. "You okay back there?"

Johnny blinked himself back into the moment and sat up. He peered over the counter and around the room. Eduardo was gone. A rotund delivery guy with a keg on a hand truck stood at the kitchen door.

"Tap that fucking thing," Johnny said. "I need a beer."

# CHAPTER 20

# THE FIRST STEPS OF AN UNSPOKEN SOMETHING

THE PASSENGER VAN arrived back from the beach at nine fifteen. From what Carrie could gather, the party picked up where it had left off, which was to say it never ended, which was to say the surf, sand, and sun had worked their hedonistic magic. The Copa crowd were radiant and ravishing and ready to get down on it. Carrie was awestruck by their stamina. She called to mind her gerontologist lexicon, searching for the appropriate label, but could only call their energy *epic*.

The old folks had been at the beach for ten hours. Bodysurfing, beer drinking, sunbathing, beer drinking, volleyball playing, beer drinking, sandcastle building, beer drinking, and a wild game of co-ed Frisbee football against a dozen UCLA fraternity boys and sorority girls that had not ended well for the college kids. One of the frat boys had been whisked away to Urgent Care with a busted nose; several sorority sisters had left the game with black eyes and bone bruises; and the biggest frat freak had taken on Tall Bob and gone home with a dislocated shoulder. A platoon of lifeguards had broken up the action before it had turned into an outright bloodbath.

No one, not a single person at the beach—not the college kids, not the lifeguards, not the passersby, not anyone—had the slightest idea that this loud and lustful crew of fabulous forty-two-year-old beach bums had just last week been a decaying and declining crew of ninety-year-old rest-homers.

And after ten hours of raucous, unruly behavior that had included Domino's making three separate pizza runs to the beach on their behalf, the Copa crowd were still famished and only too pleased to pound the keg of Sam Adams into submission while inhaling Johnny's beef brisket sliders and barbecued pork ribs. For sides, Johnny had made creamy coleslaw, jalapeno-spiced baked beans, and fresh-baked cornbread. There were pints of Ben & Jerry's Cherry Garcia ice cream for dessert.

When the Copa crew's antics—which straddled a lewd line between daring and dangerous, between unsafe and unwise, between holy-shit-are-you-kidding-me and holy-shit-don't-do-that—overwhelmed her, Carrie put her foot down. But when the men started swan diving, jackknifing, and cannonballing from the second-floor railing into the pool and the women egged them on, scoring them on degrees of difficulty, magnitude of splash, and sexiest performance, Carrie's words and warnings became lost in the lascivious hubbub.

With nothing to do but drink beer, Carrie crossed the courtyard to the keg, tapped herself a Sam, and sat next to Johnny on the far side of the pool. Together they watched the old folks give up the funk as the diving competition ended, dinner was devoured, and the poolside dance party got promiscuous in a hurry, meaning the Copa crew were bawdy as a band of strippers. Their dancing was a sexy combination of loose and lusty, everyone changing partners without missing a beat. They boogied to the music of their youth, the 1950s, when they'd been in their wet and wild twenties, and to the tunes of the 1970s, when they'd been as young as they were now. They were the only eleven people in the history of the world who'd ever grown younger, and like an X-rated runaway train, they had a head of sexual steam that couldn't be stopped.

"How long you think before the clothes come off?" Johnny said.

"I give it ten minutes," Carrie said.

"I give it five," Johnny said.

Joanna was among the randiest of the group. She seemed utterly uninhibited—her simulated sex dance with Tall Bob only a half-step from the real thing—the opposite of how Carrie remembered her mother behaving back in New Jersey. *Where in the world did she learn to move like that*, Carrie thought, *MTV?* The reason the rest of the old-timers didn't stop to watch Joanna and Bob was because they were involved in their own simulated sex dances, an ever-evolving flow-motion of copulating couples and threesomes and foursomes...and Betty and Helen getting down and dirty to the point where Carrie wanted to call out: *Jesus Christ, get a room already*.

"Your mother told me they offered you Maureen's job," Johnny said as if trying to change channels.

Carrie nodded. "I can't work at Alsiko anymore. It's closed forever and never existed. And I can't work at any other lab or hospital or university because they're going to ask me what I've been doing for the past six years, and I don't have a good answer for that. 'Me? The past six years? I was the behavioral gerontologist at an unregistered, totally illegal lab financed by both North Korea and Iran. We made a miracle drug that no one will ever know about. What have *you* been doing?'"

"So you going to take it?" Johnny said.

She heard an underlying hopefulness in his voice and turned to him. Their eyes met. She knew he never talked about his feelings but also knew he wanted her to stay and knew he knew she knew. "Yes. Two master's degrees and a PhD, part of the core team that developed the freaking Fountain of Youth drug, and I'm doing old folks' laundry."

"What old folks?" Johnny said, and they both laughed. "Sorry about the lab."

Carrie nodded as Tall Bob, reliving his hound dog days with

gusto, moved from Joanna to Invisible Helen and took off his shirt. Bernard, who for the first time ever was not wearing a suit and tie, took off his shirt too. He was the most beautiful Black man Carrie had ever seen. Sidney Poitier beautiful. Within a minute, all the men had thrown their shirts to the wind.

"I was there today, feeding the rats—I have to take care of them until the end—and I met the Pfeiffer custodian," Carrie said. "He came to find the drug and clean up the Alsiko mess I made."

"Like the fixer?" Johnny said.

"Except Russian," Carrie said. "And he plays with fire." She told him about how the cleaner had tried to burn Dionysus, but that the rat had bitten his hand instead, drawn Russian blood, and been brutally murdered on the floor of Lab No. 3. She told him how the cleaner was going to check her alibi and then either come for the drug or kill her or both or either. "So now we've got the cleaner and the fixer."

"Wolf was here today," Johnny said. "In the Copa kitchen. He tried to kill me because I'm the wild card."

"That's true. You are the wild card."

"The wildest."

He told her about how Eduardo had goaded him, invaded his personal space, tried to get him to spill the beans about Carrie and the stolen capsules. He told her he'd decided to kill the fixer with the ten-inch carver so Carrie would have time to figure out what to do about all this, but that Wolf had been too fast and too strong, and suddenly he'd been on his back on the kitchen floor, the fixer's forearm crushing his throat. He told her how he'd been thirty seconds from death when the beer guy showed up with the keg of Sam Adams and saved his life.

It was a horrifying story, of course, because at the end, Johnny nearly got choked to death. But besides that part, Carrie thought it was kind of sweet. Maybe even romantic. "The ten-inch carver?"

He shrugged a shrug that landed somewhere between *maybe*

and *nothing fucking scares me.* "He said some stuff made me lose my shit."

His tone of voice made her think the things the fixer said that made him lose his shit might have been about her. "Stuff about what?"

"You, me, him, sex, murder. Add it all up and—"

He stopped mid-sentence and pointed toward the pool. Buxom Brenda was the first Copa party girl to take off her shirt. Beach Blonde Dolores was next. Then Saddlebag Betty and Oxygen Tank Lillian. Then Invisible Helen, who was anything but invisible with her boobs bouncing in the open air. Finally, Joanna, ripped off her shirt, tossed it forty-some odd years into her past, and joined the topless dance party.

Carrie's jaw fell open when her mother's shirt came off. "Holy shit, my mother has great tits," she said out loud instead of to herself.

"They all do," Johnny said. "Especially for being ninety."

"Especially for that," Carrie said.

They laughed and watched the old folks play topless volley-ball in the pool with a colorful beach ball for a minute or two.

"I didn't see you all day Sunday or Monday morning," Carrie said. "I thought you were gone."

"I was," Johnny said.

"Where were you going?"

"Alaska."

"How far did you get?"

"Eureka."

"Pretty far."

"Far enough."

"Why did you come back?"

"Home inspection. My parole officer comes to the Copa tomorrow. I got to face him one way or the other."

She nodded. "Anything else?"

"This is the only cook job I ever had, and they like my food."

She drank her beer and looked at him. Clearly, he was not

the kind of man who talked easily about his feelings, if he talked about them at all, which he probably never did, being a tattooed ex-con-biker-butcher-cook kind of guy. But the truth was she'd never been and still wasn't much better at sharing *her* emotions. No matter, she would have to take the lead if they were going to have a conversation about this feeling they might both be feeling but would never let on they were feeling, if they were both even feeling it, which they might have been, though she couldn't be sure unless she took the lead. Or something like that.

"No other reason?" she said. "That's it? Ben Boston and cooking?"

He looked away and then found her eyes again. "I guess, I, uh, yeah, well, I couldn't leave you here alone with the fixer and now the cleaner and these maniacs. I don't run out on my friends. You know, if I had friends."

She smiled, and he smiled, and they were quiet again. Partly because they were reticent to continue down any conversational path that could possibly lead to the beginnings of anything that might mildly be considered the first steps of an unspoken some-thing—a connection or a bond or, God forbid, a relationship. And partly because the old folks had come out of the pool and were taking off their shorts.

"Skinny-dip, no choice, take it off, take it all off," Drooling Arnie said, stripping off his suit and throwing it to the side.

"About damn time," Cranky Walter said, laughing his bare ass off.

The Copa party girls didn't need to be told twice. All of them were naked in a heartbeat.

"So you came back for me, at least a little," Carrie said.

"Yeah, at least a little."

"That's good, isn't it?"

"Is it?"

"Could be, couldn't it?"

"Could it?"

It was awkward but it was on the table, right between them. They liked each other, at least a little.

"I'm going to pay Ben Boston," Carrie said.

"What?" Johnny said.

"I've been saving for six years. I have money. I'll pay Ben Boston, and then that's one less problem we have to deal with."

Johnny seemed stunned, even moved. Confused, of course, but as moved as he was confused, which was probably, Carrie imagined, the cause of his confusion.

"Why would you do that?" he said.

"Three reasons," Carrie said. "One, you tried to kill the fixer to buy me time, and that was very brave. Two, you left for Alaska and came back for me, at least a little, and that was very sweet. Three, I don't turn my back on friends. You know, if I had friends."

She held his gaze for a moment, then Johnny smiled, and they clinked glasses of Sam Adams.

"I'll pay you back," Johnny said.

"Damn right you will."

They both laughed until they realized that all eleven crazy Copa kids were standing ten feet in front of them. They were buck naked except for Nearsighted Norman, who still had his trunks on.

"We saw you laughing and talking and toasting each other and came over to tell you how happy we are to have you both here with us," Helen said.

*No doubt*, they said. *Absolutely*, they said. *Here, here*, they said.

"I propose a toast," Lillian said. "To Tattoo Boy and Carrie. You're part of the family now. We've got your backs."

*To Johnny and Carrie*, they said. *Fuck the fixer*, they said. *Best cook in LA*, they said.

They toasted with glasses of Sam Adams and then looked at Norman, who finally took his trunks off.

"Jesus fucking Christ," Bernard said.

"You're going to hurt someone with that thing," Dolores said.

And everyone laughed and *oohed* and *ahhed* because Norman was hung like a horse. He had an exceptionally large dick. Ridiculously large. Bigger than Tall Bob, who was the right size for his size, which was to say huge, though merely average compared to Norman.

When the racket subsided, Brenda said, "Speech, Norman. Speech."

Norman raised his hand, and everyone fell silent. "I was an ordinary accountant in a department store. My brother was a flashy veterinarian who specialized in cats. I got more pussy than he did."

The old folks erupted with laughter and jumped back into the pool.

*It's not an orgy yet,* Carrie thought, *but it will be soon.*

# CHAPTER 21

# MAYBE TAKE SHOES OFF AND PICK FEET IN POUGHKEEPSIE

SOME DAYS WERE JUST Gene-Hackman-playing-Popeye-Doyle-in-*The-French-Connection* days. For Tino, Monday was such a day. While the Russian coveted many of the characters Hackman had portrayed, he revered none more than the gritty NYPD detective chasing the dapper French heroin dealer in the grubby gutters and low-brow bars of New York in the 1970s. To be clear, the cleaner didn't want to be Popeye Doyle or Gene Hackman or even Hackman's version of Doyle. He wanted to be *his* version of Hackman's version of Doyle. It was that kind of Monday.

Wearing a porkpie hat that would have made Popeye proud, drinking vodka, smoking a cigar, and listening to Streisand at volumes that caused hearing loss, Tino turned the Mercedes—with his knees—into the parking lot across the street and down the block from the Foxfire Room on Magnolia Boulevard in Valley Village, maybe the best dive bar in the San Fernando Valley.

The bar from Carrie's alibi.

He'd driven from Alsiko—Ventura to Whitsett to Magnolia—the same route Carrie had taken (*said* she'd taken) to confirm her alibi timeline. Forty-five minutes leaving the lab at six thirty last

Wednesday, she'd said. And it had taken Tino forty-five minutes leaving at six thirty the following Monday.

*So far so good for Carrie Kromer*, Tino thought as he opened the Foxfire door.

Nobody really knew how long the bar had been open. The nineties? Eighties? Seventies? A hell of a long time was the general consensus. But what everyone knew for a stone-cold fact was that the place hadn't changed since day one.

Wall-to-wall wood paneling straight out of your grandparents' den. Wood-veneer cocktail tables and captain's chairs from a bygone era. Old-school bar. Leather booths and banquettes. Darts and karaoke. Video games. Cheap drinks, heavy on the pour. Diverse local crowd every night of the week, from retirees with missing teeth to local hipsters with lumberjack beards to cougars on the prowl in tight sweaters and short skirts. Granted, there were a few flat-screen TVs—a reluctant nod to progress— and some nifty neon lighting (either from the actual future or from *Back to the Future*) that added to the kitsch, but otherwise the Foxfire was physically untouched since its first day of business. More importantly, the vibe hadn't changed either. It was still open early in the morning until early the next morning. As far as Foxfire's Hollywood bona fides, the great William H. Macy's character, Quiz Kid Donnie Smith, drank like a fish in the Foxfire in Paul Thomas Anderson's 1999 movie *Magnolia*. By any measure, it was a picture-perfect slice of LA dive-bar heaven.

The place was already hopping. Most people like to poke around a new joint for a little while before getting down to brass tacks. Get the lay of the land, catch the vibe, settle into the rhythm of the room. But not Tino, and especially not Tino when he was playing Hackman's version of Popeye Doyle.

Tino found a captain's chair barstool, took a seat, ordered a vodka rocks, and started straight in with the bartenders, introducing himself as Peter Petrov, a private investigator searching for a woman in a world of trouble. The small bartender didn't work Wednesdays, so Tino lost interest in him, and he drifted down the bar. The big bartender, Justin, was the one Tino set his sights on. Carrie had said Justin would confirm her alibi, and, in fact, Justin said he worked every Wednesday, including last Wednesday. So Tino put a photograph of her on the bar.

"Do you know this woman?" Tino said like Hackman's Doyle, except Russian.

"Nope," Justin said, picking up Carrie's photo.

"Are you sure?" Tino said, instantly recognizing a bad performance when he saw one. "Maybe look closer. Maybe take shoes off and pick feet in Poughkeepsie."

"What?" Justin said, looking up from Carrie's photograph.

"Look again, Justin baby," Tino said. "I think you make mistake. I think you know this woman."

Justin looked again, closer this time, furrowing his brow like the terrible ever-aspiring actor he was in a pathetic theatrical attempt to show deep thought. "Yeah, yeah, I think I do. Yeah, wait, that's her. She came in last Wednesday about seven fifteen, drank a few beers, played some darts, sang some karaoke, left around eleven fifteen. That's her. What kind of trouble is she in?"

"Two thumbs down, Justin baby," Tino said with a Popeye sneer.

"What?" Justin said.

"Gene Siskel nail you for picking feet in Poughkeepsie," Tino said, taking the photo from Justin's hand.

Justin swelled with size and power, as if remembering that he was the bartender and this Russian pain in the ass was at his bar, not vice versa. "Listen man, I told you what I know. She was here till eleven fifteen. You don't like it, too bad for you. Now have your drink and mind your own business. This is a local place for local people. Everybody has a good time at the Foxfire. We clear?"

He turned and walked down the bar.

"That car dirty, Cloudy," Tino said. "We sit all night if we have to."

"Whatever, man," Justin said without turning around.

Tino drank his vodka and worked the room, striking up conversations with strangers, buying them drinks, asking if anyone had been here last Wednesday, showing them Carrie's photograph. The entire time, he stayed in character. No one said a word about his Popeye. Maybe because he was Russian and the collective Foxfire thought was that was how Russians behaved in dive bars in the Valley. Or maybe because it was LA and there were probably other versions of Hackman's Doyle happening in other dive bars at this very same moment.

Several patrons vaguely recalled seeing Carrie at the Foxfire last Wednesday—drinking beers, throwing darts, singing karaoke—but couldn't be sure what time she'd arrived or when she'd left.

Hours went by, and Tino's Popeye Doyle charm wore off. He became an obnoxious, aggressive Russian pest. Several people complained, and Justin (a hulking six-four and well over two hundred pounds of Gold's Gym molded muscle) came around the bar and confronted him.

"That's it, man. Time to go."

"But night is young," Tino said. "I have to find woman in picture."

"You have to find her somewhere else," Justin said and took Tino by the arm and escorted him onto Magnolia Boulevard. "If I see you come inside, I'll call the police."

"If that not drop, I open charge for you at Bloomingdale's," Tino said.

"What?" Justin said.

"You won't see Popeye coming until is too late, Justin baby," Tino said, winking.

Justin shook his head and went back inside.

That was eleven fifteen Monday night, the same time Carrie had said she'd left the Foxfire last Wednesday.

At two in the morning, the bar closed, and the final stragglers stumbled out. At two thirty, Justin locked the front door and walked to his car, an older model Acura sedan parked around the corner on Babcock. The street was empty. Not a soul in sight.

The bartender unlocked the car and grabbed the door handle and...Tino emerged from the shadows, pushed a hunting knife into Justin's left hamstring, stuck a syringe into the bartender's neck, and delivered a size-appropriate dose of Propofol. Justin struggled and Tino dug the knife in deeper. The fast-working anesthetic worked its magic. The big bartender was out in seventy-five seconds start to finish.

"Milk of amnesia, Justin baby. See you in ten minutes," Tino said.

He put the bartender in the Acura driver seat, zip-tied his wrists to the steering wheel, and then his ankles to a bar beneath the driver seat. The bloody gash in his leg leaked through his pants.

Tino sat in the passenger seat. While he waited for Justin to regain consciousness, he thought about his grandmother, a wild woman he'd called Baba Yana.

If she'd lived to see the present, then the present would have diagnosed her as bipolar or schizophrenic or both or way worse. Because she'd also been an arsonist or at least liked playing with fire, burning fields and buildings and wagons and disobedient animals. She'd been psychotically up and down—happy one minute, sad the next; calm as could be, then raging at Mother Russia—but through all her manic mood swings, and through all the flame and fire, she'd loved her grandson like there was no tomorrow. And there very nearly hadn't been.

Baba Yana had been widowed young. With no formal education and no financial fallback, she'd gone to work in a machine shop, which meant back-breaking labor ten hours a day for a handful of rubles. Somehow, she'd scraped together enough money to raise her only child, a daughter, who was raped and became pregnant (with Tino) when she was seventeen. She'd married the father out of necessity. That man had been known as The Beast. He'd moved into Baba Yana's house and begun abusing his wife, raping her, beating her, brutalizing her. And while he was at it, he also raped, beat, and brutalized Baba Yana too—sometimes in front of Tino—while his wife was away, which was often because he'd forced Tino's mother to work two jobs while he gambled on cockfights and dogfights and back-barn fistfights, which he often participated in.

When he'd directed his violence at seven-year-old Tino, something snapped in Baba Yana's bedeviled brain.

And one dark day, when Tino's mother was not at home, Baba Yana hit The Beast in the head from behind with a brick as he ate borscht at the kitchen table. While he was out cold, she and Tino dragged him to the shed behind the house. They tied him to a post, doused him with gasoline, and burned him to death. Baba Yana had let Tino light the match. The boy had been all too happy to do it.

*Good times*, Tino thought, looking over at Justin.

Thinking about The Beast and Baba Yana and Popeye Doyle and the other cruel and crazed insanity that had been his life was what made Tino tick like a bomb.

Which was bad news for the bartender, who came to at the wrong time.

# CHAPTER 22
# LET ME SEE YOUR POPEYE

TINO WATCHED as Justin realized his wrists were zip-tied to the steering wheel and his ankles were zip-tied to the bar beneath the seat, and he smiled when the bartender flew into a fit of panic-driven kicking and thrashing. The spirited outburst took a few minutes to subside and was accompanied by fear-infused screams that included phrases like *Let me the fuck out* and *Oh my fucking God* and *Fuck you, you fucking Russian fuck* and *I'll kill you, motherfucker.*

And he could hardly contain himself when Carrie's Foxfire alibi looked down at his leg, stopped screaming-kicking-thrashing, turned to Tino, and shouted, "My fucking leg. You cut my leg. I'm fucking bleeding. Oh my fucking God, I'm bleeding in my own fucking car."

"This my favorite part," Tino said, practically applauding. "Can't go to store and buy off shelf. Is priceless."

What he meant was that he liked all aspects of his job but liked one above the rest. There was absolute satisfaction across the board when it came to cleaning a mess. And there was unconditional gratification in causing the pain and suffering of those who created the mess in the first place. And there was perfect pleasure in getting paid like a Hollywood hero to do things he would happily have done for free. But the very second his targets understood the danger they were in, the hopeless finality of their peril, for Tino that was especially magical.

"Is Mastercard moment, Justin baby. Don't leave home without it."

"What?" Justin said.

He struggled again, desperate to break free. Tino could tell he was confused, scared shitless, and filled with fury all at the same time. Priceless, indeed.

"Tell me truth," Tino said.

"About what?"

"Woman in picture, Justin baby. Get with program."

He gave Justin time to think about it. It had been a few hours since the bartender had tossed Tino out of the Foxfire and longer than that since their conversation about Carrie. Justin winced at the pain in his leg. Struggled to find focus.

Then it clicked. "I told you the truth. She left at eleven fifteen."

"Let me ask question. Are you actor?"

He was a bartender in Los Angeles. Of course he was an actor.

"Yes, I'm an actor."

"Don't quit day job."

"Fuck you. I'm a damn good actor."

"Worst in LA."

Justin's eyes opened wide with what looked like indignance. His voice was filled with it. "I studied with Stella Adler. Last year, I had a two-line on *Law & Order*, and a one-line on *NCIS*. Now I'm training to be a stuntman. I have people interested in me. Agents and whatnot. I have a future in film."

"No heart. No soul. No commitment. No future. I see through you like screen door."

"I have commitment coming out of my ass."

"Have bullshit coming out ass. In *Raging Bull*, no see De Niro, only see LaMotta. That commitment, Justin baby. Two thumbs up."

"I agree with you there. *Raging Bull* is the best. That's my point. People tell me I'm one part Nic Cage, one part Keanu, one part De Niro, and—"

"One part worst actor in Hollywood."

Despite the gash in the back of his leg leaking blood by the bucket while trapped in his own freaking car, Justin sat up straight, feathers really ruffled, ego badly bruised. "I'm not the worst actor in Hollywood. You are. You think I didn't know you were doing Hackman in *The French Connection*? You think I don't know those lines? I auditioned with that monologue for *S.W.A.T.* Trust me, you are the worst fucking Popeye Doyle anyone has ever done at any time in the history of acting."

"I am not actor. I am producer. Let me see your Popeye."

"What? Now?"

"Yes, now. Show me Popeye."

The bartender's eyes rolled around his head, but he somehow got himself into character. Fueled by agony and fear and rage, his pick-your-toes-in-Poughkeepsie monologue was spot on. When he was done, he nearly cried from exhaustion or pain or maybe both, it was tough for Tino to tell.

But the Russian did not feel sorry for him. His ability to feel empathy was nonexistent. He may not have been a true producer, but he was damn sure a true sociopath. He could appreciate in his own sick and twisted way, but he could not feel.

"Is good Popeye, Justin baby. You not worst actor in Hollywood. You good actor."

"Thank you."

"No problem. Now tell me truth. How much Carrie Kromer pay you? I double."

"You'll double what she paid me?"

"I double. No trouble."

"She paid me five hundred."

Tino took a thick wad of cash from his pocket and peeled off ten hundred-dollar bills. He dropped the money in Justin's lap. Justin looked down at the grand but, of course, couldn't touch it.

"Now tell truth," Tino said. "What time Carrie Kromer leave bar?"

Justin sighed as if knowing the moment had come to save his own skin. "She came in twice. The first time, Wednesday, she told me if anyone stopped in asking if she was here, I should say, yeah, she drank a few beers, threw darts, sang karaoke, and left at eleven fifteen. But she probably left at eight. Then she came back Friday night and told me to expect a handsome Hispanic guy. I wasn't expecting a Russian. That's what threw me. At the bar, I mean. I was looking for a Latino, and instead it was you. That's why my performance was off. Can I go now? I think I need a doctor."

Tino wondered who the hell the handsome Hispanic guy could possibly be. Why hadn't Carrie said a handsome Russian guy? Everything made sense to the cleaner but that one detail. Not to worry, he would figure it out soon enough. Meanwhile, the first link in Carrie's alibi chain was broken. Tino was sure the rest of the chain would fall apart fast, and the Latino loser, whoever he was, would meet the same fate as Justin.

He took a custom-engraved, sterling-silver hip flask from his back pocket and unscrewed the cap. The smell was over-whelming.

"What the hell liquor is that?" Justin said.

"Is not liquor. Is gasoline," Tino said.

"You have gasoline in your fucking flask?" Justin said, terror creeping into his voice as if he knew for a fact that nothing good could come from gasoline in a fucking flask.

Unless you were Tino Antonov, that is. In which case many good things could come from having gasoline in a fucking flask.

Tino put his nose to the head of the flask and sniffed the gasoline as if it were a fine brandy. "You never know when is time for fire. Good to be prepared in my business."

"What the fuck business is that?" Justin said, and he started kicking like a madman.

Tino poured the gasoline all over the bartender and then all over the inside of the Acura. "I clean mess."

Justin screamed and cried and thrashed for his life.

When Tino was certain that the entirety of the bartender's existence was screaming and thrashing and screaming and crying and thrashing and screaming and crying and screaming and thrashing and screaming and crying, he climbed out of the car and leaned in through the open door.

"Is good commitment, Justin baby. Maybe have future in film after all."

Then he lit a match, tossed it into the car, and shut the door. The car ignited. Tino knew explosions were coming, so he walked away. But he couldn't resist a good fire, so he turned back to enjoy the flames.

# CHAPTER 23

# IT'S HARD TO ANALYZE THE MINUTIA OF A MIRACLE

CARRIE CLICKED through the timeline in her head as she drove to Alsiko. It was early Tuesday morning, one week since she'd thumped Old Tom and stolen the capsules. Six days since Johnny Fairfax had become the Copacabana cook. Four days since Joanna had grown forty years younger, Eduardo Wolf had seduced her in the lab, and the rest of the Copa crew had taken the drug. Three days since the old-timers had shed a collective four hundred forty some-odd years and Johnny had taken off for Alaska only to make a U-turn in Eureka (because he liked her at least a little). Two days since the joy of reclaiming their youth had become not-so-old-folks football by the pool (*where the hell had they found a football anyway?*) and she'd accepted Maureen Breen's old job. And one day since the Russian had murdered Dionysus, Eduardo Wolf had nearly strangled Johnny, the old-timers had an orgy in the pool, and she'd offered to pay Ben Boston's extortion fee—an offer she'd make good on later today when the crooked parole officer came to the Copa.

She'd planned to leave early and beat the traffic (*good luck with that*, she'd thought as soon as she'd made that part of the plan), tend to the rats, and be back at the Copa by nine, right on time to start cleaning and caring for the elderly Copacabana residents, who weren't elderly anymore.

She wasn't sure the rats would be there. For all she knew, the fixer or the cleaner had visited Alsiko overnight, when the lab was dark and quiet and empty, and *re-evaluated the evidence*—code, Carrie knew, for *killed every freaking rat in the place*.

But the rats were there. She took care of the larger community first—the two hundred or so who had not taken the drug—cleaning their cages and filling their food and water bowls. Then she turned her attention to the Greek Gods.

In one corner of the table maze, within the corral, Carrie had built a covered structure for the nine—now eight—special rats. She called it the Parthenon. It was long and narrow, like an ancient Greek temple, and Carrie had drawn Greek columns on the exterior walls to further the effect. An arched opening in the front wall allowed the rats to come and go as they pleased. It was a refuge for the Greek Gods after a long day in the glare of Carrie's scientific spotlight.

This morning, the Greek Gods were all inside the Parthenon. Carrie took a certain wireless clicker from a counter drawer, walked to the maze, and pressed the green button. Within ten seconds, all the rats were out in the corral looking up at her, waiting to be fed.

Each rat wore a custom-designed collar that vibrated when she clicked the remote. The Greek Gods had learned fast. She'd never let them down. Vibration equaled food.

The rats ate everything Carrie fed them and looked up at her for more, so she fed them again. She observed them carefully (as was her habit, profession, and nature) but did not take notes, something she always did without fail. She didn't see the point. The lab was closed and would soon be nonexistent, as in never having existed in the first place.

Since day one, Sikorski had forbidden her (and everyone else) to make copies of their notes. And he'd kept the originals locked away somewhere safe in a safe somewhere. She would leave the lab with nothing to show for all her work, which was a tragedy, yes, though if she wasn't careful, she would leave the lab dead, which put the tragedy of her lost notes in second place in the Alsiko Tragedy Sweepstakes.

Still, she *remembered* her notes by heart, and there was a pattern that had been presenting and progressing since the drug had made the Greek Gods younger: the rats were eating animal protein like all the animal protein in the world was due to disappear tomorrow. She knew rats were opportunistic eaters, consuming fruits and vegetables and meat and fish and nuts and grains and seeds and eggs and milk and candy and bugs and insects and leather and fur and all manner of small rodent carcasses. She knew this. But the Greek Gods were unusually hungry for animal protein. Over-cooked, under-cooked, not cooked ... preparation seemed secondary. They would still eat everything put in front of them, but animal protein was number one on their food chart.

When they'd devoured their second helping, she lifted each one individually and nuzzled their noses while feeling the unbelievable tautness and strength of their muscles, the perfection of their fur. That was another extraordinary thing. The Greek Gods had become obsessive groomers since they'd become younger— immaculately clean, not a blade of hair out of place. Rats, as a rule, were fastidiously cleaner than you might expect, it was true. But the Greek Gods were levels beyond that. Hyper hygienic. Stupendously sanitary. Again, Carrie was struck by the miracle of it all, though she didn't dawdle on the thought—in case the fixer or the cleaner was coming to Alsiko to fix or clean things this morning. She turned out the lights, left the lab, and drove back to the Copa.

Before she'd quit (while crossing herself and saying the Lord's Prayer), Maureen Breen had cleaned the Copa on a fixed schedule. Mondays, the first floor of the south wing—the gym, card room, and laundry room. Tuesdays, the second floor of the south wing—Tall Bob's place, Invisible Helen's, and Joanna's.

On Wednesdays, Thursdays, and Fridays, she'd work her way around the rest of the building. Week after week. All year long. When Maureen flew the coop (while rubbing her rosary and clutching her Bible), Carrie had decided not to reinvent the Copa cleaning wheel, so she got back from the lab, rolled the second-floor supply cart to her mother's room, and started there.

While Carrie made the bed with clean sheets, Joanna sat at her small makeup table and prepared to play poker with the ladies. Carrie watched her mother out of the corner of her eye. Not her dutiful daughter eye, mind you. Her behavioral gerontologist eye. She was behind Joanna, tucking in clean sheets, but could see her mother's face in the mirror.

"What?" Joanna said, catching her daughter looking at her.

"I've never seen you sit in front of a mirror and put on makeup," Carrie said. "And when I say never, I mean not even in my earliest memory."

"What is your earliest memory?" Joanna said. "Not a hazy dream that may or may not have occurred. A solid, I-was-there-and-this-happened remembrance."

Carrie made the bed a moment longer, deep in thought, then stopped. "I'm in the kitchen. I'm coloring after dinner. Daddy comes home late. You're upset that he missed dinner and didn't call. He's drunk and angry, and you have a fight. You follow him out of the kitchen. He leaves again and slams the door. Then you come back and go to the cabinet and pour every bottle of alcohol down the kitchen sink. I think I'm drawing the solar system. I can smell the smoke on his clothes, the liquor on his breath. I can hear the booze going down the drain. I was there and that happened."

"Yes," Joanna said. "It *was* the solar system. How old do you suppose you were?"

"I would say seven."

"Yes, and I was fifty-eight. Sixteen years older than I am now."

"If you think you're forty-two."

"Something like that, yes. But you're right, even as a young librarian, well before your father, well before you, I wasn't involved with blush and mascara and lipstick."

"But now you are."

"Perhaps it's a subconscious second chance to be young and attractive," Joanna said, agreeing that now she clearly was involved with blush, mascara, and lipstick. "I don't know. I'm not overthinking it. It's hard to analyze the minutia of a miracle. But it turns out makeup is lovely. I should have done it long ago. You should too, Carrie. Obviously, it's never too late to start. And it might help your self-confidence as you begin this new chapter in your life. Is that why you're watching me? The makeup?"

"That and one other thing," Carrie said.

"What other thing?"

"All of my life, you were a vegetarian. You were a vegetarian until last Friday. Now you're a full-time meat eater."

"Possibly because Mr. Fairfax is such a good cook," Joanna said, once again unable to dispute the fact that she was currently a carnivore—indeed, happy to agree. "Highly underrated, in my opinion. Cooks like Johnny Fairfax don't grow on trees."

"No, they don't," Carrie said, hoping she hadn't let any of her confused and confusing feelings for him, or *his* confused and confusing feelings for *her*, slip into her voice. "His surprise parole inspection is today."

"Do you know what time?"

"That's the surprise part of the surprise."

"It's not much of a surprise if you know you're going back to prison unless you pay an extortion fee."

"Not much."

"It's unconscionable. He doesn't make enough money to subsidize a shakedown."

"That's why I'm paying it."

"*You're* paying it?" Joanna said, turning in her chair to face her daughter. "Why would you do that?"

"I have money," Carrie said.

"That is the answer to the question, 'Can you afford to do that?'" Joanna said. "That is not the answer to the question, 'Why would you do that?'"

It was her mother's librarian tone. There would be no avoiding this conversation. No wiggling away.

"I can't explain it because I don't understand it," Carrie said. "It's not science."

Joanna stood up. She was fit and tanned and strong. And she was gorgeous. Carrie had never seen her mother this beautiful at any age, never mind sixteen years younger than when Carrie had been born, forty-five years younger than she'd been on Friday.

"Let me see you," Joanna said. She took Carrie's hands and looked hard and long into her daughter's eyes until she nodded as if she'd seen what she was searching for. "Oh my, Carrie. You're in love with Johnny Fairfax."

Carrie pulled her hands away. "No, I'm not."

"Yes, you are. You don't know it yet because it's buried deep inside you, but it is definitely there."

"It is definitely *not* there. I hardly know him. I like him at least a little. But love him? In love with him? That's ridiculous."

"That's the magic. It's in every love story ever written."

Carrie went back to the bed. She put the pillowcases on and pounded the pillows into place. "No offense, Mother, but what do you know about the magic of love? You and Daddy never loved each other. As far as I know, you've never even been in love. Yes, yes, I know, you were a librarian for forty years. You read every book about love ever written. Well, you know what? Love isn't something you can learn in books. Which means you're not exactly an expert on the subject, are you?"

And then she inexplicably started to cry.

Joanna moved her to the bed, sat beside her, and caressed her cheek. "You're right. Your father and I were never in love. But you're also wrong. I was in love once."

"You were?" Carrie said through her tears. It was exceptionally strange to her that her mother was only six years older than she was, but right about now there was nothing in Carrie's life that didn't seem exceptionally strange. "You never said anything about loving anyone. Who did you love?"

"Matthew McGraw," Joanna said.

"Who?" Carrie said.

"He was a married man. We had an affair for two years. I loved him deeply, and he loved me. He did not love his wife, and she did not love him. I was twenty-eight when it started. He was a sociology professor. We would meet in the stacks late at night. It was very romantic."

"You were in love with a *married* man named Matthew McGraw?"

"I know more about love than you think I do."

"Why didn't you ever tell me?"

"The older I got, the deeper I buried it. My marriage to your father made those feelings too painful. Better to forget and forge on."

"That's so sad," Carrie said and started crying again.

"It's in the past." Joanna put her arm around her daughter. "I have my whole life ahead of me again. This time, I'm going to get romance right. And so are you, Carrie. So are you."

At that moment, Invisible Helen appeared in Joanna's bedroom doorway. She was, in a word, stunning. The opposite of invisible.

"They're dealing the cards," she said. "Omaha hold 'em. I came to get you and saw him walk through the gate. The parole officer. He's by the pool with Johnny. And he's angry as a hornet."

# CHAPTER 24
# LIKE A CO-ED, PRISON-YARD GANG FIGHT

JOHNNY HAD FORGOTTEN how truly freaking huge Ben Boston actually was. They were standing near the outdoor dining tables beside the pool, and the six-eight, three-hundred-ninety-pound parole officer was as big as a pool house. It was as if someone had overnight constructed a Copacabana cabana ... and the cabana was Black and dressed like a million-dollar hip-hop mogul.

Boston wore tailored, golden-brown corduroys that were lightweight for LA, super soft and stylish, no doubt as expensive as they were chic. His brown and white checkered dress shirt was intentionally untucked, the trendiest of the trendy. On top of that was a sophisticated, white-cotton, spring-time sweater; a vogueish, gray-on-gray, herringbone sport jacket; and a gray, hipster, Baker Boy beret. He sported brown ankle boots with white socks. He wasn't dressed like any parole office Johnny had ever heard about. He was dressed to impress. *I got money to burn,* his ensemble said.

Johnny ran the numbers in his head. If Boston was extorting an average of two fifty a month from seventy-five parolees, that was, holy shit, close to twenty grand cash in his pocket—more than two hundred thou a year. Add in his parole-officer salary, say 70K, and it was no wonder Ben Boston looked like a forty-five-year-old Hollywood headliner.

"You at the short end of your motherfucking rope with me, Fairfax," Boston said. "I don't give a good goddamn about your job or your house or your shit-stain life. I got places to be and people to see. So you either paying the money or going to jail. What's it going to be?"

"I'm paying the money," Carrie said, crossing the courtyard to where Johnny and Ben Boston were standing. Behind her, Joanna and Helen went into the card room.

"Who the fuck is this?" Boston said to Johnny.

"This is Carrie," Johnny said.

"Who the fuck is Carrie?" Boston said to Carrie. "And what the fuck do you know about it?"

The big man took a stride toward her, and Johnny instinctively stepped between them. Without blinking, Boston grabbed the front of Johnny's shirt, lifted him in the air, and tossed him into the tables. Johnny crash-landed hard, hitting the tables and the chairs and the ground like a missile.

Johnny knew what to do: run to the kitchen, grab a carving knife, and cut this asshole to shreds. He even said it in his head. *Get a fucking knife.* But he didn't do it because Carrie said, "Johnny, don't." Like she'd read his mind.

"I work here with Johnny. I know you want three hundred dollars a month for the rest of his parole," she said. "I have the money. I'm going to pay. That's what I know about it. I pay you, Johnny keeps working here, everybody's happy."

"Fuck everybody's happy. This piss-ass, tattooed punk can rot in prison for all I care," Boston said. "Price just went up. Three fifty."

"Fuck you," Johnny said, standing again, hands balled into fists at his side. He didn't know what made him angrier—Ben Boston fucking him over or fucking Carrie over.

"Four hundred," Boston said.

"Fine," Carrie said.

She took four hundred-dollar bills from her pocket and held them out.

"Not fine," Tall Bob said, coming fast around the pool from the card room. "Is that fine with you, Walter?"

"Hell fucking no," Cranky Walter said, coming faster around the other end of the pool.

Bob's gang included Arnold and Norman. Walter and Bernard comprised the other gang.

As the men arrived in front of Big Ben Boston, the ladies lined up along the edge of the pool on the card-room side.

"The fuck is this?" Boston said.

Johnny took his place in Walter's gang. The six Copacabana men formed a semi-circle in front of the parole officer. The pool was fifteen feet behind Big Ben.

"This is the end," Bob said.

"Fuck you," Boston said, and he stepped forward to push his way through.

Except Bob was a big man too. A few inches shorter and one hundred seventy pounds lighter but a trained athlete, a major college tight end in absolute peak physical condition, stronger-faster-sharper than he was when he'd been the age he was now, which was maybe forty-three. Better than he'd been at twenty-three.

Bob pushed Boston hard, two hands to the big man's chest, shoving him backward. The parole office looked stunned by Bob's strength, taken aback by his fearlessness, by the bravado and audacity of the Copa gang. The circle closed in. Boston stepped back. Now they were ten feet from the pool.

"You got any fucking idea who I am?" Boston said to Bob and the men.

"Worthless scumbag piece of shit," Walter said. "Sound about right?"

During his first twenty-five years at the post office, Walter had also been a semi-professional boxer. He'd continued to train many years after that but given up getting in the ring for full-blown matches. It had been more than a hobby to him. It had been a way to stay in prime shape while beating back (literally) the demons that had come with year upon year of sorting and delivering the U.S. mail. Walter liked to pound people—bottom line. And he didn't mind getting thumped in return. At six-two, and two hundred thirty pounds of mail-carrier muscle, Cranky Walter had been classified a heavyweight. Strong enough and mean enough to turn semi-pro but not fast enough to win at the top. Now once again the age of roughly forty-four, the expression on his face told Johnny that Walter thought he could take a title and, fuck all else, he was ready to start by opening a can of whoop-ass on the parole officer.

"Sounds right to me," Nearsighted Norman said. He wore hip Ray Ban Wayfarers, non-prescription now that his vision was twenty-twenty for the first time ever in his life.

"Sounds fucking-A right," Drooling Arnie said.

"The fucking-A rightest," Suit and Tie Bernard said, looking as beautiful as Harry Belafonte in his prime—if Belafonte was pissed as fuck and out for blood. "Ladies?" he called across the pool.

The ladies cheered their men on. *Kick his ass,* they said. *Bust his balls,* they said. *Mess him up,* they said.

*Jesus Christ,* Johnny thought. *It's like a co-ed, prison-yard gang fight; convicts calling for violence from the sidelines.* Except this time the gang was the Copacabana men and women, fueled by pharmaceutical voodoo, braver and tougher and more focused and fearless and bloodthirsty than any prison gang he'd ever seen, standing up for *him* when no one else in his life ever had. Except Carrie, who'd stood her ground beside him as if she and Johnny were mystically bound together, as if he were her man and she were his woman. It was the first time he'd felt that feeling in his life. He looked at her. She stood with the men, part of the semicircle, a steely resolve in her eyes that said the parole officer wasn't getting away with his bullying bullshit blackmail, not this time, not on her watch, not with her man. Their eyes met for a second, and he felt their connection.

*She's beautiful*, he thought, and then he snapped out of it because Ben Boston was spewing anger like a Hawaiian volcano.

"I don't fucking swim," Boston said, turning his head to look down at the water and at the cheerleading madwomen across the pool. "So you motherfuckers are going to get the fuck out of my fucking way or I'm going kill somebody."

"You don't swim?" Bob said.

"You deaf, motherfucker?" Boston said. "I just motherfucking said I don't swim. So which one of you motherfuckers wants to die first?"

The circle was closing. The pool was eight feet behind him now.

"Every one of you motherfuckers is going to jail," Boston said. "I'm a law enforcement official for the City of Los Angeles. You fucking with the wrong motherfucker."

"He doesn't swim," Arnie said.

"Not a swimmer," Bernard said.

The pool was six feet behind Boston. He was enraged. Johnny could practically see smoke coming out of his flaring nostrils, like Boston was some kind of supercharged, WWE villain, pawing at the ground, ready to stomp someone to death.

The women were shouting and cheering. *Take him out*, they said. *Fuck him up*, they said. *Make him swim*, they said. *Make him swim, make him swim, make him swim…*

The pool was four feet behind Boston. He charged the line, three hundred ninety pounds of fire and fury. Punching and shouting and kicking. He *was* going to kill someone. He was going to kill all of them.

"I'll kill you motherfuckers," Boston said, screaming now.

But the gang held their ground. All seven of them, Johnny and Carrie included, pushed Boston back, kept him in the semi-circle, moved him closer, inch by inch, to the edge of the deep end of the pool.

*Make him swim, make him swim, make him swim...*

Everyone was swallowed in the insanity of the moment, engulfed in the viciousness of the energy, consumed with blood-lust fever. Boston was out of his mind.

*Make him swim, make him swim, make him swim...*

One foot between Boston and the pool.

"Fuck you, motherfuckers," Boston said, his voice twisted by rage...and now panic.

Six inches between the back of Boston's boots and the edge of the pool.

"Fuck you," Boston said, shrieking and swinging and swiping and punching and pushing. "Fuck you..."

Three inches from the pool. Two inches...

And then Big Ben was over the side, into the air, and crashing into the middle of the deep end of the blue water, the diving end, nine feet deep from side to side. Too deep for Ben Boston.

The parole officer flailed like a crazy man. His Baker Boy beret floated away to the side.

"He really *doesn't* swim," Norman said.

"Doesn't look like it," Arnie said.

"Looks like he sinks," Bernard said.

"Like a fucking stone," Walter said.

"Just like it," Bob said.

Johnny stood at the edge of the pool with Carrie and the men. The women watched from the other side. Ben Boston slapped the water in panic and went under. He came up once and then twice and then one more time, and then he went to the bottom of the deep end. His arms and legs thrashed wildly for fifteen seconds, his massive body twitched a few times, and then he drowned.

# CHAOS

GOD OF THE VOID BETWEEN HEAVEN AND EARTH
(AMONG OTHER THINGS)

## CHAPTER 25
# HE'S TOO BIG TO ROLL IN A RUG AND TAKE TO THE DUMP

CARRIE WAS CAUGHT between a rock and a hard place. The rock was believing that *any* of this had happened. *Any of it.* From bonking Old Tom and taking the capsules to Ben Boston dead at the bottom of the pool and every unreasonable incident and accident between the two. That was the rock.

Believing it.

The hard place was the immutable-irreversible-indisputable fact that each astounding-stupefying-impossible occurrence had really-truly-actually occurred. That was the hard place.

The truth of it.

She didn't want to believe it, couldn't believe it, and wouldn't believe it...except she *had* to believe it because not only had it happened, it was happening still.

"That is one big, dead parole officer," Bernard said.

They were ringed around the edge of the pool, the Copacabana men and women plus Johnny and Carrie, looking down at Ben Boston, now a massive mound of lifeless flesh nine feet below the surface.

"Got to be four hundred pounds," Arnie said.

"Not with his clothes soaking wet," Norman said.

"And his lungs full of water," Bob said. "He has to weigh more than four hundred pounds."

"Five hundred," Walter said. "Five and change."

There was no rending of garments, no oh-sweet-baby-Jesus-what-have-we-done bewailing, just a curious kind of quiet as they watched Boston's fancy clothes wave and sway like a seagrass meadow on a coral reef.

Carrie knew they'd committed murder. She'd grabbed the parole officer too. She'd had a hand, as the saying went, in killing him. They'd all pushed him in after he'd said he didn't swim.

Oh, sure, their trial attorney would parse words in court: *Your Honor, he "didn't" swim might have meant he could swim but chose not to. Mr. Boston never said he "couldn't" swim, which would have meant he wasn't able to swim, that he was a non-swimmer. Instead, by all testimony, the deceased said, "I don't swim." I ask the court, how were my Copacabana clients supposed to know the difference under the intensity of the circumstances, in the midst of the mad rush of this raging psychopath, who, let's not forget, was using his public office as a private criminal enterprise?*

Unfortunately, no amount of courtroom doublespeak could reverse five-hundred-plus pounds of dead weight in the water.

A week ago, she'd have called the police to report Boston's death, her logic being that cooperation might result in the prosecutor reducing the charges from murder one to murder two to manslaughter. She would have made the case that there'd been no premeditated intent to kill, that the sole intent was to stop the extortion. That would have been her course of action one week ago. *One week ago!*

But what had happened here was anything but unintentional. For God's sake, the death-squad cheerleaders had been chanting *make him swim.* Her own mother had been the head cheerleader. They should all have been racked with guilt. No matter how heinous a human being he was—*he'd been*—they had murdered him.

"I know this sounds cold, and maybe it's too soon, but I have no remorse," Helen said. "Am I the only one? Does anyone feel remorse?"

"Not me," Dolores said.

"Me either," Lillian said.

"No," Betty, said.

"Hell no," Walter said.

"I'd like to do it again," Brenda said. "It felt kind of good."

"Damn good," Arnie said.

"Say what you will," Joanna said, "but I find it totally unacceptable."

*Finally,* Carrie thought. *My mother, the lifelong librarian, will be the voice of reason, and she'll be right. It's intolerable that we murdered him, that no one, not even a criminally inclined parole officer, deserves to die like this man died, drowned to death in the Copacabana pool.*

"He's going to be difficult to remove from the water, and the longer he's in there, the more likely he'll throw the pH out of balance," Joanna said. "As a member of the pool committee, I can confirm that we maintain a proper pH of seven point four, which matches precisely the pH in human eyes and mucous membranes. This dead lump of lard is going to screw that all to hell. That, I'm afraid, is totally unacceptable."

There was a moment of silence, and then the Copa crew, including Joanna, burst into laughter. Carrie couldn't believe it. She looked at Johnny, standing beside her. He couldn't believe it either.

"This is fucking insane," Johnny said softly. "You know that, right?"

"I definitely know that. It might be the only thing I know," Carrie said. And then they held each other's eyes. "Except that you stepped in front of him to defend me. I know that too."

"After you stepped in to defend me," Johnny said.

They almost held hands. They were *this* close...but then the laughter stopped, and the moment stopped with it.

"If we don't get him out soon," Norman said, "we'll have to

empty the pool, scrub it with disinfectant, and then refill it. Pretty damn inconvenient."

"Really damn inconvenient," Bob said.

"So we have to get him out," Brenda said.

"What do we do with him?" Arnie said.

"He's too big to roll in a rug and take to the dump," Dolores said.

"He's too big to do any damn thing," Walter said.

"We can't move him," Betty said. "It's not practical. It would be like moving a dead hippo around town. People would notice."

"And if people notice him, they'll notice us," Bob said.

They all agreed. Moving Big Ben Boston, aside from out of the pool, was out of the question.

"They're going to look for him," Lillian said, lighting a cigarette. "Matter of time."

They all agreed with that too. He was a public official, albeit corrupt, and his absence would be noted.

"Well, we have to do something with him," Helen said.

"If we had a big enough box," Joanna said, "we could store him somewhere."

Carrie couldn't think straight. It was hard to consider the options because the premise was so outrageous. She thought about suggesting they throw themselves on the mercy of the court, but Johnny touched her arm, and she looked up at him.

"We have a box," he said quietly.

She nodded. It was as if they each knew exactly what the other was thinking, saying, feeling. So instead of suggesting that they turn themselves in, she said, "We can put him in the walk-in. It's big enough, and he'll be out of the pool and out of the way long enough for us to figure out what to do with him."

They all looked at each other around and across the pool.

"Good idea," Norman said.

"Damn good," Walter said.

"Excellent, Carrie," Joanna said.

"It was Johnny's idea," Carrie said, giving credit where credit was due.

"What do you say, Tattoo Boy?" Lillian said. "Will this piece of meat fit in your walk-in?"

Johnny nodded. He was, like everyone else, all in. "He'll fit."

It took six men plus Brenda and Betty to lift Ben Boston out of the water, and it was a hell of struggle even with eight of them. They took off Boston's swanky clothes and burned them in a metal trash can, along with his shoes, wallet, identification cards, cash, and Baker Boy beret. They were left with his cell phone, his car keys, and his car parked down the block—a cherry-red Chrysler 300 with the signature license plate *Big Ben*.

With the now naked dead man in the courtyard, decisions had to be made. Helen and Lillian offered to drive the Chrysler to Santa Monica, park it on some random residential street near the beach, walk to the pier, toss the keys and the cell phone into the Pacific, take an Uber to the Sunset Strip, and walk back to the Copa. They'd wear gloves, be discreet, make no mark, leave no evidence. Lillian wouldn't smoke until the parole officer's keys and phone were in the drink.

Meanwhile, Joanna and Carrie said they would clean every inch of the courtyard with Clorox, remove any shred of physical evidence that Boston had been there—fabric fibers, fingerprints, sweat, spit, anything.

The rest of them would lug the parole officer to the kitchen, put him in the walk-in, and shut the damn door.

It all went according to plan, and by the time they were done, Johnny had lunch ready. Grilled chicken quesadillas with hand-smashed black beans, red rice, fresh guacamole, homemade salsa, and a side salad with heirloom tomatoes. Ice-cold cans of Dos Equis and a bottle of Casamigos Añejo went on each table. He told the group the tequila was on him because it felt like a shots lunch—and he took the first one, thanking Carrie and the Copa crew for having his back. Everyone stood and applauded, and then they did shots, including Carrie, who'd never done a shot of tequila in her life.

Johnny poured a second round for himself and Carrie. "There's a naked Black man in the walk-in. He's big as a bear, he works for the government, and he's very fucking dead."

"I guess we have to look at the bright side," Carrie said as she and Johnny clinked glasses.

Johnny downed his shot. "There's a bright side?"

Carrie did her shot too. "Think how pissed off he'd be if he were alive."

They both smiled, but neither one could muster the same cheery spirit as the Copa crew.

"I don't think this is over," Johnny said.

Carrie nodded. "I think it's the beginning."

# CHAPTER 26

# SUPER CINEMA SETUP

EDUARDO WOLF PLAYED with puzzles to pass the time. He was adept at doing crosswords. He enjoyed jigsaws. He relished riddles. He liked any situation, assignment, mission, project, or person that challenged his mental dexterity. Which made finding the stolen capsules and eliminating every element of Alsiko evidence—animal, mineral, material, human—so that it was as if the lab had never existed an especially appealing test of his problem-solving skills. *Especially* appealing because the drug in question was a manmade miracle that had to be kept utterly-totally-entirely secret and also because Carrie Kromer had an alibi he was obligated to unravel, which meant pulling its pieces apart one by one until it collapsed. Like playing a game of giant Jenga where the loser dies a miserable death.

Two Foxfire bartenders had been working the night Carrie claimed she'd been toasting Alsiko's success. Justin—bartender number one—had been Carrie's contact, her confidant, her accomplice. Unfortunately, Justin had died in a car fire very early this morning. A tragic accident that the fine folk at the Foxfire were mourning with an all-day-all-night wake (drinks on the house) when Eduardo arrived.

The facts of the fire were suspicious. Acuras didn't explode into bonfires without professional provocation, meaning someone else had been interested in Justin—interested enough to kill him—and that was a troubling puzzle piece. He would need to keep his eye out for whoever else was poking around the Alsiko perimeter.

Bartender number two was named Brian Hood. He'd been behind the bar on the Wednesday in question and was behind the bar tonight as well. Eduardo introduced himself as Ramone Garcia, an IRS investigator—the fixer had forged official papers, of course—looking into some financial illegalities that now seemed to involve the burning Acura and the late Justin. He was looking for a specific woman (he wasn't at liberty to name names just yet) who had been at the Foxfire last Wednesday night. Justin had already confirmed that fact for him. He'd arranged to meet Justin today to see if he might answer a few more questions, but, sadly and obviously, Justin was now deceased.

Eduardo handed Brian a photograph of Carrie. Yes, the bartender remembered her. She'd had a long conversation with Justin that night, and it had stuck with him because she'd monopolized Justin's time, and money had exchanged hands. Brian had seen the transaction go down. He'd asked Justin what the hell that had been all about, and Justin had said it was a favor, no big deal, easiest five bills he'd ever made.

"Now look. Wow. Big deal," Brian said. "I should have said something to someone."

"You had no way of knowing anything illegal was happening," Eduardo said. "And you must say nothing to anyone. You may not compromise the investigation. The IRS will be most upset with you. And your life as you know it will change dramatically for the worse. Do you understand?"

"I get it," Brian said. "Don't mess with the IRS."

"Good. What else do you remember about this woman?"

Brian remembered that he'd gone outside for a cigarette

around eight fifteen and seen the woman get in a Yellow Cab Co. Prius.

Puzzles are often progressions, and Eduardo Wolf could follow sequential clues better than most. He followed this one to the actual Yellow Cab Co. Prius that had arrived at the Foxfire Room at eight fifteen last Wednesday night—and then followed it further to the actual driver. The guy's name was Joe Cabot.

Eduardo identified himself as Special Agent David Gutierrez, a fraud investigator for the Los Angeles Department of Transportation looking at Cabot as a kingpin player in the transport of unlawful substances while driving a Yellow Cab Co. taxi. Yellow Cab's cooperation, he explained, would go a long way toward mitigating the criminal charges, fines, and negative publicity heading their corporate way. With no apparent love lost for the driver, the manager contacted the Prius in question and, as directed by Special Agent Gutierrez, instructed Cabot to meet his next pickup in front of the Toyota dealership near the intersection of Lankershim and Cahuenga Boulevards.

The Prius arrived, and Eduardo slid into the backseat and pointed his untraceable Glock 19 semi-automatic handgun at Joe Cabot's head.

"Thank you, Jesus," Joe said without a trace of irony. "Perfect timing. Just what I needed. Nobody in this godforsaken city needed this more than me. What do you want? Money? Sex? Nuclear codes? The inside dope on some inside dope? I write movies, mister, and you are a gift from the Hollywood gods. I'm Joe Cabot. Who are you? No, wait, don't tell me yet. Let it build. Dramatic tension's a good thing."

He was forty-eight years old and had been knocking on Hollywood's door with a stack of spec scripts for twenty-five years without so much as a sniff of the action—not one agent willing to hip-pocket him, not one producer angling for a free option, not one down-on-his-luck director offering to buy him a cup of coffee. He'd been a lost LA soul for more than a decade. A cab driver who told himself he was still a screenwriter. A screenwriter who'd surrendered to living the low-level life of a sad-sack cab driver. He'd been drowning for years in the Hollywood riptide and now the gods had thrown him a screenwriting rope.

Eduardo leaned forward, noticed a dozen or so word game magazines haphazardly tossed onto the front passenger seat, and leveled the Glock at Cabot's face. "Drive, Joe. Drive like your life depends on it."

"Love it." Joe pulled the Prius into traffic and followed Eduardo's directions to a secluded-restricted entrance of the concrete-channelized Los Angeles River. The gate was locked with a heavy chain.

"Get out of the car and push it open," Eduardo said. "It's dummy locked. If you run, I will shoot you in both legs and drag you into the river myself."

"I'm not going to run. I wouldn't miss this for all the money in the mint," Joe said.

The cabbie got out of the Prius and did as instructed, re-dummy locking the gate behind them. He got back in the car and found Eduardo's eyes in the rearview mirror. "Awesome. They shot *Grease* here. *Chinatown*. *Terminator*. *Point Blank*. *Buckaroo Banzai*. Now what?"

Eduardo did not sense fear. He did not sense insanity. He sensed some kind of irregular relief, as if this were the end of a dark day rather than the beginning of one. Or some odd sort of eagerness, some bizarre form of enthusiasm, like the threat of violence—being shot in the legs as he ran for his life, for instance—was reason to rejoice. He even sensed some off-the-wall variety of impatience. *Impatience!* In all the years he'd been fixing insufferable situations around the world, he had never experienced a problem so excited to be solved.

"Park beneath the overpass." Eduardo pointed to where Lankershim crossed the river and merged with Cahuenga. "And get out of the car."

"Nobody can see us. Nobody can hear us. Super cinema setup," Joe said. "Can't wait for the payoff." He drove for the overpass and again locked eyes with Eduardo. "Know anything about the LA River?"

"Very little," Eduardo said.

"I researched it for a movie I wrote five years ago. It's an action thriller with space aliens and vampires and zombies surfing in the channel after it rains for forty days and forty nights. Basically apocalyptic blood sport with lots of sex. Pretty much no dialogue. Sweet romance in the middle. Couple kids trying to fall in love while the world blows up and everybody drowns. Couldn't find a producer. Too bad you're not a producer. You're not a producer, right? Because if you *are* a producer, the alien-vampire-zombie script is a box-office bonanza. Anyway, the river's more or less fifty-one miles long, and most of it flows through this concrete channel, which they built in the late thirties after a slew of floods, not unlike the one in the movie I'm telling you about. You sure you're not a producer? Here's a fun fact: Though the channel helped the city survive, the native fish weren't so fortunate. Meaning there are plenty of fish in the river, but none are native because no native fish survived the channelization. None. Zero. No river shrimp. No Chinook salmon. No three-spined stickleback. No Santa Ana suckers. Except in Santa Ana, where a sucker's born every minute. That's a joke. Pretty good one. I should use it in a script one day. Tell me you're a producer. Anyway, it's been said that some local fisherman caught a native rainbow trout in 1940. I should write a movie about that. The last rainbow trout in LA. You want to be a producer? You'll get first look."

The cabbie stopped the Prius under the overpass, killed the engine, and popped out of the car. Still pointing the gun at him, Eduardo followed, took Joe in, and found himself mildly disgusted.

The screenwriter was five-eight and heavyset, out of shape in the sense that he had not exercised for ten years. Soft. Flabby.

Puffy. He had salt-and-pepper hair that was long and unruly, and he hadn't shaved in a week. He wore blue jeans and a Cleveland Cavaliers T-shirt that looked like something he'd won without trying at a trivia night in a Burbank bar. He was slovenly from the inside out, like he'd given up on all fronts. And if this was true, then what was it about being held at gunpoint in the channel under an overpass where no one would hear him scream and see him die that had given Joe Cabot...what was it? Hope? Yes, that was it, hope. Why was this beaten-down slob of a man so suddenly hopeful?

"You have information I need," Eduardo said.

"Excellent," Joe said. "Whatever it is, I'm not telling you."

"If you don't tell me, I will kill you," Eduardo said.

"If you kill me, I'm definitely not telling you," Joe said. "Jesus, don't you go to the movies? You can't kill me yet. You won't kill me until the end...unless there's a plot twist that saves my life. And I've got one you're not going to believe."

"A plot twist that saves your life?" Eduardo was annoyed with the cabbie but also intrigued. And amused. Out of the blue, this gross little loser had somehow engaged him.

"You foreshadowed it yourself," Joe said. "In the cab. Not enough for a shared credit—that's a joke, not really—but enough for me to tip my hat in your direction, and that's nothing to sneeze at in this town. Anyway, it's a breakthrough proposal. Here it is: I play you for my life. You play me for information."

"Play what?" Eduardo said.

"Word games," Joe said. "Riddles. You kept looking at my magazines in the cab. I'm guessing you like them. I'm guessing you think you're good at them too, right? So am I. Probably better than you. So it's a challenge. I'm throwing down the word-game gauntlet, so to speak, and the audience gets to see if you can rise up and beat me. See what I mean? You pretty much have to play. It's in the script I'm going to write."

It was true. Eduardo had grown up playing word games in Spanish with his fashion-model mother. And in German with his construction-foreman father. And in French and Italian and English. The Chinese, he'd learned, did not enjoy word games so hadn't involved them with riddles. The point was he refused to believe that this little scrotum of a screenwriter could be better than he was at word games. Not plausible. Not possible.

He put the gun in his shoulder-holster. "What are the rules?"

# CHAPTER 27

# POSERS AND PROBLEMS AND PUZZLES

AS A BOY IN BRAZIL, Eduardo Wolf had been uncompromisingly competitive. He had not simply wanted to be the best at what anyone or everyone was doing or had done, he'd wanted to crush all comers, ridicule all rivals, deflate all foes. The game didn't matter as much as the humiliating defeat of his opponents. Swimming, running, jumping, boxing, martial arts, firearms, math, science, spelling, reading, writing, riddles. Every little thing had been a competition. A fight to the death. People were merely adversaries contending for his title of Top Dog of Everything in the World.

He had not been a boy with friends. And yet he'd insisted on being the best romancer as well. No easy task for a bloodthirsty, ego-driven child for whom romance meant conquest not love. But he'd been the smartest, most-talented, most accomplished, best-looking kid in the neighborhood and soon mastered the art of charm. And that, combined with sheer force of will, is why he'd always scored the best-looking girl.

As he matured, the German military taught him to intellectually control the violent nature of his ferocious disposition, to always behave as a sophisticated, well-spoken businessman in the town square, but the fixer still played every game for blood —often literally.

"I riddle you," Joe said. "If you solve it, you get one point and you ask me a question. If you don't solve it, I get one point, and I ask you one question. Then you riddle me. We get two minutes to solve the riddle. First one to five wins the game. We're playing for my life, so you have to answer the questions honestly."

"You are playing for your life," Eduardo said. "I am playing for information."

"Touché," Joe said.

"Which means it is possible that I could win the information I want, and you could win your life," Eduardo said.

"Or I could win my life and you could not win the information," Joe said.

"Or I could win the information and kill you where you stand," Eduardo said.

"You're smarter than you look."

"You are not. And so it is only fair that you go first."

"Then riddle me this," Joe said. "Name three consecutive days without using the words Monday, Tuesday, Wednesday, Thursday, Friday, Saturday, or Sunday."

Eduardo thought for a minute and then smiled. "Ah, Joe. If this is the best you can do, then you should tell me what I want to know and let me kill you now."

"Thirty seconds."

"Yesterday, today, and tomorrow. One point for me."

Joe shrugged it off. The game was just getting started. "What's your question?"

Eduardo took Carrie's photograph from his pocket. "Did you pick up this woman at the Foxfire Room at eight fifteen last Wednesday night?"

Joe looked at the picture, thought for a moment, and nodded. "Yes, I did."

"Where did you take her?"

"One question. Rules are rules."

"Indeed," Eduardo said. "Two fathers and two sons went fishing. They were at the lake all day and only caught three fish. As the sun set, one father said, 'That's enough for all of us. We'll each have one fish.' How can this be possible?"

Joe paced back and forth. One minute went by. Then half a minute.

"Fifteen seconds," Eduardo said. "Ten, nine, eight, seven, six, five, four ..."

"Got it," Joe said. "One father, one son, one grandson. Two fathers, two sons."

"I start with an easy one, and you nearly fold under the pressure. Your immediate future does not look promising," Eduardo said. "One point for you, and a question."

"What's your name?"

"That is the question to save your life? My name?"

"One-one. Game's to five. Plenty of time to save my life."

"I am Eduardo Wolf."

"Listen up, Eddie. It's about to get hot, and as my mother said, if you can't take the heat, stay out of the kitchen."

Eduardo was a master of self-control, but he felt his jaw tighten ever so slightly. This screenwriting, cab-driving piece of human garbage had burrowed under his skin. "My name is Eduardo. Never Eddie."

"You like baseball, Eddie? Because I got some chin music coming your way. A little bit of brushback."

"Baseball is an idiot's game."

"Three playing cards in a row," Joe said. "Name them in order with only these clues. A two to the right of a king. A diamond to the left of a spade. An ace to the left of a heart. A heart to the left of a spade. Two minutes."

Above them, an endless flow of traffic cruised across the overpass. The blare of horns, the roar of engines, the thump-thump-thump of countless tires as they hit a certain separation in the pavement.

It took Eduardo all of ten seconds to solve the riddle. But he waited to offer the answer and instead used the remaining time to remember his Uncle Dietrich—his father's brother—an electrician with a gift for cards. Blackjack had been his game. His uncle had been a chronic gambler, an internationally known card counter with a suitcase full of disguises. But once he'd been identified by the casino—his disguise busted in Vegas or Atlantic City or Nassau or Singapore or London or Paris, or any of the relevant Rivieras—he'd be prohibited from playing the tables. He'd never married or had children of his own, so he'd taught Eduardo everything he knew—legal and illegal—about beating the house at its own rigged game. But as good as he'd been at blackjack, it was card tricks and card games and all kinds of card conundrums that were his special talent. Eduardo had worshipped his Uncle Dietrich and been an attentive and accomplished student. Particularly when it came to posers and problems and puzzles.

"Thirty seconds," Joe said.

One family evening in particular came to mind. Everyone had been involved in a five-thousand-piece jigsaw that when finished would cover a four-foot-by-six-foot table. The goal for the game-crazy family had been to finish the jigsaw in one night. They'd been drinking beers and eating brats and having a grand time. Everyone except ten-year-old Eduardo and Uncle Dietrich, who'd been across the room in their own world, lost in a deck of cards and all the tricks and puzzles they could pull from it. After an hour, Dietrich had stood and announced *It has finally happened, the boy is better than me.*

"Ten seconds," Joe said.

"Ace of diamonds, king of hearts, two of spades," Eduardo said. "I have two points. Here is my question: Where did you take this woman after you picked her up at the Foxfire on Wednesday night at eight fifteen?"

"Valley. Reseda. Two-story older building on Sherman Way

between Reseda and Wilbur. Tax guy on the first floor. Dropped her in the lot on the side."

"The lab."

"Two-one," Joe said. "Time to tie it up."

"A man wants to enter an exclusive club, but does not know the password," Eduardo said. "He waits by the door and listens. A club member knocks. The doorman answers and says 'twelve.' The club member says 'six,' and is allowed to enter. A second member comes to the door and knocks. The doorman answers and says 'six.' The club member says 'three,' and is allowed to enter. The man had heard enough. He knocks on the door. The doorman answers and says 'ten.'' The man says 'five,' and is not allowed into the club. What should he have said?"

As Joe paced back and forth, Eduardo realized this was the most fun he'd had since arriving in Los Angeles. Throwing darts at Sikorski had certainly been pleasurable. And taking down the tattooed wild-card cook had been very nice indeed until the beer man interrupted what would have otherwise been quite a lovely outing. But neither event compared to the word-game competition for the cab driver's life beneath the Lankershim-Cahuenga overpass.

"Got it," Joe said with five seconds to spare. "The guy should have said 'three.' The doorman's code is the number of letters in the word."

"Excellent," Eduardo said. "And your question?"

"Who are you and what the hell is it with this woman?" Joe said.

"That is two questions."

"Pick one."

"Because I'm enjoying myself, I shall answer them both. I am an international corporate fixer. When there are unresolvable issues that must be resolved with whatever means are necessary, then I am contracted to fix that problem. The woman in question has stolen a drug from a foreign pharmaceutical company. The drug reverses the aging process and must be returned, and all evidence of its creation destroyed."

Joe smiled with delight. "Eddie, I don't think you understand what this means to me. Writers wait all their lives for a story like this to fall from the sky. I'm going to write this script, and my life is going to change."

Eduardo laughed. "Unless I'm the first to five, in which case, your life is going to end."

Joe laughed too, though as if he didn't find it as funny as the fixer found it.

They were alone in the world, trading riddles in the channel while thousands of cars zoomed across the overpass above them. Not every riddle was answered correctly or even answered at all. But just when it seemed like one or the other of them was ready for a breakthrough, likely to take a significant lead and put some puzzle pressure on their opponent, a riddle would baffle them and the game would be tied again. Three-two. Three-three. Four-three. Four-four.

And then Joe asked a tough one. "Name the eight-letter word that can have a letter taken away and the seven letters remaining make a word. Then take another letter away and the six letters remaining make a word. Then keep on doing that and the remaining letters still make a word until there is one letter left and it makes a word."

"Joe, I commend you," Eduardo said. "That is a championship riddle, a riddle no one should be able to answer in twenty minutes, let alone two."

"So game, set, match?" Joe said, with a mix of hope and relief. "My life is saved?"

"I'm afraid not," Eduardo said. "The word is *starting*. Take away the second 't' and you have *staring*. Take away the 'a' and you have string. Take away the 'r' and you have *sting*. Take away the 't' and you have *sing*. Take away the 'g' and you have *sin*. Take away the 's' and you have *in*. Take away the 'n' and you have I. Unfortunately for you, I happen to know this one."

"Jesus."

"He can't help you now. But I can."

"What do you mean?"

"I propose a rule change. The game must be won by two points. Both players must agree."

"Win by two, yes, I agree, win by two."

"My turn."

On they played. When their favorite riddles, those they'd committed to memory because remembering those particularly problematic puzzlers was also remembering that they'd solved them, when those riddles were exhausted, they turned to the word game magazines on the front seat in the Prius.

Though they kept score, the tally became an afterthought. The riddles and answers were drugs in their veins, the personal questions that followed almost as addictive. Eduardo had long ago acquired the information he needed to crush Carrie's alibi, so he asked Joe questions about living the lousy life of an invisible LA screenwriter, a life Eduardo had before this day under the overpass known nothing about. He came to find Joe's lonely subterranean existence fascinating.

The cab driver lived in a cheap, one-room rental on a sad street in Panorama City and hadn't left Los Angeles in twenty-five years. He lived exclusively on fast food—breakfast, lunch, and dinner, every meal for that same quarter century...he'd never so much as made himself a sandwich. He played video games for days at a time. Drank gallons of black coffee but no alcohol. Smoked pounds of pot but not cigarettes. Peripherally followed sports but had no physical hobbies. Instead, he consumed word-game magazines by the dozens and spent hour upon hour writing movies he knew no one would read. When he wasn't writing, he was driving the Prius, hoping beyond hope that inspiration, the *story of the year*, would one day slide into the back seat of his cab and change his world.

That day was today, and he, Eduardo, was that inspiration,

and the stolen Fountain of Youth was the one movie in a million Joe had been waiting for.

"How can a fairy tale that's been told for centuries be the story of the year?" Eduardo said after solving a riddle and winning a point.

"Because this is Hollywood," Joe said, "where the highest form of filmmaking is to take the most well-known and popular stories in history, in this case the fucking Fountain of Youth—a dream shared across all nationalities, all races, all ages, all colors, all creeds, the tallest of tall tales—and tell it a new way, give it a fresh twist, an exciting spin that no one saw coming. You're talking Tinseltown religion, Eddie. Pre-sold, box-office gold. That's what everyone here prays for. The once-in-a-lifetime chance to discover a story like the one you told me."

It wasn't just Joe's sorry screenwriting saga that intrigued him. Eduardo was completely self-aware that he was sharing his own life with Joe. No one in the world knew anything about Eduardo Wolf. His personal life was a mystery in a black hole. And as the word game went on and on, Joe ran out of meaningful questions and began asking things like, *What's your favorite food? What's your favorite color? Who was the first girl you ever kissed? What's the one thing in the world that scares you the most?* Eduardo shared more of his true self with Joe than he had with anyone on the planet. To the fixer, it felt like they were becoming friends, though the feeling was unfamiliar.

The score was fifteen-fourteen, Eduardo ahead by a point.

"I saved this riddle for last because it's my young nephew Diego's favorite. He's a pirate enthusiast back in Brazil. Beautiful boy," Eduardo said. "There are three treasure chests on a Caribbean island. Each chest contains one hundred coins. The first chest has one hundred gold coins, the second chest has one hundred silver coins, and the third chest has an equal split of fifty gold coins and fifty silver coins. Each chest is labeled, but all are labeled incorrectly. You are allowed to pick one coin from one chest, after which, you must correctly identify each of the three chests to win the treasure. What should you do?"

Joe racked his brain, summoning every last ounce of word game power in his soul, but the seconds clicked by until one hundred twenty of them were gone.

"It's a tough one, Eddie," Joe said. "Plus, it's got pirates, which is always a bonus in Hollywood. Might take me another ten minutes. No way I solve it in two."

"Allow me," Eduardo said. "Take a coin from the chest labeled fifty-fifty. If you pick a gold coin, then you know that chest must contain all gold coins. It can't be the fifty-fifty chest because all the chests are incorrectly labeled. So the chest labeled silver must be the fifty-fifty. And the chest labeled gold must be the silver. If you pick a silver coin, then that chest must contain all silver coins, the chest labeled silver must be all gold, and the chest labeled gold must be the fifty-fifty."

"Yeah, that's a good one, no doubt. You win by two, fair and square," Joe said. "You're not really going to kill me, are you, Eddie? We're friends now. You can tell Diego all about the two of us playing word games under the overpass. You can say we got down to the end, and you pitched his favorite riddle, and I couldn't solve it for the life of me. It'll be his story of the year."

In less time than it took to blink, the fixer pulled his Glock 19 and put a bullet in the middle of Joe's brain.

"I don't have a nephew named Diego," Eduardo said as the screenwriter fell dead to the ground.

# CHAPTER 28

# FOR A GENIUS, YOU'RE AN IDIOT

CARRIE ARRIVED at the lab early Wednesday morning to care for the rats. Yes, it was dangerous to be here now that Stuart was a dead man, Leo was a dead man walking, and she was a dead man on deck. But the rats were alive—not yet been burned by the cleaner or eradicated by the fixer—and she remained responsible for feeding them, cleaning their cages, and with regard to the Greek Gods, for monitoring their behavior.

This morning, however, she'd realized it was *her* behavior that needed monitoring. While watching the Gods march through the maze like a fearless pride of lions, she became acutely conscious of a curious development regarding her own confidence, which was that her self-image had improved as her behavior had deteriorated.

Already a trained scientist by the time she'd entered middle school, Carrie had evaluated her own life like a lab experiment and extrapolated the data to conclude that the human population was divided into two columns. In column one were *the people at the party*. In column two were *the wallflowers*.

The people at the party were self-defining. They had the confidence to be out among the masses, laughing and singing and crying and playing and working and living up to, and often beyond, the cultural expectations of normal human folk. Or at least had the confidence to *act* like they had the confidence. The athletes and the actors. The bankers and the brokers. The leaders and the followers. The husbands and the wives and the children. All the general populace living in the sunlight.

The wallflowers did not have the confidence to walk in the sun. They hugged the walls at home, in school, at work, and in life. They stayed in the shadows and did not socially engage the people at the party if they could help it. If the wallflowers shared a defining characteristic, it was that they did not believe they belonged at the party. They lacked the self-esteem necessary to push themselves off the wall and join the crowd living life in the light. *I'm a wallflower because I'm supposed to be one, because I deserve to be one* was what wallflowers told themselves.

This was the dictionary definition of Carrie, and no one saw it more clearly than Carrie herself, who'd been self-aware at an unusually early age and only became more mindful of her low self-image as time ticked by. She wasn't pretty, athletic, fashionable, sexy, popular, or cool. She wasn't anything but smart. And smart didn't get you off the wall and into the party. Smart kept you on the wall. Smart reminded you every day that you were a goody-two-shoes-science-geek-rat-girl, and that was all you were ever going to be. Smart focused your scientifically trained mind on what you didn't do, what you couldn't do, what you'd never do, who you'd never be. Smart sealed your low-confidence deal. Smart exacerbated your low self-image and perpetuated your low self-esteem. Smart forever labeled you an unattractive loser with no normal social life for the rest of time.

And then Carrie had conked Old Tom on the head and stolen the capsules. Within a week, she'd had a close encounter with the Latino fixer and a confrontation with the Russian cleaner. She'd done shots of Casamigos Añejo. She'd lied about her alibi, given the stolen drug to her mother and the Copa crew, and had a tattooed, ex-con butcher turn his bike around in Eureka and rumble a thousand miles back to LA just to see her.

As a result of her unscrupulous behavior, Johnny Fairfax, who as recently as one week ago wouldn't have given Carrie a second glance, was now at the beginning of the onset of whatever was the commencement of the launch of a possible relationship. He was giving her a second glance and then some. And he liked what he was seeing. She could tell by the way he looked at her. And she felt good about it...felt good about herself feeling good about herself. Which was a concerning contradiction because she was also feeling horrible about her behavior.

*It's all so terribly confusing,* Carrie thought as she scooped rat shit into a baggie with a small laboratory utensil, *though nothing a shot or two of tequila won't fix. Haha. But seriously, it makes no scientific sense. Theoretically, as one's behavior improves, gets societally better, it follows that one's self-esteem improves concurrently. There's no justification for this symbiotic relationship to work in reverse. As one's behavior declines, gets worse, one's self-esteem by necessity should decline. But look at me. I've behaved badly, worse than I could ever imagine myself behaving, and I'm pushing off the wall and joining the party. Since I started down the road to ruin, my sense of self has changed for the better. I'm not the same plain Jane I used to be. I mean, I'm no Kate Upton, but I have nice hair and good skin and a pretty smile. I have respectable tits. Not as big as my mother's but definitely above average. No one's tossing me out of a wet T-shirt contest, that's for sure. Hey, to some guys, pear-shaped means sexy. It means the bigger the cushion, the better the pushin'. Oh my God, I would never have said this about myself a week ago. But Jesus Christ, it's true. I've got a cushion worth pushin'.*

She wasn't used to the idea of herself as a law-breaking liar. Wasn't used to the idea of herself as attractive to men, any men, forget a man like Johnny Fairfax. Wasn't used to these thoughts running rampant in her brain, to the feelings she was feeling. She was sure they were real, but they didn't fit her yet. They were like a cartoon baseball cap too comically big for her head. A cap that covered her ears and her eyes and made everyone laugh. A cap that made *her* laugh. And so, she laughed to herself. Except she didn't laugh to herself. She laughed out loud so that the Greek Gods could hear her.

"What could possibly be so funny at a time like this?"

She looked up. Sikorski stood on the other side of the table maze. She'd been so lost in her new sense of self, so engrossed in the removal of rat shit from the Parthenon, that she'd somehow missed his entrance into the lab. Plus, both of his feet were wrapped in towels, which might also have had something to do with his stealth. His clothes were wrinkled and ragged, he hadn't shaved or washed his hair, which was wilder than usual, another dimension of Einstein altogether. His deep-set eyes were badly bloodshot, like he hadn't slept in a week, which, of course, he probably hadn't. In short, he looked exactly like a dead man walking, albeit one with towels wrapped around his feet.

"You look terrible, Leo."

"I feel worse."

"What are you doing here?"

He pulled a gun from his pocket. "Cause and effect."

"I'm not thinking much like a scientist these days," she said. "You'll have to explain that to me."

"I look terrible because I am terrible. And I'm terrible because you ruined my life. And because you ruined my life, I'm here to obtain your confession. You're going to confess that you stole the capsules."

He took a pen and a piece of paper from his other pocket and tossed them toward her. They landed on the table maze, in the corral, beside the Parthenon. The Greek Gods were huddled in the temple, out of sight.

"You ruined your own life," Carrie said. "You took money from the Chinese and told them they were your exclusive investor. And then you took money from the Russians and told them *they* were your exclusive investor. And then you conveniently forgot to mention that fact to either one of them, that you had another exclusive investor besides them. How's that for cause and effect?"

"I had no choice. The Chinese told me they wouldn't invest another dime without concrete results. This was well before the rats reversed, and I needed additional funding to get where I knew we had to go. The Russians were happy to help. I employed each of them as insurance against the other. With so much at stake, the Chinese would protect me from the Russians, and the Russians would protect me from the Chinese."

"For a genius, you're an idiot."

"For a genius, I'm armed and dangerous. I took the liberty of writing your confession for you. All you have to do is sign it."

She lifted the piece of paper. It was handwritten in his scientist scratch. "I, Carrie Kromer, behavioral gerontologist for Alsiko Labs, hereby confess in full to the outright theft of the capsules that provided proof-positive age reversal identifiers in the subgroup of rats designated the Greek Gods. I stole the capsules of my own free will and destiny and am solely responsible for their rightful return. I accept whatever retribution results as a consequence of my crimes and misdemeanors.'"

"Too strong?" Sikorski said.

"I'm not signing it because I didn't—"

*Bang.* He fired in her direction. The bullet hit the wall of cages behind her. It was loud and terrifying. She'd never been that close to a gun that had been shot.

"Stop saying that," Sikorski said, eyes crazed with anger and frustration. "I know you took them. You destroyed everything I created. I'm going to kill you, Carrie. But first you're going to sign the goddamn confess—"

He was out of his mind, and she absolutely believed him when he said he was going to kill her, so before he could finish his sentence, she shoved the entire table maze into his body with all the adrenaline and fear-fueled power she could summon. It hit him hard below the waist, knocked him off his feet, and crashed down on top him, pinning him on the lab floor.

He was immobilized under the table maze up to his chest. His left arm was trapped beneath the heavy slab of wood, but somehow his right arm was still free. He'd lost his grip on the gun, but it had fallen to the ground nearly within reach of his right hand. He was too weak, and the table maze was too heavy for him to move off his body.

So he went for the gun.

He stretched and wiggled and stretched and wiggled and stretched. His fingers brushed against the grip.

Carrie watched Sikorski's hand inch closer and closer to the weapon. But she wasn't thinking about getting shot. She was thinking about the clicker in her hand.

The side wall of the table maze had broken off when it hit Sikorski's body and crashed to the ground, and the interior maze boards had come undone, out of their slats, and fallen away. Sikorski's upper chest, neck, and head were directly opposite the Parthenon with no barriers between them.

Carrie thought long and hard about good and evil, right and wrong, moral and immoral, legal and illegal. She thought long and hard about whether to help Sikorski out from under the crushing weight of the table maze or whether to leave him trapped in the lab and hope someone else, maybe the tax preparer from downstairs, would arrive in time to save him.

She thought long and hard about whether or not it was in her best interests to let Sikorski live in the first place, since there was no reasoning with the scientist anymore. He'd lost his mind. He *knew* she'd stolen the capsules, and he was going to kill her for it, period, end of Sikorski saga. Leaving him to die would be an act of self-defense. But what about killing him herself?

She thought long and hard about remorse and regret. If she was feeling all of those things, then why did she also feel so good about Sikorski being entombed? She used to know the difference between acceptable behavior and behavior beyond the pale. But now she was torn between her past self, her present self, and her future self. Was she a good person or a bad person? Was this yet another defining moment in her irreversible transition from nice to naughty? The Carrie from a week ago would have been overwhelmed with guilt. *That* Carrie wouldn't have considered any option other than saving Sikorski. *This* Carrie was looking for a way out of the messy web in which she was caught.

She thought long and hard about all of this, except Sikorski was so very close to grabbing the gun and shooting her in the head, so "long and hard" turned out to be three seconds of consideration. Self-defense was the verdict. *If I let him live, he kills me*, she thought.

She walked around the table maze and put the gun in her purse. Then she positioned the clicker beside Sikorski's face and pushed the button.

*Click-click-click-click-click-click.*

The Greek Gods emerged from the Parthenon. Apollo's leg had been injured in the crash, and he was limping. Even so, he and the rest of the rats sniffed their way across the table maze to Sikorski, whose eyes opened wide with terror as the rats encircled him. They were cautious at first. As if confused. Uncertain. They'd felt the vibration from the collar and knew it was time to eat. But where was the food? *What* were they supposed to eat? They inched forward, hunger driving them.

Sikorski screamed like a hurricane as the rats ripped the skin off his face and neck and devoured the fleshy red meat beneath the epidermis. He tried to swat them away with his one free hand, but he was too weak, and they were too fast, too determined, too hungry, and then too crazed with bloodlust.

After a while, Sikorski stopped screaming. He gurgled like a man drowning in his own blood, like a man who'd been eaten alive by rats, and then he died.

When the Gods had their fill of the dead scientist, Carrie

collected them one by one and put them in a small travel cage. She did not deal with the bloody mess on the lab floor.

*Sikorski was a dead man one way or the other*, she thought with Tino and Eduardo Wolf in mind. *I'm not proud of doing their dirty work, but now that it's done, it's only fair they return the favor and clean him up.*

# CHAPTER 29
# NOT GOOD NEWS IF COUNTING FLAGS

THERE WERE FOUR RED FLAGS, and that was four too many for Tino. The first was Sikorski, who'd been lying about the stolen drug and all things big and small surrounding its unfortunate disappearance. But the lies weren't the red flag. The bloody pinholes in Sikorski's arms and legs and face were the flag. Someone had used the pharmaceutical scientist as a pincushion just prior to Tino torching the man's feet. Coincidence? At the time, it had been too soon to tell. Now, it was feeling less and less like serendipity.

The second red flag was Stuart Langston's arm, which had been ground to bone dust up to the biostatistician's elbow when they'd found him burned to a crisp in his car. Of course, the timing of the crash was suspicious, but it was possible that someone beyond the Alsiko circle had held a grudge against Langston and acted on it as Tino was arriving to clean the mess. But that was seeming less and less likely. Car crashes didn't grind arm bones to dust.

The third red flag was Brian Hood. After Tino eliminated Justin (and his better-than-average Popeye Doyle), he'd returned to the Foxfire and spoken with the other bartender working the night the capsules were stolen. Brian had looked at the photo of

Carrie and told the cleaner she'd left early in the evening in a Yellow Cab Co. Prius, a fact that had blown Carrie's cover to bits. Not only that, but Tino hadn't been the only one asking about the woman in the photo. Brian had told the same story to a Latino IRS investigator.

*Is third red flag,* Tino had thought . *Not good news if counting flags.*

The fourth red flag was Joe Cabot. Pretending to be Cabot's infuriated ex-brother-in-law-blast-from-the-past to whom the cabbie owed money, Tino had put pressure on the dispatcher— meaning he'd wrapped his arm around the man's neck and squeezed it like an African python—and discovered Cabot's cab had picked Carrie up at the Foxfire and taken her to Alsiko the night the drug was taken. The dispatcher gave up Cabot's cell phone, home address, and work schedule rather than be terminally asphyxiated. Tino had everything but the cabbie, who'd been found shot in the head under the Lankershim-Cahuenga overpass, meaning Cabot himself wasn't the red flag. It was that he'd been murdered.

Monday, before he'd gone to the Foxfire, Tino had been to the parking lot down the street and spoken with the night-shift attendant. She'd confirmed Carrie's car had indeed been parked there the night the capsules were stolen—it had pulled in at five past eight and pulled out at eleven twenty-seven. But since he'd also confirmed a Yellow Cab Co. cab had not driven Carrie from the lab back to the lot—only from the Foxfire to Alsiko—the cleaner had to make a return visit to the lot attendant to determine how Carrie got back to her car. Did an accomplice pick her up at the lab? Carrie's alibi was already in tatters, but as a matter of methodically cleaning the mess, no stone could be left unturned. Unturned stones often covered tangential evidence— stains and maggots pointing arrows back at the original mess he'd been sent to clean. Even these loose and lateral connections had to be scrubbed from the face of the Earth.

The night-shift attendant was a seventy-two-year-old, once-upon-a-lifetime-ago Vegas showgirl named Elaine Godspeed. From the time she was a little girl back in Bakersfield, her life had been all about dance. Captivated by the Radio City Music Hall Rockettes, she'd left home at sixteen and run right to Las Vegas to dance with the stars and find her fame and fortune. Unfortunately, she'd found cigarettes and booze and drugs. She'd danced for years in the casino shows, first on the Strip, then off the Strip, and then way off the Strip, where she'd spent a decade stripping (a way-off-the-Strip stripper) for alcoholic gamblers who'd bet the ranch and crapped out.

When her body had lost its commercial appeal, she'd followed a drug-dealing con man to LA. He'd died of an overdose, and she'd bounced from town to town until she landed in a shabby mobile home park in Sylmar, a sunny city of one hundred thousand shoved up against the San Gabriel Mountains at the northernmost edge of the San Fernando Valley. Historically known for its olive orchards (and illegal street drag racing), Sylmar had seemed a likely landing pad to Elaine, who'd been drinking gin martinis with extra olives for breakfast, lunch, and dinner since she was seventeen. She'd washed them down with cigarettes, which she chained smoked like a locomotive, and whatever pills she was popping that particular week. She was a hardcore, gravel-voiced, smart-mouthed broad, which was why the parking lot manager had hired her to work the night shift down the street from the Foxfire—that and because no one else who spoke English had applied for the job.

It was noon on Wednesday when Tino arrived at the Waco Mobile Home Park on San Fernando Road in Sylmar. Like all the rental units in the decomposing park, Elaine's mobile home was no longer mobile. It was permanently affixed to its concrete pad. A front deck of rotting wood ran the length of the dilapidated single-wide. The trailer itself was fading-rusting-peeling grungy blue. The roof was stained and dented and beat to hell. Windows were smeared with smoke from the inside. There were pots of dead plants near the front door. Other discarded, corroded junk was stacked in unruly piles up and down the deck. It was a sad sight to see, and yet the decaying immobile home was still standing. Kind of like Elaine herself.

Tino had met the Vegas showgirl when she'd checked the parking lot log—before he'd put on his Popeye Doyle persona, zip-tied Justin to the Acura steering wheel, and burned him to death. The woman had smelled like a smokestack and seemed harmless to Tino at the time, meaning she was not evidence that needed cleaning.

*But times change*, Tino thought as he pulled his Sig Sauer pistol with the 9mm silencer.

He stood on Elaine's deck and looked around the immediate neighborhood of deteriorating trailers. No one was out and about. He placed a gloved hand on the doorknob. The door was locked but flimsy as cardboard. It gave way easily, and Tino stepped inside.

"You again. Him again. It's a threesome," Elaine said. "No problem. I'm a party girl from way back."

Tino shut the door. The trailer was as ragged on the inside as it was on the outside. Ancient wood paneling the color of malted milk covered every surface that wasn't a cracked and washed-out, sky-blue vinyl cushion or a cream-colored kitchen appliance. The interior was deceptively smaller than it appeared to be from the exterior, and the smoke made it hard to breathe.

To Tino's left was the eating area, a sky-blue vinyl booth straight out of a 1960s diner. Elaine sat in the booth facing the front door and the Russian, drinking a gin martini with extra olives and smoking a cigarette. An overflowing ashtray was on the table in front of her. Other overflowing ashtrays were scattered about as well. She'd pulled the curtains, and the low-level lighting gave the place a sickly amber glow. The place was a dump.

To the right, on the same side of the single-wide as the front door, was the kitchen sink, the stove, and the refrigerator, all part of the same counter. Across from the kitchen was a sky-blue vinyl banquet-sofa. Seated at the end of the sofa was a handsome Latin man with an untraceable Glock 19 semi-automatic handgun.

# CHAPTER 30
# BORIS BADENOV AND ANTONIO BANDERAS

"LONG TIME, AMIGO," Tino said with enmity, pointing his Sig at the fixer.

"Not long enough, comrade," Eduardo said with acrimony, pointing his Glock at the cleaner.

Though the men renewed their mutual contempt without blinking, there was no racial derogation in their greetings. *Amigo* and *comrade* were simply nouns offered in lieu of actual names they both had no interest in learning since whatever name they learned would be a pseudonym anyway.

"Lose the lights and pass the popcorn. Boris Badenov and Antonio Banderas know each other," Elaine said.

"I should have killed you in Antwerp," Tino said.

"I should have killed you," Eduardo said.

"You should have killed each other," Elaine said, sucking in the top half of her cigarette and washing it down with a swig of martini. "Save us all a heap of heartache. What the hell happened in Antwerp?"

"My client buy one hundred million dollars in diamonds from his client, and diamonds disappear after payment is made," Tino said. "Let me tell you, when one hundred million in diamonds disappear, is big mess."

"When an international transaction of this magnitude is interrupted, there are only so many men with the capability of repairing the damage by any means necessary," Eduardo said. "My comrade is one. I am another. It's a small fraternity. By the way, I found the diamonds, in case you were wondering which one of us is more capable."

"I find diamonds," Tino said.

"Your memory fails you, comrade," Eduardo said. "After I seduced the duchess and discovered where she had secretly sequestered the diamonds, I informed you of their location and sent you to retrieve them like an errand boy."

"Maybe in TV movie adaptation, amigo," Tino said, turning to Elaine. "But in real life, I burn duke with Zippo lighter, he tell me where duchess hide diamonds, and I find them. Not need help to clean mess." He turned back to Eduardo, and his voice filled with disgust. "Must be hard to carry ego around world. So big and heavy."

"Lighter, I'm sure, than your inferiority complex," Eduardo said, "which weighs at least as much as your envy, though less than your pride."

Tino detested many things about Eduardo Wolf, but none more than the fixer's self-assured panache, his top-tier style, his upper-crust class, his easy-going savoir-faire. It was all so effortless for the Latino. The James Bond flair. The long line of women waiting to share his bed. But it was his smug romantic magnetism that especially annoyed Tino, who had to pay women for sex (and did so regularly).

The Russian had been born a working-class brute, and a working-class brute he would always be. No amount of cash in a suitcase spent on German cars or Italian clothes or Russian vodka or Rodeo Drive jewelry could change the fact that Tino was Timex and Eduardo was Rolex. The cleaner coveted the fixer's class, culture, and sophistication, character traits he knew he'd never naturally possess. The way women—including the goddamn duchess—went wild for the Latino was a permanently pinched nerve in Tino's pride.

"Can't imagine what you are doing in this trailer, amigo," Tino said, swallowing that piece of pride and refocusing his priorities.

"I was thinking the same thing, comrade," Eduardo said. "Why are we *both* here?"

"Bad luck is the answer to that one." Elaine inhaled the bottom half of her cigarette into her lungs and washed it down with the remains of her martini. "When I was a girl in Bakersfield, my nickname was Lucky Lainey. It was meant to be ironic. Like calling the class idiot Einstein. All my life, up to and including right now, if I didn't have bad luck, I'd have no luck at all."

"I have question for you, Lucky Lainey," Tino said.

"I also have a question for you," Eduardo said.

"And I have one for both of you." Elaine stood up and gestured at the sink, where the gin and vermouth waited on the counter. "Who wants a martini?"

"Sit down," Tino and Eduardo said at the same time, pointing their guns at her.

"Worst party I ever went to," Elaine said, sitting back down on the banquette.

"I'm asking about this woman." Tino put his photo of Carrie on the table in front of Elaine.

"And I am asking about the same woman." Eduardo put *his* photo of Carrie next to Tino's photo of Carrie.

The cleaner and the fixer looked at each other and at their matching photos. *Double red flag* is what their expressions said.

"Tell me what remember about last Wednesday night," Tino said to Elaine.

"Yes, last Wednesday," Eduardo said. "That is the night in question. Tell me what happened with this woman."

Tino couldn't believe it. Neither could Eduardo.

"She parked her car around eight," Elaine said. "Came back to get it like eleven thirty. I told you that when you came to see me at the lot. We checked the log, remember? I did it with both of you. Hey, wait, is this some kind of cloak-and-dagger romantic triangle? Because I'm not getting in the middle of you two clowns and her. Been there, done that. Jealously is nobody's good news."

"How did she get to lot late Wednesday night?" Tino said to Elaine. "Did she walk from Foxfire? Did she take taxi?"

"Did she get a ride from someone else?" Eduardo said.

The men glared at each other with expressions of incredulity. How could they be seeking the same information from the same woman at the same time in the same trailer?

"Outside accomplice?" Tino said to Eduardo.

"It's possible. She's smart," Eduardo said to Tino.

"But she is weak. I will break her," Tino said.

"I will seduce her before you break her," Eduardo said. "She's attracted to me."

"Again with the women," Tino said.

"It's my cross to bear," Eduardo said.

"She came in a cab," Elaine said. "Green and white. United Taxi."

"So many people park in lot," Tino said.

"How is it you remember this woman that night?" Eduardo said.

"She paid me five hundred bucks not to tell anyone," Elaine said, standing again. "That's five down the drain for whoever she is. Sorry, sister. Hey, how about a round of martinis on me?"

"Sit down," Tino and Eduardo said at the same time.

"Stolen capsules belong to my client," Tino said.

"In fact, they belong to *my* client," Eduardo said.

"My client is Sikorski sole investor," Tino said.

"*My* client is Sikorski's sole investor," Eduardo said.

"Can you hear it? That's the fat lady singing for Sikorski," Elaine said.

"Not good," Tino said.

"Not at all," Eduardo said.

"If you had drug, you would not visit Elaine," Tino said to Eduardo.

"If you had it, neither would you," Eduardo said.

"If I had it, I would have taken it by now," Elaine said, lighting a cigarette and looking mournfully into her empty glass.

"When I find capsules, your client will be angry," Tino said.

"When I find them, your client will be furious," Eduardo said.

"If I call Sikorski and find them myself, *then* can I make my martini?" Elaine said.

Both men looked at the former showgirl.

"Evidence with big mouth," Tino said.

"Bad luck for Lainey," Eduardo said.

"Is there another kind?" Elaine said.

They shot her point blank in the chest. She fell back in the booth, dead on contact, smoke curling up from the cigarette in the ashtray.

"I should have killed you in Antwerp," Tino said.

"I should have killed you," Eduardo said.

# CHAPTER 31
# HEAVE HO, ON WE GO

THE WHOLE TIME Johnny was busy with breakfast he was thinking about the dead man in the freezer. Big Ben Boston was buck naked and had a creepy frosting of ice crystals on his skin. Johnny did his best to behave as if it were just another Wednesday morning, but while he prepared blueberry pancakes with maple-glazed ham steak, fresh-squeezed orange juice, and high-octane coffee, he couldn't stop glancing at the freezer door and replaying the death of the parole officer in the pool while the Copacabana cheerleaders howled on the sidelines. In his two most violent moments—smack dab in the middle of murdering the junkie thief and the skinhead convict—he hadn't been as bloodthirsty as the Copa crew when they'd drowned Ben Boston.

The whole time Johnny served breakfast at the poolside tables he was thinking that a loss of appetite would be the normal response after drowning a corrections-department employee. Even though Boston had been as dirty as dirty got, the guy had worked for the government. And they had killed him. Johnny had supposed the Copa crew would think about that in the privacy of their own minds, and after a night of deep and powerful retrospection, introspection, meditation, and contemplation, the result would be a more complete under-standing of the irreversible fact that the parole officer was on ice (or that ice was on the parole officer), and they were truly fucked and so would not be especially hungry.

But the Copa crew ate like Johnny had served the last fresh blueberry in California, like the final pig on the planet had been butchered and this was the end of breakfast anywhere with maple-glazed ham steak on the menu. They ate with voracious gusto and between bites cracked wise with sexually suggestive jokes and risqué stories of the lustful lives they intended to live now that they had their lives to live again. Not one of them seemed to give a second thought to Ben Boston.

"How can you act like it never happened?" Johnny said gently to Lillian as he refilled her coffee cup. "Like he's not dead in the freezer?"

"Snap out of it, Tattoo Boy," Lillian said. A wink softened the sting of her voice. "That fat fucker's in the rearview mirror. Heave ho, on we go."

The whole time Johnny corralled the Copa crew into the passenger van he was thinking that having a bad plan to deal with the dead man was the same as having no plan at all. He'd always had plans to cover up his criminal behavior. Every crim-inal made plans. Plans were part of committing the crime. If you were going to murder a guy, you made a plan for after the murder. But there was no plan in place for Ben Boston, and no plans to make a plan. Instead of making a plan, the gang were going to the Museum of Death on Hollywood Boulevard, where they would see, according to the museum's own literature, *the world's largest collection of serial killer artwork, antique funeral ephemera, mortician and coroners instruments, Manson Family memo-rabilia, pet death taxidermy, crime scene photographs, and so much more!*

"Going to the Museum of Death is not a plan," Johnny said to Joanna, the last one into the van. "What are we going to do?"

"We're not sure, Mr. Fairfax," Joanna said. "We're hoping the museum provides us some kind of creative vision. That is the plan. Seek inspiration at the Museum of Death. We'll be back by lunch, and then we shall see what we shall see."

The whole time Johnny cleared the tables and cleaned the kitchen he was thinking about how Carrie should have returned from the lab hours ago. Where the hell was she? What was taking so long? But the answers to those questions were bad news—the fixer or the cleaner was waiting at the lab, and Carrie was dead in a ditch somewhere in Agora Hills—so to shift his focus, he prepared the fifty-plus ingredients required to make his very own, one-of-a-kind, special-occasion Hillbilly Chili.

To achieve the massive culinary masterpiece he'd created with an Appalachian serial killer back in the prison kitchen, Johnny maxed the volume on the kitchen boombox. His thick and-meaty, rock-and-roll meal in a bowl included three kinds of meat, five kinds of beans, three kinds of mushrooms, four kinds of peppers (two roasted), fresh tomato puree (no canned crap for this challenging chili), two kinds of flour, a dozen different spices, beef stock, chicken stock, two kinds of wine, two kinds of beer, homemade chili powder, and a multitude of other ingredients large and small. His rowdy and raucous preparation allowed him to move from worrying about Carrie to reflecting upon *why* he was worrying about her—and how surprisingly happy he was to have someone to worry about in the first place for the first time.

As he washed and dried and cut and sliced and chopped and sautéed and roasted and blended and soaked and drained and boiled and heated the endless items that made the chili so hill-billy, he relived his week-long whirlwind relationship with Carrie. Much of what he recalled made him smile, including their first encounter, last Thursday night, when they'd met at dinner at the end of his first day on the job, and it had been clear they couldn't tolerate each other and never would. But then an endless parade of unbelievable, unimaginable, unpredictable, improbable, implausible, and impossible things had happened, and he and Carrie had inconceivably connected on an emotional level he'd never thought existed inside him.

Unfortunately, reliving the chronological events of the last week, all the unthinkable things that had been said and done, led him back to yesterday's murder of Ben Boston, the cheerleaders chanting for the parole officer's death, and their absolute lack of remorse in the aftermath. Johnny, in contrast, was overflowing with second thoughts. He wanted to share them with Carrie and see if she could make sense of the insanity since he couldn't seem to.

But she still wasn't back from the lab, and he knew the police would be coming to the Copa sooner rather than later, searching for one of their own who'd gone missing in action. They would find their parole officer in the freezer, looking like a four-hundred-pound chocolate snow cone, and Johnny would take the rap because he was an ex-con with a violent history.

"The cops are coming," he said out loud to himself.

"The cops are here," Carrie said.

# CHAPTER 32
# A CLUSTERFUCK FOR THE AGES

JOHNNY TURNED TO CARRIE. The relief and happiness he'd felt at the sound of her voice disappeared in a heartbeat. Two LAPD detectives stood beside her.

Both cops were Hispanic women. Identical twins. Carbon-copy cops. Absolutely duplicate physical appearance. Zero differentiation. Impossible to tell one from the other or the other from the one. Exact same clothes worn the exact same way. Same lip gloss. Same nail polish. Same detective badge on their belts in precisely the same place. Same dark sunglasses. But what really dropped Johnny's jaw were their matching, stunning, long, and tightly woven ash-blonde dreads that reminded him in the most unsettling way of the twin henchmen who'd worked for the Merovingian in *The Matrix Reloaded*, except that the detectives were real women with real badges and real guns, not fictional characters in a sci-fi action-thriller trilogy Johnny had seen a dozen times. Real or not, Johnny was speechless. He thought his mouth might have fallen open, but he wasn't certain about that. He hoped not.

"This is Detective Ramos," Carrie said, moving to the boombox and lowering the volume.

"Ronda," the twin on the left said.

"And this is also Detective Ramos," Carrie said.

"Rowena," the twin on the right said. "You can close your mouth now, Johnny."

*Shit…open.* "You know my name?"

"We know your whole low-life criminal history," Ronda said.

"You a badass, Johnny. In a stupid way," Rowena said.

"Dumb-as-a-fucking-rock badass," Ronda said.

"Two-time-ex-con, dumb-as-a-fucking-rock badass," Rowena said.

"What do you want?" Johnny said.

"We want to know where Ben Boston at," Rowena said.

As if surfing the same wavelength, the detectives moved in opposite directions, deeper into the kitchen, touching things, lifting things, opening drawers and cabinets, easing their way into full-on LAPD search mode.

Johnny tried to play it cool but, being a natural-born hothead, playing it cool was one of his worst character traits. He looked at Carrie. She seemed calm, although maybe that was because she'd had no experience with the police whatsoever and wasn't sure where this was going. He, on the other hand, had a lifetime of experience with law enforcement and knew *exactly* where this was going, which was nowhere good.

"How should I know?" he said.

"You were his last appointment," Ronda said.

"He never showed up."

"He parked out front this shithole and called his office," Rowena said.

"Said he was going in to see you," Ronda said.

"Said you were in violation of your parole," Rowena said.

"Said he was sending you back up," Ronda said.

"So he's still parked out front?" Johnny knew full well that Helen and Lillian had left Ben Boston's cherry-red Chrysler 300 somewhere safe in Santa Monica.

"Sounds like you know he's not," Rowena said.

"Sounds like he changed his mind," Johnny said. "Went to see someone else."

He couldn't stand the way the detectives were crawling all over his kitchen, their hands on everything. And the way they traded off single sentences freaked him out.

"Never got to any appointments after you," Ronda said.

"Sounds like maybe you a lying ex-con," Rowena said. "Sounds like maybe you moved his damn car after you did what you did."

"I didn't do anything," he said.

"We about to find out if that's true," Ronda said.

She walked behind the counter and stood by the stove, next to Johnny, who still had multiple pots and pans in play. She grabbed a large spoon off the counter and went to stir a pot. He took the spoon right out her hand before it made contact with what he was cooking.

"You can't search this place without a warrant," he said. "I know my rights."

"Yeah, you do," Rowena said from across the kitchen. "You know all about your rights. Which means you also know you about one damn minute from being arrested for obstructing an investigation with probable cause."

"What probable cause?" he said.

"Ben Boston was taking you in, so you took him out," Ronda said. "You got motive coming out your ass."

"And you got a violent nature," Rowena said.

"I'm a cook."

"You a convict," Ronda said.

"Ex-convict."

"Which is why we going to look around and see what the hell happened to your parole officer, see what you did to him." Rowena arrived at the walk-in freezer.

Johnny's face fell a few inches, and he knew the twins both saw it. It was a dead giveaway. The walk-in was where the two-time ex-con had hidden the body.

Ronda looked at Rowena. "Bullseye."

"You best believe it." Rowena took hold of the handle.

Johnny knew he could take the twin standing next to him. Grab her gun and shoot her and her sister in their identical heads. Of course, he also knew that would solve everything for a total of three seconds. Then, what was already a clusterfuck for the ages, would become Hell on Earth.

After the cops were dead, he could put Carrie on the back of his bike and ride to Canada, where they could live a life on the lam in the vast Canadian wilderness. He'd once heard from a convict the Royal Canadian Mounted Police were not as hard-core as American cops, and he pictured them on their horses, trying to chase down the Harley as it disappeared into the Canadian forest. That vision was replaced by another vision of Johnny and Carrie living off the land in the Canadian Rockies, putting up pup-tents, building campfires, and fishing for salmon in the same stream as grizzly bears.

The images came fast, spinning madly into view and then whirling away the next instant. Johnny wondered if this was his life flashing before his eyes. Not the life he'd lived so far. The life he could have lived with Carrie in Canada after he'd killed the twin detectives.

*That* thought—the life-flashing-before-his-eyes thought—was demolished in less than a second when he remembered that Detective Rowena Ramos had her hand on the freezer door, and his actual life was about to change for the worse in the worst way.

But then Carrie came out of nowhere, slid between the walk-in and the detective, put her back against the door, and leaned on it so that Rowena couldn't open it without physically moving Carrie out of the way.

Everyone was momentarily stunned. Even Carrie.

"I suggest you move your ass off that door, Ms. Kromer," Rowena said.

"I suggest you get a warrant," Carrie said.

The detective leaned in and hissed like a snake. "Get off the damn door."

Carrie leaned in right back at her. Their faces were a foot from each other. "Get a damn warrant."

And in that moment, Johnny was so stinking proud of Carrie that he wanted to kiss her more than he'd ever wanted to kiss anyone ever. It was a thought so revelatory in its emotional depth, especially in the middle of this madness, that he repeated it to himself just so he could hear it in his head. *I want to kiss her more than I've ever wanted to kiss anyone ever.*

"You got any idea what the judge is going to think of you?" Ronda said to Carrie.

Carrie kept her eyes locked on Rowena, who was still only a foot from her face. "I have no criminal record at all," she said. "I'm a model citizen. The judge is going to love me, especially when I tell him your search is inadmissible because you didn't get a warrant first, even though we very clearly asked you to more than once."

After a few tense seconds, Rowena backed away. "We going to get a warrant, Ms. Kromer. You can bet your ass on that."

"Meantime, we going to leave a squad car out front so you don't take off with Ben Boston's body," Ronda said. She moved out from behind the counter and joined her sister in the middle of the kitchen.

"Then we going to close this place down and tear it apart until we find what the fuck you did with the man," Rowena said.

The detectives backed toward the door, eyes on Johnny and Carrie.

"All these old motherfuckers going to be out on the street because you shot your damn mouth while your girlfriend obstructed police business," Ronda said.

"Tell it to the judge," Johnny said.

And then the detectives glided through the kitchen door as if floating through air, practically translucent, like *The Matrix Reloaded* twins, and were gone in a glimmer.

# CHAPTER 33
# CRAZY-TOWN TALK

THE COPACABANA passenger van arrived as the Ramos twins were driving away. Carrie met her mother beside the pool as the crew came home from the Museum of Death and told her about the detectives and their impending search warrant. An emergency meeting of the kitchen committee was quickly called.

"How much time before they get back with the warrant?" Walter said when the committee was assembled in the kitchen.

Carrie, Johnny, Joanna, Bob, Walter, and Brenda stood by the open walk-in door, looking in at the enormous, partially frozen, nude body of Big Ben Boston.

"They got to talk to their captain," Johnny said. "Talk to the DA. Talk to a judge. Maybe the captain's busy. Maybe the DA's in court. Maybe the judge is playing golf and they got to wait until he finishes eighteen. Happens more than you think. Could take half a day. Maybe more. My guess is they'll be back by dinner."

"You can't be here when they show up," Carrie said to the committee members. "I mean everyone. The police can't see you."

"That's a concern, of course, Carrie," Joanna said. "But before we worry about that, we should decide what to do with the body."

"We'll need a crane to get him out of here," Bob said.

"And a dump truck to move him," Brenda said.

"He's big as a water buffalo," Walter said.

"Or a buffalo filled with water," Joanna said, and the committee laughed.

"Mother, please," Carrie said.

"You have to laugh," Joanna said.

"Or you drown in your tears," Bob said.

"Or just drown," Brenda said, pointing at Ben Boston.

They laughed again. When they stopped, there was a lengthy discussion about the problematic prospects of hiding the massive dead man anywhere at the Copa. Or anywhere at all. But Carrie couldn't focus on the particulars because she was thinking about something one of the Ramos twins—Rowena; no, Ronda; no, Rowena; no, Ronda; no, Rowena; no, Ronda; definitely Rowena; or possibly Ronda—had said to Johnny before evaporating into the shimmering Hollywood heat. *All these old motherfuckers going to be out on the street because you shot your damn mouth while your girlfriend obstructed police business.*

The first part, the *all-these-old-motherfuckers-going-to-be-out-on-the-street* part, was concerning because the old motherfuckers weren't old anymore, yes, but mostly because the idea of them out on the street where everyone could see them would result in a paradigm shift the likes of which humanity hadn't seen since the discovery of fire.

But the second part, the *you-shot-your-damn-mouth-while-your-girlfriend-obstructed-police-business* part, was the eye-opener because, well, was it so obvious to the detectives that Carrie and Johnny were in a relationship? Did she and Johnny give off the public vibration that they were boyfriend and girlfriend? Was Johnny subconsciously telling the world she was his significant other? Was she unknowingly accepting the assignment? If so, was it obvious to everyone or only to the detectives, who were trained to see subtle signs? Did all the people in her orbit think she and Johnny were an "item," as her mother might say?

Forget the bit about *shooting her mouth* even though she'd never shot her mouth ever and was now doing it at the cops. And forget the bit about *obstructing police business*, which she was unequivocally doing in all senses of the word *obstructing*. Forget about both of those. It was the girlfriend thing that had her mind whirring like a blender.

"...not a window anywhere we could squeeze him through," Bob said.

"...put him in one of those metal POD containers and truck him to San Pedro," Walter said.

"...load him on a freighter to France," Joanna said.

Carrie had never been anyone's girlfriend. She wasn't even emotionally or intellectually convinced she was Johnny's girl-friend—*of course she wasn't*—but rolling that thought around her head gave her the warmest feelings. Her mind drifted into a hazy river of romantic visions. She saw herself with Johnny on some sailboat in Santa Barbara, sun setting into the ocean, breeze blowing through her hair, dolphins jumping beside the boat, steel drums, exotic cocktails. She was laughing and holding his hand. The images were fleeting, but the feelings stayed with her.

And then the conversation went in a direction that obliter-ated all the images and feelings in one fell swoop.

"It's a lot of meat," Brenda said.

"Four hundred pounds," Bob said.

"Cook it up, probably taste like pork," Walter said.

"Maybe like beef," Brenda said.

"Most likely chicken," Joanna said.

"Everything tastes like chicken," Bob said.

They all laughed, though it was more a thoughtful chuckle than a full-on, that-was-funny guffaw.

"Stop this conversation right now," Carrie said and looked at Johnny for support.

"That's crazy-town talk," Johnny said, taking Carrie's side.

But the kitchen committee was onto something, like sharks that smelled blood in the water.

"You'd have to butcher him," Walter said.

"Cook him up," Bob said.

"Then eat him," Brenda said.

"Eliminate the evidence in a most delicious manner," Joanna said.

"Do you hear yourselves?" Carrie said. "Do you even know what you're saying? Hello? Anybody home? You cannot butcher Ben Boston."

The committee turned to Johnny.

"Can you butcher Ben Boston?" Bob said to Johnny.

"I mean, I don't know. I, uh, well, I mean..." Johnny said.

"He's a dead, fat-ass cow," Walter said. "You ever butcher a dead fat-ass cow?"

"Lots of times," Johnny said, swallowing his voice.

"So you *could* do it," Brenda said.

"I mean, yeah, I mean, I could," Johnny said.

"But he wouldn't," Carrie said. "Nobody is butchering Ben Boston. We're not savages."

"That's fine, Carrie," Joanna said. "We'll wait for the police to return with their search warrant, and then we'll all go to jail for the murder of a parole officer. And while we're there, the world will discover the existence of the miracle drug you took from the illegal lab and administered to your mother and her friends with the assistance of your ex-convict boyfriend. Does that sound like a better option to you at this point in time?"

*Jesus Christ*, Carrie thought. *There is it again. Is there a sign on my forehead? Do they all think Johnny's my boyfriend? Am I the only one who doesn't see it?* Carrie looked at her mother, at the committee, at the dead body, at Johnny, at her mother, at the committee, at the dead body. Her voice was soft. Incredulity wrestled with horror. "Do you understand what you're talking about?"

"Talking about Ben Boston burgers," Walter said.

"What do we do with the bones, chef?" Bob said to Johnny.

Johnny looked at Carrie. Their faces filled with resignation. They'd lost the battle *and* the war. "Bake them until they're brittle, then bust them into pieces with a mallet and put them in the meat grinder until they're white powder. Then scatter them up and down Sunset Boulevard, where they'll get lost in all the rest of the white powder."

"Let's lift him onto the counter," Joanna said, gesturing toward the body.

Walter nodded, looked at Johnny. "Sharpen your knives, hombre."

# CHAPTER 34
# ONE WITH THE KNIVES AND THE MEAT

IT WOULD BE the challenge of a lifetime. A sick and twisted challenge, no doubt, but the challenge of a lifetime for a rock-star butcher like Johnny Fairfax. No butcher he'd heard of in any kitchen anywhere at any time had ever done anything remotely like butcher a Ben Boston. Johnny would be the first. And though he was reluctant to admit it and didn't want to do it, he was up for the challenge. Plus, he couldn't say no with so much on the line...not the least of which was his manhood. The last thing in the world Johnny wanted was to be called a pussy. So, yes, he would butcher the body.

Joanna recruited additional manpower to get the parole officer out of the walk-in and onto the chopping block, and soon the mammoth dead man was in position. Johnny looked at the sheer size of the bloated body and knew Walter had been right: the parole officer was somewhere between the size of a fat-ass cow and a fat-ass hog. He would need help. Someone to keep him focused. Someone to encourage him, inspire him, keep him chopping and carving and cleaving when the going got ugly. As the residents left the kitchen to fill in the others and make plans within plans, he took Carrie by the arm.

"I can't do it alone," he said. "I need you."

She looked into his eyes. "You need me?"

"I really fucking do." He held her hand in a way that he'd never held anyone's hand before.

"Then I'm really fucking here." She held his hand right back.

They could have kissed, but they didn't. Instead, Johnny lifted his twenty-two-inch butcher meat saw in one hand and his Full Tang meat cleaver bone axe in the other. He turned to the big body and stood there. He was stuck in time and space. It was true, the first cut into a human being really was the deepest, not to mention the hardest. He could feel the beginnings of nausea. Sixty frozen seconds ticked by.

"Take off your shirt," Carrie said softly.

"My shirt?"

"Take it off."

He pulled his eyes away from the parole office, looked at her, and nodded. "You and me?"

"Me and you."

She gave him her bravest and most determined smile, and it unlocked something inside him. Or rather, it unleashed something inside him. Something powerful. Something primal. Something fueled by the pounding of his heart and the fury of the life he'd lived to this moment. Something he could never deny for the rest of time.

"You were gone so long," he said, taking off his shirt and getting down to the bad business of carving up the dead man. "I thought something happened."

Something *had* happened, she said, and she told him about Sikorski coming to the lab with a gun; how he'd wanted to kill her for stealing the drug but instead got his legs crushed under the table maze; how the rats had not been fed and she'd held the clicker beside Sikorski's head; how the rats had eaten his face off; how she'd left him bloody and dead for the fixer and the cleaner.

Some smaller part of him listened to her words, nodding to the beat of her story as if Guns N' Roses *Appetite for Destruction* were blasting in his ears instead of her voice. He could hear himself making comments back to her—*then what?... no way... you're kidding?...that's crazy*—but it was an out-of-body sensation because most of him had slipped into the zone and become one with the knives and the meat.

He started with the head, removing it with the bone axe and meat cleaver. If he hadn't been racing the police, he might have taken the time to remove Ben Boston's brain, as it was considered a delicacy in some cultures. But he *was* racing the police, so the parole officer's head went straight into a large pot of boiling water.

He took off the hands and feet, then the arms and legs, sawing and cleaving and chopping through bone and tendon and muscle. Blood went everywhere. He and Carrie were covered with it. She took the body parts from him, wiped the gore from his face, caressed his sweating, tattooed chest with her hand. Her touch energized him.

She told him how she'd left the lab and gone to the Foxfire to see if Justin—her alibi bartender shill—had held his ground; how she'd discovered that not only had he given ground, he was dead, burned to a crisp in his car; how it had to have been the cleaner, who liked to play with fire and had burned rats as a boy back in Russia.

Johnny made sounds that said he was listening while he opened Ben Boston's torso, cracked through the rib cage, and cut out the organs. He knew old people liked liver—though the Copa crew wasn't actually old anymore—so he put it to the side. Everything else went into a plastic bag he would burn in a trash can before dinner.

He was magician and master craftsman. Artist and wizard. Houdini and Picasso. Gandalf and Slash. The clock was ticking, but he couldn't hear it. All he could hear was the sound of his blades cutting through tendon and ligament and bone...and Carrie telling him about the Yellow Cab Co.

What she was saying was that after the Foxfire fiasco, she'd called her Yellow Cab Co. driver, an odd man named Joe Cabot, the second leg in her alibi, to see if he'd held it together under pressure from the fixer and the cleaner; how she'd discovered that Cabot had been shot to death; how his body had been found beneath the Lankershim-Cahuenga overpass, one perfectly placed shot to the middle of his forehead; how it had to have been the fixer because the saucy Latino was perfect that way.

Johnny heard the bit about the saucy Latino, heard the heat in her voice, but let it go because the parole officer was now butchered into manageable pieces—two forearms, two biceps, two thighs, two calves, one torso. Boston's head and hands and feet were boiling in a large pot. Johnny considered making a stock from the liquid (for soup and sauces), but then thought that might be a step too far. *It's enough just to butcher the meat*, he thought. Meanwhile, the oven was pre-heating to bake the bones.

Johnny was aware Carrie was cleaning the mess as fast as he made it. She was a working whirlwind behind and all around him, bleaching and mopping and wiping and scrubbing and scouring. While she cleaned, she told him how after she'd called the cab company, she'd called the parking attendant at the lot down the street from the Foxfire, a smoky and boozy broad named Elaine; how she'd paid Elaine five hundred bucks to be the last line of alibi defense; how the line had been erased, meaning when Carrie couldn't reach Elaine, she'd called the mobile home park office and learned Elaine had been found dead in her trailer, shot twice in the chest.

Johnny understood Carrie's cover was blown to bits and that soon the fixer and the cleaner would come for the drug and for her and for all of them. He didn't think Carrie required an immediate response to this new fact of life. He thought she needed to get it off her chest. He nodded because he had things he needed to get off his chest too, though now was not the time for that because now was the time to take the meat off the bone.

He peeled back Ben Boston's skin and exposed the flesh. Carving the parole officer into smaller cuts was gritty, gruesome work. When the meat was divided into similar cuts on the counter, the bones were washed clean, sawed into pieces, and placed directly into the high-heat oven. In Johnny's mind, when the bones went in and the head, hands, and feet were at a hard rolling boil, that was the moment the butchering ended and the cooking began.

Every pot and pan in the place was in play. All the spices in the rack had a part in the performance. Johnny put much of the meat into the grinder. He'd looked at Ben Boston's driver license when they took his soaking wet wallet out of his pocket and noticed the parole officer's full name was Benjamin Charles Boston.

*Literally ground chuck,* he thought.

He crushed fresh garlic. He sautéed leeks. He grilled peppers. He chopped onions. He made sauces and rubs galore. He was everywhere at the same time, prepping and cooking and cooking and prepping. When one dish was done, he was immediately on to the next dish. There was no break. There was the food and the police and the search warrant and nothing else. He took the ground chuck and made burger patties and meatballs and meatloaf. He made sausages of all nations—andouille, Italian, Polish, and Irish. He made breakfast sausage patties with maple syrup. He left some of the ground meat loose for tacos. He made a dozen pot pies. He made Bolognese. He made trays of lasagna and moussaka. He cut some of the meat into cubes for stew. He shredded some for barbeque. He cooked the rump until it was fall apart tender and put it in the Hillbilly Chili.

He caught glimpses of Carrie working behind him and beside him, cleaning the kitchen, washing the pots as he finished with them, wrapping and labeling and freezing the food, predating the containers so the police would have nothing to hang their hats on. They were silent and in sync, doing a macabre dance of blood and bone, tendon and tissue, meat and mayhem that would have made Angela Lansbury and Len Cariou proud. It was as magic as it was tragic. Johnny felt it in his soul, and he thought Carrie felt it too.

When the last pot had been washed and dried and hung on the rack, when the last pan had been scoured and scrubbed, when the knives and spoons were spotlessly clean, when the kitchen had been polished to a gleaming sheen, Johnny took the garbage can with the organs and the skin and the blood into an alley behind the Copa, poured gasoline in the can, and set the contents on fire. It was nasty, no doubt, but then it was ashes, and he washed them down the alley sewer. Then he cleaned the garbage can with bleach and hid it among the trash cans of the neighboring buildings.

He returned to the kitchen, where Carrie was going through every inch of the room *again*, looking for any sliver of micro-scopic evidence—blood, hair, skin—any shred, scrap, strip, crumb, or fragment of what was once the parole officer, re-doubling her efforts to sanitize and sterilize the kitchen and all its accoutrement.

The bones were brittle enough to crush with a hammer. He put all the tension of the last week into each swing and smashed the ever-loving shit out of Ben Boston's baked skeletal remains. The grinder turned the pieces to powder. The blender turned the powder to bone dust. They poured the bone dust into baggies, and Johnny took them to Sunset Boulevard and scattered the dust in the hot Hollywood breeze like they were someone's ashes, which they more or less were.

When he got back from the boulevard, Carrie was cleaning the grinder and the blender *again*. When she was done, they could have been brand-new, commercial-grade gear straight out of the box.

Johnny looked at the clock for the first time in a long time. Five thirty. Six nonstop hours of kitchen madness. He looked at Carrie, and she looked at him. They were filthy, sweat-soaked, and covered with dried blood. They needed immediate showers. Their clothes had to be burned in the next breath. They were in every way exhausted.

"The hard part's done," Carrie said. "Now comes the hard part."

Johnny nodded. "Yeah. Now we have to eat him."

# CHAPTER 35
# PLENTY OF MEAT TO EAT

CARRIE WAS SETTING the tables beside the pool when Detectives Ronda and Rowena Ramos arrived with a search warrant, four uniformed police officers, and a woman Carrie didn't recognize. On the one hand, it didn't appear that the woman was with the police, though on the other hand, it kind of did.

Johnny was grilling sausages and burgers. A pot of Hillbilly Chili bubbled on the grill's gas burner. Baskets of homemade potato chips and bowls of green salad sat on the rolling cart beside the grill.

The Copa crew had not made an appearance since they'd left Johnny alone in the kitchen to butcher the parole officer seven or so hours ago. Carrie had no idea where they were or what they were doing.

These were the observable facts of the matter at six fifteen on Wednesday at the Copacabana. There was nothing about this set of circumstances that didn't make Carrie crazy with concern.

First, the police were here with a search warrant. The Ramos twins had it in for Johnny, and they didn't like Carrie. They would check every inch of the Copa for clues simply out of spite.

That in and of itself was bad news. Second, Johnny was cooking the butchered remains of the man the cops were looking for. Putting it like that, in its most simple terms, made Carrie want to vomit a little in her throat. Third, where the hell was everyone? If they showed up for dinner looking forty instead of ninety, then the game would be busted so wide open that even the fixer and the cleaner wouldn't be able to fix and clean it.

The Ramos twins and the cops came around the pool to the grill. Carrie crossed to meet them and stand with Johnny. The unidentified woman stayed behind the pack of police, taking pictures of the pool and the courtyard, poking around in a way that unsettled Carrie even more.

Ronda presented Carrie with the official paperwork. "Signed, sealed, and search, Ms. Kromer."

"Stay out of the way till we done," Rowena said.

Ronda leaned over Johnny's grill. "This what you feed old folks?"

"They like meat," Johnny said.

As if Johnny had shouted *And...action!*, the card room doors opened across the courtyard on the far side of the pool, and the Copa crew came into the light. It was all Carrie could do not to laugh and cry and gasp and shout *What in the ever-loving hell is this?*

Joanna and Arnie and Bob and Lillian and Norman and Dolores and all of them were in full wardrobe and makeup that depicted them as ancient old folks. Bernie and Brenda and Helen and Walter and Betty and all of them had somehow, maybe by voodoo, transformed themselves back to being in their nineties. They were crooked and bent and slow and unsteady. Even Bob, with his ramrod spine, look gnarled by age. They were glassy-eyed and confused and muttering to themselves. Arnie was drooling. Some were in wheelchairs, others used walkers and canes. Their hair was gray. Their skin was pale. Their clothes were sad. Their faces were sadder. It took them forever to come around the pool to the tables. Without acknowledging the police, they took their seats and waited to be served.

The detectives gave instructions to their team—first floor first, second floor second, room by room by room by room. Then they all put on latex gloves and dispersed into the building, looking for any trace of the missing parole officer. Rowena and Ronda went straight into the kitchen—no doubt, Carrie thought, making a beeline to the freezer.

When the cops were out of earshot, Carrie and Johnny served dinner. Carrie looked at her mother, who'd aged fifty years in seven hours. "What the hell, Mother?"

"You can thank Dolores, dear. She did hair and makeup in Hollywood for fifty years. She made us old again. To Dolores, the queen of disguises," Joanna said, lifting a glass of fresh-squeezed lemonade toward Bleach Blonde Dolores. All three tables followed suit, toasting the makeup artist.

Then they all dug in for dinner. After two minutes, it was clear this was not anyone's idea of normal. No, no, no. Eating human meat was far *better* than anyone's idea of normal. It was the best tasting food any of them had ever eaten. The best burgers. The best sausage. The best chili. They said it over and over. *Unbelievable flavor...so rich...so juicy...so succulent...so tender...melts in your mouth...incredibly delicious...like a dream...could eat it all day, every day.* They ate chili cheeseburgers and chili cheese sausages by the score. They put chili on their chips. They ate chili by the spoonful. They could barely talk, they were eating so hard. But they could and did moan and groan like it was fantabulous sex they were having instead of a meal made of Ben Boston.

At one point in the feeding frenzy, Walter stood up, banged the table, and said, "Best meat of my life. Listen here, Fairfax. You shot the damn moon this time."

Carrie had never seen her mother eat with such gusto, such fervor, such passion. Joanna consumed two large chili cheese-burgers, two chili cheese sausages, and two additional bowls of chili. Carrie had to remind herself that her mother, the lifelong librarian, had been a strict vegetarian...until she'd taken the drug.

Carrie ate chips and salad. She couldn't bring herself to bite into a Ben Boston burger, couldn't force a forkful of chili past her lips. She watched in horror and shock as the Copa crew, disguised as the old people they used to be, pounded down dinner like a pride of hungry lions. She saw Johnny lift a burger, but he couldn't do it either. Their eyes met. He was as shell-shocked by the whole thing as she was.

*Jesus Christ*, she thought, *they're eating Ben Boston.*

As Carrie tried to swallow the idea of it, the woman with the camera who'd come in with the police tapped her on the shoulder.

"Never saw old people eat like this before," the woman said. "New one on me. Usually they pick at it, move it around the plate, take a bite here and there. My father's eighty-eight. In a home. Eats like a bird. They all do. Flock of birds. This is a pack of hyenas. Know what I mean? It's like they're not really old."

Carrie had to blink herself back to reality. *What kind of opening statement is that?* "This group has an appetite."

"Francine Fontana." Her Nikon hung from a strap around her neck. She had a pocket pad and was taking notes.

"Carrie Kromer."

While Fontana scribbled and scrawled, Carrie looked her over. She was fifty years old or close to it. Long dyed red hair. She was a big woman. Five-ten and heavy set, with big boobs. Every ounce of her being gave off the vibe she'd been around the block more times than she cared to count.

"I'm an independent crime reporter," Fontana said. "Free-lance. Lawyers chase ambulances. I chase search warrants. Espe-cially murders and missing persons, which more times than not turn into murders. I knew Ben Boston. Piece of work. So when he went missing and the cops pulled a warrant to search this place, I asked the twins if I could tag along."

"I have nothing to say, Ms. Fontana."

"Not yet maybe. But you will. You know why?"

"I can't imagine."

"Because I know you worked at Sikorski's lab."

Carrie was silent. She could feel brain cells imploding and exploding inside her head.

"I'm sitting in a bar next to this crackpot who looks like a Hollywood mad scientist," Fontana said. "He throws down two, three, maybe four Jack Daniel's and Coke and tells me he's celebrating. I tell him happy birthday, and he tells me no, he's a pharmaceutical engineer and he's celebrating a new drug. A wonder drug. That's what he's celebrating. A wonder drug he invented. He won't tell me what it does, but he tells me he knows it works because it worked on the rats. He tells me the woman who runs the rats can scientifically confirm the drug works. He tells me the scientist rat woman knows for a fact the wonder drug works and can prove it. The scientist rat woman's name is...let's see...oh yeah, Carrie Kromer. Which is, coincidentally, your name."

"Is there a problem here?" Johnny said, standing beside Carrie in a protective way.

"Tell your two-time ex-con boyfriend to back off," Fontana said.

*Oh my God*, Carrie thought. *Is there anyone in the world who doesn't think he's my boyfriend?*

"That's right, Fairfax. I did my homework. You got means and motive written all over your face. Big Ben had it in for you, so you got rid of him," Fontana said. "Maybe the twins find something, maybe they don't. But we both know you did it. Don't we, Carrie? I'm calling you Carrie because we're going to be besties these next days, weeks, and months. You can call me Fran. The truth is, you're my Pulitzer. You and Sikorski and the wonder drug that works on rats. You're on my speed dial, girlfriend."

Then she followed the twins into the kitchen.

When every last morsel of meat was gone, Carrie and Johnny

served brownies with homemade vanilla bean ice cream and chocolate sauce for dessert. The Copa crew drank several gallons of high-octane coffee to wash down the sugar. Immensely satisfied, they sat around the tables, talking softly, staying more or less in old-folks character as the cops went room to room. The men smoked cigars and drank brandy. So did the women. They were the most eccentric band of nonagenarians remade as Gen Xers disguised as nonagenarians on the face of the Earth. Then again, they were the only band of nonagenarians remade as Gen Xers disguised as nonagenarians on the face of the Earth.

Carrie cleared the tables and realized she wanted a cigar and a brandy. She'd never smoked a cigar or drunk a brandy. She knew it was wildly out of character, but she also knew her character was changing and more changes were coming as these agitated circumstances settled themselves. What the changes might be, how her new character would reveal itself, she couldn't imagine. But one thing was now clear to her, and she said it to herself: *I'm not a good person anymore.* Except she said it just loud enough for Johnny to hear.

"You are to me," he said.

She was at the rolling cart. He was at the grill. The Copa crew were behind them. The Ramos twins and the police were crawling around the building. But for Carrie, at this moment, there were only two people in the universe.

"You mean it?" she said.

He took a step toward her, like in the movies where the hero wraps the heroine in his arms and kisses the daylights out of her, but before he could do any of that, the uniformed officers arrived back in the courtyard.

They stood nearby, talked softly, removed their gloves. It was clear from their facial expressions and body language they'd found nothing incriminating, no miniscule minutia that pointed to foul play involving the parole officer. The detectives met them a few minutes later. They spoke quietly. Carrie could see the twins had found less than the officers. Their disappointment was exceeded only by their frustration.

To her surprised, Carrie enjoyed a moment of pride at her ability to cover the tracks of their collective crime—a wave of satisfaction at the detectives' expense. She was stunned she could be proud of something like obstruction of justice or someone else's exasperation. *I'm a long way from the girl I was in New Brunswick.*

The four police officers headed for the front entrance, done for the day. Ronda and Rowena walked over to Carrie and Johnny by the grill. Fontana stopped halfway between the two. The Copa crew smoked cigars, drank brandy, and took in the show.

"You on our shit list, Fairfax," Rowena said to Johnny.

"We be on your ass every damn day," Ronda said.

"We moving our office right into this rat hole," Rowena said.

"Make this chump dump Hell on Earth," Ronda said.

"You grilled your last burger," Rowena said.

"What's that they say, Tattoo Boy?" Lillian called out like an old, deaf woman. "They want you to grill them a burger?"

Laughter at the tables. Wise-guy snickering that sounded odd coming from ninety-year-olds.

"Great idea," Norman said. "Make it a double, with chili and cheese."

More laughter, less reserved this time.

"Better yet, Mr. Fairfax," Joanna said, "give them the recipe so they can make some at home."

The laughter dam broke wide open. Carrie was horrified by their smart-mouthed humor, stupefied by her mother's misbehavior. But she also realized no one in their right mind, not the Ramos twins or anyone anywhere, would ever dream of making any kind of connection between the burgers and Ben Boston. There was no line to draw between the two. It would be like finding a link between a shoelace and a rhinoceros. There was simply no computation to make. No *there* there.

"Do what you have to do," Carrie said to the twins. "Johnny has nothing to hide."

"But plenty of meat to eat," Arnold said.

Again, the old folks cracked up like unruly grade-school kids pulling the wool over a substitute teacher's eyes.

The detectives glared at the group and marched away. Francine Fontana caught Carrie's attention, made the universal hand gesture for a phone at her ear, and said, "Call me." Then she blew Carrie a kiss across the courtyard and vacated the premises with the twins.

A minute went by. No one spoke or moved.

And then Bob stood up and applauded, not as a beaten-down, weary old man, not as a bewildered and befuddled shoe salesman, but as a badass miracle of science. "Well done. Well done, Carrie and Johnny."

Everyone stood and clapped their hands. *Bravo*, they said. *Huzzah*, they said. *Hooray*, they said.

The heartfelt ovation took Carrie's breath away. She and Johnny shared a beautiful smile. She wanted to reach for his hand but realized there was still business to take care of. She took the plastic container of capsules from her pocket. Based on her estimates with regard to the schedule and strength of the doses the Greek Gods had taken, she said, it was time for the second human dose.

It had occurred to her any discussion as to whether or not they wanted to continue with this course of medication was unnecessary and absurd. She reminded them that with the rats, it had taken what she figured was the equivalent of three human doses to lock in the reverse-aging effects and said again she didn't know for a fact how many doses it would take for humans, though by her best reckoning, she imagined it couldn't be less than the number of doses she'd stolen.

"How many is that, dear?" Helen said.

"Three," Carrie said.

Joanna poured herself another brandy, held the snifter in one hand and the capsule in the other. "To the second time around."

They held their snifters in one hand and their pills in the other. "The second time around."

Then they took the drug with brandy and celebrated their resurrected youth, Ben Boston a scrumptious bump in the road behind them.

# EROS

GOD OF SEXUAL DESIRE (AMONG OTHER THINGS)

# CHAPTER 36
# SHIT THAT WOULD MAKE EVEN RAY BRADBURY'S HEAD BLOW UP

JOHNNY AND JOANNA were in the kitchen. It was Monday morning, eight a.m. Carrie had left for the lab at seven forty-five to care for the rats. The Copa crew were busy with the business of being medicinal marvels, which this morning had meant taking the passenger van to Griffith Park at sunrise for a Mount Hollywood half marathon. No matter that none of them had ever run a half marathon. They'd awoken with reams of aggressive energy, hungry for brute physicality, and met by the pool before sunrise and decided to just do it.

*They could be Nike poster people,* Johnny had thought as the van pulled away, *if they weren't pharmaceutical freaks of nature.*

Joanna had stayed because it was eight a.m. Monday morning, and eight a.m. Monday morning was when she met with the cook and organized the week's menu and shopping list. The Copa crew would be back for a late breakfast, so she had time to meet with Johnny and, as she'd said to him as she'd waved goodbye to the van, *talk things through and reflect.*

Johnny had never been one for talking things through, never reflected on a single damn thing he'd done. He'd lived his life in the fast lane—except for the years in prison, of course. And the thing about living his crashing smashing life at Harley Davidson speed was that he'd never had time to think about the bad shit behind him because he was already freewheeling head-first-forward into the bad shit ahead.

But now, *now*...there was no way to keep going without looking back. This wasn't bad shit or weird shit or crazy shit. This was ungodly shit. This was paranormal shit. This was shit that would make even Ray Bradbury's head blow up.

Which was why Johnny said, "Yeah, sure, I'll talk it through and reflect. Where do you want to start? Killing Ben Boston, butchering Ben Boston, or eating Ben Boston? Or maybe we could start with the fact that you're almost ninety, except now you're forty-two. Or how about the fixer, or the cleaner, or *The Matrix* twin detectives? Or we could start with the super rats Carrie brought home from the lab. You pick."

"Very good. I pick love," Joanna said.

They were standing on either side of the counter, Joanna's big binder of menus and shopping spreadsheets between them, recipe cards and food magazines scattered around.

"Love?" Johnny said. Of all the topics to consider from the past week of insanity, this was the last one he'd expected. And to discuss it with Carrie's mother? He had never discussed love with anybody's mother, including his own.

"Yes, Mr. Fairfax. Love," Joanna said. "Do you know what it is?"

"Do I know what love is?"

"Do you?"

"Yeah, I know what it is. Everybody knows what it is."

"What is it?"

"What is it?"

"That's what I'm asking?"

"Yeah, so, okay, good. So, love, yeah. Love is, well, what it is —I mean, what love is, is love is love, yeah, that's what it is. I mean, love is when two people love each other, when two people are in love. That's what love is." Johnny hoped his answer would be enough to change the conversation but knew it wouldn't come close.

"A generally accepted definition is that love is an intense feeling of deep and overwhelming affection based on any and all of kinship, personal ties, admiration, common interests, or sexual desire and attachment to someone," Joanna said. "Or, quite possibly, it's simply nature's way of tricking people into reproducing. That last bit is a joke, Mr. Fairfax. You really do need to lighten up."

Johnny made himself smile at Joanna's joke, despite not feeling especially jovial. Throughout his life, he'd often thought love was a bullshit ideal that people lied about to get something or to get out of something. This past week, however, he'd been forced to revisit that thought, and the whole revisiting-his-thought thing had left him wondering what the hell had happened to him in the first place since he had never been a revisit-his-thoughts kind of guy—not in prison, not out of prison, not ever.

"That's what I meant," he said.

"The reason I'd like to talk this through is because I believe you have fallen in love with my daughter," Joanna said. "I believe this happened over the last week, and I'd like to reflect on the events that brought you together in order to establish whether the feelings are real or fleeting, since I also believe this is your first time in love, and it's likely you don't understand what you're feeling, taking into account you are who you are. She's my daughter, after all, and I don't want her to get hurt. Although, I must confess, Mr. Fairfax, to my surprise, she seems rather smitten with you as well. So, do you love my daughter?"

"What?" Johnny said, aware he hadn't said *No, I don't*.

"Do you love my daughter?"

"I mean, I don't, I never, I can't, I mean—"

"Consider me your guide to the moon and back," Joanna said. "The answer is: Oh my stars, yes. You are most certainly in love with my daughter."

"You can't tell like that. No freaking way. How can you tell?" Johnny said, knowing he was feeling something he'd never felt before but couldn't define it as love because that was a feeling he'd never felt before.

"There's a flashing neon sign on your forehead you can see from the San Diego Bay," Joanna said.

"Prove it," Johnny said. No way could Joanna see he was in love with Carrie just by the look on his face.

"Fine. You must answer two questions without thinking," Joanna said. "I imagine that will come naturally for you."

"Two questions, no thinking, no problem," Johnny said.

"Would you do anything to protect her?"

"Yes."

"Can you imagine spending the rest of time by her side?"

"Yes."

"There you have it. Proof positive."

"It can't be that simple."

"It's the most complicated thing in the world until it isn't."

"It's only been a week. It can't happen that fast."

"It is the slowest thing in the world until it becomes the blink of an eye," Joanna said. "Look in your heart, Mr. Fairfax. Venture deep into its hallways. The truth is waiting for you to find it."

The truth was Johnny had not looked into his own heart in, well, he'd *never* looked into his own heart. But he did now, and what he found there, the depth of the emotionality in his very own heart inside his very own self, left him thunderstruck. He was sweating. His heart pounded. His head spun.

"Jesus Christ," he said. "It's like a fucking pipe bomb going off in my chest."

"Have you seen a pipe bomb go off?" Joanna said.

"When I was fifteen. I robbed a convenience store in the middle of the night with an army vet who'd done five tours in Afghanistan and had PTSD that wouldn't quit. He was the one who robbed it. I was just a kid looking for action, along for the ride. Anyway, he'd made a pipe bomb and blew the store to shit when we ran for it. The explosion hit the gas pumps out front, and they went up like a world war, flames fifty feet in the air. So, yeah, that's what's going on in my chest."

"That, Mr. Fairfax, is the most unusual, certainly, but also the most accurate definition of love I've heard in quite some time."

They were quiet for a moment, Johnny shuffling papers on the counter between them.

"Now what?" he said.

"Now you talk about your feelings so you can understand them, so you can tell my daughter what's in your heart without mentioning grand theft and pipe bombs, which in and of itself is a fascinating encapsulation of love. Grand theft and pipe bombs."

"Fascinating, indeed. Although there are several aspects of this conversation I find even more compelling." Eduardo Wolf stood just inside the kitchen door, holding his Glock 19 while applauding them.

"Eduardo fucking Wolf," Johnny said with hatred. He could feel the fixer's forearm on his throat. He instinctively made a fist, thought about reaching for a knife.

"Several aspects," Joanna said, "means you've been listening a good long while."

"Good and long enough to learn the half-wit cook is experiencing either an infantile infatuation or a violent video game attraction for Carrie Kromer, who stole an experimental drug from an illicit lab funded by my client, who would like their pharmaceutical property returned and all evidence of its existence erased from reality,"

Eduardo moved toward them. He wore a gray suit, blue dress shirt, and no tie. Skintight, black leather gloves.

"Good and long enough to learn you are Carrie's mother, a remarkable occurrence given you appear to be in your early forties—"

"Forty-two," Joanna said.

"—and your daughter is thirty-five. So the solitary conclusion is that Carrie gave the drug to you because, and I do not say this lightly, it works. Though it doesn't simply work. It works wonders."

Eduardo stopped in front of Joanna. Johnny reached across the counter, intending to throttle the fixer, but Eduardo leveled his gun at Johnny's chest, and he froze.

"If you kill Mr. Fairfax, my daughter will disappear with the capsules, and you'll face your client emptyhanded, an important piece of evidence left unfixed by you."

Eduardo laughed. "I believe you are correct about your daughter, and so business before pleasure—pleasure, in this case, defined as permanently eliminating living evidence." He took a phone from his pocket and placed it on the counter. "Where is she?"

"I don't know," Joanna said.

"Even if I did, I wouldn't tell you shit," Johnny said. The fixer's gun was still pointed at him, so there was nothing he could do but be belligerent, a talent he possessed in spades.

"These are your answers?" Eduardo said.

Johnny and Joanna traded glances and said nothing.

"I am disappointed." Eduardo put his hand around Joanna's throat and squeezed. Harder and harder. Tighter and tighter. Joanna instinctively put her hands on Eduardo's arm, but he was too strong for her. He held her up and in place while he choked the life out of her, Glock still pointed at Johnny.

"Perhaps you should change your mind, Johnny. Joanna will suffocate in a moment, and it will be your fault," Eduardo said. "You will have to explain that to Carrie, of course. Something along the lines of *If only I'd told him where you were, she would be alive right now. Instead, I said nothing, and now she's dead.* I'm sure she will understand."

Johnny waited three defiant seconds and then broke. "She's at the lab."

Eduardo released Joanna. She gasped air into her lungs. The fixer brushed her hair back from her face, lifted the phone off the counter, found the number for Alsiko, and handed the phone to Joanna. "Call her. Ask her where she's hidden the capsules."

Joanna made the call. Eduardo never took his eyes off her—or his Glock off Johnny.

"Carrie, it's your mother. I'm with Mr. Fairfax and Eduardo Wolf. Yes, I'm catching my breath. I'm fine. Mr. Wolf insists on knowing where the capsules are. I believe he's going to shoot Mr. Fairfax if you don't tell him what he wants to know. Yes, I see." She pulled the phone from her ear and said, "They're in her purse."

"Tell her we're on our way—you, me, and Johnny," Eduardo said. "Tell her to wait for us. Tell her I will trade your lives for the capsules. Tell her if she's not in the lab when we arrive, I will kill you both. Tell her you will die exceptionally cruel InSinkErator deaths. She'll understand."

Joanna relayed the message and clicked off the call. "She'll wait."

Eduardo smiled. "Excellent. You can convince her I'm an infinitely higher-class catch than this moron, ex-con cook."

"My daughter would never fall for you. Physically, emotionally, intellectually. In any way real or imagined," Joanna said, regaining her composure and using her strongest librarian voice.

"And you believe this lifelong loser, who has never done anything right, you believe she would give her heart to someone like him?" Eduardo put the Glock on the counter, took a zip tie from his pocket, secured Joanna's wrists.

Johnny peripherally heard the conversation about his own ineptitude versus Eduardo's Rudy Valentino proficiencies but couldn't entirely focus because he was thinking about the fixer's gun on the counter. Yes, the counter was wide, and the Glock was beside Eduardo, but Johnny believed he could get to it before the fixer.

*He's right*, Johnny thought. *I've never done one fucking thing right in my entire life. But that's about to change. This is the moment I've been waiting for. The moment every fucked-up fuckup has been leading me to. It's all been about this fixer asshole and his fucking gun. All I have to do is grab it and shoot him. That's it. Save Joanna, save Carrie, save everyone. If I do that, everything turns around. All the mistakes, all the bullshit will be behind me, and all the good shit will be straight ahead. I'll have a clean slate, a new life. This day is the day I start over, and that's all I ever wanted, a second fucking chance to be the man I should be. This is it. I know it. I can feel it. This. Is. It.*

He lunged for the gun, stretching out across the counter, eyes focused on the Glock, arms reaching ... but with the reflexes of a wild cat and the calm of a hurricane's eye, Eduardo lifted the gun before Johnny could grab it.

Johnny belly-flopped hard, face-planting on the counter, busting up his nose, which spurted a stream of blood from both nostrils on impact.

With Johnny's chest still flat on the counter, Eduardo placed the barrel of the gun on Johnny's forehead and said to Joanna, "My point personified."

Without moving his head, Johnny looked up at Eduardo, then over at Joanna, his nose spilling blood all over the place. *Not it,* he thought, heart sinking for the countless time in his rash and reckless life. *Not. Fucking. It.*

# CHAPTER 37

# FROM RUNAWAY TRAIN TO HELL IN A HANDBASKET

CARRIE CONCLUDED the call with her mother and thought, *I have made a major mess.* Sikorski was still dead on the lab floor, his bloody face eaten away by the Greek Gods, his lifeless body crushed beneath the weight of the table maze, his empty eyes open, looking far into the rich-and-famous future that should have been his. She was surprised the fixer or the cleaner had not made his gruesome remains disappear by now, but she wasn't focused on the mess that used to be Sikorski. She was instead thinking about the mess that was Johnny and her mother in Eduardo's car on their way to the lab.

She had to wait for them to arrive. Had to. Her mother's life hung in the balance. Johnny's life too. If Eduardo hurt either of them, she would never live it down. She thought of her mother in Eduardo's car, and her stomach turned. She thought of Johnny in Eduardo's car, and her heart ached. She thought of Eduardo and his Glock 19, and the back of her neck got hot.

*Stop it*, she thought. *Now is not the time to think about making love to a spicy Latin man in the back seat of his rental car while he's holding a gun. Stop thinking about that right now.*

Instinct told her the drug wouldn't be an adequate trading chip. The fixer would take the capsules and kill all three of them without blinking. She needed more. She needed Sikorski's personal notes.

*Click, click, click, click, click...*

Francine Fontana stood fifteen feet across the lab, camera in hand, photographing the macabre scene like the freelance crime reporter she was, getting shot after shot of Sikorski and Carrie and the wall of rats behind them.

"Where do I start?" Francine said, moving around the lab, catching creepy closeups and offbeat angles of the death scene. "*Times*? *Weekly*? *Metro*? *CityBeat*? *Daily News*? How about the *Daily Journal*? Turn the lawyers loose. Or maybe go national with *True Crime*. Sell the rights to Warner Brothers. Or HBO for one of those eight-part specials. Or go network and make it a Movie of the Week. Do I shoot for prime time or late night cable? Partner up with Jane, my screenwriter friend, and let her write a movie that will make us millions? The problem I have covering a murder with wonder drugs, test-tube rats, and cryptic characters is there are so many media outlets in LA, so many publications, every last one looking for a page-one stunner, that I don't know where to start. And the story...that's a whole other can of what-the-hell-do-I-do-first-next-or-ever. Do I start with the dead drug scientist on the floor with his face eaten off or the laboratory rat girl standing over his body with the guilty look on her face? Tell me, Carrie. Where do I start?"

As a matter of reflex, Carrie concluded she needed a new equation to survive the unexpected weather. Meaning Francine Fontana was a force of unpleasant nature. There would be no stopping her. No distracting her. No bribe big enough to turn back her distasteful tide. There was nothing she could do to protect herself, her mother, Johnny, or her Copa family. Francine would tell their ghoulish story to the world and they would all suffer the consequences from now to infinity. There was nothing Carrie could do. And then there was.

As soon as the thought crossed her mind, she knew it would change the speed of her moral decline from runaway train to hell in a handbasket. Because the only way to stop Francine Fontana was to kill Francine Fontana.

But that wasn't the thought that had Carrie's ethical degradation spiraling downward toward the devil. Sure, she'd tagged Old Tom and stolen the capsules; had her hands on Ben Boston when he'd gone into the pool; cleaned the carnage in the kitchen after Johnny had butchered his parole officer into recipe-ready cuts of meat; and held the clicker beside Leo Sikorski's face to call the Greek Gods to breakfast. Yes, no doubt, that had all happened.

But she could make the argument she hadn't hurt Old Tom too badly—*Sorry, Old Tom*—and the capsules had gone to good use at the Copa. And she could also make the argument other people had pushed Ben Boston into the deep water too. She could further make the argument Johnny had done the butchering while she had simply tidied up the room. She could even make the argument she'd not known for sure what the rats would do when they heard the clicker and saw Sikorski. Except for Old Tom, in each instance, there was a narrow case to make that she was an unlucky bystander when the crimes were committed. But there was no such case to be made for what Carrie was contemplating now, which was personally and intentionally—with unequivocal premeditation—to write, sign, seal, and deliver Francine's death warrant.

She simply could not allow the freelance crime reporter to memorialize her and her mother and Johnny and the Copa crew —freeze them forever in the pages of *True Crime*—as some kind of murderous, cannibalistic, freak-show circus. If she had made a major mess up until this moment, she would not make even *more* of a major mess for the rest of time.

Her one way out was to tell Francine everything—or nearly almost everything—and tag her as evidence to be eliminated by Eduardo Wolf, who was due to arrive at the lab any minute. She knew the underpinnings of her soul—honor, honesty, integrity, intelligence, and decency—were on the line and that one tiny tap, such as sentencing Francine to death, would send her head-first into the Abyss of Lost Souls for forever and a day.

*But so be it*, she thought.

"At the beginning, Francine," she said. "You start at the beginning."

It was a longer story than Carrie had realized, with many moving parts and quirky characters, and Eduardo Wolf was on his way, and she wanted Francine to hear every last bit, so she didn't linger or embellish or elaborate. Instead, she told Francine to hold all questions until the end, which made Carrie smile to herself because the end *for* Francine would be the end *of* Francine.

The crime reporter recorded the entire telling of the tale on her phone. And though she uttered not one word, her face said everything her voice didn't—the story, no, the *saga*, was as unbelievable as it was disarming. As preposterous as it was engaging. As outrageous as it was revolutionary. Like discovering the cure for cancer on one side of the street and finding a tree that grew thousand-dollar bills on the other side.

When Carrie reached the end of the story, which was Francine standing in the lab listening to the end of the story, she said, "And I realized it wouldn't be enough to trade the capsules for my mother's life, for Johnny's life, for my life. I realized I needed Sikorski's notes to close the deal with the fixer."

"You could manufacture the drug in another lab," Francine said.

"No one would know," Carrie said.

"You'd make millions."

"Billions."

"Not to mention the Pulitzer I'd win."

"Not to mention," Carrie said and heard footsteps coming down the hall.

She didn't know if Francine heard them. She didn't think so because the crime reporter was imagining aloud her life as the celebrated journalist who'd told the story of the miracle medication and then sold it to the world at barely discounted prices, becoming even richer than J.K. Rowling. Francine was so busy being famous in her own future, talking about the Hollywood Hills home she'd purchase with the drug proceeds, that Carrie could tell she didn't hear the Lab No. 3 door opening.

*Here they come,* Carrie thought. *My mother, Johnny, and the fixer.*

The door opened. Francine stopped talking and turned to see who it was.

*No Pulitzer Prize in your future, Francine.*

Except it wasn't her mother and Johnny. And it wasn't the fixer. It was the cleaner. Faded blue jeans, blue Nikes, blue T-shirt, blue baseball hat, dark sunglasses, Sig Sauer pistol with 9mm silencer. Looking, Carrie thought, like some LA hitman from a network TV series set in Southern California.

Tino seemed surprised to see someone other than Carrie in the lab. But he seemed more surprised to see Francine than he was to see Sikorski crushed under the table maze with his face chewed to shit.

The three of them stared at each other. But soon Carrie realized neither Tino nor Francine were staring at her. Soon Carrie realized they were staring at each other. Although, *staring* did not seem nearly a strong enough word for what was happening between them. They were fixated on each other. Although, *fixated* wasn't the right word either. They were infatuated with each other. Check that, *infatuated* didn't define it. *Captivated, enamored,* and *enraptured* were all words Carrie considered and rejected with the others because none of them, either individually or collectively, seemed nearly strong enough for what was happening between Tino and Francine.

What was happening between the fixer and the crime reporter, what had happened instantaneously, like a gasoline explosion that obliterates the block, was unbridled-unadulter-ated-unrestrained-uncontrolled-uninhibited animal lust. Tino and Francine weren't just attracted to each other; they were fully fucking each other with the expressions on their faces and the language of their bodies. Being in the same room with them while this was going on made Carrie nauseous. If it weren't for the cleaner's Sig, she might have left the lab to find a toilet to puke in.

"Are you going to introduce me to your sexy friend, Carrie baby," Tino said, taking the last of Francine's clothes off with his eyes, "or am I chopped liver?"

"More like Russian caviar," Francine said, her voice dripping with the promise of lewd love making.

*So gross*, Carrie thought. "Tino, meet Francine, a freelance crime reporter covering the story of the missing capsules. Francine, meet Tino, the cleaner sent to make the mess disappear. Did I mention she knows the whole story and that makes her evidence?"

"That make her hotter than one minute ago," Tino said.

"Someone sent you to find the capsules Carrie stole and clean this all up?" Francine said, gesturing around the lab and down at Sikorski.

"Take big man to do big job," Tino said, practically grabbing his junk.

"How big?" Francine said, practically rubbing her nipples.

*If they don't stop, I'm going to hurl*, Carrie thought.

"There is couch in Sikorski office," Tino said, practically unzipping his fly. "Maybe need to find out now."

"There's something else in Sikorski's office we need to find first," Francine said. "Sikorski's notes. I'm coming over there to introduce myself. Don't shoot me."

She crossed the lab floor and whispered in Tino's ear. Then Tino whispered in her ear. Then back and forth again. They whispered and laughed and laughed and whispered. Their bodies were very close. He had his arm around her, his hand on her ass. They breathed on each other's necks. Their lips were as near as they could be to touching without touching. Carrie couldn't hear a word, but she could see the sign, which flashed *Bad News—Bad News—Bad News—Bad News*.

Just as Carrie could feel the barf in her throat, Tino turned to her and pointed the Sig at her face. "Where Sikorski notes, Carrie baby? Answer like life depend on it because life depend on it."

"I don't know," Carrie said.

"What about his office?" Francine said. "Locked cabinet? Secret safe?"

*Two against one, and I'm the one.* "No. I looked."

"Why should I believe?" Tino said.

"Because if I lie, you'll kill me," Carrie said. "If I tell the truth, you won't kill me because you'll still need me to tell you if those notes are the real notes when you find the notes. So the reasonable deduction is that I'll tell you the truth."

"She's right," Francine said. "We need her for the time being."

*Fuck you for the time being.* "Maybe he hid them in his house," Carrie said. "That's the next logical location."

"Where Sikorski live?" Tino said.

"I don't know. Ask him," Carrie said, pointing at the late Sikorski.

Tino and Francine looked at the dead scientist, then back at Carrie.

"His wallet," Carrie said. "Jesus, Francine, aren't you a crime reporter?"

Francine made a face that said *You're the one on the wrong side of the gun, girlfriend,* and they all moved the table maze off the grotesque Sikorski corpse, flipped it (what-was-left-of-his) face-down on the lab floor, and took the scientist's wallet and keys out of his pockets.

Francine removed Sikorski's license, read the address, and turned to Tino. "7800 block on Owensmouth in Canoga Park. Fifteen minutes from here if we catch the lights."

"You drive, Carrie baby," Tino said, waving the Sig at her face. "Francine and Tino talk business in back seat."

Carrie remembered what Eduardo Wolf had said about her

not being in the lab when he arrived with Joanna and Johnny. *They will die exceptionally cruel InSinkErator deaths.* "I can't leave."

Tino put the barrel of the Sig on Carrie's forehead. "Don't be stick in mud." He winked at Francine. "If you catch my sexy drift. Stick in mud."

Francine caught his drift and then some. They shared a lewd look.

*So gross,* Carrie said to herself while thinking she was dead when she got to Sikorski's house and when they got to the lab, her mother and Johnny were dead too.

# CHAPTER 38

# YO FUTURE IS FUCKED

JOHNNY DROVE Eduardo Wolf's lap-of-luxury Lincoln Continental to Reseda. The fixer sat in the back, behind Joanna, holding the Glock to her head. By any measure, their immediate circumstances were dire. Yet Johnny wasn't thinking about their immediate circumstances. Not directly. He *was* thinking about them indirectly because he was directly thinking about the first time he'd been to prison and had the distinct honor of meeting a man known throughout the California penal system as the White Zulu.

Matthias Monroe. A Black man from the notorious LA neighborhood known as Watts who claimed he was descended from a long line of Zulu kings. Not surprisingly, everyone called him Zulu. What was striking about Zulu was that he'd been born albino. Stark white. Not white the way white people were white. Much whiter than that. Not even white the way Johnny and Edgar Winter were white. No, much whiter than that too. Zulu was white the way white paint was white. Bright white. Dazzling white. A shocking white Black man.

When he was nineteen, Zulu had murdered three people in cold blood—his girlfriend and the couple she'd been cheating on him with. The albino had followed them to a mobile home in

Anaheim, found them in bed together, and blown them into bloody pieces with a shotgun. He'd been sentenced to life without parole. In prison, Zulu had taken up the art of palmistry and become famous for reading the futures of fellow inmates.

Johnny had arrived at Zulu's table in the prison yard when the fortune teller was sixty-nine years old. By then, he'd read the palms and foretold the futures of thousands of inmates, many of whom had sworn by the accuracy of the albino's predictions and prophecies, which were as legendary as Zulu himself.

*You will open a convenience store on Chandler Boulevard in Burbank, where you will be robbed five times. The fifth time, you will be shot in the neck.*

*You will have three children, one of whom you will name Brandon. That child will be a girl who will hate you forever.*

*In a past life, you were once a woman named Nancy Reagan, though not that Nancy Reagan, so you developed migraines from explaining year after year that no, no, no, no, no, you were not that Nancy Reagan. Eventually the migraines drove you insane, and you died in a mental hospital and were reborn a criminal. Sadly, this will happen to you again.*

The albino's readings had been long and dramatic. Never less than an hour. Usually two. All the inmates in the yard would crowd around Zulu's table to hear him opine upon the past, present, and future lives of whoever's palm he was reading. It had been like going to the movies or to a Broadway show right there in the prison yard. Must-See TV—except much of what he foretold somehow came to pass. So when it had been Johnny's turn for a reading, the crowd stood three deep, and the buzz in the yard was *This should be epic.*

Johnny had placed his hands palm up on Zulu's table. The albino had taken Johnny's hands and looked deep into the lines on his palms. The crowd was silent. The show was about to start. Everyone had settled in for a marathon, especially Johnny.

Finally, Zulu had exhaled, looked around the circle of inmates, and then into Johnny's eyes. *Yo past and present don't mean shit, Fairfax, because yo future is fucked,* he'd said. And then he'd gotten up and walked away as the crowd parted.

*What?* Johnny had called after him, stunned by the impossible brevity of the reading.

*Yo future is fucked, Fairfax,* the albino had said without turning around.

Which was why Johnny was indirectly thinking of their dire circumstances. The albino had been spot on. Fast forward to the present. His future was indeed fucked.

"...of course, I did not enjoy being choked half to death," Joanna said, "but at the same time, there's something exhilarating about being held hostage. Being in the middle of a deadly drama.         Murderous-international-pharmaceutical-criminal intrigue is something lifelong librarians such as myself can only read about in the espionage novels that fill our stacks. A librarian *actually* living this kind of adventure is profoundly improbable—there exists an ever-growing mountain of books to shelve, papers to organize, and subjects to research, after all. But you'd have to agree, wouldn't you, Mr. Wolf, that improbable has been redefined, that the line between fiction and non-fiction, between fantasy and reality, has been blurred, if not erased? These are exciting times for librarians, no doubt."

"Turn here," the fixer said to Johnny.

Johnny pulled the Lincoln into the Alsiko side parking lot, found an empty spot—there were plenty now that the lab was shuttered—and killed the engine. Eduardo had disabled the security system during an earlier visit (when he'd introduced Stuart Langston to a game called *Fun With The InSinkErator*), so they got out of the car, went into the building, and up to the lab without issue, although having a loaded Glock at their backs might have been a bit of an issue for Joanna and Johnny.

They went straight to Lab No. 3, Carrie's rat lab, where they found Sikorski's dead body on the floor.

"Who's this?" Joanna pointed down at Sikorski's back.

"This is the late Dr. Leo Sikorski," Eduardo said, turning the body over with his foot.

They recoiled at seeing Sikorski's face eaten to the bone, but there was no time to discuss the lifeless mess that had once been the pharmaceutical genius who put the Fountain of Youth in a capsule. Eduardo ordered them out of Lab No. 3, and they went through Alsiko, room by room, looking for Carrie. She was nowhere to be found. There was one lab left. Sikorski's production lab. Lab No. 1. They opened the door from the hallway and stepped into the room.

"Police. Freeze, motherfucker," Ronda said.

"Don't know who the fuck you are, Ricardo Montalbán," Rowena said.

"But drop that motherfucking gun right now," Ronda said.

The twins were across the room. Weapons drawn and pointed toward Johnny, Joanna, and Eduardo. Badges easy to see on their belts. Dressed identically. Double trouble.

Eduardo didn't flinch. And he didn't drop his Glock. "Officers, welcome to Alsiko. I don't believe I've had the pleasure."

"Detective Ronda Ramos," Ronda said.

"Detective Rowena Ramos," Rowena said.

"Now drop the damn gun," Ronda said.

"And move away from Fairfax," Rowena said.

"Who's about to be arrested for the murder of whoever the fuck that is in the other room without his motherfucking face," Ronda said.

"Not to mention the murder of Ben Boston," Rowena said.

"Who came to the Copa to cancel this asshole's parole," Ronda said.

"But disappeared off the fucking face of the Earth instead," Rowena said.

"Delicious man, Mr. Boston," Joanna said, winking at Johnny.

"I didn't kill that faceless fucker, and I didn't kill Ben Boston," Johnny said.

"You in violation of your parole, either way," Rowena said.

"The rest you best believe we going to make stick," Ronda said.

Johnny was trapped. Eduardo was behind him, planning to kill him (and Joanna and Carrie). The detectives were in front of him, planning to send him back to prison. He looked around the room for a way out. The perimeter of the large lab was all counters and cabinets and rolling metal shelves filled with pharmaceutical laboratory gear that looked a lot like *Star Trek* to Johnny. The windows had been blacked out so the world wouldn't know what Leo Sikorski was doing up here.

Four wide worktables stood in the middle of the room between them and the twins, each one covered with test tubes and glass containers and more electronic pharmaceutical equipment.

Near the detectives, one corner contained dozens of gas cylinders, a heady cocktail of ammonia, hydrocarbon chloride, nitrous oxide, sulfur dioxide, methane, acetylene, propane, butane, hydrogen, helium, and other hydrocarbon and elemental industrial gases used by manufacturers in oil and gas, petrochemicals, power, mining, metals, medicine, biotechnology, nuclear power, and pharmaceutical research, development, and production.

"I have decided not to surrender my weapon," Eduardo said, putting the barrel of the Glock on the back of Johnny's head. "Instead, I've decided *you* will surrender *your* weapons."

"Is that right, asshole? Because I've decided you drop that fucking gun or we start shooting," Ronda said.

"Going to get loud and proud in this motherfucker in one more minute," Rowena said.

"Be that as it may, it is unwise to the point of foolish to discharge firearms in such close proximity to industrial gases," Eduardo said, gesturing at the cylinders, "some of which are highly flammable, others of which are highly explosive, and most of which are both."

"Who in the fuck *are* you?" Rowena said.

"And what in the fuck are you doing here?" Ronda said.

"I am Eduardo Wolf, and I have come to fix the problem," Eduardo said.

Johnny shook his head at the detectives as if to say, *Don't go there. You don't want to know the rest. Trust me. You really don't.*

"No shit," Ronda said.

"Want to share with the rest of the class just what the fuck the problem is?" Rowena said.

"I think the immediate problem is you," Eduardo said.

"That's fucking funny," Rowena said.

"Because we think the immediate problem is you," Ronda said.

Joanna subtly grabbed Johnny's arm. "I think it might be more interesting to complete this conversation in the dark."

And she reached behind her and turned off the lights, drowning the room in absolute, pitch-black darkness.

The moment the lights went out, Joanna pulled Johnny hard and fast to the ground. He heard a gunshot right above his head. Then three more gunshots. Then three more. And then three more. He heard glass smashing and heavy things crashing to the floor. He could see bursts of gunfire going back and forth but couldn't focus because Joanna was dragging him to a door. And then, they were through the door and in the hallway and on their feet and sprinting through Alsiko, Lab No. 1 in a roaring firefight behind them.

They raced down the stairs and outside into the parking lot. They could still hear gunshots on the second floor. *It's a fucking war zone up there,* Johnny thought as they ran toward Eduardo's Lincoln. It occurred to him they didn't have the key to the Lincoln or to any car, so they were really just running from the building, from the detectives, from the fixer. Just running.

When they reached the Lincoln, they were blown off their feet as the entire second floor of the building exploded. Pieces of roof and glass and laboratory rained down into the parking lot. Fire shot out of where the windows used to be. It was exactly like a high-powered bomb went off in Lab No. 1 and took all of Alsiko with it.

*Some of which are highly flammable, others of which are highly explosive, and most of which are both,* Johnny thought. *Fucking right about that.*

Still on the ground, car alarms going off around them, parking lot littered with debris, he laughed aloud.

"Something strikes you as funny, Mr. Fairfax?" Joanna said.

"They're dead," Johnny said. "The twins and the fixer. Nobody lives through a shitstorm like that—*nobody*. It almost killed *us*, and we're out here. Point is, the albino got it wrong. My future's not fucked after all."

## CHAPTER 39
# COCK IS ROCK

SIKORSKI LIVED on Owensmouth Avenue near Elkwood Street in Canoga Park, twenty minutes from the lab—fifteen if you caught the lights, so twenty because no one caught the lights in LA. His house was a modest mid-century ranch with a touch of Tudor. The front yard was entirely white pea gravel. Scrubby shrubs close to the house added nothing to the exterior décor, which was sad to the point of miserable. Like so many Southern California homes, the garage was the most prominent feature— two cars wide and jutting toward the street, meaning you arrived at the garage before you ever got to the house. The front door was around the side of the garage and farther back from the street.

As Carrie pulled Tino's Mercedes into Sikorski's driveway, it occurred to her that Walter White, the cancer stricken drug dealer from *Breaking Bad,* played to perfection by Bryan Cranston —who had real roots in Canoga Park, it just so happened— would have chosen this very house for his meth lab had the series been set in the San Fernando Valley and not New Mexico. It also occurred to her that Johnny and her mother were likely dead by now.

*I'll be dead next,* she thought.

They'd taken Sikorski's wallet and keys, checked his Volvo for important papers, and found exactly nothing that mattered. So they'd grabbed his garage remote and left the lab.

Carrie turned into Sikorski's driveway and hit the remote button. The door went up, she rolled the Mercedes into the garage, and closed the door behind them. To the world at large, nothing would look amiss at Sikorski's house. Same old, same old. Doors shut. Blinds drawn. Lights low. Nobody home? Somebody home? No way to tell the difference, and who would care to check? Probably no one knew Sikorski had even lived here. Definitely no one would know they were here now. So no one would know they ever left.

Except Carrie wouldn't be leaving. She'd be dead inside the house, and the police wouldn't find her for weeks and weeks. Her corpse would be rotting and rancid by then—maggots and whatnot. Perhaps even as bad as Sikorski's corpse in the lab—not counting the fact his face had been eaten by super rats.

The side of the garage not occupied by Tino's Mercedes had been set up as a gym—free weights, a treadmill, an old-school machine that looked like a Hollywood Transformer robot stuck in the middle of transforming, and a heavy bag for when Sikorski needed to let off steam. There was dust and decay on all the gear. Sikorski had never lifted a weight in his life, never walked on the treadmill, never hit the heavy bag. He'd been a ninety-eight-pound weakling, mad-scientist genius who'd spent the entirety of his life inventing a Fountain of Youth drug. Exercise had never been part of his daily routine. There had never been time for that. Science and pharmaceutical engineering had consumed him day after day for years upon years.

*Now, of course, his daily routine consists of being dead,* she thought.

Carrie, Tino, and Francine went through the garage into the house. A part of Carrie was astounded she was actually here. Before she'd stolen the capsules, the idea that she would ever set foot in Sikorski's home had been absurd. He would never in a million years have invited her, and she would never in a million years have accepted his invitation. They didn't like each other. They were not friends. She and her rats had been nothing more than unknown variables plugged into his complicated pharmaceutical equation until they'd become solutions, which had in turn led to success, which had in turn led to a miracle, which had in turn led to the death and destruction of Stuart Langston and Sikorski himself, and any minute now, Carrie too.

The house had no style. Not in the sense that Sikorski had failed to make his mark in mid-century, say, or modern or colonial or craftsman or even eclectic. But in the sense that no recognized style applied. There was simply no style to the house. Carrie imagined Leo probably had no idea where his disparate furniture had come from. He had to have purchased the tables and lamps and chairs at some point in time or maybe different points in time, but she was certain he wouldn't have been able to recall what he bought or when or where he bought it or how much he had spent.

*Aside from sitting on his sofa—alone in the dark, no doubt— making the chemical calculations that created the world's wildest wonder drug,* she thought, *he probably didn't know he had a sofa.*

Thinking that thought was when Carrie realized they'd been looking in all the wrong places for Sikorski's important papers. Since they'd been inside the house, they—meaning Carrie while Tino kept the silenced Sig pointed in her direction while Francine had her hands all over Tino—had found a locked file cabinet, a locked desk drawer, and a large, locked cashbox. All three secured locations were, in order, shot, jimmied, and smashed open. The suppressed sound of the 9mm silencer was somehow more terrifying to Carrie than the sound of an unsilenced round.

*No one will hear the bullet exploding from the pistol and blowing my brains all over Sikorski's living room. Mine will be a sad, silent murder.*

The file cabinet held all of Sikorski's home information—

closing and legal documents; gas, power, water, phone, and cable bills; receipts and various communications; insurance, real estate taxes, and mortgage materials; car service records, payment reports, and ownership papers; and other mundane organizational archives that had nothing to do with Alsiko. The desk drawer was filled with his lab and personal banking information. The chemical engineer had multiple accounts that funneled money back and forth and round and round. There were two dozen different checkbooks—*none of which will do him any good now*, Carrie thought. The cashbox contained mementos from Leo's life.

His high school yearbook, signed by classmates—most of whom referred to him as *Leo the Loon*. His first driver license. Incredibly, he looked identical at sixteen to how he looked as a grown man. Turns out he'd been a mad chemical genius with Einstein hair even when he was a pimply teenager. Concert tickets to see Lionel Ritchie, of all fucking people. A mood ring. A gold medal from a grade-school science-club competition. A rubber-banded stack of love letters from a girl named Cynthia. A rubber-banded stack of love letters from a boy name Gorman.

*What a mess of a man*, Carrie thought. *Confused all his life about everything except chemistry. No wonder he did equations alone in the dark, sitting on a sofa he didn't even know he had.*

That's when she realized they'd been looking in the wrong place.

She turned to Francine and Tino. The reporter had wrapped her arms around his left arm and was rubbing her body against him, whispering in his ear, kissing his neck, flirting like a Figueroa Street hooker. She was calling him her Russian bear, and he was—for reasons utterly inexplicable to Carrie—calling her Bambi.

"It's not here. We have to go back to the living room."

"Okay, Carrie baby," Tino said. "I shoot you in front of TV watching *Law & Order* episode where woman is shot in front of TV watching *Law & Order* episode. What call that, Bambi?"

"I call it my ironic Russian bear taking care of business," Francine said.

"I call it a hunch," Carrie said.

They went into the living room. Carrie crossed to Sikorski's sofa. Stacks of paper were piled on magazines piled on more stacks of paper piled on more magazines piled on more stacks of paper. She was impressed the coffee table had not collapsed under the weight of the reams of paper piled upon it. She sat on the sofa and went through the stacks.

Near the top of the center pile was a loosely paperclipped set of pages that featured chemical equations from top to bottom, side to side, and front and back. Schematics and drawings accompanied the mathematics—the detailed work of a bizarre little man who'd seen the world through a peculiar prism of biology, chemistry, physics, and pharmaceuticals. The formula for a miracle. The recipe for Leo's wonder drug.

"Tell me truth, Carrie baby," Tino said. "Is Sikorski notes?"

"Yes," Carrie said. "Sikorski's notes."

"Bingo," Francine said, taking the papers from Carrie. "Oh my, we will rule the world."

Then she tossed the papers back on the coffee table and moved to the cleaner. She started kissing him in a hot and passionate way. He responded big time. Their hands were all over each other. Francine rubbed his crotch. Tino massaged her tits and squeezed her ass. He pulled her shirt off. She pulled his shirt off. She slid out of her pants, went to her knees, unbuckled his belt, unbuttoned his pants. They dropped to the floor. Somehow, the cleaner kept the Sig pointed at Carrie throughout the foreplay. Francine stood again, in front of him, her back to Carrie, and they started making out, dry humping to beat the band. Their kisses were excessively wet and sloppy. Tino put his gun under Francine's panties and ran the barrel up and down the crack of her ass. They spoke dirty to each other throughout, saying things like *Fuck me with your gun* and *I want big tits for lunch*. While they undressed each other and drooled on each other and pawed each other like dogs in heat, Tino kept one eye on Carrie. Even winked at her.

It was the grossest sexual display Carrie could have imagined. A kind of low-brow Russian porn. Much worse than the porn she'd seen in college, where once at a fraternity party (she *still* regretted attending), the frat boys had hired three porn actresses to get it on while everyone cheered. And once in the ladies' dorm, when the geeky girls of the Women's Physics Club had rented several porn flicks to see what all the fuss was about. She'd never got to the fuss because all she could only think about were the actors' parents and what *they* were thinking about, knowing their kids had grown up to be porn stars.

Anyway, she hadn't wanted to watch the college porn at Rutgers and didn't want to watch the Russian porn happening live, right now, in Sikorski's living room. But Tino and Francine were like a human train wreck without clothes, and Carrie couldn't turn her eyes away. So instead she said, "Jesus Christ, get a room already."

Tino came up for air. "Good idea, Carrie baby. Tie her to chair, Bambi. Use cord from lamp."

Francine was flushed and breathing heavy. Her neck and face were wet with Tino's sexual slobber. Wearing only a lacy bra and panties, she put Carrie in a chair to the side of the sofa and tied her hands and feet with the long cord of a nearby lamp.

Tino watched in white boxers, hard-on like a tent pole. "Hurry, Bambi baby. Cock is rock."

Francine finished cording Carrie to the chair, went back to Tino, wrapped herself around him, and they left the living room. Seconds later, Carrie figured they'd found Sikorski's bedroom because she could hear their animal sex sounds wafting down the hallway into the living room like forest-fire smoke.

Carrie thought she would have to sit in the chair and listen to them screw until they were done, at which point the cleaner would come back to the living room, probably naked, and shoot her in the head. But Francine, distracted by impending sex with her Russian bear, not to mention the discovery of the pharmaceutical notes that would make her a billionaire, had done a poor job of tying Carrie's hands.

Carrie squirmed and wriggled her wrists free, except her sweater got twisted and tangled in the cord. She fought with the entwined mess for a jumpy-jittery moment, then thought, *I never liked this sweater,* and slid her hand and arm out of the sleeve, untied her ankles, lifted Leo's priceless papers off the coffee table, grabbed Francine's camera on her way out the door, and ran for her life.

# CHAPTER 40
# A RUMP TO REMEMBER

THE JOY JOHNNY felt at the fact those fuckers were fried to fragments by a precarious cocktail of industrial gases and gunfire was more than mitigated by the additional fact that no one at the Copa had heard from Carrie since she'd left to feed the Greek Gods first thing Thursday morning. Johnny had called her a dozen times since he and Joanna had escaped from the lab, but Carrie hadn't answered. He was worried sick someone—the cleaner, no doubt—had intercepted her at Alsiko before he, Joanna, Eduardo Wolf, and then the twins had arrived...and that something horrendous had happened to her. *And that he had not been there to save her.*

This was a new feeling for him. Johnny had never truly cared about anyone except, well, Johnny. Throughout his short, shallow, angry, bitter, violent, criminal life, he'd come first, last, and only. So caring about Carrie more than he cared about himself was like an earthquake in his heart and soul, an interior tectonic smash-up that shook him to the bone. There was so much he didn't understand about living a loving life. It was like his heart was speaking to his head in Chinese. He couldn't catch a word but had a sense of the powerful feelings in play.

He paced and paced, thinking about it until his brain hurt,

until he couldn't stand one more minute of pacing, one more instant of doing nothing to find her. Then he climbed on his bike, ready to roar helter-skelter across Los Angeles, a desperate one-man search-and-rescue operation. Where, exactly, he would look for her he had no idea. All he knew was that he had to do something, go somewhere, try and keep trying.

Just as he kicked the Harley in gear, Carrie pulled up in an Uber.

He ran to her. Somewhere mid-stride he realized she was running to him too. They came together on the sidewalk in front of the Copacabana and embraced like soulmates who hadn't seen each other in years. He didn't kiss her because he was still catching his breath—he hadn't exhaled since the lab blew up while he and Joanna were sprinting across the parking lot. And because he was too overwhelmed with relief to think about kissing her. And because he was just too nervous to kiss her. That was a new feeling for him as well. He'd never before been nervous about kissing a woman. So why was he so damn jumpy about kissing Carrie? He had butterflies in his stomach, for fuck's sake.

He walked her into the Copa, and the gang, sitting at the tables, discussing Joanna's adventure with Johnny at the lab, bounded up and over to them. They all met by the pool, and Carrie told them the story of Tino and Francine, up to and including her getaway—with the notes and the camera—while the cleaner and the reporter humped each other in Leo's bedroom.

Johnny didn't know exactly how the Copa crowd would react to Carrie's account. He thought they would be relieved and overjoyed—like he was—but he wasn't expecting the exultant eruption that followed the story's finale. The men lifted Carrie and Johnny onto their shoulders and danced them around the courtyard, while the women sang "Celebration" by Kool and the Gang like it was some kind of 1980s whacky Jewish poolside wedding. The fact that Tino and Francine were still out there didn't stop them from reveling in Eduardo Wolf's explosive demise at the lab.

Betty blasted the Bluetooth, Johnny and Carrie were lowered to the ground, and there was celebratory dancing in the courtyard. Not normal celebratory dancing. No, no, there was nothing normal about it. The Copa crew's dancing had become more frequent, progressively primitive, increasingly tribal, unmistakably sexual, unambiguously violent, unilaterally unrestrained, relentlessly euphoric. They danced alone, in pairs, and in groups, bodies glistening with sweat, eyes on fire. It was mesmerizing and disturbing at the same time.

Johnny stayed by Carrie's side throughout the dance. He had this feeling inside his heart that he would never leave her alone again. He didn't know what to make of this feeling, and he didn't know if she was feeling the same way about him, but it seemed she was as entranced by the gang's euphoria as he was, and she stayed by his side as much as he stayed by hers, so maybe she was feeling something too. He hoped so more than he could remember ever hoping for anything.

"It's like watching Woodstock," he said.

"Except we're in Hollywood and not Upstate New York," she said.

"And the women aren't topless."

"Yet."

"Yet."

And then the women, all of them—Joanna, Lillian, Betty, Dolores, Helen, and Brenda—as if tuned to a wavelength only they could hear—took off their shirts and bras and danced topless around the pool. Then Arnie, Norman, Bernie, Walter, and Bob ripped off their shirts too. And then everyone's clothes came off, and they were dancing naked in the sun, sweating like steam engines, wild and primeval and aggressive. Ten minutes, fifteen, twenty ... and then the dance was done, and they jumped into the pool, laughing at their own silliness like grade-school kids at recess.

They swam to the edge of the pool closest to Johnny and Carrie.

"What's for lunch, Tattoo Boy?" Lillian said. "We're hungry as hippos."

"I could eat a fucking hippo," Walter said.

"Don't even have to cook the damn thing," Bob said.

"Homemade ziti with tomatoes, arugula, mushrooms, black olives, and roasted red peppers. Caesar salad on the side. Fresh-baked rosemary breadsticks," Johnny said.

"Fiddle-faddle," Brenda said. "We want man meat."

"Man meat and more man meat," Bernie said.

"Make it a man-meat parade," Arnie said.

"Parole-officer protein," Dolores said.

"Let's eat the fat man until the fat man's gone," Norman said.

"What cuts of Mr. Boston do you have on hand, Mr. Fairfax?" Joanna said. "Something substantial yet simple to prepare."

Johnny looked down into the water, where the naked Copa crew were calling for human flesh like a nest full of just-hatched carnivorous birds. "I could make a stew."

"Big Ben beef stew," Walter said.

"Excellent. What with it?" Betty said.

"Basmati rice? Cornbread?" Johnny said.

"Does that sound like man meat to you?" Arnie said.

"No salads," Helen said.

"No carbs," Dolores said.

"No fruits," Arnie said.

"No nuts," Walter said.

"No vegetables," Bernie said.

"First canon of the kitchen," Brenda said. "Feed the people what they want."

"And what they want is meat," Betty said. "Man meat."

"You mean man meat with the man meat?" Johnny said.

"Man meat with the man meat and more man meat in the middle," Bob said.

Johnny was culinarily confused. In all his years working in

kitchens across LA, he'd never heard anyone ask for meat with their meat and more meat in the middle—forget the fact the meat they were demanding was his dead parole officer. "Well, I guess, uh, how about beef stew and meat loaf?"

"How about a rump steak to round things out?" Dolores said.

"The man had a rump to remember when it comes to fine dining," Helen said.

"Beef stew, meat loaf, and rump steak," Lillian said. "Bring it on, Tattoo Boy."

"Go, Johnny go," Bob said.

"Johnny be good," Norman said.

Then they laughed and splashed and splashed and laughed.

Johnny and Carrie walked to the kitchen, the Copa crew whooping it up in the water behind them.

"What the hell happens when they eat the last bite of Ben Boston?" Johnny said.

Carrie shrugged. "All I know is there's no good answer to that question."

# CHAPTER 41
# TO AVALON AND ON

AS FAR AS Carrie was concerned, lunch was ludicrous. Primarily because the Copa crowd consumed a parole officer baked, broiled, browned, barbequed, roasted, sautéed, fried, and grilled with marvelous means, but also because the midday meal didn't end until after the sun had set in the west. The old folks feasted for seven hours with insuppressible appetites, insatiable gusto, and voracious epicurean zeal. Every dish had a name because the gang had insisted Johnny name them. And as the dishes were delivered and their names announced, they stood and cheered their chef de cuisine and sang the praises of his food. Johnny cooked nearly every bit of Ben Boston he'd butchered. Carrie was his expediter, sous chef, and front-of-house manager.

Somewhere around four o'clock, lost in the demented dining delirium, after serving what he'd called Fabulous Fat-Man Fricassee, Johnny turned to Carrie and said, "Jesus Christ, I'm cooking for cannibals."

Carrie had thought it might happen like this because the Greek Gods, now living at the Copa, had turned on Apollo, injured when the table maze crushed Sikorski, and eaten him down to his little rat bones. Meaning there were now seven

Greek Gods, and Carrie understood these seven wanted nothing but red raw rat meat. Carrie would feed them other meat (at this point, they would eat nothing but meat), they would sniff around the bowl, and then look up at her as if to say, *Hey, this isn't rat* before finally feeding.

But the seven-hour meal was mostly memorable because as it ended, Helen said, "Tonight, we revel in the arrival, safe and sound, amen and hallelujah, of Carrie Kromer and Johnny Fairfax."

*Huzzah, huzzah*, they all said.

"We dance like devils in the City of Angels," Brenda said.

*Huzzah, huzzah ...*

"We praise the pills," Arnie said.

*Huzzah, huzzah ...*

"We applaud the papers," Betty said.

*Huzzah, huzzah ...*

"We acclaim the camera," Bob said.

*Huzzah, huzzah ...*

"We party like it's 1965," Bernie said.

*Huzzah, huzzah ...*

"To Avalon and on," Dolores said.

*To Avalon, huzzah, huzzah ...*

Dolores, who had done Tinseltown hair and makeup for decades, still read the trades every day, which was how she knew the perfect place to party. The hottest, hippest, most historic dance club in LA.

Avalon Hollywood.

Located on Vine Street, near the corner of Hollywood Boulevard, Avalon was a vast venue that during its long, storied life had been known as The Hollywood Playhouse, the WPA Federal Theatre, El Capitan Theatre, The Jerry Lewis Theatre, The Hollywood Palace, and The Palace. Stretching gloriously back to its 1927 opening, the Spanish-Baroque-style building had hosted all the top talent of the time throughout time. Lawrence Welk and The King Sisters. Groucho Marx and

Louis Armstrong. Fred Astaire and Ginger Rogers. Judy Garland, Liberace, and Jimmy Durante. Frank Sinatra, Sammy Davis Jr., and Dean Martin. Diana Ross and the Supremes. Nirvana, Nine Inch Nails, and Soundgarden. The Beatles' first West Coast performance. The Ramones' last show ever. Richard Nixon's Checkers speech, for pity's sake, had been televised from here.

With all of them in mind, it was fait accompli that the Hollywood and Vine venue was the perfect place for the Copa crew to celebrate the reclamation of their youth, the expiration of the fixer, the appropriation of Sikorski's papers, the confiscation of Fontana's camera, and the safe-and-sound salvation of their brilliant young scientist and her talented chef boyfriend. They would meet at ten in the courtyard, take the van to Avalon, and dance until dawn.

Carrie helped Johnny clean the kitchen, worrying aloud about the Copa crew making a scene at such a well-known nightclub. There would be security cameras by the doors, above the bars, maybe even in the bathrooms. There would be bouncers all over the place, eyes peeled for problems, ready to remove misbehavers by force, meaning head-first onto Vine Street.

There would be no hiding in plain sight this time. If the old folks did anything crazy, like taking their clothes off and dancing naked on the bar or starting a barroom brawl or commandeering the DJ booth, the police would be called, questions would be asked, charges would be filed, revelations would be revealed, ages would be disclosed, and the world would discover the miracle medicine.

After *that* uproar, the authorities would follow the clues to Ben Boston, Leo Sikorski, Stuart Langston, Ronda and Rowena Ramos, and the others who'd probably perished as part of her alibi: Justin the bartender, Joe the cabbie, and Elaine the parking-lot lady. Not to mention that although the fixer was dead, the cleaner was very much alive. Which meant they should all stay in and stay together instead of making a public appearance at Hollywood and Vine.

Johnny agreed it was risky business to be out and about and told Carrie the only way to stop them was to convince Joanna it was a dumb idea.

"She's a librarian, right?" Johnny said. "Librarians deal with dumb ideas better than anyone. You tell her how it is, she'll shut that shit down. She's our last line of defense."

So when the kitchen was clean, Carrie marched across the courtyard to her mother's door to make the case that dicey dancing at Avalon was too precarious a proposition to permit. She even said it in her own mind. *I'm putting my foot down, Mother. Avalon is out of bounds.*

She knocked on Joanna's door and waited, playing the conversation in her head so she wouldn't be flustered once she was face-to-face with her mother.

"Who is it?" Joanna said.

"It's me," Carrie said.

"It's open. I'm in the bedroom."

Carrie went into the apartment, walked to the bedroom, and stopped flat in the doorway. The opening lines of her argument had been on the tip of her tongue, but they evaporated like morning mist because Joanna was in bed with Norman and Bernie. They were all naked.

"Mother," Carrie said in an instant state of shock.

"It's not what it looks like, dear," Joanna said.

"It's not?" Carrie said.

"No. Bernie goes both ways," Joanna said.

"I always did," Bernie said.

"I'm usually a one-way street," Norman said. "But for Bernie, no harm done."

"No harm done?" Carrie said. "Are you people crazy? You're having sex with each other. You're all ninety years old."

"Yes, except we're forty-two again," Joanna said. "Don't be a prude, Carrie."

"This kind of thing's been happening since the Bible," Bernie said.

"The Bible? Really?" Carrie said.

"Not in so many words," Norman said. "But there's a lot of sex in the Good Book. People begatting and begetting, page after page. They lived in the desert, no Netflix, no SiriusXM, no Mall of America. All they did was screw. No one complained."

"Job complained," Bernie said.

"And you see where that got him," Norman said.

"Absolutely," Bernie said. "Biblical scholars around the world agree that if Job had done a three-way, he'd have been a hell of a lot less uptight about things."

"Biblical scholars around the world do not agree that Job should have done a three-way," Carrie said. "Three-ways are not part of any kind of biblical scholarship."

"And that's the problem with religion," Bernie said.

"In a nutshell," Norman said.

Joanna laughed. "These two have been making me happy for years, dear. I thought this might be a nice way to thank them for their friendship."

"The nicest, Jo Jo," Norman said.

"Friends forever, Joey," Bernie said.

Carrie just stood there, not knowing what the hell to say.

"Do you want to join us, dear?" Joanna said.

"What? No. Gross. No," Carrie said, snapping out of it.

Then she told them why she was here, though she had to concentrate because Norman's horse dick was out in the open, and it was a conversation stopper.

They shut her down out of hand. They were going to Avalon to celebrate and that was that. Although Joanna did see the benefit of someone staying behind to hold down the fort.

"And on that note," Joanna said, "I believe we're ready for round three. So off you go, Carrie. See you in the courtyard at ten."

Carrie hurried the hell out of there so she didn't have to actually watch her mother have sex with Norman and Bernie. And she didn't stop hurrying until she reached her apartment. She shut the door behind her and leaned against it, fighting the incorrigible vision of a random Ivy League doctoral presentation in which an artist's rendering of Job in a three-way was the topic of scholarly debate.

When the vision passed, she fed the Greek Gods, fell asleep for a while, took a shower, and got ready—reluctantly—for a night on the town.

Since she'd never gone clubbing at Avalon (or anywhere), what to wear was a dilemma. She didn't have clubbing clothes. She cycled through everything in her closet—tried everything on, took everything off, then tried it on again, then took it off again. On the third pass, it occurred to her that for the first time in her life—or at least for the first time in a long time, so long she couldn't remember the last time—she was not dressing for herself. She was, she realized, dressing for Johnny.

*Oh my God, it's true,* she thought. *I want him to think I'm pretty. No, not pretty. Sexy. I want him to think I'm sexy. I want him to be attracted to me. I want him to be as attracted to me as I am to him. Oh my God, it's true. I'm attracted to him. He attracts me. He's a flame, and I'm a moth. Oh shut up, you idiot. You sound like a high school poet geek girl in love with a bad-seed butcher dropout. In love? What? Are you stupid? You don't know anything about love. Shut. Up. Oh my god, it's true.*

She'd never dressed for anyone ever. Not even the Bolivian biology boy who she'd unapologetically seduced when she was a teaching assistant. Nope, she had not dressed for him on the very day of seduction. The plain-Jane truth was she had never dressed for *herself.* Clothes had never been and were still not a point of focus for her. She'd had school clothes when she was in school. And when she joined the workforce, she'd had work clothes. But party clothes? No. Dancing clothes? Hell no.

The one possible exception was a black, smocked-waist maxi skirt, flowy and breezy and comfortable as could be. She'd bought it for a garden party she'd been unexpectedly invited to but never attended because she'd realized there would be no walls to lean against in a garden, a sticky situation for a wallflower. The skirt did a good job of hiding her hips—*or as Mother would say, as good a job as a pear-shaped woman can hope for.* It was the only skirt she owned that she could dance in. Or move as though she were dancing since she was decidedly not a dancer.

She matched it with a black-and-blue silk blouse she'd bought at Bloomingdale's in a moment of weakness, thinking she might wear it to the lab on a Casual Friday, if Sikorski ever instituted a Casual Friday, before deciding it was too silky for Alsiko and hiding it in the back of her closet.

*Back to this business about dressing for Johnny Fairfax,* she thought. *Despite anything I may or may not feel for him, and that he may or may not feel for me, I will not sexually humiliate myself—like my mother, for God's sake, by changing the way I dress, or undress, for a man, even if that man is Johnny Fairfax. I simply will not.*

She looked at herself in the mirror, hair down around her shoulders, light red gloss on her lips, flowy-breezy black skirt, silk blouse—and unbuttoned one more button to show some cleavage.

# CHAPTER 42
# I LIKE THE WAY YOU DANCE

JOHNNY STOOD BESIDE THE POOL, five straws in hand. One of the straws had been cut shorter than the others. The men were preparing to ceremonially select who would stay behind and defend the fort in case the cleaner came for Carrie, the camera, the pills, and the papers.

Bob, Walter, Bernie, Norman, and the women were waiting for Arnie, who arrived dressed in black from head to toe (like a ninja) and promptly circumvented the selection by volunteering to take the watch while the rest of the gang got their groove on at Avalon. Arnie offered to man the guard because the cleaner was Russian, and Arnie had lost fifteen family members in the Katyn massacre of 1940, when Stalin's Soviets had murdered 22,000 Poles—officers, intelligentsia, landowners, lawyers, business-men, government officials, priests—and buried bodies in the Katyn Forest.

Arnie Bialik, it turned out, had joined the service in 1942, on the day he turned eighteen, to deliver some personal Russian retribution.

"I was an American Marine, a stone-cold killing machine," he told the Copa crew in the courtyard, "and I'm stronger and smarter and faster and meaner than I was then. So please, go.

Dance, have fun, and allow me the pleasure of killing the cleaner. One last payback for what the Soviets did to my family. Believe me, I'll be having as much fun as you. Maybe more. And then Fairfax can cook us some Soviet stroganoff with real red Russian beef."

There was some back and forth about safety and so on, but Arnie argued that at five-nine, one hundred sixty pounds of wiry muscle, and trained by the military in weaponry, hand-to-hand combat, knife fighting, and martial arts, he would clean the cleaner's clock. Johnny didn't hear it all, couldn't fully concentrate on their conversation, because Carrie was crossing the courtyard in a flowy-breezy skirt and silk blouse, and his heart was skipping beats all over the place. Not one beat here and there but bags of beats with every step she took toward him.

His heart had never-not-once skipped a single beat. So what the hell was it doing skipping multiple beats while Carrie came around the pool? She was drop-dead beautiful, so that had to be it, right? Yes and no. He'd been with other beautiful women in his life, and his heart had held onto all its damn beats. Maybe it was the insanity he and Carrie had shared since he'd become the Copa cook. Or because their fathers had both died on the days they had turned twenty-one. Or her patience with him. The way she looked at him. The way her smile left him breathless. Maybe all of that. All he wanted to do was take her in his arms and kiss her a hundred times. He couldn't remember ever wanting to do that with any other woman. What was happening to him? Was he changing his stripes? It couldn't be. He was Johnny Fairfax, badass, ex-con, butcher-chef. His heart didn't skip beats.

*Jesus Christ, is this what fucking love is like?* he thought as Carrie arrived at his side. Together, they caught the tail end of the Arnie-covers-the-Copa conversation.

"...and if he doesn't come," Arnie said, "then we have plenty of time to dance together. We're not getting any older, if you haven't noticed."

The Copa crew laughed, agreed to let Arnie take the watch, and walked away to the van.

"What was that all about?" Carrie said to Johnny as they followed the gang.

"Arnie's going to stay and kill the cleaner with his bare hands to avenge his family that got murdered in Poland during World War Two," Johnny said.

"Of course he is," Carrie said. "World War Two revenge is right up Arnie's alley."

She smiled, and his heart soared. He hoped she was as attracted to him as he was to her. He'd showered and put on his best rock-star clothes—tight, black, Frank Zappa T-shirt, faded jeans, Harley Davidson boots. That they were polar opposites no longer concerned him. They were simply Johnny and Carrie, riding out the craziest story either one of them had ever heard.

"Let's take the bike," he said, "in case they close the place and we split early."

"I think closing the place is a given," she said. "Where would we go?"

"Anywhere we want," he said.

They climbed on, she wrapped her arms around his waist, and they followed the van to Hollywood and Vine.

Avalon was wall-to-wall clubbers, many below the age of twenty-five—thanks to the every-Thursday Tiger Night event. The 3D laser light show on the dance floor was an insane, multi-colored, *Star Wars* firefight in deepest, darkest space. Pulsing ray-beams shooting out sideways from the walls. Psychedelic lightning flashing down from the ceiling. Smoke and fog erupting everywhere like volcanic geysers. Ultra-super-high-tech stage with rigging and trusses like the bridge of a starship. Shaved-head DJ gyrating to his unremitting alien beat like Jean Luc Picard on purple microdot, his Federation light show an awe-inspiring U2 concert on steroids.

Electronic dance music pounded out of the countless speakers and hit the dancers in the chest like a hundred jackhammers. It was jet-engine loud, physically addictive, tangibly hypnotic, viscerally irresistible. If you were anywhere in the club, your body was moving. The mix was wild wizardry, swirling and whirling and climbing and diving in musical scales made of magic because the crowd, every last one of them, was lost in space and time, dancing on some distant, drug and alcohol powered parallel plane in which nothing existed except the beat, the bodies, and the buzz.

Johnny figured there were hundreds of people on the dance floor. But it was hard to see the room all at once, and it felt like more than a thousand. The Copa crew swept him and Carrie into the middle of the crowd and danced around them with crazy energy fueled by the unremitting rhythm, the adrenaline of their recovered youth, the carnivorous potency of the pills pulsing in their veins.

Despite the super-nova stimuli coming at him from all directions, Johnny couldn't take his eyes off Carrie. She'd told him she didn't dance, but she moved like Sade in "The Sweetest Taboo," the smoothest of smooth operators.

Johnny didn't dance either. Okay, maybe once in a blue moon in some greasy backroads bar when he'd been stoned out of his brain and drunk on tequila and was trying to get laid by some random biker chick who'd been even higher and drunker than him and looked good enough in the dark. Okay, maybe then. But even then, he'd barely moved a muscle, as if he'd been too cool for the beat.

He muted his style not so much as to actually be too cool for the beat, but so that he wouldn't look foolish. Because not looking foolish when you ran with Johnny's crowd was even more important than being too cool for the beat.

Anyway, he'd told Carrie Avalon wasn't his kind of club. And Carrie had said she didn't even have a kind of club, so Johnny thought it was remarkable they both seemed to be having such a fabulous time dancing together in a club that wasn't their kind of club.

*It's the "together" part,* he thought. *It has to be.*

It occurred to him that though they came at things—like dancing in a nightclub or carving up dead parole officers—from opposite sides, he and Carrie somehow always met in the middle. And though he was no deep thinker, he thought that might be the point—they were meeting in the middle without giving up any important parts of themselves, and they were still who they were when they were together.

There was no break in the music, no rest, not for a second, and the funny part was Johnny and Carrie found themselves moving more and more and more until they were dancing all out like the clubbers around them—wild and free, spinning and swirling, bumping and grinding, laughing and laughing and laughing and laughing—no way to stop the delirium; no chance to catch their breath; past, present, and future suspended in free-falling flight by the lights and smoke and thumping-throbbing-banging bass.

So they kept dancing, and soon the Copa gang faded into the mad morass of bodies until they were lost somewhere in the solar system and there was no one anywhere in the world except Johnny and Carrie. And still they kept dancing—shake, rattle, and rolling with the same passion and spirit and energy and, yes, joy, as the other clubbers.

Johnny wanted to talk to Carrie, to tell her how happy he was to be with her, but he knew she wouldn't hear him. It was like they were dancing directly in front of a monstrous, soccer-stadium sound system, and the stadium was filled with one hundred thousand metalheads, and the band was Black Sabbath, and they were screaming-shrieking loud.

Even so, he leaned down and shouted in her ear, which passed for whispering on a Thursday night in Avalon, "I like the way you dance."

She shouted back in his ear, "I like the way *you* dance."

She smiled at him, and her smile was just devastating. So he leaned down and shouted again. "You have a pretty smile."

But there was something about the tone of his voice, the drop-dead-deep-honest emotion in the words, that made *you have a pretty smile* sound a whole lot like *I've never cared about anyone in my life the way I care about you. Please don't ever leave me.*

And it seemed to him she'd caught the truth of his tone too because she smiled at him again and reached up to his ear. He hoped she might say *I care about you too*, but instead she shouted, "I have to use the ladies' room, and I want you to come with me because I'll never find my way back, and I don't want to lose you."

He shouted in her ear, "I don't want to lose you either."

They looked into each other's eyes for what seemed like twenty minutes but was actually two seconds, then they weaved and wedged their way off the dance floor, went down some corridors, turned left and right and right and left, and entered a hallway where the music was soft and the lights were low.

They stood at the ladies' room door, and he said, "I'm here."

She looked into his eyes, took his hand, and pulled him inside.

# CHAPTER 43

# THIS WAS REAL. THIS WAS RAW. THIS WAS NOW

IN HIGH SCHOOL, losing her virginity to and with Daryl Sasso in his suburban New Brunswick basement while looking up at his World War Two model jet fighters had not been an impulsive act. Carrie had considered the consequences in detail, both for her and for the pimply, militaria-loving swimmer. She'd listed the potential positive outcomes versus the prospective negative aftermaths, charted the general and individual reactions she expected from her peers across all social strata. She'd thought it through, planned it out, and discussed it in advance with Daryl. They had checked their calendars to find an otherwise unoccupied weekday afternoon and turned up the basement thermostat so they would not be cold.

At UCLA, when she'd seduced Alonzo the Bolivian biology boy, that was also not an impulsive act. She had watched him in class, checked his schedule against hers, knew when and where the handsome Latin boy would be and how he'd get there and back. She'd manipulated his biology homework, making it just ever so much harder than the other freshman so he would need help from his grad-student teaching assistant. She'd lit candles in her dorm room and opened a bottle of red wine. She'd washed her sheets. The lights were already low when they arrived. There was soft music playing. It had been premeditated, calculated, and orchestrated. Deliberate and designed.

Pulling Johnny into the Avalon ladies' room was the most purely impulsive thing she'd ever done. Up until the very moment he'd said *I'm here,* she'd had no true idea she was going to make love to him in the bathroom. Yes, sure, she'd been feeling connected to him. And yes, sure, she'd admitted to herself she was, to her astonishment, physically attracted to his smoky, smoldering, tattooed, rock-star, ex-con, biker-bad-boy butcher looks. And, yes, sure, she'd been less inhibited on the Avalon dance floor than she'd ever been in her life—smocked-waist maxi skirt swinging like she was some kind of wild hippie woman doing some kind of wild-hippie-woman fertility dance, hair whipping around her head, hips shaking like an earthquake, hot and bothered and bothered and hot. But having sex in the ladies' room of a packed dance club? On a Thursday? No way that was happening.

Except it *was* happening.

Three long-legged young women were applying lipstick at the sinks, hair streaked blonde, makeup for days, dresses so short they might as well have worn nothing at all. Carrie caught them out of the corner of her eye as she pulled Johnny into the middle stall. She was sure the women had seen them in the mirror because all three stopped mid-lip. Not one turned around or said a word, but their mouths fell open in unison as their gazes followed the couple into the stall.

Before the stall door had even shut, Carrie was all over him, and he was all over her. The sexual kindling that had been sparked and sizzling below the radar burst instantaneously into passionate flames as the door closed behind them.

They kissed furiously, touching and grabbing and grinding with mad passion. She'd never been this turned on. Not even with Alonzo, and that had been, as far as her limited experience could take her at the time, good sex. But here she was blazing with sexual heat, nerves raging with lust as his hands went up and under her smocked-waist maxi skirt and took hold of her ass, pulling her toward him.

It was more than lust, of course. She cared for him and felt that he cared for her too. But her emotions were wound tight in the same crazy web of passion that burned her skin.

He unbuttoned her silk blouse and unhooked her bra. He kissed her neck, put his tongue on her breasts. Even when she masturbated—*Yes, yes, even pear-shaped girls masturbate, Mother*, she'd once said when Joanna came home early from work and caught Carrie using the librarian's vibrator—even then, while dreaming of some impossibly sexy Latin lover, her body wasn't the high-voltage live wire it was with Johnny Fairfax in the Avalon ladies' room.

He took off his T-shirt. She kissed his tattoos, ran her tongue over them, rubbed her breasts against them. This wasn't anything at all like her imagined lust for Julio Iglesias or Enrique, his fine-looking Latin son. This wasn't dreamy desire for Antonio Banderas or illusory longing for Andy Garcia. It wasn't wistful yearning for Javier Bardem or melancholy craving for Benjamin Bratt. This was real. This was raw. This was now. This was personal and powerful beyond her visions and reveries. This was physical heat like she'd never thought possible, sensual passion she'd only seen in movies and weekly television dramas.

He put his hand between her legs and her heart pounded in her head. She unbuckled his Harley Davidson belt, unbuttoned his pants, pulled them down to his ankles. He was hard. It took her breath away. She lowered his Jockeys down to his knees and heard him groan. For reasons no amount of her scientific experience could explain, this made her even hotter.

He kissed her, raised her right leg so that her foot rested on the rim of the toilet, and pushed gently inside her.

She held him, kissed him, surrendered to the heat, lost herself in time, brain spinning inside her skull, eyes shut and yet bursting from their sockets, stars shooting, sirens blaring, body shaking and grinding and thrusting and thrusting and thrusting. She heard herself say, *Don't stop, don't stop, harder, harder, don't stop, yes, yes, yes, yes,* and scream with elation at the moment of her orgasmic explosion. She felt his body spasm and jerk and ripple.

They stayed together, breathing hard, foreheads touching, kissing each other, holding on like they might never let go.

But then she said, "We can't stay here, Johnny."

And he said, "But I want to stay here forever."

She kissed him and kissed him, and they came apart and straightened themselves and opened the stall door.

The three long-legged women who'd stopped mid-lip still stood at the sinks, accompanied now by a dozen men and women who'd come in to enjoy the show. As Carrie and Johnny made their curtain call, the crowd spontaneously began to applaud and cheer.

Carrie blushed but wasn't embarrassed. Quite the contrary— she'd never been prouder of anything she'd done than she was of fucking Johnny Fairfax in the Avalon ladies' room. To confirm that feeling for her, the men and women in attendance gave high fives to the copulating couple as they walked out of the restroom and into their uncertain future.

# CHAPTER 44
# KING OF THE MEAN STREETS

A METAL STORAGE chest stood along the west wall in Lab No. 1. Sikorski used the chest to hold the volatile chemical combinations with which he was experimenting—in case they detonated or burned or became noxious or poisonous or presented some other kind of hazardous reaction. Beside it, Eduardo Wolf hugged the ground, on the losing end of a ferocious firefight in the dark with Detectives Ronda and Rowena Ramos. By calculating the reverse trajectories of the bullets coming at him, the fixer could tell the twins were cutting the angles in the lab, boxing him in so they could take him out. Carrie's mother and the idiot Copacabana cook had escaped when Joanna turned out the lights. Eduardo admitted the situation was dire. He was fast running out of options. Soon he'd be out of ammunition. Soon after that he'd be dead.

Except he'd been trained by the KSK and the BND to make blueprints in his mind's eye of every room he ever entered. He'd been doing it almost unconsciously all of his adult life. So he knew precisely where the industrial gases were located and which of those gases would cause the most immediate and furious explosion. He climbed into the chest, police bullets smashing all around him, fired his Glock 19 at the cannisters, and closed the metal lid.

Which was why he was walking across the Copacabana courtyard on Thursday night instead of being dead like the detectives, who were blown to bloody bits in the Alsiko conflagration.

He'd come for the capsules. Earlier in the evening, he'd cased the Copa and seen the residents leave in the van, Carrie and Johnny behind them on a Harley. All dressed for a night on the town. He had no idea where they were headed, not that it mattered. What mattered was that he would eliminate them, all of them, when they returned.

But first he would find the stolen drug. He stopped beside the pool and gathered his thoughts. Regardless of how he organized, categorized, or characterized them, one thought came before the others: Constantine Antonov.

The Russian was here for the missing miracle drug. No doubt about it. They'd arrived at Lucky Lainey's trailer at the same time asking the same questions about the same people for the same reasons. Which meant Sikorski had been duplicitous with his client, Yelchin, and whoever the cleaner's client was, most likely Pfeiffer, the Russian drug conglomerate. This was very bad news for Sikorski, of course, but equally bad news for any shred of evidence left behind, meaning there would be no evidence left behind.

Killing the Copacabana residents held no intellectual appeal. They were miracles of science, living proof that Sikorski's drug would change the path of all humankind. Eliminating them seemed senseless as a philosophical exercise, repugnant from a moral perspective, and appalling from any sort of historical standing. Professionally, however, he would do it without blinking. It was his occupational obligation. A job to be done. He was well paid to fix problems. This was a problem to be fixed.

Sadly, there would be no pleasure in taking their lives. Nor would he enjoy killing Carrie Kromer. She'd been courageous in the face of her fear, and he respected that. To honor her bravery, she would die quickly and without pain. That would not be the case for the cook. Johnny Fairfax would suffer for his obstinate idiocy. Eduardo would torture him for a good long while before snuffing out his worthless, miserable life. He would savor each moment of Johnny's pain, revel in the ex-con's agony, delight in the moment of his excruciating death.

But even the joyful anticipation of killing the cook couldn't relocate the Russian from the front and center of the fixer's mind. Eduardo Wolf did not like Constantine Antonov. The cleaner's crass style, crude manner, unpolished behavior, and unsophisticated approach to the profession they shared was nothing short of infuriating. How could anyone act with such disregard for their own self-respect?

Even now, standing beside the pool, just thinking about the Russian made his heartbeat quicken, his jaw tighten, his hands form fists. No one annoyed him like the Russian annoyed him. They had confronted each other several times over the years, and each time Tino had burrowed under his skin like a tick. And quite like a tick, the effects of the cleaner's bitter bite lasted long after Eduardo was rid of him. Worse yet, seeing the Russian again—the actual moment of seeing him in Lucky Lainey's trailer—had instantly brought back the painful irritation the fixer had felt in Antwerp, the last time the two had tangoed.

If only there were a way for the fixer to return the favor— leave behind some lingering level of exasperation the Russian could carry for months and years like a venereal disease. And then it came to him. So simple a solution. So obvious an answer. Eduardo would recover the capsules, kill everyone at the Copa, and delegate the cleaning to the cleaner. Tino would be left with all the guts (literally) and none of the glory. The Russian would be Eduardo's water boy and nothing more.

Eduardo imagined the Russian's first thoughts would be *Fuck capsules, fuck Copa, fuck fixer. I don't clean his fucking mess.* But his next thoughts would negate his first thoughts because his next thoughts would be *Fuck me. I am fucked Russian cleaner*. Tino would have no choice but to clean the mess Eduardo had made because telling Pfeiffer that he, the cleaner, could neither find nor deliver the stolen drug to them because their competitor's agent, the fixer, had in fact found and indeed delivered the stolen drug to *them* would be very bad news.

But Tino *also* telling his client that he, the cleaner, had left the evidence behind and done nothing to clean the mess would be beyond bad news. Quite possibly it would be the-end-of-Tino bad news. So to avoid that unwanted outcome, the Russian would *have to* burn the Copa and the corpses to cinders —no matter how much it infuriated him to do so. It might even be true, Eduardo imagined, that the Copa fire would be the first fire in forever the cleaner wouldn't enjoy, and that Tino would remember that joyless fire for the rest of his life. If Eduardo was exceptionally fortunate, compelling the cleaner to clean the mess while not allowing him to recover the capsules might pour water on the joy of *all* the Russian's fires for the rest of time.

Eduardo was delighting in the idea of polluting Tino's passion, when the quiet of the courtyard was broken by a man's voice.

"Looking for these, you rat-bastard Rooski?"

*Again with the Russian?* the fixer thought as he turned to the voice. The man was dressed in all black. Forty years old. Five-nine or ten. One hundred fifty, maybe sixty pounds of what appeared to be perfectly wired muscle. Indeed, the man seemed to be unnaturally fit.

*One of the residents*, Eduardo thought. *One of the miracle men left behind to protect the castle from a Russian invasion—or an unwanted visit from the fixer.*

In his right hand, the miracle man held a ten-inch carving knife. In his left hand, a medicine vial.

"If those are the stolen capsules," Eduardo said, "then I am undeniably looking for them."

"You don't look Russian," the man said. "And you don't sound Russian."

"That is because I am not Russian," Eduardo said.

"If you're not Russian and you're looking for these, that makes you the fixer, Eduardo Wolf," the man said. "Which is an unexpected piece of the puzzle since Johnny said you were dead, blown up in the lab."

"I enjoy puzzles," Eduardo said. "And if this one makes me the fixer, who does it make you?"

"The Marine who's going to carve you up and serve you for dinner," the man said. "Arnie Bialik."

Eduardo smiled not because he knew the Marine had meant the carving-and-serving part literally as well as figuratively but because Arnie's challenge transported him back to when he'd been a boy in Brazil and had taken on all comers who'd contested his crown as King of the Mean Streets.

He'd never been able to turn down a fight to the death. As far back as he could recall, he couldn't resist the thrill of a thrown gauntlet, the battle of strength and skill, of finesse and force, of one man's capacity for suffering over another's. His heart would fill with adrenaline and pump it furiously through his veins, fueling his iron will and ferocious focus. His spine was made of steel. He had been born this way. He had no regrets and made no apologies for the lives he'd taken. He'd always looked forward to the fight.

It was a glorious evening. Clear skies. Barely a breeze. Cool, dry air. Eduardo removed his blue sport jacket, revealing his shoulder holster—Glock on the left, extra magazines on the right. He folded the jacket neatly and placed it on a chaise lounge.

"You going to shoot me, you gutless fucking fixer?" Arnie said.

"In my neighborhood, you did not bring a gun to a knife fight." Eduardo unclipped the holster and placed it next to the jacket. Then he reached behind him and pulled a hellish, special-forces Gerber Ghoststrike knife from a concealed-carry sheath attached to his belt. The badass blade glistened in the moonlight.

"In World War Two, I cut thirty throats like yours," Arnie said, sliding the vial into his pocket and crouching into ready position.

"Not like mine." Eduardo edged forward with deadly poise. He led with his right hand, his knife hand, blade up and in front to protect his face and neck, moving it in unpredictable patterns, back and forth and up and down, circles this way and that way, so that the Marine couldn't anticipate where the blade would be.

Experience had taught him there were no winners in a knife fight. Everyone got cut. Everyone bled. But one bled worse than the other. The strategy was to play defense, to slice through muscle and nerve and artery when your opponent attacked, to be patient and focused, to be hyper-alert, to show no fear, to expect pain and blood.

They circled each other, slashing and jabbing, neither man over-committing, both men maintaining balance and vision, keeping their opponent in front of them.

Eduardo realized quickly that the Marine was exceptional, equally trained, equally skilled, matching him move for move, waiting for him to make the first thrust.

"World War Two you said?" Eduardo said.

"Europe. Front lines," the Marine said.

"That would make you ninety-five years old."

The men kept circling, jabbing, slashing, trying to force the other fighter to commit, to attack, to expose an arm, to open a flank. Eduardo could feel the tension in his legs, up and down his back, in his arms.

"Ninety-six," the Marine said.

"Fit for your age," Eduardo said.

Clockwise, then counterclockwise, then clockwise, then back again, the fixer's blade a foot from the Marine, moving, moving, moving, probing, testing, taunting, waiting for weakness, a slip, an opening. And then he saw it. When they danced count-clockwise, the Marine's right hand, his knife hand, moved forward three to five inches, an unconscious miscalculation for the fixer to exploit.

"Clean living," the Marine said.

"And a pharmaceutical substance that doesn't belong to you." Eduardo reversed course.

"A drug worth fighting—"

Eduardo lunged forward, looking to slice through the Marine's right wrist, to sever the nerve and open the arteries. But the Marine was ready for the attack. The forward movement of his blade hand as the men moved counterclockwise had been a tactic, an intentionally planted weakness. He was lightning fast in his defensive reaction, sliding beneath Eduardo's blade, using a vicious, backhand slash to cut the fixer deep on the inner forearm. Blood poured from the wound. Eduardo jumped back, instinctively moved the knife to his left hand.

"That has to hurt," the Marine said. "Deep and clean. I see bone."

It did not hurt. Eduardo's capacity for pain was freakish, essentially superhuman. From the time he'd been a boy in Brazil, the other kids had been thunderstruck with fear and awe at his ability to withstand extreme discomfort, to endure impossible agony without so much as a grimace or a groan. He'd learned to compartmentalize the pain in that part of his body under duress, to cordon off any emotional response, to ignore the flashing, screaming nerves, the blood, the break, the burn.

Eduardo said nothing. Followed his training. Showed zero emotion. Focused on what his injury had awakened in his opponent. And what he sensed in the Marine was *bloodlust*. Not simply the amped-up, adrenaline-fueled desire to finish the fight with the vicious death of an enemy, a kind of bloodlust the fixer sensed in his opponents many times over the years. No, this was something different, something the fixer had not seen before. This was some kind of inhuman, cold-hearted hunger for the blood itself. It was an all-consuming sensation in the Marine, pulsing in his veins with every beat of his heart. It was, Eduardo thought, a weakness to be exploited.

Though he was equally skilled and deadly with a blade in either hand, he let the knife in his left hand act as a lure, a decoy. He pretended to be less adept with his weapon, weakened by the Marine's attack, and growing weaker as he bled out. And though he had blocked the pain of the bleeding gash in his right forearm, he let that arm go limp, exposing the right side of his torso. He slowed his dance, appeared unsteady, off-balance, unstable.

The Marine became impatient, a shark with blood in the water.

*Soon,* Eduardo thought. *Soon.*

And then the Marine lunged, fast and strong, carving knife thrusting toward the fixer's exposed right side. Any normal man would have been mortally wounded in that violent split-second attack.

But Eduardo was waiting for him. He slid to his left, grabbed the Marine's right wrist with his right hand, pulled him forward so he was unexpectedly off balance. In that same split second, Eduardo pushed his blade deep into the Marine's lower right abdomen.

Stunned and badly wounded, the Marine tried to pull away, to retreat and reconsider his position. Eduardo couldn't believe how strong he was, how fast, how fierce, how impervious to pain. But the fixer was unusually strong as well, remarkably fast, equally determined. He held onto the Marine's right wrist, continued pulling him off balance, punched the knife in a second time.

Still the Marine did not go down. Eduardo twisted his blade, sliced upward and side to side. The miracle man battled back. The fixer led him by the wrist, holding on for his life, both men fighting furiously. He thrust the blade in again. The Marine staggered but would not fall.

*He is not human,* Eduardo thought. *Any other man would be dead. The drug has made him something more than human.*

He pulled the blade out and slammed it in again. The Marine dropped to his knees. Eduardo dropped with him, pushed the knife deeper into his right side.

There were two more minutes of struggle, then two minutes of stillness and, then the Marine let go of the carving knife and fell forward, dead before his face hit the ground.

Eduardo was exhausted. Badly injured. He looked at his arm and knew he needed immediate medical attention—he'd lost a tremendous amount of blood and was bleeding out still. He removed his belt and tied a tourniquet above the nasty gash the Marine had cut into him. He was too weak, too damaged, too fatigued to kill Carrie and the cook and the rest of the Copacabana residents. He would repair, reassess, and return soon to eliminate the remaining evidence.

He reached into the Marine's pocket—what was his name? Arnie Bialik? Yes, that was it—he reached into Arnie Bialik's pocket, retrieved the stolen vial of capsules, forced himself to regain composure, strapped on his shoulder holster, slipped into his sport jacket, and walked across the courtyard as if nothing of consequence had occurred.

# NEMESIS

GODDESS OF REVENGE (AMONG OTHER THINGS)

# CHAPTER 45
# IN THE NAME OF HOLY VENGEANCE

CARRIE CLIMBED ABOARD THE HARLEY, wrapped her arms around Johnny's waist, and let the afterglow of the evening wash over her like a midsummer Malibu wave. She'd had three orgasms in the Avalon ladies' room—she knew it was three because she'd heard herself scream out *oh shit, that's one...oh my God, that's two...Jesus fucking Christ, that's threeeeee*—but that wasn't the reason she was feeling so warm and wonderful. *Okay, fine,* she thought as Johnny pulled the bike away from the club. *That's part of the reason.* But the deeper-truer-greater source of the wellspring of purring happiness in her heart was the profound sense of emotional bonding she felt for Johnny.

She had laughed and danced and downed shots of tequila with Johnny and with the Copa crew and her Avalon Ladies Room Fan Club until who even knew what time it was. And with that had come the sensation that—she couldn't believe it but was sure it must be true—she was just like a Person at the Party. But in her next breath on the back of the bike, she realized the feeling she was feeling had nothing to do with being a Person at the Party and everything to do with...falling in love.

*Oh, for Pete's sake, Carrie, you're a scientist,* she thought. *So how about you think this through scientifically before jumping off the fall-*

*ing-in-love bridge. You don't just reach instantaneous conclusions when it comes to something so personally monumental as falling in love. You think it through, you process the signs and signals, you examine the evidence, and then you make a determination. So, biologically speaking, it's accepted science that there are three major motivators for falling in love: libido, connection, and partner preference. Check, check, and check. And as far as chemistry is concerned, the primary neurochemicals that control these primal drives are testosterone, estrogen, dopamine, oxytocin, and vasopressin. Meaning, check, check, check, check, and check. Now, sharpening the focus down to a single subject—me—psychologically and physiologically, this feeling of euphoria I'm feeling, combined with the release of the previously mentioned cocktail of chemicals in my brain can, in fact, make falling in love feel like an addictive rush, which is what I appear to be experiencing at this very moment. That said, when adding excessive amounts of tequila and fucking in a public restroom to any equation, it is considered good laboratory practice to appreciate the possibility scientific reasoning, not to mention results, go right out the window. Meaning, it's possible I'm falling in love with Johnny Fairfax, but it's also possible I'm falling in love with the idea of falling in love with Johnny Fairfax. And further, it's possible that both outcomes are simultaneously true. And further still, I goddamn hope they are.*

Johnny pulled the Harley to the curb in front of the Copa. The passenger van parked behind them. It was three a.m. Friday morning. Carrie was exhilarated but tired to the bone.

*Except tired isn't the right word.* "I'm spent," Carrie said. "That's what I am."

She and Johnny waited by the front gate and watched the Copa crew come out of the van.

"Me too," Johnny said. "Spent."

"I've never been spent before."

"Feels good."

"Really good."

"We'll have to get spent again. Maybe not in a nightclub bathroom next time."

Even after everything they'd done and been through and shared, she could feel herself blushing. "I'm so glad there's going to be a next time."

She saw the same happiness, the same heartfelt attachment, in his eyes. But before she could say something about it, put it on the table, so to speak, the Copa crew were at the gate.

There was nothing spent about them. They'd taken over the Avalon dance floor, ruled the Avalon bar, dominated the Avalon evening—nonstop insanity from the moment they'd hit the floor—and they were still wired, dancing off the van to music only they could hear. They were exhilarated, invigorated, energized...and famished.

"Fire up the frying pan, Tattoo Boy," Lillian said. "I got a hankering for—"

"Oh my God. Look." Betty pointed at Arnie's body.

They saw Arnie on the ground in a pool of blood, and the joy drained from their faces.

Everyone ran to him. Carrie knelt beside his body, took his wrist, put her fingertips to his neck, put her face beside his nose and mouth. Though she was a behavioral scientist and not a physician, she knew enough to know that lying in a pool of his own blood without a pulse, without breathing, was the behavior of a dead man.

She'd known Arnie for years (as an elderly man), liked him a lot, and didn't want to jump over the emotions she knew she was feeling—grief, anguish, sadness, shock, horror, distress. But Arnie had put the capsules in his pocket for safekeeping, and the cleaner had come to collect them. Carrie checked Arnie's pockets. Nothing. Empty.

"He took them," she said. "The cleaner killed Arnie and took the capsules."

The Copa crew shot straight past sorrow to anger and rage. They circled the body, danced around it like some kind of alien war tribe.

"Fuck the cleaner," Walter said.

"Kill the cleaner," Bernard said.

"Hang him," Bob said.

"Shoot him," Norman said.

"Cut his throat," Brenda said.

"Crush his skull," Helen said.

"Shred his skin," Dolores said.

"Break his bones," Betty said.

"Drink his blood," Lillian said.

"In the name of holy vengeance," Joanna said, tears of rage in her eyes, "we do solemnly swear to slaughter the cleaner."

*Slaughter the cleaner*, they all chanted. *Slaughter the cleaner. Slaughter the cleaner.*

"It wasn't the cleaner," Johnny said.

The tribe stopped in its tracks.

Carrie followed the smeared trail of Arnie's blood. It seemed as if he'd pulled himself fifteen feet across the courtyard toward the outdoor dining room, perhaps trying to get to the first aid kit in the kitchen, before he couldn't pull himself another inch and died.

Johnny stood where Arnie had first fallen. Carrie walked to him and looked down. In his own blood, with his own hand, Arnie had written one word: *fixer*.

Rage roared through the Copa gang. There was nothing Carrie could do to stem their emotional typhoon. So she waited for it to pass and looked at Johnny. *This will go from bad to worse*, her eyes said. He nodded. They no longer had to speak to understand each other.

"The fixer is dead," Joanna said. "Mr. Fairfax and I were there when the lab exploded. No one could have lived through a detonation of that magnitude."

"While he was bleeding to death," Carrie said, "Arnie took the time to tell us it wasn't the cleaner, and believe me, he'd have known the difference. You all would. They're night and day. So given Arnie's message, written in his own blood, we have to allow for the possibility there was at least one way Eduardo Wolf could have survived."

They were quiet, but Carrie felt them seething with violence, burning with grief. She sensed each one of them running the new equation in their mind, all of them coming to the same result.

"It was the third and last dose that locked in the age-reversal result of the drug in the Greek Gods, is that correct?" Joanna said.

"All the evidence points that way, yes," Carrie said. "But this is uncharted scientific territory. There's no map for this medication."

"Map or no map, we have to take the third dose," Betty said.

*The third dose*, they chanted. *The third dose. The third dose.*

"Yes, yes, but how do we do that if the fixer has the capsules?" Norman said.

"He'll be back," Lillian said. "They both will. The fixer and the cleaner."

"We're unfinished business," Dolores said. "Evidence to be destroyed before the case is closed."

*They'll be back*, they chanted, dancing again around Arnie's dead body. *They'll be back. They'll be back.*

"That's the good news," Brenda said.

"Damn good," Walter said.

"We'll be ready for them," Bob said. "Especially the fucking fixer."

"He has to bring the drug with him," Helen said.

*Bring the drug*, they chanted. *Bring the drug. Bring the drug.*

"Why would he do that?" Johnny whispered to Carrie.

"Because he won't have a choice." Carrie crossed the court-yard to her apartment, looking once over her shoulder at the Copa crew, who danced around the dead body of their fallen tribal warrior, chanting *in the name of holy vengeance* again and again and again and again.

She went inside her apartment, walked to her bedroom,

pulled open the drawer on her bedside table, and removed the black business card Eduardo Wolf had handed her in the lab eight days ago after he'd killed Stuart in the InSinkErator while he was breathing on her neck and making her swoon.

She called the number. While she waited for the fixer to answer, the Copa crew chanted in the courtyard, *In the name of holy* vengeance, *In the name of holy vengeance. In the name of holy vengeance.*

"He fought like a soldier and died like a man," Eduardo said.

"I want the capsules," Carrie said.

*In the name of holy vengeance. In the name of holy vengeance."*

"You may not have them," Eduardo said.

"Then I will make my own. Millions of them," Carrie said.

Silence. She knew the fixer had understood precisely what she was saying.

*In the name of holy vengeance. In the name of holy vengeance.*

"You have Sikorski's original notes," Eduardo said.

"His final chemical equation," Carrie said.

*In the name of holy vengeance. In the name of holy vengeance.*

"It does not belong to you," Eduardo said.

"Maybe it belongs to Pfeiffer," Carrie said. "I could call the cleaner and ask him."

Silence again. She could feel the fixer's anger.

"What do you propose?" Eduardo said.

"A trade. The capsules for the formula and the lives of my friends."

"I accept. Where and when?"

"The Copa. High noon."

The fixer hung up without another word. Carrie took a breath, hardly holding on to the fast-receding memory of her and Johnny drinking, dancing, and screwing at Avalon, and went back to the courtyard. *High noon?* she thought. *What is this, a Western?*

The Copa crew had gathered wooden tables from the card room and piled them in a helter-skelter stack. Arnie's body had been laid peacefully on top. They were placing Arnie's personal possessions on the table around his dead body, as solemn as dying thunder.

Johnny met her by the pool.

"What are they doing?" she said.

"Building a funeral pyre," he said. "They're going to burn Arnie, drive his ashes to the ocean, and scatter them over the water. Let the wind carry them all the way to Poland, where he can rest in honor and peace for all eternity. That's their plan."

"Of course it is," she said.

She and Johnny sat on a poolside chaise and watched the bonfire burn.

# CHAPTER 46

# BEST WRITING FOR AN IMAGINARY DETECTIVE SERIES INSIDE CARRIE'S BRAIN

AFTER ARNIE'S ashes had been collected into a porcelain ginger jar donated by Dolores; after Johnny had grilled, roasted, and pan-fried the very last butchered bits of Ben Boston; after the Copa crew had devoured their early-morning meat and headed for the hidden beaches of Malibu so Arnie's remains could be cast and carried around the globe; after Carrie and Johnny had been too tired to clean the kitchen, not to mention the scorched residue of the improvised funeral pyre, and had fallen asleep in each other's arms on a poolside chaise; after the first light of day had awoken them and they'd kissed like crazy and made love again; after all that, it was eight thirty, Friday morning, and the homicide detectives had arrived.

Eric Flore and Steve Higgins were, Carrie thought, right off the Hollywood casting couch. Detective Flore was fifty, salt-and-pepper hair with a speckled goatee to match. Detective Higgins was ten years younger. Surfer blond and ocean-blue eyes.

*They could be the stars of their own homicide detective TV series,* Carrie thought, *if they weren't busy being actual homicide detectives.*

Despite the homicide nature of their detective-ness, Carrie was too dreamy to dial herself in. She was sure it was the tequila and the dancing and the sex, not to mention the funeral pyre in the courtyard. Plus, she'd hardly slept. Her world was in free-falling flux. She'd lost control of her own storyline. Some unknown power of the universe was writing the scenes of her life, crafting her dialogue, moving disparate characters in and out of her topsy-turvy world. Dreamy didn't begin to describe the chaos swimming in her head and heart. She was peripherally aware Johnny was speaking with the detectives, but her comprehension of their conversation was negligible because she was imagining herself guest-starring on the hit Flore and Higgins TV show *SoCal Slow Burn*.

She wasn't sure if it was network or Netflix, but she was the visiting antagonist-of-the-week who'd stolen a miracle drug from an illegal lab, administered the drug to her mother and her mother's friends, been "involved" with a succession of violent deaths, fallen head over heels for a two-time ex-con cook, lied to the police, matched wits with professional hitmen, and was in deep denial of her dangerous circumstances as the law-enforcement noose tightened around her neck. Or maybe that was her real life. Who could tell at this point?

"Miss Kromer," Flore said. "Care to join us?"

"We boring you?" Higgins said.

"Carrie," Johnny said.

"What? No. I'm sorry." Carrie fought through her fog. "Were you saying something? You were. You were saying something."

"We were saying we found your name in a fireproof file cabinet that survived the explosion," Flore said.

"We were saying there were three dead bodies in the lab, one that we haven't identified yet, and two that we have," Higgins said.

"We were saying the two we identified were LAPD," Flore said.

"Detectives Ronda and Rowena Ramos," Higgins said.

"We were saying that not only are they tied to you because

they're dead in your lab, but they're tied to Fairfax and his missing parole officer, Ben Boston," Flore said.

"We were saying we think the two of you are in it up to your assholes, and that means multiple homicides, including two of LA's finest," Higgins said.

"We were saying the smart play would be to get out ahead of this thing and cooperate like your lives depended on it because they do," Flore said.

"We were saying the other name in the file cabinet was Stuart Langston," Higgins said. "We reached out, but he's been missing for more than a week."

"Did Langston do it and go off the grid, or is he dead like the dude in the lab?" Flore said.

"We were saying who's the unidentified dead dude in the lab?" Higgins said.

"The one with his face chewed to shit," Flore said.

"We'll identify him soon—teeth, fingerprints, whatever," Higgins said, "but it'll be positive points for you if you save us the time and aggravation and tell us who he is."

"We were saying it's time to talk the talk," Flore said.

Carrie looked at the detectives and nodded she understood it was time for her to come clean and tell them what she knew, which was everything about everything since she'd bashed Old Tom on the head.

"I want to help you, Detectives. I really do," she said, "but I don't know what in the world you're talking about."

*There's something exciting about being on the wrong side of the law,* Carrie thought. But then she immediately clarified that for herself. *Not in a good way. In a bad way. Very bad. Bad exciting.*

She glanced at Johnny and knew by the look in his eyes he would give nothing away either. They were in this together to the end. She wanted to kiss him so bad she could practically taste his tongue.

"What about you, Fairfax?" Flore said. "Care to add anything to Kromer's nothing?"

"I haven't seen or spoken to Mr. Boston in, I don't know, five or six days, something like that, so I can't help you there," Johnny said. "Don't really remember."

Higgins took out a little pad, flipped the pages backward in time. "You met with your parole officer a week ago, last Friday, at which time he scheduled a home/work inspection for that following Tuesday, which is when he called his office to say he was here and headed inside."

"That's the last time anyone saw him," Flore said.

"The next day, Wednesday, Detectives Rowena and Ronda Ramos came to the Copacabana to investigate the unexplained disappearance of your parole officer," Higgins said.

"And were told they'd need a warrant," Flore said. "I got to wonder why in the hell they would need a warrant to find a missing parole officer who had it in for a two-time ex-con cook with a documented inclination for violence. Don't you, Fairfax?"

"It's a free country, Detective Flore," Carrie said, "but not that free. The police can't just rip a place apart without cause. Mr. Boston never showed up here. Johnny told those detectives that—we both did—and they wouldn't take our word for it. So they had to get a warrant. If I'm not mistaken, that's the way the law works."

"They wouldn't take your word for it? No kidding," Flore said. "A lying criminal and his smart-mouth girlfriend? Who wouldn't believe the two of you?"

Adrenaline pushed through Carrie's veins. *You got that right, cop*, she thought. *I am his smart-mouth girlfriend.*

"The detectives returned Wednesday evening with a warrant, searched the premises for signs of the missing parole officer, and left unsatisfied," Higgins said.

"By unsatisfied you mean with nothing," Johnny said. "You mean they left with nothing because he was never here."

"Thursday morning, there were reports of a massive explosion in the San Fernando Valley on Sherman Way in Reseda,"

Higgins said. "Fire and police on the scene discovered three bodies in the wreckage of an unlicensed, unregistered pharmaceutical lab. The Ramos twins and one unidentified male."

"Did we mention him, the one without his face?" Flore said.

They went on for ten more minutes, reciting by date and time the odd occurrences that had led them to the Copacabana, to Carrie and Johnny. She heard them say they'd reported the illicit lab to the FDA but lost focus and missed much of what they said after that because she turned the channel from the real-life homicide detectives in the Copa courtyard to their hit TV series *SoCal Slow Burn*, in which she was this week's guest-starring villain.

As was always the case in these cases, the end of the episode was bad news for the bad guy. Flore and Higgins, as they always did, identified the dead body in the lab from dental records, pulled his address, and searched his house. The ensuing trial was lurid, scandalous, and sensational—what with the stolen wonder drug, the man-eating rats, the professional hitmen, and the sex in the Avalon ladies' room. The verdict was guilty on all counts. The sentence was prison for as far into the future as Carrie could see.

The good news was the episode was nominated for an Emmy in the category of Best Writing for an Imaginary Detective Series Inside Carrie's Brain because the heartbreaking subtext of the story—the emotionality that connected the audience to the villain for the entirety of the dramatic hour in spite of her smart mouth and dastardly deeds—was the romantic relationship she'd finally found after living her whole life as a lonely, science-geek, rat-girl wallflower was over before it ever had a chance.

That's when Flore answered his mobile, had a quick conversation, whispered something important to his partner, and Higgins snapped her back into the moment by saying they'd return sooner rather than later but had to go because that was the lab calling to report a positive ID on the faceless dead body was imminent.

The moment they were through the front gate, Carrie said, "We have to get to Sikorski's house before they do. My sweater's still there."

"What about the funeral pyre?" Johnny said.

"Sweater first," Carrie said, "or I get my Emmy in prison."

# CHAPTER 47
# EVERY MAKE AND MODEL OF MURDER YOU CAN IMAGINE

WITH CARRIE'S arms wrapped around him, Johnny rode the Harley to Sikorski's house in Canoga Park, smack in the middle of the 7800 block on Owensmouth Avenue. He parked around the corner from the dead man's mid-century ranch so no one would be able to trace the bike back to him or Carrie or the Copa. It was still Friday morning. There was no one on the street. Carrie left her purse in the saddlebag on the back of the bike, and they walked past Sikorski's house, looking for meddlesome neighbors.

The coast was clear, and they cut quickly down the narrow slip of crabgrass between Sikorski's ranch and the house next door and arrived in the backyard without anyone witnessing their trespass.

The yard was fenced and, like forty thousand other LA houses trying to beat the heat, had an in-ground pool—low-budget concrete with a deep end, a shallow end, a diving board, and a curvy slide.

*Kids lived here before Sikorski did,* Johnny thought. *I would've slept on that slide if this was my house. Who doesn't love a freaking slide?*

The water was murky—no one had cleaned or used the pool

in quite some time. A few unattractive trees were placed here and there across the yard. Their only purpose, it seemed to Johnny, was to drop leaves everywhere. A few random flower beds were dead to the world. A rusted grill and a worn-out picnic table had been abandoned years ago. An electric leaf blower rested on top of the table, its long cord plugged into an outlet on the back of the house. Johnny imagined Sikorski was about to blow leaves off the patio and away from the pool but got distracted and gave up before he started. Tall, thick, unruly hedges ran the full perimeter of the fence line, creating a sense of unmanicured dystopian privacy.

*Not so Sikorsky couldn't see them*, Johnny thought. *So they couldn't see him.*

They got their bearings for a minute, then Johnny looked at Carrie, and she nodded. He moved to a kitchen window and got ready to bust it in. But before his elbow hit the glass, the back door opened, and Francine Fontana stepped out of the house and onto the back patio, armed with a .357 Magnum.

*Dirty fucking Harry*, Johnny thought. *Blow a hole in your chest you could ride my Harley through.*

Francine was fifteen feet from them, revolver aimed in their direction, Carrie's sweater in her other hand. "Looking for this, girlfriend?"

"Yes, I am," Carrie said.

"Not a great color for you." Francine tossed the sweater to Carrie.

"Beside the point, Francine, don't you think?" Carrie said, catching the sweater.

"I think the point is, you brought your ex-con lover boy along for the ride," Francine said. "I think the point is, two birds with one stone, the stone being my Magnum."

Johnny had never been called anyone's *ex-con lover boy*. He liked it. Tough and sexy at the same time. He wanted to let it sink in, *ex-con lover boy*, but instead he thought about how he was going to get the gun out of Francine's hands before anything tragic happened. He took a step toward Carrie.

Francine pointed the .357 right at his face. "Don't move until I tell you to, Fairfax. Got it?"

"Think so," Johnny said, and took another step to Carrie, beside her now. "Don't move until you tell me to."

"I assume your Russian boyfriend went to the Copa," Carrie said.

"Fifty-fifty whether you came here to collect your sweater or stayed home to guard Sikorski's notes," Francine said. "I said here. He said there. I win. You lose. Either way, I mean. You lose either way."

Johnny had not liked this woman the first time she'd shown up at the Copacabana with the Matrix twin detectives. He liked her a lot less now that she was pointing a .357 at his head. *I need a moment. That's all I need. One fucking moment.*

"I'm not telling you where the notes are," Carrie said.

"Here's the thing about love, girlfriend," Francine said. "It makes you do things you promised yourself you'd never do. Take me, for instance. I've been a crime writer for more years than I care to admit. I've seen every make and model of murder you can imagine. Worst of the worst. Told myself I'd never kill anyone any time for any reason. And then I met my Russian bear. Now, I'm going to kill someone right here, right now, if you don't tell me where you hid the notes."

"You can't kill me, Francine," Carrie said. "You'll never find them without me."

Francine took two steps toward them and aimed the .357 at Johnny's chest. "Not you, Carrie. Him. Your lover boy. He's dead in five, four, three, two—"

"Okay, fine. You win," Carrie said.

*Give me one moment,* Johnny thought. *Is that too much to ask? One goddamn moment.*

"I'm listening," Francine said.

"First floor," Carrie said. "First room on the right as you come through the gate. Used to be Betty's apartment. Now it's the gym and the guest room. It's under the mattress in the bedroom."

"And my camera?" Francine said.

"With the notes," Carrie said. "So now you don't kill us, right? You have what you want, you just let us go."

"Hold that thought, girlfriend," Francine said, and took her cell phone from her pocket. She made a call, held the phone to her ear, the .357 still aimed at Johnny. Her voice did a one eighty, from murderous crime writer to flirtatious sex kitten.

*Jesus Christ*, Johnny thought. *She's phone fucking him while she points her gun at me. First time for everything. How about first time for one fucking moment?*

Francine told Tino about the notes and camera under the mattress, then she listened for a while, then she said she would give him her full report in person. She explained that by "in person" she meant while she was fucking him later, after she killed these two losers and he collected her camera and the notes and met her at Sikorski's house. Then she told him the other sexual things she would do to him, some of which were disgusting and gross, even to Johnny, then she hung up.

"Congratulations," Francine said. "I'm not going to kill you."

"That's good," Carrie said.

"Not really. Not for you. They'll call it murder-suicide," Francine said. "You shoot Fairfax in the head, then blow your own brains out. Both of you dead in the pool. No prints on the gun. LAPD will let it go like a hot rock."

"Don't do it, Francine," Carrie said. "Nothing's worth killing people."

"I used to think the same thing," Francine said. "But billions in my bank account and global fame for changing the course of human history? I don't know...I think that's worth killing people for. Especially a geek like you and a loser like Fairfax. Now move to the edge of the pool, nice and slow."

Johnny glanced at Carrie and it was as if they'd had a long

conversation over a cup of coffee at the local Starbucks about Francine and her .357 and Sikorski's notes and the capsules and the cleaner and the fixer and Avalon and the Copa and the funeral pyre and the lines that connected them and everything between those lines. At the end of it, she gave him an imperceptible nod, a nod no one else could have seen, a private nod. And in that private nod, Carrie said, *I believe in you, I have confidence in you, I need you, I trust you, I love you, and I know you can save us both if you can get a moment. Here comes your moment.*

"What's your story here, Francine?" Carrie said.

She and Johnny were now side by side at the edge of the deep end, the barrel of the Magnum on the back of his head.

"She don't have one," he said.

"You came to Sikorski's house to find the notes you couldn't find in the lab," Francine said. "You and Fairfax had a nasty argument, you shot him in the back of the head, then did yourself. Classic crime writing. Thank you very much."

"Thin as the paper it's written on," Carrie said. "Lazy crime writing, thank you very much. If I'm your editor, I'm sending you back for rewrites."

"You think so?" Francine said, but she seemed taken aback, offended by being called a lazy crime writer.

"I know so," Carrie said. "What kind of nasty argument would Johnny and I have that would make me shoot him in the back of the head? That's a plot hole any self-respecting crime writer would fill before moving on with the story. I'm surprised, really. I thought you were better."

Francine was silent. The .357 still at the back of his brain, Johnny imagined her thinking through plot lines, trying to create one on the fly. Carrie had bumped her off balance.

"I have one," Carrie said. "I was jealous because I found out you were fucking him behind my back."

Francine laughed out loud, and in the exact split second of that laugh, Johnny spun, grabbed her arm, and flung her far out into the deep water. She splashed down hard, revolver still in her hand.

Without blinking, Johnny ran to the picnic table, lifted the plugged-in electric leaf blower, and threw it at Francine.

Nothing happened, except Francine wiggled and jiggled like she'd been tickled. It was obvious that she wasn't a good swimmer. Treading water while keeping the gun pointed at them, while flailing her way to the metal pool ladder was a chore and a half.

"I still have the gun, you fucking idiots," Francine said, spitting water. "Don't fucking move."

"We should run," Carrie said to Johnny.

"We should stay," Johnny said.

"I don't think so," Carrie said, and tugged at his arm.

"Trust me," Johnny said.

Francine reached the side of the pool and grabbed the metal ladder with her left hand. She placed the gun on the lip of the edge, too close to her for Johnny or Carrie to get it, and took hold of the ladder with her right hand, becoming part of the circuit for the voltage in the water.

The electric current surged through the crime writer, searching for a path to ground. Her eyes opened wider than wide, and her eyeballs practically popped out of their sockets. Her back arched, her body shook violently, her head bobbled up and down with abandon. Five seconds. Ten seconds. Fifteen full seconds of current shooting through her heart. Only then did Johnny pull the cord from the wall.

Francine released the ladder and splashed backwards into the pool, looking up at the sky, seeing nothing, literally dead in the water.

"How did you know?" Carrie said.

"When I dropped out of high school, I worked weekends with my old man's brother, building pools. He made a big deal about grounds and closed circuits and voltage and currents. It's not the voltage, he told me two hundred times. It's the current looking for a route to ground. That's what'll kill you. Being part of the circuit."

"She was part of the circuit. A route to ground."

"Dead ground."

"Really dead."

She took his hand and leaned her head on his shoulder, and together they watched Francine's fried body float across Sikorski's pool.

# CHAPTER 48
# IT WASN'T A NAIL OR A SCREW OR A SPLINTER

TINO CLICKED off the call with Francine and wondered, *How should I kill her?* He was standing in the Copa courtyard, in front of the scorched remains of what appeared to be a funeral pyre. There was no one else here.

*Must have been big blaze,* he thought, wishing he'd been there to watch the flames dance, wistfully remembering the hypnotic magic of the Acura fire, when Justin the bartender had burned alive in his own car. *Maybe burn Bambi too.*

From the first lecherous moment they'd seen each other in the lab, there had been no doubt in his mind he would kill Francine. It was true that he'd lusted for her in that same breath —she was buxom and bawdy, his favorite female features—but being in Sikorski's lab had made her part of Sikorski's mess.

*Maybe cut throat.*

While acknowledging she would die, he'd also been picturing her tits in his face and wondering how much she would charge him to have sex with her. That she'd turned out to be as physically attracted to him as he was to her had been a delightful development. That she'd fucked him without money changing hands had been an unexpected surprise. That she'd liked it and wanted it rough had been an improbable pleasure that had ignited his imagination, supercharged his libido, and subconsciously sanctioned him to dream with her out loud about their future together.

*Maybe suffocate with plastic bag.*

The dream had been that they'd be rich beyond measure. They'd be fantastically famous. They'd fuck each other hard and rough three times a day on their personal yachts and their private planes and in their massive mansions spread around the globe. They would drink expensive champagne. Drive luxurious sports cars. Wear designer clothes made just for them. They would own priceless paintings framed with diamonds. Throw outrageous parties on the tops of skyscrapers. The paparazzi would worship them. Their wedding would be televised in every nation, their story told in every language. The world would adore them. They would be crowned the king and queen of all Earth for bestowing eternal youth upon the human race.

*Maybe shoot in head.*

Dreaming about such a life had been perversely exciting, not to mention homicidally motivating. Francine was intoxicated with lust and power, inebriated with murder and mayhem. She wanted to kill Carrie and the cook herself, she'd said. Wanted to do her part, earn her keep, carry her weight. Wanted her Russian bear to be proud of his Bambi. Who was he to deny her this indulgence, her expression of her love for him and the fantabulous life they would create together? Their future was set in stone, except for the fact it was never going to happen.

*Maybe stab in heart.*

Whatever she felt for him he did not feel for her. He was incapable of intimacy, unable to process what others referred to as emotions. His universe was measured in binary code. Two feelings only. Pleasure and pain. Every encounter was one or the other...or one until it was the other. Francine had been pleasure until she wasn't. She'd seduced him and entertained him. But she had not moved him because he was not moveable.

*Maybe push gasoline-soaked towel down throat and light match.*

That one made him laugh out loud. He turned away from the funeral pyre, how he'd kill Francine Fontana finally decided, and went to the first room to the right of the Copacabana gate. The gym and guest room. Carrie had hidden Sikorski's notes and Bambi's camera under the mattress. He would collect what belonged to the oligarchs and burn the Copa and everyone in it to the ground. Talk about pleasure.

He opened the door and stepped into the gym. There was a treadmill that had not been trod upon in years. A rack of free weights no one had lifted in longer than no one had treaded upon the mill. Yoga mats and big exercise balls. Blocks for an aerobic step class that had never stepped a step. One wall was mirrored with a ballet barre. Tino stopped before the mirror and touched the bar.

As a boy in Russia, where ballet was as popular as basketball, he'd taken dance classes for an entire year. He'd understood the athletic artistry of it all, learned the proud history of the Bolshoi, and committed to memory its most famous ballets. "*The Sleeping Beauty, Swan Lake, La Bayadere, The Nutcracker, Spartacus*," he said, holding the barre and looking at himself in the Copa gym mirror. But ballet was not for him. He couldn't wait to get home and burn rats.

He opened the door from the gym to the bedroom. Queen-sized bed on the opposite wall of the door. Two night tables, each with a small lamp, on either side of the bed. Closet with sliding mirrored doors. Dresser and Barcalounger with a reading table and floor lamp. Tino thought the room looked like an old faded photograph, the colors dulled and dying with the march of time.

He knelt beside the bed, lifted the mattress six inches with his left hand, slid his right arm into the space above the box spring, and swept it from side to side, feeling for the notes and the camera.

Something was odd. The box spring had a one-foot wood-plank edge all around its perimeter but had been hollowed in the middle. The mattress had just enough lip to support it so it wouldn't sink and sag into the open center, where the springs should have been.

"What kind of crazy fucking bed is—"

He screamed in pain, couldn't finish the sentence because something very sharp cut him very deep on the top of his hand.

"Fucking *fuck*—"

He screamed again as something else cut him hard on the underside of his wrist, opening the radial and ulnar arteries that bring blood into the hand.

He felt the blood spurting out of his wrist. On his knees now, he shoved the mattress to the side to free his arm and check his wounds. He imagined it was a loose nail or a screw or a ragged-jagged splinter left by whatever fucking idiot had removed the middle of the box spring.

It wasn't a nail or a screw or a splinter.

It was the Greek Gods.

"You fucking rats," Tino said, grabbing his wrist, trying to stop the bleeding. "Don't look at me, you fucking-fucking rats."

But the Gods *were* looking at him. All of them in a row, staring up at him. It was ridiculous to think they remembered him, that they recalled the cleaner killing Dionysus, hurling their comrade against the wall of cages and then crushing him with his foot. But to Tino, it seemed as if that were exactly the case.

He was still on his knees, wrist bleeding badly, chest against the bed, mattress shoved aside, box spring open, Gods in a line. Two rats jumped at the same time, screaming out of the box spring as if shot from little canons. They hit the cleaner in the face, one biting him hard on the cheek, tearing his skin open. The other hit him flush in the left eye, shredding the eyeball with its razor teeth, puss and blood and ocular fluids flowing everywhere.

The cleaner screamed and fell backward, shocked and stunned but conscious he was forever blind in that eye, bleeding everywhere, knowing he had to get up and get out...and yet wanting to stay and kill the rats until they were fucking-fucking dead.

But the rats were relentless. He reached for them, grabbed at them, tried to get them off his face. He forced himself back to his knees, and two more rats hit him in the head. Then three more hit him in the chest. Seven rats biting through his clothes, through his skin, biting, biting, biting...

He fought to his feet and staggered to the doorway, the rats crawling all over his face and head, his arms and chest, sinking their teeth into his flesh, tearing him open piece by piece.

Two stutter steps and he was in the gym, his one working eye blurred with blood. He tripped over an exercise ball, crashed to the floor, cracked his head on the side of the rack of free weights, opened a nasty gash, knocked himself not quite out but unable to get back up.

There was nothing he could do. He was on his back and the rats were all over his face and head, his arms, his hands. Slicing him to shreds.

One of the Gods bit him in the neck, rupturing his carotid artery. The cleaner spasmed on the floor, sensed his blood shooting into the air. He felt himself fading into death. The pain was agonizing, excruciating, infinite.

In his mind, he could see Baba Yana, his feral grandmother. She was waiting for him at the gates of Hell.

His last vision was of himself tied to a stake in the town square, thousands and thousands of rats watching him burn for the rest of time. And then the room went dark. Not because he was dead, though death would come soon enough, but because one of the Gods had ravaged his other eye.

# CHAPTER 49

# THE DEAL IS DEAD, LONG LIVE THE DEAL

"I WAS HOPING THIS WOULD HAPPEN," Carrie said. "I wanted it to happen. I lied about the notes and the camera, where they were, and crossed my fingers this exact thing would happen. I willed it to happen. Does that make me a bad person?"

"Makes you my hero," Johnny said.

"It was premeditated," Carrie said.

"Means more that way," Johnny said.

They were in the gym, looking down at the cleaner, who was exceptionally dead on the ground, face up, or rather what-was-left-of-his-face up. Skin and flesh gone, eaten to the bone. Eyes horrendous black pits. Blood everywhere.

After what had happened at Sikorski's house with Francine, and knowing Tino was at the Copa, but not knowing if he'd still be there when they arrived, they'd climbed quietly through Johnny's bedroom window and went room by room, Johnny wielding a crowbar, looking for the Russian, hoping to surprise him and take him out.

Instead, the cleaner had surprised them. Or at least Johnny, since Carrie had arranged for Tino's grim death-by-supernatural-rats in advance.

"I'll butcher the body," Johnny said, hoisting the Russian over his shoulder.

"I'll clean the blood," Carrie said, following Johnny out of the gym.

Johnny went to the kitchen. Carrie went to the cleaning closet.

She was surprised how casual their decisions had been—*I'll butcher the body; I'll clean the blood*—as if it were just another day at the Copa, when, truth be told, she realized as she gathered the mop, bucket, bleach, and rubber gloves, it actually *was* just another day at the Copa.

She collected the Greek Gods, gave them fresh water and love, put them back in their box spring habitat, and covered them with the mattress to keep them safe and warm.

Her phone chimed, notifying her she'd received a text message. It was her mother.

Joanna typed: *Swigging rum and skinny-dipping with dolphins in Pacific. They came to carry Arnie's ashes to Poland.*

Carrie replied: *There are no dolphins in the Baltic Sea.*

Joanna replied: *There will be when they get there with Arnie's ashes.*

Carrie replied: *How do you know they'll go to Poland and not Miami?*

Joanna replied: *They told us so.*

Carrie replied: *You believe you can communicate with dolphins?*

Joanna replied: *I'm forty-two again. I swig rum and believe I can do anything. Don't you? Back by dinner. I can positively talk to dolphins.*

Carrie put her phone back in her purse, slung the strap over her head so the purse hung across her body, and put her mind to cleaning the bloody mess that had once been the cleaner.

*The more things change,* she thought, *the more they stay the same. That's what people say. It's an immutable law of cultural physics. After everything that's happened, I'm still arguing with my mother about the silliest things. Talking to dolphins for Chrissakes. It doesn't get sillier than that.* But then she caught herself, literally stopped cleaning and stood straight up. *But that turns out to be broad bullshit. There's a new sheriff in town, people. A new law of cultural physics, and this is it: the more things change, the more they freaking change. Period. I'm cleaning up the bloody remains of a human being who was eaten by super rats. And. I'm. Okay. With. That. That's me totally changing. That's not me staying the same. My mother is forty-two years old and has cannibalistic tendencies. There's nothing staying the same about that kind of change. For all I know, she actually is talking to dolphins. The drug reconstituted her chemistry to make her younger and eat man meat; why couldn't her chemistry be reconfigured to speak dolphin?*

And then her phone chimed again. Another text. Carrie rolled her eyes and took her phone out of her purse. But it wasn't her mother. It was Johnny.

*Come to the kitchen. Bring Sikorski's notes. Hurry.*

She ran to her room, slid her underwear drawer clean out of the dresser, collected the notes she'd taped to the backboard, put them in her purse, and hurried, like the text said, to the kitchen.

She wondered why Johnny would text her that message. What could be happening that she would need to bring the notes and have to hurry? The cleaner was dead and wasn't popping back to life on the butcher block. Not without his face.

And then she remembered.

She'd arranged to meet the fixer at noon, to trade the capsules for the notes and their lives. *High noon,* she thought. *That's what I said. High fucking noon. It has to be him.*

And it was. Eduardo Wolf—black slacks, black short-sleeved T-shirt, impenetrable sunglasses, and a bandaged arm—had knocked Johnny mostly unconscious and tied his wrists and ankles to a support column. Johnny was shirtless, bleeding from his nose and ear. He would have a horrible black eye, but he was not dead.

"Did you bring the capsules?" Carrie said.

She was scared of the fixer and worried sick about Johnny, but she was determined to keep it out of her voice, off her face, away from her eyes. Plus, Eduardo Wolf looked smoking hot in his tight tee and dark shades, and she absolutely could not let that lust bubble up right now.

*No swooning*, she thought. *Don't you dare swoon.*

Eduardo took two steps toward the counter, and lifted a six-inch boning knife—sharp point, badass narrow blade. "Did you bring Sikorski's chemical equations?"

"Capsules first," Carrie said.

"I think not," Eduardo said.

"No capsules, no notes," Carrie said.

"No notes, no Fairfax," Eduardo said.

He put the point of the boning knife in the middle of Johnny's chest, on the un-inked skin between the words *Beast* and *Chef*, and applied just enough pressure to make Johnny wince without breaking through the skin.

"We had a deal," Carrie said, trying to stay focused.

"The deal is dead; long live the deal," Eduardo said.

He pushed the blade a touch harder, still not drawing blood but causing Johnny pain he could not silence.

"Fuck you," Johnny said. "Fuck this motherfucker, Carrie. Don't give him shit. He's going to kill me either way."

"I will certainly kill Fairfax if you don't give me Sikorski's notes," Eduardo said. "I may or may not kill him if you do. That, in essence, is the new deal. What's it going to be, Carrie? You have ten seconds to decide. Ten, nine..."

Though it was Johnny's life on the line, it was her life that passed before her eyes. Her profound and pivotal moments, her Earth-shattering, ground-shaking, life-shaping moments—all of it rushing onto her internal monitors, overloading her senses, simultaneously intersecting at her emotional mountaintop, creating a creepy-crazy, hyper-conscious, nuclear-fusion aware-ness of the people who'd pushed her along the path of her days.

"Eight, seven..." Eduardo pressed the blade just hard enough to draw first blood.

Johnny screamed but only for a second. "Fuck you, you fucking fixer. Fuck you."

"Six, five…" Eduardo inserted the boning knife one sixteenth of an inch into Johnny's chest.

Her father's dead-drunk, verbal-violent abuse. That terrible day at the pool with her mother, Carrie in a one-piece on the diving board, ashamed of her pear-shaped figure, afraid to dive, afraid to fail in front of the other children. Stuart Langston coming on to her that first day in the lab. The Brazilian biology boy dripping candle wax onto her belly with the lights low, Fleetwood Mac in the background. Daryl Sasso's mother calling downstairs to the darkened basement, asking if everything was all right while Daryl ejaculated and Carrie thought about the real-life pilots who'd flown the World War Two jet fighters, a mental attempt to numb the physical pain of her first fuck. The day she knew the rats were younger and the drug worked. Riding on the rear of Johnny's Harley, her arms around his waist, hair blowing in the wind, cheek resting against his back, the happiest she'd been in her entire life.

"Four, three…" Eduardo said.

She looked at the fixer—no, through him. Could see the whole of her world and knew lust was no longer her primary emotional motivator. What moved her now was love. She was no longer hugging the Wall of Life. She was a Person at the Party. Johnny, the most unlikely of men, had stood by her side, taken her hand, won her heart, and guided her into the warmth of the sun.

"Two, one…" Eduardo said. The muscles in his arm tightened as he prepared to push the boning blade deep into Johnny's chest.

"Wait," Carrie said. "The notes are in my purse."

The fixer waited.

Carrie opened her purse, pulled out Sikorski's gun, and shot Eduardo Wolf in the balls.

He went down like a sack of cement, dropped the knife, and

grabbed his bleeding nuts, too stunned and in too much pain to make even a sound.

"Jesus Christ," Johnny said. "When did you get a fucking gun?"

She told him about when Sikorski had come to the lab to deliver what he'd called *cause-and-effect* justice. When he'd looked like a dead man walking, his feet wrapped in towels. When he'd said that for a genius, he was armed and dangerous. When he'd fired a shot in her direction. When she'd pushed the table maze on top of him and clicked the Greek Gods to his face. When she'd grabbed his gun off the ground and put it in her purse. That was when.

"Jesus Christ," Johnny said again. "Why did he have towels on his feet?"

While they were both wondering about that, something she'd learned from her father—who'd occasionally imparted a little wisdom between bouts of drunken abuse—came to mind. She was a schoolgirl. It was after class. Instead of soccer or ballet or band or theater, he'd taken her to his university lab, where one of his experiments was proceeding poorly, and told her *a good scientist finishes what they start, whether they like the result or not.*

With that in mind, she walked to the fixer and shot him five times in the chest.

It was a result she liked.

# CHAPTER 50
# PROBABLY THE THIRD SHOE

BUTCHERING Ben Boston had been a monumental challenge. First of all, the son of a bitch was the size of a water buffalo. Second of all, he weighed as much as a water buffalo filled with water. Third of all, at the time, *three fucking days ago,* Johnny's experience of carving a dead man into commercial cuts for cooking had been zero. Fourth and final of all, the dead man on the butcher block had been Johnny's very own parole officer—who he'd had a hand in drowning. How, Johnny had wondered while standing over that mountain of a man, was he supposed to ply his trade under *those* kinds of conditions?

But by the time he was cutting the last of the cleaner into cubes for a classic Russian stroganoff, he'd already sliced and diced the fixer into ground chuck for a tasty *Picadinho'A Brasilera,* into flank steaks for grilling with a bright Brazilian *chimichurri* marinade, and into bite-sized bits for a spicy *Feijoada,* a classic Brazilian beef and black bean stew to die for—especially if you were Eduardo Wolf.

*I'm getting the hang of butchering people,* he thought.

And then he said it out loud to Carrie. "I'm getting the hang of butchering people."

"Don't tell anyone besides me," Carrie said.

They both laughed, though neither one found it funny.

She told him she'd finished disinfecting the gym and guest room, cleaning every speck of Russian DNA off every surface with heavy-duty bleach and an industrial scouring pad.

Now they were scrubbing the kitchen, collecting the bullet that had ripped through Eduardo Wolf's nut sack, bleaching the floor where he'd bled out and died, searching for that one sneaky drop of Brazilian blood that, if discovered by the homicide detectives, would trip their investigation wire and lead to the discovery of means and motive and end with misery.

Now they were labeling and pre-dating the fresh cuts of man meat, washing the pots and pans and knives Johnny had used to carve the cleaner and the fixer into cannibal cuisine.

Now they were carrying the bags of human skin and blood and organs to the alley, dropping the gore into a metal garbage can, pouring gasoline in the can, and lighting a fire that would burn the evidence to untraceable ash.

Now they were dumping the can and spraying the ash with a hose, washing it away down the alley.

Now they were back in the kitchen, crushing the bones Johnny had baked until brittle, grinding them to nothing, and discarding the dust down a Palm Avenue sewer.

Johnny worked beside her throughout the day. Though he was absorbed with the grizzly task at hand, he couldn't take his eyes off her. They didn't speak until they were done, until there was no trace of anything that would call attention to whatever. And then he said he needed five minutes to breathe before preparing dinner, and they went to the courtyard and sat in lounge chairs beside the pool, waiting for the Copa gang to bid the dolphins adieu on their journey across the oceans and around the world to the Baltic Sea, somehow carting Arnie's ashes with their flippers.

"You think it's over, all this crazy shit?" he said.

"We still have to deal with the homicide detectives," she said.

"I meant after them," he said.

"I have a feeling there are more shoes to drop," she said. "But I can't even guess what they are."

"Me too," he said. "Me either."

Their cell phones rang within a few seconds of each other. They answered, listened, talked, clicked off their calls, and took a thoughtful minute.

"Who was that?" Johnny finally said.

"Ross Marino, FDA," Carrie said. "He wants to meet me at the lab, what's left of it, Monday morning. He has profound questions for me. That's what he called them. Profound questions."

"Can't fuck with the FDA," Johnny said. "Those dudes are serious."

"As a heart attack," Carrie said.

"So that's one shoe," Johnny said.

Carrie nodded. "Who called you?"

"David Dixon. My new parole officer," Johnny said. "Told me he was Ben Boston's best fucking friend. Said he thinks I'm part of the reason he went missing and wants to get in my face first thing Monday morning."

"That's the other shoe," Carrie said.

The front gate opened, and the Copa crew waltzed through to the courtyard. They were stark naked and drinking Captain Morgan Spiced Rum from half a dozen bottles.

"Jesus Christ," Johnny said. "Fucking dolphins stole their clothes. Took them to Poland. You know the world's gone to shit when you can't trust dolphins."

"When they take the third pill, all of this, everything that's happening, gets locked in forever," Carrie said.

"Probably not a good thing," Johnny said.

"Probably the third shoe," Carrie said.

Johnny and Carrie told them the three-act story of the crime reporter, the cleaner, and the fixer, how they'd died the dreadful deaths they'd deserved, how Eduardo and Tino (but not Francine) had been butchered and were on this evening's menu.

At the end of act one, the part with the leaf blower, the Copa crew grabbed two chairs, put Johnny in one and Carrie in the other, lifted them into the air, and marched them around the pool, singing "Ding Dong the Witch is Dead."

At the end of act two, the part with the cleaner and the rats in the gym, they formed a dance line and crisscrossed the courtyard singing "Trololo," a Russian sing-song sing-along with no actual words that Johnny thought was the weirdest song he'd ever heard.

And at the end of act three, the part with the fixer being shot once in the balls and five times in the chest, they formed a circle, put Johnny and Carrie in the middle, and sang "The Girl From Ipanema."

All one hundred percent certified nude.

For Johnny, it was a serious serving of surreal on top of surreal with a side of surreal smothered in surreal sauce. He was being celebrated for murdering, butchering, and cooking three people by a naked tribe of cannibals who'd swallowed a miracle that made them half as young as they'd been. His two turns in prison paled in comparison. The impossible shit he'd seen and done during his crazy-life-lived-on-the-far-fringes-of-normalcy couldn't hold a candle to what was happening now. The whole scene was insanely insane.

Once upon a time, he'd have reacted with panic and anger and violence. But he sensed those days were over and done and gave up trying to wrap his mind around it. This was his life and it was better now than it ever had been, despite everything that had happened and was happening still.

And the reason was Carrie. She was the eye of the hurricane that had made landfall in his life, a category-five emotional monster. He found her eyes as the Copa crew serenaded them for their murderous behavior.

She reached up and whispered in his ear, "This is so far outside the box that I can't see the box."

"I'm okay with that as long as I have you," he said, which

was incredible because not only had he never felt that way about a woman before, he'd never felt that way before, period. And articulating those feelings out loud in real time? No freaking way. He'd discounted the possibility. After all, these were the feelings of a good and honorable man, not a badass ex-con butcher. The only explanation he could think of was Carrie was changing him, and he was changing because of her, because he wanted to change for her, because he wanted to be a good and honorable man to her. It was a soul-rocking self-revelation, a personal epiphany that shook him like an earthquake.

The Copa crew finished the final chorus, and Joanna said, "So, did the fixer bring the capsules?"

"He did." Carrie took the vial from her pocket.

"No time like the present," Helen said. "Spread the good news, why don't you?"

Carrie handed the vial to Johnny. He walked around the circle and gave everyone their third and final capsule. Then he moved back to the center and stood beside Carrie.

The Copa crew lifted their left legs as if resting them atop a wooden cask, held up their bottles of rum, and saluted each other and Carrie and Johnny with one word they said several times back and forth.

*Captain. Captain. Captain. Captain. Captain. Captain. Captain. Captain...*

Then they looked at Johnny and Carrie, held their poses, and waited.

Johnny realized the tribe was expecting a return salute. It was the first time he could remember anyone wanting him to be a part of their club. So what if they were a family of pharmaceutical freaks of nature who ate like ravenous cannibals? So what if they eschewed clothing and screwed each other silly for fun and friendship? So what if they built funeral pyres and talked to dolphins? They liked him for who he was...and they loved his cooking. For the rest of his life—and there was a good chance most of it would be lived behind bars when word of what had gone down got out—no one would appreciate him the way the Copa crew did.

He looked at Carrie, and she looked at him.

She lifted her left leg and said the word. "Captain."

Johnny laughed out loud. It was fucking madness, all of it, but it was madness he could live with because of her. He lifted his left leg. "Captain."

The Copa gang cheered like pillaging pirates and swallowed the drug with a pull of rum.

# ZEUS

GOD OF JUSTICE (AMONG OTHER THINGS)

## CHAPTER 51
# UNINHIBITED APPETITES ACROSS THE BOARD

MONDAY MORNING, nine o'clock. Carrie leaned against her car and looked across the lot to what was Sikorski's lab before it had been blown to shit. She was waiting for Ross Marino, the FDA agent who'd said he had *profound questions* for her. There were other cars in the lot. Unmarked FDA vehicles—vans and trucks and sedans that might as well have been outfitted with neon signs flashing *Official government business. Proceed with caution.*

The second-floor exterior walls and roof had been badly damaged—in some spots completely demolished—giving Carrie a view of the FDA investigators going through the Swiss-cheese wreckage. Her heart broke a bit at the thought of all the rats who'd perished in the blast, but there was no going back on that score. The rats were gone. Stuart was gone. Sikorski was gone. The cleaner was gone. The fixer was gone. The Ramos twins were gone. Ben Boston was gone. Justin the bartender was gone. Elaine the parking lady was gone. Joe Cabot the cab driver was gone.

Even the cut-rate accountant who'd rented the first floor below the lab was gone, although he wasn't dead. He'd simply moved out while city engineers determined whether the remaining structure was architecturally sound for occupancy or the ceiling would crash down on the accountant's cut-rate customers.

Over the weekend, she'd failed to come to terms with emptying a revolver into a man's chest after shooting him in the testicles. Not because she was struggling with it, but because the weekend had been wild enough to make even something like that an afterthought.

Her mother and the rest of the Copa cannibals had become ravenous for, well, everything. Uninhibited appetites across the board. Friday had been a nonstop pool party, with skinny-dipping and volleyball and drinking and dancing and feasting and sex. The tribe had been communally frisky. Different people with different partners in different corners of the courtyard all afternoon and into the night. Throughout it all, Johnny had cooked Brazilian and Russian specialties using recipe-appropriate cuts of beef. The tribe couldn't get enough meat. To wash it down, Bob and Walter had filled a fifty-gallon garbage can with house-made sangria strong enough to kill a cow. They'd drunk every drop and passed out from gluttonous exhaustion at three o'clock, Saturday morning.

They'd been up and at it again Saturday at eight. Breakfast was served—Russian sausages and Brazilian hash and eggs made with spicy Eduardo Wolf ground chuck. A hit and a half. Every last bite consumed.

Only then had the Copacabana Olympics begun. It was friendly competition because they were a tribe, it was true; but it was also fierce, the events themselves often death-defying displays of courage and folly. The Cannonball Competition, for instance, had seen the men jumping off the second-floor roof— twenty-five feet of courtyard between them and the pool—and smashing down into the water. Points were given for style and splash. There were handstand races and gymnastic routines and spectacles of speed and strength. Carrie vacillated between amazement and horror at how fast and strong they'd become. Maybe not superhuman, but not normal human either.

Lunch was more man meat. Then more Olympics. Then a meat-filled, mid-afternoon feast (Brazilian empanadas). Then more Olympics. Then dinner, a masterful, multi-course, multinational menu comprising human meat and nothing but human meat. Then an Olympics awards ceremony with gold medals for all, naked dancing, and drinking until dawn.

As the Sunday sun had come up, Carrie and Johnny passed out in each other's arms and slept for three hours. The tribe woke them because they were starving again and wanted a substantial morning meal—protein on top of protein—to power them through the project of the day: conceiving, writing, producing, directing, and starring in a full-length feature film shot entirely with smartphones. They would post the film after dinner (edit the footage and add music), project it on a white sheet hanging down from the second floor railing, and view it at midnight while drinking champagne in the pool.

To make it interesting, each member of the tribe had taken a turn directing a ten-minute block. They'd written a script they called modern-day surfer-western porn. To Carrie's astonishment, the tribe had finished the film, stripped each other naked, splash-landed into the pool, and watched their cinematic creation on the hanging sheet, cheering the actors, writers, directors, producers, editors, and the craft service and catering crew—Carrie and Johnny—who'd taken a bow during intermission.

All of that was the reason murdering a man had taken a back seat in Carrie's brain. Only now was she ready to reconcile the shooting, though she'd need to do it in the next thirty seconds because an agent she assumed was Ross Marino had exited the building through the side door and was crossing the lot toward her.

# CHAPTER 52
# ALL ABOARD THE FDA EXPRESS

I SHOT *Eduardo Wolf one time in the nuts and five times in the chest,* Carrie thought, *and that is murder in the first degree, very bad news in a legal sort of way. But looking at it from the point of view of a behavioral scientist, which I happen to be, I know for a fact, meaning I can feel it in the pulsing of the blood in my veins, that it is simultaneously the last step in my personal evolution from pear-shaped wallflower to badass bitch who has orgasmic sex in nightclub restrooms with her biker butcher boyfriend, who carves dead human beings into commercial cuts of recipe-ready beef, so fuck you and the horse you rode in on, Ross Marino, you FDA dirt-bag ass-wipe.*

This long-time-coming self-realization made her laugh out loud as Marino arrived at her car.

"Enjoying yourself, Ms. Kromer?" Marino said.

"Not especially, Agent Marino," Carrie said.

They nodded at each other, as if agreeing that whatever game was going to begin had just begun.

"Couple ground rules," Marino said, "so we don't trip off the track before the train leaves the station."

She could tell he wasn't from Los Angeles. There was nothing about him, physically or philosophically, that said surf and sun. Not even from Southern California or anywhere in California or from the West Coast at all. In fact, she was ready to bet the house he was a wrestler from New Jersey or Wisconsin or Pennsylvania or Ohio or someplace where wrestling held sway in the high-school hallway and local sports page.

*His glory days*, Carrie thought.

The FDA agent was fifty-something, under six feet tall by several inches, and thick as a tree. His arms were too thick for his sport jacket. His neck was too thick for his shirt collar, which was unbuttoned, no tie. His thighs were too thick for his slacks. His wrists too thick for a watch. Fingers too thick for his wedding ring, which Carrie imagined he kept on top of his dresser in a shallow dish with his keys and wallet and state-championship wrestling medals.

"Let's hear them," she said, trying to sound assertive and calm but feeling less confident than she'd felt just thirty seconds ago. He seemed more CIA than FDA.

"I know who you are, and I have a considerable sense of what happened in the lab," Marino said, "so we're going to dispense with the pleasantries and talk truth to truth. I'll ask you honest questions, you'll give me honest answers. If you don't, I'll know because I possess an internal bullshit meter that screams like a siren in my head when I've heard one iota less than the truth, and I'll hold it against you in a way that will ruin the rest of your life, such as it might have been had you told me the truth in the first place. Do you understand?"

"All aboard the FDA Express," Carrie said. *Don't let him take your ticket. He knows who you are and what happened in the lab? Jesus Christ, could he have picked a worse way to begin the ground rules?*

"Not exactly the express," Marino said.

"Not exactly the express?"

"Not exactly the FDA."

"Stop the train," Carrie said, her stomach turning inside out and upside down.

"Too late," Marino said. "We already left the station."

"Who's we? Can you at least tell me who I'm riding with?"

"I work for a shadow department of a cloak-and-dagger FDA division that nobody knows about, including the cast and crew of the FDA itself. Several senior senators receive underground reports on a need-to-know basis, but they would dispute, deny, and disavow any knowledge of our existence with their last senatorial breath. So no, I can't tell you who we are because we're not anyone."

"You're not even here, are you?"

"I'm not even Agent Marino."

"But I can call you Agent Marino for the purposes of this conversation?"

"I've been called worse."

"What do you do in the shadows of the FDA, Agent Marino? If you can tell me without killing me."

"I can tell you to a point. Beyond that, I'll have to inject you with a fatal dose of clonidine or maybe moxonidine."

"Drugs being your primary weapon."

"Our primary weapon is information. We're involved with pharmacological counterintelligence. We keep a global eye on drugs being researched and developed, both above and below board, and those that have already been escorted through the system and are being bought and sold nationally and internationally, to ensure none of them pose a threat—financially, medicinally, morally, or culturally—to the citizens and corporations of the United States and its allies. In a pharmaceutical sense, we secure the safety and well-being of humanity."

"Except for injecting people with drugs that cause coronary failure, you mean."

"Except for that, yes."

She was in over her head and she knew it. Marino was the end of the game. The part of her that was a science-geek girl from New Jersey wanted to give up, give in, and get it over with. There were worse ways to go than an FDA assassin syringe. Tino could attest to that. So could Eduardo Wolf. And Sikorski. And Stuart Langford. And Francine Fontana. Except their attesting days were done. She opened her mouth to tell Marino about the drug and the Copa and the craziness that had happened since she'd bopped Old Tom and stolen the capsules, but the part of her that had fallen for Johnny Fairfax, that had cruised on the back of his bike, that had fucked him in the Avalon ladies' room, *that* Carrie refused to cooperate with the drug police.

"If you have a considerable sense of what happened in the lab, then you probably know more than I do," she said.

"I don't doubt it," Marino said. "We keep a close eye on our competitors, Yelchin and Pfeiffer being two prime examples of worldwide, government-operated pharmaceutical outfits under our surveillance. Are you familiar with those names?"

Carrie swallowed and shook her head.

"It was a rhetorical question," Marino said. "I know you're familiar with them. Would you like to know how I know?"

It was the last thing in the world she wanted to know, but she nodded anyway.

"Both of those drug conglomerates dispatch a specialist when their undercover shit hits the fan. The Chinese use a freelance fixer who goes by the name of Eduardo Wolf in Southern California. The Russians have an in-house cleaner who calls himself Tino Antonov. He lives in Los Angeles. The San Fernando Valley. Studio City, to be precise. I know you've met these men because we track them when we determine they're attending to company business, which we indeed determined. What's unusual here is that both companies had undercover shit hit the fan in your lab. Both men spoke directly with you and your colleague, Stuart Langford, who is missing in action and probably dead, and with Dr. Sikorski, who is as dead as a man can be. You, however, are not dead. And that is profound question number one. Why are you not dead, Ms. Kromer?"

And with that question, Carrie knew the Big Lie was coming. It wasn't here yet, but it was just around the conversational corner. The Big Lie was the ace up her sleeve. And having a Big

Lie ace up her sleeve swelled her confidence, which had gone flat as a flounder.

"Maybe they thought I knew something that could help them," Carrie said.

"Which brings us to profound question number two," Marino said. "What is the something you know? What is the drug?"

"I want to help you, Agent Marino. I really do. But I can't."

"Reason being?"

"Sikorski was crazy about secrecy. During development, each person only knew the piece they were building. None of us knew the nature of the drug. None of us had access to his overarching vision. He was the only one who knew what the final pharmaceutical product would be."

"Not the only one," Marino said. "Yelchin and Pfeiffer had seats at Sikorski's table, which probably came as a big damn surprise to both of them since they don't play nice with each other. So they had to know what he was building because they were funding him with banned-nation money and dispatched the fixer and the cleaner to make a bad outcome better—better in this case meaning they blew up the lab and the mad scientist with it, not to mention two LAPD detectives and some passive peripheral players they perceived as too risky to leave alive. You, on the other hand, were somehow too risky to eliminate. And if it wasn't because you knew what the drug was, then it had to be something else."

"Like what?" Carrie said.

"Like profound question number three," Marino said. "Like Sikorski's notes."

*Here it is*, Carrie thought, *the Big Lie*. "You mean his personal notes?"

"His chemical equations. His final formulas. His personal notes, yes," Marino said.

"What about them?"

"Do you have them?"

"Do *I* have them?"

"Yes. Did you find them at Sikorski's house? I think you went there looking for them. By the way, I couldn't help but notice the dead crime reporter in the pool with the electric leaf blower. Did you kill her after you found the notes or before? Is that why Wolf and Antonov kept you alive? Because you had, and still have, the notes?"

"I've never been to Sikorski's house. It had to be Wolf and Antonov who killed the reporter. Maybe *they* found the notes."

"I know Wolf and Antonov well. Over the years, I've shared the same pharmaceutical airspace on multiple occasions. When the fixer and cleaner leave dirt and debris on the floor, the FDA sends me in to sweep up after them. If they had the notes, you would be dead. You're alive because *you* have the notes—or because they thought you did. So profound question number three, Ms. Kromer. One more time. Do you have Sikorski's final notes?"

*Oh great*, Carrie thought. *First the fixer, then the cleaner, now the sweeper.* "I don't know why they kept me alive. I don't have the notes."

Marino stared straight through Carrie's eyes and burned a hole in the back of her head. Then he looked away, up at the sad remains of the second floor, his team at work in the wreckage. He nodded as if he'd had her pinned on the mat in the district finals but she'd somehow slipped away for a point. "Right now, this actual minute in real time, I have an air-raid siren screaming in my head. Do you know what that means?"

"Your bullshit meter is broken?"

"It means you have one chance to tell the truth or I change the trajectory of your life for the rest of time."

"Or I go to the press."

"Or you come work for us."

"Excuse me?" Carrie said. *Oh my God. Did the Big Lie work well enough to get me a job offer with the FDA? Why, yes. Yes, it did.*

"We have a complex in Virginia," Marino said. "Half a dozen

state-of-the-art pharmaceutical labs. One of them has your name on it."

"Why my name?" Carrie said.

"You're lying to me, Ms. Kromer," Marino said. "I think you know the precise nature of the drug—what it is and what it does. I use the present tense because I think the drug has already been successfully built and tested and that its realization coupled with some kind of Sikorski financial funny business is what impelled Yelchin and Pfeiffer to send the fixer and the cleaner to your front door. Both those cretins have also vanished from the board, so I think they either killed each other or were sent to fry bigger fish—after, of course, eliminating all the evidence. Except you because, again, they thought, like I think, you have the formulas and equations to replicate whatever pharmacological voodoo was happening in the rubble up there."

"Wait...you're offering me a job?" Carrie said.

"Torture is frowned upon as a governmental inducement, to tell the truth, and I think there's no other way for me to encourage your voluntary assistance," Marino said. "And though there are few things I'd enjoy more than an hour with you and my kitbag of medieval dental instruments, that option is not available to me. So, yes, I'm offering you the opportunity to continue and complete Sikorski's work, only this time for your country."

"In an undercover FDA lab?" Carrie said.

"Rigged like the bridge of a starship," Marino said. "With a crew to match."

"But I'm not a chemist," Carrie said. "I'm a behavioral scientist."

"You'll have dozens of top-tier pharmaceutical chemists at your beck and call," Marino said. "Surely, as a behavioral scientist, you can coordinate their scientific behavior."

"Will I get paid?" Carrie said.

"Like the queen of Bessarabia," Marino said. "We're the United States government. We print as much money as we need.

Plus, there will be some small yet significant net profit participation on your end. Which, if the drug, whatever it does, is as efficacious as Yelchin and Pfeiffer and the FDA believe it might be, could make you one of the wealthiest women in the history of humankind."

"I never liked going to the dentist anyway," Carrie said. *Jesus Christ, holy shit, oh my God, the bridge of a freaking starship with a crew to match! What I could do with my very own crew!*

"Without cooperation and/or evidence, I have no way to progress beyond this point, and there are other FDA matters pressing, so this window closes Wednesday," Marino said. "If you accept the offer, the world becomes your oyster without any further questions. If you decline, you live the rest of your life toiling in obscurity, unemployable in your field once our internal smear-campaign apparatus demolishes your personal and professional reputations. It's a no-brainer, Ms. Kromer. So profound question number four—consider it a bonus—is: Do you have a brain?"

He handed her a white business card with a black, embossed phone number but no name or other identifiers—for the first time, she noticed he was wearing latex surgical gloves.

*Not right now,* she thought, as blown away as the lab. *But I will by Wednesday.*

# CHAPTER 53
# FUCK YOU, UNCLE FUCKING JOHN

MONDAY MORNING, nine o'clock. Johnny sat in the same parole office, in the same first floor waiting area, in the same chair, flipped through the same fishing magazine he'd lifted off the same coffee table, and landed on the same full-page photograph of the same river fish being pulled from the same river. But this time, he did not think, *I'm that fucking fish*. This time, he thought, *Fuck you, Uncle Fucking John*.

While it was true Johnny's birth mother had vanished into the fog of oblivion after consigning her two-year-old son to Merry and Patrick Fairfax, it was also true her identity had not remained a mystery. Her name, Johnny had learned later, was Isabella Rotolo. She had an older brother named John, who was a grifter, a scammer, a car thief, and a criminal.

When John had gone up the river for grand theft auto (his second time), he'd coincidentally arrived at the very California State Penitentiary where in precisely three weeks and three days Johnny would finish his first stint for breaking and entering and assault.

It had taken three days for the men to find each other in the yard, though they hadn't exactly found each other. It was the inmates who'd caught the crazy resemblance first and brought the men together. They'd stared at each other in disbelief. For Johnny, it was like looking into a mirror twenty years in his future. For John, it was a mirror into his past. They were spitting images of each other. Carbon copies. Which led to amazement and laughter and busting of balls. It was later, after the horseplay, that the stories began. And once they did, they took on a life of their own.

*How can you look exactly alike and not be related?* everyone in the yard wanted to know. The inmates had demanded to hear both John and Johnny's family sagas from the beginning to see what kind of connection could be made between the two. John had gone first—where and when he was born and reared, who his parents were and what had happened to them, and that he had a younger sister, Isabella, who'd gotten pregnant when she was fifteen, had a baby boy when she was sixteen, and had to give the kid away when she was eighteen.

"Gave him to some redheaded butcher down the block," John had said. "Dude's wife had a name like Merry Christmas. Hard to remember. Long time ago."

Johnny's jaw had fallen open and hit the ground. It was a full two minutes before he could speak. The yard went silent, sensing profundity, and then it had been Johnny's turn—his birth mother had given him away when he was a two-year-old toddler to the butcher and his wife down the street, Patrick and Merry, who'd raised him as a Fairfax.

John had shaken his head. "You little shit, you're my nephew. Your mother was my sister. Isabella Rotolo. I was there when she dropped you off. She was eighteen and broke. No father in the family photo. I gave her forty bucks to get you going. You were fucking doomed if she kept you, so she gave you to the butcher so you'd have half a chance. Guy was a dick, so I don't know what kind of chance you had with him, but that was then and this is now. I'm your Uncle Fucking John."

There'd been back-slapping and cheering in the yard as a family was reunited before everyone's eyes. Some of the badass convicts had actually cried. It was the most emotional thing that had happened in the prison for as long as anyone could recall.

For the next three weeks, Uncle Fucking John and Johnny had been attached at the hip. Johnny had a million questions about Isabella. But she and her big brother had lost contact after dropping the boy at the butcher's house—to the point of never speaking again—so John could only tell Johnny about Isabella as a girl growing up. It was the story of a broken home and gangs and drugs and petty crime and early pregnancy and truancy and juvie court and on like that until Isabella had been left with no choice but to give up her son and run for her life.

"Last I heard, and this is going back thirty, forty years, she went east—New York, I think. But then I heard Boston, so I don't fucking know where she is," John had said. "She was a piece of work. Tough kid, I'll tell you that."

Johnny had taken some comfort knowing his mother was a tough kid. But the big news was that Isabella had named her son after her brother. Their baby pictures were freaking identical. Twins separated by nineteen years.

"We're the same, you and me," John had told Johnny. "You got my name, and you got my luck, meaning hard luck or bad luck or no luck at all. Never catch a fucking break. It's in our blood. Both of us. The Rotolo Curse. I'm never catching one, and neither are you. That's just the way it is. Who gives a goddamn anyway, right? Fuck them. That's what I say. Fuck them all."

*No, fuck you, Uncle Fucking John,* Johnny thought, still staring at the fish on the hook in the magazine. *I'm catching a break one day soon. It's my turn. I can fucking feel it.*

"Johnny Fairfax," the receptionist said. "Mr. Dixon will see you now. Room 210. Top of the stairs, turn right, end of the hall on your right."

Johnny arrived at the end of the hall. To his left was Ben

Boston's office. The door was open, and Johnny could see inside. Nothing had been moved or changed or touched—except by the police, Johnny figured, who had no doubt been through Boston's desk drawers and file cabinets investigating the parole officer's inexplicable disappearance.

Dixon's door was closed, but Johnny could hear someone playing an unamplified electric guitar in the office. Without power, the sound of the strings was faint and thin, but Johnny could tell it was the kind of breezy pop music that made him want to puke. He knocked.

"It's open, Fairfax," Dixon said.

Johnny opened the door and stepped in. The space was identical to Ben Boston's room across the hall. Same sad gray tones on the walls and floor and ceiling. Same secondhand, Army-issued furniture salvaged from World War One.

*Or some war a long fucking time ago,* Johnny thought.

David Dixon stood in front of his desk, unplugged electric guitar strapped over his shoulder, rocking like some kind of jazzy Justin Timberlake jerkoff. It wasn't Justin Timberlake personally who made Johnny want to wretch. He'd never met Justin Timberlake. It was the music Justin Timberlake represented. That white-boy-fancy-dance-hip-hop-bebop bullshit music that had prepubescent girls around the globe singing the songs and dancing the dances and screaming their little guts out as if Justin Timberlake himself was about to jump off the stage and kiss them on the mouth.

Dixon even looked a little like Justin Timberlake. Thin and wiry. Wavy brown hair. He was smooth and dapper, not unlike Ben Boston. Clean blue jeans, crisp white dress shirt, tweed vest. One of *those* fucking guys. A hipster-with-a-tweed-vest guy.

*Except no fedora, thank fucking God,* Johnny thought.

He started to speak, but Dixon shook his head, meaning silence, meaning do not talk until instructed, until parole officer permission is granted. He was in the middle of a song or a riff or something and didn't want to be interrupted.

Johnny stood by the door and waited. And waited. And waited. Four full fucking minutes. He hated this pop dance shit. *Dixon knows that. He has to. He's torturing me as a way of introducing himself.*

When the music mercifully ended, Dixon nodded as if to tell himself how damn good he was. Then he turned his attention to Johnny.

"Before we clock in and get going as ex-con and parole officer, I want to know what the hell happened to Big Ben," Dixon said. "He was my friend for fifteen years. We *owned* this end of the building. You understand what I'm telling you? We cut our teeth together. Went through hell. Came out on top. Cream always rises, Fairfax. But what it doesn't do is fucking disappear without a trace."

"I don't know what happened to him."

"Bullshit. You were his next—and, turns out last—call. He had you on his shit list. Told me you were going back to the big house for violating your parole."

"He scheduled an inspection and never showed up."

"He was parked outside your building. So my question is pretty fucking simple. How do you make a man the size of Ben Boston disappear?"

*One bite at a time.* Except he opened his mouth and said it out loud too. "One bite at a time."

"Is that supposed to be funny?" Dixon said.

"Not really," Johnny said.

The parole officer considered Johnny for a moment, then took his guitar off, placed it on a little stand tucked in the corner of the room, and gestured for Johnny to sit in one of the chairs in front of his desk. Dixon sat behind the desk, facing Johnny.

"I've been through your file, Fairfax," Dixon said. "You did, in fact, violate your parole, and Big Ben was about to make you pay for that sin against society. I'm reading his notes and thinking, *that's all she wrote for Johnny Fairfax.* I'm done, you understand what I'm telling you? Ben's gone, I'm done, and you're toast. That's my decision five minutes, literally, five minutes before you stepped into my office. You're going back inside for the rest of your life."

Johnny's heart stopped beating and his lungs stopped breathing because his brain stopped sending signals because it was busy blowing up because his pop-star parole officer had just said he was sending Johnny back to prison.

"And then my wife calls, worried about her brother, and when my wife calls worried about her brother, that means a change of plans for everyone involved, including you. Especially you," Dixon said. "Because if Momma ain't happy, ain't nobody happy, meaning happy wife, happy life. And vice versa in fucking spades."

Johnny was confused. He was going back to prison; he wasn't going back to prison. He couldn't get his lungs to work. Hadn't taken a breath in what felt like hours. And if you can't breathe, then you can't speak. So Johnny said nothing.

"My brother-in-law's sort of a dick but not in a bad way, if you know what I mean. Kind of a sad sack fuckup. Bartender for thirty years. Upscale joints. Calls himself a mixologist. Dreams about owning his own steakhouse. So I encourage him to quit his gig and follow his steakhouse dreams. I was just making conversation, for shit's sake. But he actually listens to me and quits his job and invests his life savings—sells his house, cashes in his retirement, puts up his last dollar—in a steakhouse somewhere outside Redding, north end of the Sacramento Valley, county seat of Shasta, other end of the universe, eight hours from LA if everything goes right. Green rolling hills is what he tells me it looks like, whatever the fuck that means. Redding, California. That's where my brother-in-law bets the ranch on a steakhouse went out of business five years ago."

"He's not a chef?" Johnny said because he didn't know what the hell else to say.

"Can't cook his way out of a can of soup. But you can. Says so in your file. Says you're a cook."

"Hellcat in a kitchen."

"Butcher too. Steakhouse after steakhouse after steakhouse. Cook and butcher. Butcher and cook." Dixon said. "So my brother-in-law hires a steakhouse chef from—"

"I can't go back in. Can't do it. Don't send me back."

"Listen to the story, Fairfax. My brother-in-law hires a steakhouse chef from Kansas City to set up and run the kitchen. Pays him a ton of dough. Guy flies to Redding, gets the place ready for opening night, which is this fucking Friday, flies back to Kansas City, loads his shit in a U-Haul, drives it back to Redding, and gets in a five-car crackup outside Vegas. Takes his head clean off his body. He's dead on impact. Did I mention my brother-in-law opens this fucking Friday? So he's screwed, and my wife thinks it's *my* fucking fault for encouraging her brother to follow his fucking steakhouse dreams. My wife thinks it's *my* responsibility to fix it before Friday or she moves to Redding to help her brother save his sinking ship. 'You will never see me again, David,' she says to me. And I believe her. So you're going to be the head chef at my brother-in-law's steakhouse in Redding. That's my fix."

"What?"

"It's the chance of a lifetime for a two-bit, two-time ex-con like you. Clean slate. Fresh start. I'll handle your transfer to a Shasta County parole officer. I'm the prince of paperwork, so that's not a problem. My brother-in-law's paying top dollar, and the job comes with a three-bed, two-bath house overlooks a lake. Room and board. Check and check. It's a get-out-of-parole-free pass. Do you fish, Fairfax?"

"No."

"Time to learn."

"I need to think about it," Johnny said.

"What part of 'the place opens Friday' did you not understand?" Dixon said. "Or did you forget the bit about you going back to prison if Redding's not on your radar?"

"I got to clean shit up," Johnny said. "I can't drop everything on a dime and—"

"Wednesday morning. You say no, you go to prison. You say yes, you live the rest of your life grilling steaks in the green rolling hills of Redding. Talk about catching a break."

"Yeah, steakhouse chef. Hard to believe," Johnny said.

But he was thinking, *Fuck you, Uncle Fucking John.*

# CHAPTER 54
# THERE ISN'T A SCRIPT BECAUSE THERE ISN'T AN ENDING

CARRIE WENT to check the Greek Gods and felt something was different before she could identify what it was—like shivering before a cold wind blows or sensing ripples on the surface of a glassy pond seconds before a turtle slips into the water.

And something *was* different. The rats had not finished their morning meal. There was meat in their little bowls. Not a lot but some. The first time since what she'd come to call the "decisive dose" had been administered. Still, it was a lesser observation.

And then, as Carrie cleaned the bowls, Zeus took a running start to leap out of the box spring and caught his little foot on the edge. It threw him off balance in the air, and he landed hard on the floor. He bounced back up like nothing had happened, and, yes, it was trivial, given the rat had jumped out of the enclosure like an antelope, but it had happened. The first physical slip since the decisive dose. Again, a minor moment to be recorded in a journal and nothing more.

She couldn't concentrate on these inconsequential aberrations anyway because since she'd returned from her encounter with Agent Marino, all she could think about was the FDA lab with her name on it. And because it was all she could think about, she'd avoided Johnny the rest of that morning.

How in the world could she begin *that* conversation? After all they'd been through, how could she tell him she'd been offered a job in Virginia that was too good to turn down? And that the job was so far off the radar she probably couldn't tell him exactly where she would be?

*Where in Virginia?*

*Sorry, Johnny. I can't tell you that.*

Before she could conclude the conversation in her mind, it was time to help Johnny prepare lunch—and have the conversation for real, the point being she had no idea how the conversation would end.

The Copa gang had gone parasailing in Marina del Ray at the crack of dawn. Carrie had seen them off. As they'd piled into the passenger van, Joanna had said they would be back by two and would likely be famished. An order had been placed for double-bacon chili cheeseburgers made with Russian ground beef and blazing-red-hots made from spicy Latino sausage meat.

Carrie stood in the doorway and watched Johnny work the way some people sit on the edge of the bed and watch their lover sleep and breathe. She loved watching him work. He was grace and grit in the same second. A rampaging bull and an elegant dancer. Every step purposeful, hands moving independently yet in seamless harmony. A working man who'd had bad breaks and hard luck and paid his debt to society. Most of America would never get past the fact he'd been to prison twice. But she'd had more fun with Johnny than she'd ever had before him. It was possible, she realized now, she'd *never* had fun before Johnny. Much to her own surprise, being with a two-time ex-con didn't count for shit on the Scorecard of Life. On the Scorecard of Life, it turned out, love and respect and friendship were what counted.

Meaning it would be harder than she imagined, given her current Scorecard of Life, to tell Johnny she was moving across the country to start a top-secret laboratory and complete Sikorski's miracle drug for the FDA.

Johnny turned and saw her in the doorway. They moved to each other. Embraced and kissed. She sensed it was more than an I'm-so-happy-to-see you kiss. More than an I'm-so-lucky-to-have-finally-found-you kiss. It was a kiss tinged with sadness. It was a kiss goodbye.

"What's wrong?" Carrie said.

"You tell me," Johnny said.

*He feels what I feel*, she thought. *He knows me better and more deeply than anyone has ever known me.*

"It was your meeting, wasn't it?" she said.

"Yes. And yours too, right?"

"Right."

"Something bad happened?"

"Yes, no, yes, no. Something good that could also be something bad."

"Me too."

So he told her about David Dixon and his sad-sack, fuckup-brother-in-law's steakhouse in Redding and the decapitated chef and if he didn't say yes on Wednesday, he was going back to prison.

And she told him about Agent Marino, who wasn't even Agent Marino, and the shadow department of the cloak-and-dagger FDA division that protects America and its allies from evil drugs and the job offer in Virginia and the window closing Wednesday and the bonus question, which was did she have a brain.

"You're the smartest person I ever met," he said. "You have to take it."

"I know. But Virginia is so far away."

"So is Redding. I mean, not as far as Virginia, but still pretty fucking far."

"Head chef at a steakhouse. It's what you've always wanted. You have to take it."

"I know."

And they embraced again, holding each other like this was the last day of life on Earth.

"I'm going to miss you so much," she said, and could barely get the words out, her voice was so soft and sad.

"I'm going to miss you too," he said, his voice cracking with emotion.

"I'm going to miss you both," a woman's voice said from the other side of the kitchen, "but I'll get over it."

She was smoking a cigarette and leaning against the door frame. Fifty or so years old. Long, frizzy blonde hair straight out of a bottle. Chinos and platform sandals and a button-up blouse. Bangles on both wrists and rings on every finger. Dark sunglasses that shaded the whole upper half of her face. The cigarette was in her right hand. In her left hand was a small voice recorder.

"I mean, don't get me wrong," the woman said. "I cry at sappy movies just like any girl next door. But you two have to be the cheesiest Hallmark moment I've seen in decades. Really, we're not making money in Tinseltown with that kind of sentimental shit. Not in this day and age."

Johnny and Carrie came out of their embrace.

"Who are you?" Johnny said.

"Jane Kinsey," the woman said.

"He means who the hell *are* you?" Carrie said.

"And what the hell are you doing in my kitchen?" Johnny said. "That's exactly what I mean."

"I'm a screenwriter," Kinsey said. "I write low-budget, true-crime movies that play on late-night cable so the stations have something to run between commercials. I have a partner who feeds me material. She's a journalist. A crime reporter. Maybe you heard of her. Francine Fontana. Ring any bells? How about funeral bells? Does it ring any funeral bells? It should. They found her fried in a backyard pool, electrocuted by a plug-in leaf blower someone tossed in after her. The backyard, the pool, and the leaf blower belonged to a pharmacological chemist who made designer drugs. Guy's name was Sikorski. I'm using past tense because he's dead too. Lot of dead characters in this story. Have you noticed that? More often than not, that's the thing about true crime. Lots of dead characters in the story."

She took a deep drag and smiled as if to say, *Ball's in your court, kids.*

There was something about the smug in Kinsey's smile that made it hard for Carrie to swallow. Like Francine's screenwriter friend knew something Carrie didn't. Like Kinsey was two steps ahead of the game.

"Why should it ring funeral bells for *us*?" Carrie said.

"If you're going to play dumb, Carrie, this will take all afternoon," Kinsey said. "Same for you Johnny. Let's at least make an effort to keep up."

"You know our names?" Johnny said.

"Did you just miss the part about not playing dumb?" Kinsey said. "Yes, I know your names. I know everything about this story. Francine was my partner-in-crime, so to speak. She delivered the true stories, I fictionalized the scripts, and we split the proceeds. I have her notes. All of them. I am, as they say, up to speed insofar as miracle drugs and fixers and cleaners are concerned."

*Not all the way up to speed*, Carrie thought.

Kinsey wouldn't know the Copa crew were eating human meat because Francine hadn't known the Copa crew were eating human meat. Because Carrie had left that tiny tidbit out when she'd told Francine *nearly almost everything* that day in the lab.

Carrie thought about using the current Copacabana meal plan to her advantage—killing Kinsey and having Johnny butcher and cook and serve the screenwriter that very evening. *Dinner and a movie all on the same plate.* But another consideration was bothering her as well.

"Late-night cable?" she said. "Really? That's the best you can do? After all we've been through, you think we're only as good as late-night cable? Let me tell you something, Jane-whoever-the-fuck-you-are. We're holding out for a feature film."

"Big story, big screen," Johnny said.

"Big screen, little screen...so far there isn't any screen because there isn't a script because there isn't an ending," Kinsey said.

"Ending?" Carrie said.

"How does it end? The story. What's the ending?" Kinsey said. "What happens to the two of you? To the not-so-old-anymore folks in Copa Town? You have to know the ending if you want to write a movie."

Carrie looked at Johnny, not needing to say, *Should we tell her about the jobs?* He nodded, not needing to say, *You go first.*

So Carrie told Kinsey about Agent Marino and the FDA lab with her name on it in Virginia. When she was finished, Johnny told Kinsey about Dixon and the steakhouse job offer in Redding.

"That is the greatest ending ever," Kinsey said. "No, no, the *two* greatest endings ever coming together to make the one, most perfect ending ever to the most incredible true-crime caper I've heard in years."

"We didn't take the jobs yet," Johnny said.

"You have to take them," Kinsey said. "That's the end of the story. You go to Redding, she goes to Virginia, fade out, the end."

"What if we don't take them?" Carrie said, though in her heart she'd already accepted Marino's offer.

"Yeah, what if we stay?" Johnny said without conviction because his mind was already on the way to Redding.

"Then the homicide detectives crawl so far up your asses they can look out your eyes, assuming your new parole officer makes room for them. Because, trust me, he's going to be up there too," Kinsey said to Johnny before turning to Carrie. "And the FDA drags your name through the mud until the only job you can get is greeter at some douchey-discount big-box store in the middle of a creepy Kansas cornfield. You have to take the jobs. You have no reason to stay."

"We have each other," Carrie said, holding Johnny's hand. She meant it with all the blood in veins, but their fate had already been decided. Someone had placed a brick on the wrong side of the scale.

Kinsey shook her head and moved into the kitchen. She stopped at the counter and took a breath. "Let me explain something to you. You can't stay together. It was never in the cards. You are not now and were never meant to be. From the moment you met, you were meteors burning through the sky, too hot and too fast to last. You had to melt down and crash-land in the ruins of romance, and you have. The most spectacular, starry-eyed flameout in recent cinema history..."

On and on she went, selling them the true ending of their story. Selling and selling and selling. An Olympic salesperson. A blue-ribbon award-winner. Somewhere in the middle of Kinsey's pitch, Carrie was reminded of a story her father had once told in the car on their way to his lab at the university, about the owner of a general store on a two-lane at the edge of a small town in the vast middle of nowhere. A traveler came into the store looking to purchase a can of something cold to drink and discovered nothing but bags of salt—shelves and shelves of bag after bag of salt. "Excuse me," the traveler said to the owner, "do you have anything for sale in this store besides salt?" Without looking up from the magazine he was reading behind the counter, the owner said, "Not that I can think of." The traveler shook his head in bemusement and said, "Well, you must be really good at selling salt." The owner looked up and said, "Me? No. But the salt salesman? Man, can he sell salt."

"So that's it," Kinsey said. "Johnny goes to Redding to fulfill his destiny as a steakhouse chef, and Carrie goes to the lab in Virginia to change the fate of mankind with a miracle. You both feel it. You know it's true. The grand finale."

Carrie and Johnny looked at each with sadness and love but no regrets. Kinsey was correct. They'd never had and never would have a chance to reach the horizon.

"Fade out," Johnny said.

"The end," Carrie said.

# CHAPTER 55
# LOOSELY THE BEGINNING

THE EFFICACY of the miracle drug turned out to be somewhat less than miraculous. Which meant even Carrie's casual observations recalibrated the landscape of her life—the way an earthquake retunes the topography it rattles and rolls. Which meant the end of the story was not set in stone, meaning it was malleable, meaning it was, in fact, loosely the beginning, meaning Carrie woke up at six thirty, Wednesday morning, to discover the age-reversing effects of the drug had done a Houdini on the Greek Gods.

It was an expression her father had used in his Rutgers lab when a result he'd hoped for presented itself in a sort of scientific tease—here one moment, gone the next. That elusive conclusion, the one that had appeared with promise and vanished without reason, had *done a Houdini.*

The rats were older than they'd been when they were younger than they were. They had aged a little rat lifetime overnight. The drug had abandoned their little rat bodies with alacrity and vengeance—without mercy or warning. Leaping like impalas across the African plains was a muddy memory in their little rat brains, which could barely traverse the most straightforward maze. Their little rat eyes were pallid and foggy.

Their appetites anemic. Their fur thin and brittle. They were failing physically and behaviorally. Fading with every morning minute that ticked by.

By eight thirty, Hermes and Hebe were dead. Lyssa by eight forty-five. Five minutes later, Nemesis died in Carrie's hands. Chaos stopped breathing two minutes after that. Eros expired at eight fifty-five. Zeus, king of the Greek Gods, waited until the stroke of nine, and then his heart stopped beating and he followed the others to the Great Rat Garbage Scow in the sky. They'd died of old age. They were gods and then they were ancients and then they were dead.

Carrie thought it possible, even probable, that some manifestation of age re-reversal might present in one or several or all members of the Copa tribe. The thought alone made her weak in the knees. To calm herself, she went back to her scientific roots. Although likely, regression was not a given. The drug and its effects remained an experiment under review, a trial in progress —a small sample, an abbreviated timeframe. Nothing could be labeled a done deal. Still, it was an outcome that had to be considered since it had risen in the rats with such fierce finality, with such surprising acceleration.

She had to tell Johnny. There was no one else she could talk to, or rather, *wanted* to talk to. No one else she wanted to share her life with. Johnny Fairfax was the one and only man in the world for her. That's how she felt right at that emotional moment, with the Greek Gods dead and bad news for the Copa gang around the corner. Johnny was her true love. And he was leaving her for some stupid steakhouse in Redding. And she was leaving him for some lousy lab in Virginia.

Her face flushed. Loss and regret and grief washed over her. She left the rat room for the kitchen. Her phone rang while she was crossing the courtyard. It was Agent Marino.

"It's Wednesday," Marino said. "Is there a lab in Virginia with your name on it?"

*There's no small talk with Marino*, Carrie thought. *No warming up whatsoever.* The answer was on the tip of her tongue. *Yes,* was the answer. *Yes, I'm going to Virginia, where people will call me the pharmacological queen of Bessarabia.* She had thought about it and thought about it and thought about it, and that was her answer. It had to be. It would be the mistake of a lifetime not to go.

"No," she said. "I've had enough science to last me the rest of my days."

She heard silence on Marino's end. Not surprised silence. More like frustrated silence. Aggravated silence. Irritated silence.

"I'm going to ask you one last time." Marino said. "Do you have Sikorski's notes?"

"And I'm going to tell you one last time," Carrie said. "No, I don't."

"Good luck at Walmart. You'll look swell in the blue vest," he said and clicked off the call.

She was amazed by how easily she lied, by how complete a liar she'd become. Lying was a useful survival tool, it turned out.

*Who knew?* she thought as she came through the door into the kitchen.

Johnny stood in the space between the ovens, cooktops, and counter, his back to her. He had pots and pans in play, but he was frozen, unable to cook or move a muscle. He sensed her presence and turned to her. There were tears in his eyes. He wasn't weeping or sobbing or rending his garments, but his eyes were red and wet with sadness.

He pointed at them. "This is the first time I ever cried in my life."

They rushed to each other and embraced-embraced-embraced, like they were glued together for the rest of time.

"I'm so fucking sad about not seeing you again," he said. "I don't know how to keep going without you. It's not about being a chef. It's about *being with you* and being a chef. I'm not taking the steakhouse job. I'm not going to Redding. I'm going with you to Virginia."

"You can't skip on your parole for me."

"Already did. Dixon called me this morning. I told him thanks but no thanks. Told him Redding was too fucking far for me."

"What did he say?"

"I'd be back in prison by the end of the week."

"What did you say?"

"Told him I'd appeal."

"You'll lose."

"That's why I'm going to skip. Marino told you it was top secret. They'll never find me. I'll be your janitor. Cleanest top-secret lab in Virginia."

"I'm not going to Virginia."

"What?"

She told him about the drug losing its potency and the rats dying of old age, about the possibility of the miracle unraveling in her mother and the rest of the tribe. She told him about her wanting to be there for them when they re-aged—*if* they re-aged. But mostly she told him about wanting to spend the rest of her life by his side.

They kissed like true lovers and held each other until Carrie felt them becoming one body, one spirit, one mind, one life. It was what she'd always imagined love felt like.

"What do we do now?" she said.

"We wait for them to come back from the tunnels," he said.

"Tunnels?"

He told her the Copa gang had driven off at the crack of dawn to explore the famous underground Prohibition tunnels of Los Angeles, eleven miles of passageways that had led to speakeasy bars in basements of buildings housing otherwise innocent storefronts like drug stores and barbershops. The King Eddy Saloon had been reimagined to sell pianos. There were tall tales of the tunnels being used by police to transport prisoners through LA, of bankers moving cartloads of cash, of coroners and gangsters dumping dead bodies.

"There's an elevator behind the Hall of Records on Temple

Street, but almost nobody goes underground," he said. "If they do, there's bars and chains to keep them in the main tunnel and out of the endless offshoots because, officially, with earthquakes and stuff, the side tunnels are closed to the public."

"Did you tell them that?" she said.

"I told Lillian while the rest of them loaded hacksaws and chain cutters into the van."

"What did she say?"

"'We're not part of the public anymore, Tattoo Boy.'"

Lillian was right. Carrie knew it. The public didn't grow old twice. She wanted to prepare them, to comfort them, but there was nothing she could do right now.

"So we wait until they come back," she said.

Johnny nodded. "And for Dixon to make his move."

The wait for Dixon ended at eleven forty-five. The prince of paperwork had made his move, requesting and receiving an immediate emergency transfer to Redding, the woman from the parole office said. Her name was Cynthia Norris. She was Johnny's new parole officer. She said she was a lifer at the end of her long, hard parole-officer road, she was stepping down in six months, and the last thing in the world she wanted was for Johnny Fairfax to ruin her swan song with petty bullshit. To that end, Norris noted, Johnny's file stated he had a steady job and a place to live.

"Is that still the case?" Norris said.

"Yeah, it is," Johnny said.

"Bully for you. Stay put and keep your nose clean. I'll check in a week or so after I run through the rest of Dixon's cases...and also Ben Boston's cases. They're trying to kill me before I retire so they don't have to pay my pension," Norris said.

"I feel you," Johnny said.

"Peachy," Norris said and hung up.

## CHAPTER 56
# SHE WANTED THEM ALL TO BE KEEPERS

THEY WAITED LONGER for the Copa gang. Eight days after the Greek Gods had expired, the tribe began to re-reverse, to age in fast-forward.

Though it was hard for Carrie to watch her mother and the rest reload the years—hard and fast and through and through—she believed in her heart it was for the best. If they'd stayed younger, remained the stronger-faster, cannibalistic versions of themselves, it would have required a Herculean effort, day after day, to keep them corralled, out of the real world, away from normal human society, far from those who grew older as time marched on, from those who didn't source their protein from other human beings.

As it was, with the drug losing steam by the hour, the Copa gang soon required the same level of all-out care they would have demanded if they'd remained young—though without having to be corralled. They weren't going anywhere wild with walkers and wheelchairs.

*Either way,* Carrie thought, *young or old, they need epic quantities of help.*

She and Johnny did it together. A two-man job across the board. He planned the menu, did the shopping, cooked the meals, and scrubbed the kitchen. He cleaned the courtyard, hauled the bed and bath and cleaning supplies up the stairs, folded the laundry when Carrie was busy with someone who'd fallen down and could not get up. It was hard physical work to care for the elderly.

But it was harder emotionally. And Johnny was there for that part too. He was a shoulder she could cry on, a lover she could laugh with, a best friend she could tell her deepest secrets to knowing he'd keep them close and take them to his grave.

He was still a badass butcher and a hellcat in a kitchen. That was his nature, and it had not changed. He was still Johnny Fairfax. But there was no denying the metamorphosis in his heart, no refuting the solemn sea change of his soul. Before the Copacabana, he'd lived his life without meaning. And drifting unmoored through the years had been as hard *for* him as it had been *on* him. Without guidance, without friendship, without love, he'd mistakenly substituted his nature for his purpose, and it had landed him in prison twice. It had made his life small and angry and violent and empty. But at the Copa, he'd discovered, often against his will, his purpose was not to be an angry violent criminal living life on the edge of law-abiding society. He'd been wrong about that all this time.

His purpose was to be a caregiver.

That, he had learned to his profound surprise, was his true gift. The purpose of his life, he'd discovered, was to use his gift, his heart—which he'd found beat every day with love and compassion—*and* his hellcat-badass nature to care for those who could not care for themselves. To never give up on them.

That, he'd realized in his one and only epiphany, was his true calling, the reason he was on this Earth. Caregiver. It filled his heart with goodness without transforming his nature. He remained a tattooed badass, but now it came from a place of meaning. She loved him more every single day.

And so it was with the Copa crew. Her feelings for them deepened as they re-aged, as they became the people they'd been when they were old before they were young. Before they were cannibals. Norman needed his thick glasses. Lillian reconnected with her oxygen tank—and kept right on smoking. Walter was crankier than he'd been when he was cranky before he was crankier—and he'd been cranky as shit to begin with. Bob couldn't remember five minutes ago. Dolores, Betty, Bernard, and Brenda were wrinkled and dimpled and old-old-old. Helen was so ancient and small that Carrie could look right at her and wonder out loud where Helen was.

She missed Arnie. They all did. Even Tall Bob, who had only echoes of Arnie in the thick fog of his memories, missed the Arnie he thought he remembered.

One time, Carrie caught him crying for no reason and hurried to comfort him. "Bob, Bob, why so sad? Tell me what's wrong."

"I miss my friend Arnie," Bob said. "Did I have a friend named Arnie? I did, didn't I?"

"Yes, you did, Bob. We all miss him."

"What happened to him? I feel like something bad happened to Arnie. Where is he?"

"The dolphins took his ashes to Poland."

"He died?"

"Yes. He was defending the fort, and he died in battle."

"He was brave."

"The bravest."

"The dolphins took his ashes to Poland?"

"They did."

"I don't know what that means, but it sounds very nice."

"It is, Bob. It's very nice."

She had the same conversation with him three days in a row.

The most challenging aspect of Carrie's new life as full-time Copacabana housekeeper and nursemaid was watching her mother deteriorate for the second time. It had been thrilling for Carrie to know Joanna as a forty-two-year-old superwoman. Joanna had been an older parent, so Carrie had never known her as young and physically vibrant. Intellectually vibrant, of course.

Joanna had remained the sharpest knife in the shed even as her body failed. But for Carrie to see both sides of her mother aligned in harmony—even cannibalistic-freak-show harmony—that had been special indeed, the impossible luck of Carrie's life.

But that luck had run dry. Carrie had already seen her mother age, had already lived through Joanna's pain and frustration and pain and pain. And now she was watching it happen again. Joanna's body breaking down, her spirit fighting to live through her own physical degeneration. The cane. The walker. The wheelchair. The agony. The helplessness. The hopelessness. The dying. The dreadful dying.

It was worse this time around. Not because there was something different about her mother, but because there was something different about *her*. The first time Joanna had aged, Carrie had been too dependent upon her mother, too emotionally intimidated, to offer the kind of decisive comfort Joanna needed. But then she'd clobbered Old Tom and stolen the capsules and lived the great adventure of her life, and it had empowered her in all the ways she'd dreamed of as a wallflower rat-girl geek. She'd pushed off the wall and was living in the light of the sun. She could open her heart without fear, offer her love without condition, and accept it without judgment. The care she gave now came from a place of inner strength and confidence. It was pure. It was genuine. It was beautiful. Finally, she felt she deserved to be at the Party of Life.

One night, when she was helping her mother from the wheelchair to the bed, Joanna looked into her eyes and then through them into her soul. But this time, maybe for the first time, her mother's unwavering, calculated, and penetrating stare did not chill her, did not send shivers up and down her neck, did not close her off and shut her down. This time, Carrie smiled, realizing—again, for the first time—this was how Joanna said, *I love you, my one and only child*.

"What happened to my pear-shaped girl?" Joanna said.

"She's here, Mother. But now she feels good about things."

"That's love, my darling."

"I know."

"It turns out Mr. Fairfax is not transient after all."

"No, Mother. He's a keeper."

It was this discussion that impelled Carrie to create a pharmaceutical laboratory in what had been Johnny's apartment. She realized she wanted to live a lifetime loving her mother this way, being loved by her mother this way in return. Experiencing this profound feeling for only the last few painful months of Joanna's life was not acceptable. She wanted Joanna to be a keeper too. And the more she thought about it, the more she realized she felt the same way about the rest of the Copa crew. She wanted them all to be keepers. She could not bear to watch them die, one by one, while she stood on the sidelines knowing she could keep them alive if she put her mind to it.

So Johnny moved in with her, and his place began its laboratorial renovation.

But a lab alone would not suffice. She'd need a chemist to run Sikorski's equations. Someone with questionable ethics. Someone she could bribe with the promise of a billion-dollar payday. Someone who'd leave the FDA out of their chemical calculations. Someone as reluctant as she'd be to notify the authorities—*any* authorities, even the meter maids—about the comings and goings in her clandestine Copacabana drug lab.

She had such a scientist in mind.

His name was Adam Flynn. A tall, skinny Bakersfield boy who'd skipped high school entirely and matriculated as a full-time student at USC at age fourteen. He'd earned a bachelor's, a master's, and a PhD in organic chemistry at seventeen. Added another PhD in molecular biology at nineteen. Graduated from the USC medical school at twenty-one. Gone to the USC school of law while at med school (because medical school was easy for him and he'd reasoned being an attorney might help him evade the law in the long run) and passed the bar at twenty-two.

He was, in every sense of the word, a genius. It was as if the universe had given Flynn an absurdly large portion of superior intellect at birth but had neglected to supply him with even a miniscule measure of morality.

Though neither scientist was capable of forming friendships, Flynn and Sikorski had been laboratory associates. They'd worked in the same labs, occasionally at the same time, on a handful of occasions over the years, and were familiar with each other's genius. Early on, Sikorski had considered hiring Flynn to work in his illicit lab. That was how Carrie had met him. As Alsiko's resident behavioral scientist, Sikorski had also tagged her with being the lab's director of Human Resources, so round one of interviewing Flynn had fallen to her.

Flynn had been out of work at the time. *Between labs* was how he'd put it. The reason he was between labs, he'd said, was because he'd been booted from his last university research job for building an illegal meth lab in a dark university sub-cellar. A wandering maintenance man had discovered it by accident. Flynn had been threatened with legal action and worse. But acting as his own attorney, he'd threatened countersuits that ran to the tens of millions of dollars and promised concurrent reams of negative publicity shoved straight up the university's ass. In the end, both parties had agreed to separate silently and say nothing about the settlement to anyone at any point in time in the future, ever. Being an attorney *had* helped him evade the law in the long run after all.

He'd been completely unashamed to tell Carrie the story. No sense of ethics. No concern for principles. No fear of immorality.

Sikorski had decided against hiring Flynn because—Carrie recalled with astonishment—the man did not have the requisite amount of integrity...*for Sikorski,* the man who ran an unlawful lab funded by banned nations without telling the banned nations there were other banned nations in on the funding. Flynn did not have enough integrity for Sikorski.

But he had enough for Carrie.

Flynn was a genius who could build drugs like nobody's

business. He was available, he did not shy away from unlawful projects, and Carrie had his contact information. She reached out, he was interested, and they met at a coffee shop on Melrose Avenue—her, Flynn, and Johnny, who Carrie introduced as the Director of Lab Security.

She told Flynn about Sikorski's drug, about its miraculous age-reversal attributes, about its curious cannibalistic side effect (which they would have to eliminate), that perhaps the drug should be designed for weekly dosage—as opposed to three doses and done forever, since forever was not the occurring result of three doses. She told him about the potential payday, about his generous cut, about being among the richest humans who ever lived, about the obvious and inherent danger of this kind of history altering project. She told him his buy-in for the billions would be providing his incognito expertise and, by whatever no-questions-asked means necessary, supplying the required laboratory equipment.

When she was done setting the scene for Flynn, the scientist turned to Johnny. Not Carrie. Johnny. "Explain to me the job of the Director of Lab Security."

"If I get the feeling you're out of line at the lab—you don't actually have to be out of line, I just have to get the feeling you are—if I get that feeling, I'm going to open your head with a meat cleaver, butcher your body into commercial cuts, fricassee the fuck out of your flesh, and serve you to the cannibals," Johnny said. "Does that explain it?"

Flynn took them in for a moment, then smiled. "When do we start?"

On the return ride to the Copa, seated on the back of Johnny's Harley, her arms wrapped around him, two things occurred to Carrie.

The first was Jane Kinsey, Francine Fontana's screenwriting partner-in-true-crime, who'd been calling Carrie for news. Was Johnny grilling steaks in Redding? Was Carrie sequestered somewhere secret in Virginia? What was the end of the story? Carrie had not returned her calls. But now she concluded it would be in everyone's best interest to keep Kinsey close. A rogue hyena screenwriter on the loose in LA with their story in hand was a bad idea by any measure. So Carrie would call Kinsey and tell her the truth of the ending—that she and Johnny had declined their dream jobs and stayed in LA to love each other and care for the Copa crew. Kinsey, of course, would detest that ending and balk at the idea of Hollywood falling for such a sappy script, a romantic comedy in which the romance was so absurdly dreamy and the comedy so outlandishly fierce. But as a novel, yes, as a *novel*, Carrie would convince Kinsey the tall tale would make a wild-and-crazy book, as dark as it was adoring, as brilliant as it was bizarre, and fortunes could well and still be made by knocking on Hollywood's adaptation door.

Carrie would explain she had a lawyer on board, had registered the rights to the story, and was in the market for a ghostwriter. Being the ambulance-chasing scavenger she was, Kinsey would sign up to write the book with Carrie rather than walk away with no story at all. There would be no walking away with a rogue hyena like Kinsey.

Sitting side by side, Carrie could ensure the novel ended precisely at the point where she and Johnny cohabitated at the Copa. Sitting side by side, Carrie could make the actual writing of the book take years and years. She could drag it out until Kinsey lost interest. And if she didn't lose interest, then, well, with Kinsey under contract, Carrie could at least mitigate the worst of the worst of the story. Meaning more passion. Less murder. More romance. Less eating people. Or maybe no eating people. Maybe just leave the eating-people part out altogether. Maybe just the wonder drug and the love affair and enough blood and guts to keep the crime crowd turning pages. It wouldn't be a novel based on a true story. (Wasn't that the Hollywood phrasing?) It would be a book inspired by actual events. Or maybe leave the eating-people part in. No one would believe it anyway.

Flynn would be the beginning of a new story and none of Kinsey's concern. Flynn would not be in the novel. Flynn would be in the lab. His role would demand a short leash. And one would be fitted for him.

Which brought Carrie to the second thing, the realization that following the formula and reproducing the drug without the undesired side effect would require multiple trials. Consequently, she would need new rats.

So she got some.

# THANK YOU

I hope you had as much fun reading *Cooking for Cannibals* as I had writing it because I had a blast. If you did, it would be fabulous if you could help other lovers of dark comedy and crime thrillers and, well, dark comic crime thrillers find the book by leaving a review and sharing the laughs.

Honest reviews of my books help introduce them to new readers. I would be deeply grateful if you could find a few minutes to post a positive review about *Cooking for Cannibals*. It only takes a minute to leave an upbeat word or two. Thank you for doing that.

# YOU HAVE NEVER. MET
# AN ALIEN. LIKE
# THIS ONE.

**"Leder's Extraterrestrial Noir is a blistering sci-fi crime thriller that disintegrates genre boundaries and opens the floodgates for messed up hilarity and weirdly relatable adventure!"**

An extraterrestrial crashes into a suburban cul-de-sac Colonial, absorbs every binary bit of information ever chronicled in all of human history, rearranges its molecules to present itself as a couple of late and legendary film noir superstars, then immediately displays an appetite for debauchery, depravity, decadence, and destruction, seducing the family into its psychopathic criminal orbit with irresistible Hollywood panache, alluring sexual charisma, and inconceivable intergalactic powers....all in the name of saving them from their inevitable emotional, marital, and financial ruin.

But super-genius-daughter Mike Devine figures out fast that the extraterrestrial's principal plan is to employ its unfathomable interplanetary muscle and implode the planet. Which leaves the fate of her family, not to mention the world, in her twelve-year-old hands.

**"If you like giddy, gruesome, edge-of-your-seat tall tales that cross the line and outer space, then blast into orbit with Rich Leder's unputdownable rocket of a read!"**

Get Extraterrestrial Noir today and strap in for the ride!

# HERE'S ANOTHER HILARIOUS DARK COMIC CRIME THRILLER FROM THE DELIGHTFULLY BIZARRE IMAGINATION OF WRITER RICH LEDER

**A deranged dog. A death-defying shakedown. A disastrous development.**

Dan Miller may be a smooth-talking swindler, but he's still in the hole. So when his malicious moneylender comes to collect, digging up $75K is going to take a miracle. Lucky for him, his latest client can breathe life into the dead. Reunited after their mother's passing, Dan and his strait-laced brother hatch a lucrative plan to resurrect a coke-addled dentist's beloved poodle. But when the undead dog goes bloodily off-script and a wannabe-comedian cop starts chasing them, the Miller brothers bring their mother back from the dead to gather the gory pieces.

Get Let There Be Linda today and laugh out loud at Leder's zany, hysterical, irreverent, and heart-stopping story!"

# ALSO BY RICH LEDER

<u>ROMANTIC SHADES OF FUNNY</u>

Juggler, Porn Star, Monkey Wrench

<u>DARKER SHADES OF FUNNY</u>

Let There Be Linda

Cooking for Cannibals

Extraterrestrial Noir

<u>KATE MCCALL CRIME CAPERS</u>

Workman's Complication

Swollen Identity

Emboozlement

Gottiguard

*For all the readers who want to laugh at dark comedy but pause
thinking maybe they shouldn't while simultaneously sensing that
whatever it was they just read was meant to be funny and, in the end,
really was, so, yeah, whatever, they're laughing at that shit anyway.*

*For all of you.*

# ABOUT THE AUTHOR

Rich Leder's screen credits include 19 television films for CBS, Lifetime, and Hallmark and feature films for Lionsgate Entertainment, Paramount Pictures, Tri-Star Pictures, and Left Bank Films. He has published eight novels through Laugh Riot Press.

He has been the lead singer in a Detroit rock band, a restaurateur, a Little League coach, an indie film director, a literacy tutor, a magazine editor, a screenwriting coach, a commercial real estate agent, a wedding guru, and a visiting artist for the University of North Carolina Wilmington Film Studies Department, among other things, all of which, it turns out, was grist for the mill.

Contact Rich through his website: www.richleder.com